PRAISE FOR
THE SECRET CROWN

"A dizzying, thrill-laden chase for treasure through Bavaria, with the coolest heroes since *Lethal Weapon*."
—Andrew Gross,
New York Times bestselling author of *Eyes Wide Open*

"Chris Kuzneski has mastered the art of the quest novel, bringing to life lost treasures, exotic locales, and fresh conspiracies, as his trusty duo of Payne and Jones rely on their elite military training to slay bad guys, solve riddles, and save the day."
—Lisa Gardner,
New York Times bestselling author of *Love You More*

"Hugely entertaining, an adventure made for the big screen—with secret codes, priceless artworks, and a search for treasure. Kuzneski seamlessly blends historical fact with ingenious fiction. Once you start, you'll be hooked!"
—Joseph Finder,
New York Times bestselling author of *Buried Secrets*

"Nobody blends fascinating history and pulse-pounding action like Chris Kuzneski. *The Secret Crown* is smart, funny and impossible to put down—so impossible that I finished the book by candlelight during a power outage. The book is *that* good!"
—Jeremy Robinson,
bestselling author of *Threshold*

"An adventure brimming with mystery, intrigue, and humor. Kuzneski stirs together thrills, chills, and laughs in equal measures to serve up a rollicking, fun read."
—Boyd Morrison,
bestselling author of *The Vault*

continued . . .

"A fast and furious thrill ride with the perfect amount of history and humor blended in."

—Raymond Khoury,
New York Times bestselling author of *The Devil's Elixir*

SWORD OF GOD

"A nonstop locomotive of a thriller that had me burning the midnight oil 'til breakfast."

—Vince Flynn,
New York Times bestselling author of *Kill Shot*

"Action-packed and full of suspense . . . will keep you guessing, chuckling, terrified, and utterly riveted."

—Gayle Lynds,
New York Times bestselling author of *The Book of Spies*

"As convincing as it is terrifying."

—James Rollins,
USA Today bestselling author of *The Devil Colony*

SIGN OF THE CROSS

"Makes you wish it would never end."

—Clive Cussler,
New York Times bestselling author of *The Jungle*

"Like *The Da Vinci Code* on steroids."

—Thom Racina,
USA Today bestselling author of *Deep Freeze*

"A lightning pace. This story really flies!"

—Tess Gerritsen,
New York Times bestselling author of *The Silent Girl*

"One of those perfect bookstore finds. I was hooked at the first sentence."

—John Gilstrap,
New York Times bestselling author of *Threat Level*

continued . . .

THE PLANTATION

"Ingenious . . . a rip-roaring page-turner . . . Chris Kuzneski's writing has the same kind of raw power as the early Stephen King."

—James Patterson,
New York Times bestselling author of *Cross Fire*

"The most action-packed, swiftly paced, and tightly plotted novel I've read in a long time."

—Nelson DeMille,
New York Times bestselling author of *The Lion*

"Excellent! High stakes, fast action, vibrant characters, and a very, very original plot concept. Not to be missed!"

—Lee Child,
New York Times bestselling author of *The Affair*

THE
SECRET
CROWN

CHRIS KUZNESKI

BERKLEY BOOKS
New York

THE BERKLEY PUBLISHING GROUP
Published by the Penguin Group
Penguin Group (USA) Inc.
375 Hudson Street, New York, New York 10014, USA
Penguin Group (Canada), 90 Eglinton Avenue East, Suite 700, Toronto, Ontario M4P 2Y3, Canada
(a division of Pearson Penguin Canada Inc.) • Penguin Books Ltd., 80 Strand, London WC2R 0RL,
England • Penguin Group Ireland, 25 St. Stephen's Green, Dublin 2, Ireland (a division of Penguin
Books Ltd.) • Penguin Group (Australia), 250 Camberwell Road, Camberwell, Victoria 3124, Australia
(a division of Pearson Australia Group Pty. Ltd.) • Penguin Books India Pvt. Ltd., 11 Community
Centre, Panchsheel Park, New Delhi—110 017, India • Penguin Group (NZ), 67 Apollo Drive,
Rosedale, Auckland 0632, New Zealand (a division of Pearson New Zealand Ltd.) • Penguin Books
(South Africa) (Pty.) Ltd., 24 Sturdee Avenue, Rosebank, Johannesburg 2196, South Africa

Penguin Books Ltd., Registered Offices: 80 Strand, London WC2R 0RL, England

This is a work of fiction. Names, characters, places, and incidents either are the product of the author's
imagination or are used fictitiously, and any resemblance to actual persons, living or dead, business
establishments, events, or locales is entirely coincidental. The publisher does not have any control over
and does not assume any responsibility for author or third-party websites or their content.

THE SECRET CROWN

A Berkley Book / published by arrangement with the author

PUBLISHING HISTORY
G. P. Putnam's Sons hardcover edition / January 2012
Berkley premium edition / August 2012

Copyright © 2012 by Chris Kuzneski, Inc.
Cover photographs: Gold bars © Stock Connection Distribution /
Alamy. Corridor © Jo Miyake / Alamy.
Cover design by Nellys Lang.

ISBN: 978-0-425-25040-2

BERKLEY®
Berkley Books are published by The Berkley Publishing Group,
a division of Penguin Group (USA) Inc.,
375 Hudson Street, New York, New York 10014.
BERKLEY® is a registered trademark of Penguin Group (USA) Inc.
The "B" design is a trademark of Penguin Group (USA) Inc.

PRINTED IN THE UNITED STATES OF AMERICA

10 9 8 7 6 5 4 3 2 1

ALWAYS LEARNING   PEARSON

PROLOGUE

For years he had been paid to protect the king. Now he had orders to kill him.

And it needed to be done today.

Without witnesses. Without wounds. Before he could slip away.

Tracking his target from the nearby trees, he watched Ludwig as he left the castle grounds and strolled along the shoreline. The king wore an overcoat and carried an umbrella, protection from the threatening skies that had blanketed the region for much of the day. Normally, the sun wouldn't set until quarter past nine, but the approaching storm made dusk come early.

A storm that would wash away any signs of foul play.

The assassin checked his watch and noted the time. Ten minutes to seven. Dinner would be served at eight and not a moment before. If his target was late, an alarm would be sounded and a search party would be formed. That much was certain. This was a turbulent time in Bavaria, and Ludwig was the central figure in all the drama, somehow loved and hated at the same time.

Some viewed him as a hero, a brilliant visionary who could do no wrong. Others saw him as a paranoid madman who had bankrupted the royal family with his flights of fancy. The assassin realized the truth was probably somewhere in between, though he couldn't care less about politics. He was there to do a job, and he would do it without mercy.

"Go to the boathouse," he whispered to his partner. "Signal me if we're alone."

His partner nodded, then crept through the woods without making a sound. They had positioned themselves along the northeastern shore of Lake Starnberg, the fourth-largest lake in the German Empire. Created by Ice Age glaciers, it extended fourteen miles from north to south and two miles from east to west. This time of year, the water was too cold for swimming, effectively trapping Ludwig along the coast with no means of escape.

Without a boat, the lake offered no sanctuary.

Without a miracle, Ludwig would be dead before dark.

The assassin smiled, confident in his ability to finish the job. In recent days, Ludwig had been followed by a team of guards whose sole task was to protect him. Not only from his enemies but also from himself. But this night was different. Bribes had been paid and arrangements had been made that would guarantee his isolation. As expected, the lone obstacle would be Ludwig's psychiatrist, a man of advanced years who watched over his patient. The assassin would strike him first. And then he would turn his attention to Ludwig, the fabled Swan King.

The assassin glanced at the boathouse, waiting for his partner's signal. The instant he saw it, he slipped behind his two targets, effectively cutting them off from the safety of the castle grounds. And he did so silently, careful not to give away his position until he was close enough to strike. In a matter of seconds, he had cut the distance to twenty feet.

Then fifteen.

Then ten.

As he narrowed the gap to five feet, his focus shifted to the makeshift weapon he held in his hand. Plucked from the nearby shore, the stone was brown and jagged and stained with mud.

A moment later, it was covered in blood.

The doctor fell at once, unconscious before he even hit the ground. His skull shattered by the blow, his ribs fractured from the fall. Yet neither injury proved fatal. Minutes would pass before the doctor would take his final breath, his lifeless body dragged into the depths of the cold lake where he would eventually drown—punishment for the role he had played in the charade.

In the meantime, the assassin had more important things to worry about. Before leaving the royal palace in Munich, he had been given an assignment unlike any other. Two tasks that he needed to complete before he returned home. Two tasks that would rescue his kingdom from financial ruin and ensure its future for decades to come. Two tasks that would not be easy.

Get Ludwig to talk, and then silence him forever.

1

❖

Klaus Becker stood perfectly still, careful not to attract attention as he eyed his mark from his concealed perch in a nearby tree. Some less-experienced gunmen would have used military-grade optics to guarantee a killshot from this range, but what was the challenge in that? To him, if his prey didn't have a sporting chance, Becker wanted no part of the fight.

That was the code he lived by, the one his father had taught him.

The one he hoped to teach his kids someday.

Unfortunately, that day would never come because he would soon be dead.

Unaware of his impending fate, the forty-year-old cocked his head to the side and squinted as he stared down the barrel of his rifle. Suddenly, the world around him blurred and the only thing that mattered was the mammoth target that had roamed into his field of fire. Weighing over six hundred pounds, the Russian boar had two deadly tusks that were nearly twelve inches in length. Highly intelligent and often cantankerous, wild boars were common in central Europe, but they rarely reached this size. Only mature males in the harshest of climates ever grew so large, which was the main reason that Becker had traveled here for a few days of hunting.

He wanted his shot at some sizable game.

The snowcapped peak of Zugspitze, the highest mountain in Germany, could be seen to the west. It was part of the Bavarian Alps, which stretched across the region like a massive wall and formed a natural border with Austria to the south. The rugged peak could be climbed via several different routes from the valley below, the one that cradled the town of Grainau, but none of the trails interested Becker. As an experienced hunter, he knew Russian boars would forage for food in the thick groves below the timberline—the highest elevation where trees and vegetation are capable of growing—so he positioned himself in the middle of the forest, far from the hiking trails and far from any interlopers.

Out here, it was Becker against the boar.

Just like he had hoped for.

After taking a deep breath, Becker made a slight adjustment to his aim and then pulled his trigger. Thunder exploded from the barrel of his Mauser M98 hunting rifle as the stock recoiled against his shoulder. A split second later, the boar squealed in agony as the $9.3 \times 64mm$ bullet entered its left flank and burrowed deep into its lung. Remarkably, the boar remained standing. Without delay, its survival instincts kicked into flight mode. Since the gun blast had come from its left, the boar bolted quickly to its right, disappearing into the undergrowth that covered the forest floor.

"Scheiße!" Becker cursed as he jumped out of his tree stand.

To kill his prey, he would have to track it on foot.

Following the blood trail, Becker moved with alacrity. Despite their girth, boars weren't fat like domestic pigs and were surprisingly fast—able to reach speeds of more than fifteen miles per hour. Carrying a rifle and dressed in camouflage, Becker couldn't even travel that fast on a bicycle. Still, given the amount of blood he found on the hillside, he knew this was a race he would eventually win.

With every beat of the boar's heart, it was a little bit closer to dying.

And Becker wanted to be the reason it did.

Five minutes later, he caught up with the wounded boar in a natural cul-de-sac, formed by the steep incline of the mountain and a pile of fallen rocks and trees. Years of experience had taught Becker about the dangers of injured animals, especially when they were trapped. He knew if they felt threatened, they would attack with every bit of strength they had left. And since Becker didn't want to get run over by a six-hundred-pound bowling bowl with sharp tusks, he stopped a safe distance from his target and raised his rifle to finish the job.

"Steady," he whispered in German. "I'm not going to hurt you."

The boar snorted loudly and focused its beady eyes on Becker while a soft growl steadily grew from deep inside its throat. Sensing what was about to happen, the boar decided to get aggressive. Suddenly, without warning, it lowered its head and charged forward, reaching its top speed in only a few steps. Becker expected as much and adjusted his aim, compensating for the boar's pace and the shrinking distance to his quarry. Without flinching or jumping out of the way, Becker calmly pulled the trigger, confident that he wouldn't miss.

Fortunately for him, his aim was true.

The bullet tore through the boar's skull and plowed through its brain, killing it instantly. One moment it was charging at Becker, the next it was skidding to a halt on its belly—as if someone had turned off its power via remote control. Just to be safe, Becker fired a second shot into its brain before he approached his prey for a closer look.

Although he had seen plenty of Russian boars in hunting magazines, the pictures didn't do the animal justice. This beast was huge. Coated in thick brown fur with stiff bristles, it had a large snout, sharp tusks, and a muscular torso. Becker walked around it twice, poking it with his rifle, making sure it was truly dead. The last thing he wanted was to be gored by an animal on its deathbed. He quickly realized that wouldn't be a problem with this boar.

Finally able to relax, Becker laid his weapon off to the side and touched the boar with his bare hands. There was something about a fresh kill—when the body was still warm and the blood had not yet dried—that satisfied something deep inside Becker, a primal urge that had been embedded in his DNA by long-lost ancestors who had hunted for food, not sport. Whether it was the adrenaline rush from the chase or the power he felt when he ended a life, hunting was the only time he truly felt alive.

Ironically, it was the thing that led to his death.

The first time Becker heard the noise, he didn't know what it was. He paused for a moment, scanning the terrain, making sure that another animal hadn't smelled the blood and come looking for a meal. He knew these mountains had wolves and bears and a number of other creatures that would love to sink their teeth into a fresh chunk of meat—whether that meat came from a boar or a hunter. Either way, Becker was ready to defend his turf.

But he wasn't ready for this.

Before he could run, or jump, or react in any way, the unthinkable happened. A loud crack emerged from the ground beneath his feet and the earth suddenly opened. Becker fell first, plunging deep into the man-made cavern under the forest floor. He was followed by dirt, debris, and finally the boar. If the order had been reversed, Becker would have lived to tell the tale with nothing more than a few cuts and bruises, because the massive boar would have cushioned his fall. But sometimes the universe has a wicked sense of humor, a way of correcting wrongs in the most ironic ways possible, and that's what happened in this case.

A split second after Becker hit the ground, the boar landed on top of him.

Two tusks followed by six hundred pounds of meat.

If Becker had survived his fall, his discovery would have

made him a wealthy man and a hero in his native Germany. But because of his death, several more people would lose their lives as the rest of the world scrambled to discover what had been hidden in the Bavarian Alps and forgotten by time.

2

✤

Thirty feet below the surface of the Ohio River, the man probed the riverbed, hoping to find the object before a lack of oxygen forced him to ascend. He had been scouring the rocks for more than four minutes, which was a remarkable length of time to be submerged without air—especially considering the adverse conditions of the waterway.

Thanks to a midweek thunderstorm that had caused minor flooding in the region, the current was unusually swift. It tugged on his shoulders like an invisible specter. To remain in place, he had to swim hard, his arms and legs pumping like pistons. Eventually, all of his movement stirred up the sediment around him, turning the bottom of the river into a murky mess.

One moment it was as clear as vodka; the next it looked like beer.

Equipped with goggles that barely helped, he probed the silt for anything shiny. He found an empty can and a few coins but not the object he was looking for. Yet he didn't get frustrated. If anything, his lack of success sharpened his focus and made him more determined. This was a trait he had possessed since childhood, an unwavering spirit that kept him going when lesser men would quit. A quality that had lifted him to the top of his profession.

A trait that made him dangerous.

In the darkness behind him, something large brushed against his feet. He turned quickly and searched for a suspect. Weighing over twenty pounds and nearly three feet in length, the channel catfish had four pairs of barbels near its nostrils that looked like whiskers. Known for its ugliness and indiscriminate appetite, the catfish swam next to him for several seconds before it darted away. All the while he wondered if the fish had swallowed the sunken treasure and was simply there to taunt him. During his years in the Special Forces, he had heard so many fish stories from Navy personnel that he didn't know what to believe. Even if only one percent of them were true, then anything was possible underwater.

No longer distracted by the catfish, he continued his search. From the burning in his lungs, he knew he had less than a minute before he would have to surface—and he refused to do so empty-handed. With a powerful kick, he propelled himself closer to the riverbed, careful not to scrape himself on the rocks that dotted the terrain. Then, using his boat's anchor as a starting point, he allowed the current to push him downriver for a few seconds so he could gauge its strength. Since it was strong enough to move him, a 240-pound man, there was no telling how far it might have moved the artifact. Ten feet? Twenty feet? Maybe even fifty?

Or would its size and shape prevent it from being affected at all?

From experience he knew weapons sank fairly straight, regardless of the force of the river. Drop a gun or knife in a body of water, and it would sink directly to the bottom— even in a strong current. But something this small? He had no idea where it would land or what it would do when it got there.

In the end, all he could do was guess and hope for the best.

Careful not to stir up more sediment as he coasted along, he let the river guide him, hoping it would lead him in the right direction, praying it would take him to the treasure. With every passing second, his lungs burned more and more until it felt like he had inhaled a flame.

Time was running out, and he knew it.

If he didn't give up now, he would soon be dead.

Reluctantly, he tucked his legs underneath him, ready to launch himself from the riverbed, when he felt something metallic under his foot. Without looking, he reached down and grabbed it, then propelled himself toward the world above. Time seemed to stand still as he stroked and kicked his way through the murky water, unsure where he was or how far he had to go until he reached the river's surface. The instant he did, he gasped for air, filling his lungs with breath after breath until the burning subsided. Until he knew he would survive.

Then, and only then, did he notice the world around him.

The city of Pittsburgh to his east. The football stadium to the north.

And the crowded boat that had waited for his return.

"So?" someone asked. "Did you find it?"

Too tired to speak, Jonathon Payne simply nodded and lifted the lost bottle opener over his head. The instant he did, the partygoers erupted—not only would they be able to open the remaining cases of beer, but most of them had wagered on the success of his mission.

"Shit!" shouted David Jones, who had lost big money on his best friend. Although DJ had served with Payne in the military and knew what he was capable of, he didn't think anyone could find such a small object on his first dive into the murky river. "Hold up! Let me see it."

Payne swam slowly to the boat and handed it to Jones. "Please don't drop it again."

"What do you mean *again*? I didn't drop it the first time."

"Well, someone did, and it happened on your watch."

"My watch? Why is it *my* watch? It's *your* boat."

Payne used the dive ladder on the back of his yacht to climb out of the water. Per tradition, he threw a party on the last weekend of summer to commemorate the end of the boating season. After today, his boat would be dry-docked for the cold months ahead.

"As captain of this vessel, I'm putting you in charge of the bottle opener."

Jones handed him a towel. "And what if I decline?"

"Then you're in charge of cleanup."

"Screw that! I don't do garbage. I'll guard this opener with my life."

"Yeah," Payne grunted, "I had a feeling you'd say that."

To the outside world, the two of them didn't appear to have much in common, but that had more to do with their looks than anything else. Payne was a hulking six-foot-four. Muscles stacked upon muscles, his white skin littered with bullet holes and stab wounds, his brown hair perfectly disheveled. He had the look of a gridiron legend, an ex-athlete who had lived his life to the fullest but still had more worlds to conquer. Born with a silver spoon in his mouth, he'd decided to sharpen the handle and use it as a weapon, serving several years in the military until his grandfather died and left him controlling interest of his family's corporation.

Unfortunately, he had been craving adventure ever since.

Jones, too, was an adrenaline junkie, but he looked more like an office clerk than an officer. Known for his brain instead of his brawn, he possessed the wiry build of a track star, someone who could run a marathon without breaking a sweat but wouldn't stand out in a crowd. Although his mocha skin and soft facial features made him look delicate, Jones was lethal on the battlefield, having completed the same military training as Payne.

In fact, the two of them used to lead the MANIACs, an elite Special Forces unit composed of the top soldiers from the Marines, Army, Navy, Intelligence, Air Force, and Coast Guard. Whether it was personnel recovery, unconventional warfare, or counterguerrilla sabotage, the MANIACs were the best of the best. The boogeymen no one talked about. The government's secret weapon. And even though they had retired a few years earlier, the duo was still deadly.

"By the way," Jones said, "I heard your phone ringing when you were underwater. What a *fabulous* ringtone. Is that a Menudo song?"

Payne growled and shook his head in frustration. A few weeks earlier, someone had figured out a way to change the ringtone on Payne's phone through a wireless connection. No matter what Payne did to stop it—including purchasing a new phone and even changing his number—the culprit kept uploading the most embarrassing ringtones possible. Apparently, the latest was a song from Menudo, the Puerto Rican boy band that had launched many pop stars.

"Did you answer it?" Payne asked, confident that Jones was guilty.

Jones laughed. "Of course not. I'd *never* touch your phone."

3

⚜

The city of Pittsburgh sits at the confluence of three rivers, which helps explain why there are more bridges (446) in Pittsburgh than in any other city in the world—including the previous record holder, Venice, Italy. From the deck of *Greek Gold*, Payne could see the Allegheny River to the north and the Monongahela River to the south. The two waterways converged near the giant fountain at Point State Park. It marked the beginning of the Ohio River and was a popular gathering place for people of all ages, especially in the summertime.

As a teenager, Payne used to visit the park with his grandfather, who had founded Payne Industries and built its headquarters across the river atop scenic Mount Washington. Despite his duties, his grandfather managed to find the time to raise Jon after Payne's parents died in a car crash. Back in those days, when the steel industry was still the driving force of the local economy and the rivers were way too filthy to swim in, they used to play catch along the water's edge, not too far from old Three Rivers Stadium. Now when Payne gazed at the revitalized North Shore, he saw two of the most scenic ballparks in all of sports, the Carnegie Science Center, a World War II submarine (the USS *Requin*), and the newly opened Rivers Casino.

No wonder a national poll named Pittsburgh the most livable city in America.

Still wet from his swim, Payne slowly made his way through the boisterous crowd, receiving hearty congratulations as he passed. Half of the people were from work—mostly lower-level staff from Payne Industries who were being rewarded for their performance. The other half were business contacts and their guests. Payne was a generous host and got along with just about everybody, yet he rarely felt like he belonged. Except for Jones, there was no one on board he thought of as his friend. He was equal parts upper class and blue collar but felt stuck between the two worlds, unable to fully connect with either of them. Not that he was complaining. Payne loved his life and realized how good he had it. Nevertheless, there was a part of him that longed for what he had given up to run his family's company.

The action, the adventure, the threat of danger.

Everything missing from his current life.

Glancing at his cell phone, Payne noticed the missed call had come from an unlisted number. Based on experience, he knew it was probably someone from his former life.

Business contacts, especially those calling the chairman of the board of a major corporation, wanted their numbers to be recognized in case he was screening his calls. But that wasn't the case with military personnel—particularly the operatives Payne had met in the MANIACs.

They were more concerned with protecting information than supplying it.

"Who was it?" Jones asked.

Payne shrugged and typed in the passcode that unlocked his phone. "I don't know. It came from a restricted number."

Jones arched an eyebrow. "Maybe it was Ricky Martin."

Payne ignored the Menudo reference and checked his voice mail.

"Not even a smile? Come on, man. That was funny."

Payne plugged his ear and turned away, trying to hear his message. Behind him, the party raged on louder than it should. Music thumping from his speakers. People laughing and dancing and blowing off steam. Tiny waves lapping against the sides of his boat while his best friend yapped in his ear. Despite it all, he heard the message. Years of training had honed his focus.

"This is Kaiser," said the voice. "Call me A-SAP."

No wasted words. No wasted syllables.

Call me as soon as possible.

Payne swore under his breath. This wasn't good news. It couldn't be.

If Kaiser was calling, something bad had happened.

· · ·

Payne and Jones had known Kaiser for a decade, but didn't really know him.

Not his real name. Or where he lived. Or if he had a family.

But if they needed *anything* from the black market, he was the man to contact.

According to legend, he was an ex–supply sergeant who had retired from the U.S. Army when he realized he could make a lot more money on his own. He started his operation in Germany near the Kaiserslautern Military Community, the largest U.S. military community outside the continental United States. Known as K-Town, it houses nearly fifty thousand people. Originally, he catered to these displaced men and women, providing simple things from home that they couldn't get on their own. Food, clothes, movies, books—all at a fair price.

Then the Internet came along and competed for his business, forcing him to dabble in other things: weapons, smuggling, and phony IDs. Pretty much everything *except* drugs.

Over the years, Payne and Jones had done so much business with Kaiser that he'd eventually invited them to dinner to show his appreciation. In his line of work, face-to-face meetings were a rarity, but Kaiser knew if either man wanted to track him down, they could do it within a week. Not because he was sloppy or failed to take precautions, but because Payne and Jones were *that* good at their jobs. He figured, if they could find and eliminate terrorist strongholds in the mountains of Afghanistan, then they certainly could locate him in Germany.

With that in mind, he did whatever he could to stay on their good side.

But up until now, he had never called them in America.

Jones noticed the concern on Payne's face. "What's wrong?"

"Nothing's wrong."

"Are you sure?"

"Not really."

Jones lowered his voice to a whisper. "Who was it?"

Payne subconsciously glanced over his shoulder. "Kaiser."

"Kaiser? Was he returning a call of yours?"

"Nope."

"Then something's wrong. Kaiser wouldn't call unless something's wrong."

"Not necessarily. Maybe he's in the States and wants to grab dinner."

Jones grimaced. "Did he *say* he wants to grab dinner?"

"Not in so many words."

"Then what did he say?"

Payne cleared his throat. "'This is Kaiser. Call me A-SAP.'"

"Good Lord! Someone's dead."

Payne couldn't help but laugh. "Relax, princess. We don't know that."

"Speak for yourself. I can tell. Someone's dead."

"Here's a thought. Why don't I call him before you panic?"

"I'm not panicking. I'm predicting."

"Well, it *sounds* like you're panicking."

"Come on, Jon. You know me better than that. If anything, I'm excited about the possibilities. Watching you swim for kitchenware isn't exactly rousing."

"That's funny. I don't remember you volunteering for the job."

"That's because I don't drink and dive."

Payne smiled at the pun. "Touché."

"And even if I did, there's no way I was going to jump in *that* water. Let's face it: You're gonna smell like fish for the rest of the weekend."

Payne smelled the towel draped around his neck. "Please tell me you're joking."

Jones shook his head. "Let's put it this way. You're a good-looking billionaire and no women have flirted with you since your return. What does that tell you?"

"It tells me that you think I'm good-looking."

"What? That's not what I meant."

"So what are you saying? It was a Freudian slip?"

"No, Jon. My point is that you smell."

"Compared to normal?"

"Exactly."

Payne pressed the issue. "In other words, you *usually* like the way I smell."

"What?"

"You think I'm a good-looking, good-smelling guy."

"Stop it! Quit putting words in my mouth."

"Dude, I'm not putting *anything* in your mouth."

Jones blushed, worried that some of the other guests might have overheard the comment. At first he was going to speak up and defend himself, then he thought better of it. No matter what he said, it was going to be taken out of context and used against him. So he stood there, silent, waiting for Payne to let him off the ropes. But Payne wasn't done throwing verbal jabs.

"What's wrong, DJ? Did I embarrass you? Or are you jealous?"

"*Jealous?* Of what?"

"That another guy phoned me. I swear we're just friends."

Jones laughed to himself, surprised that Payne was still busting his balls. Normally, Jones was the childish one in their friendship, always joking at inappropriate times, and Payne was the adult. The sudden role reversal made Jones wonder if his friend had stayed underwater a little too long.

"On that note," Jones said, "I'm going to get a drink."

Payne smiled in victory but couldn't resist a knockout blow. "I think we're out of daiquiris. But if you'd like, we can probably get a pink umbrella for your beer."

4

✤

Despite groans of protest from his guests, Payne lowered the volume on his stereo—low enough to return Kaiser's call, yet loud enough to prevent eavesdroppers—then strolled to the far end of his boat. Some people might have viewed him as paranoid, but not Jones. Years of experience had taught them the value of secrecy. One of their superiors at the Pentagon used to say, "the smallest of leaks can sink the biggest of ships," and they knew this to be true.

In their world, small leaks were often plugged with bullets.

Using his encrypted cell phone, Payne dialed 0-1-1, followed by the country code for Germany, and then Kaiser's number. A few seconds later, he was chatting with the man who ran the largest black-market network in all of Europe.

"Thanks for getting back to me so quickly," Kaiser said. "I wasn't sure if a man of your stature would return a call from someone like me."

Payne smiled. "Why wouldn't I? I talk to assholes all the time. Including DJ."

Kaiser laughed loudly. Very few people had the guts to tease him, and even fewer had permission to do so. Payne was one of the chosen few. "How long has it been? Two, maybe three years?"

"Gosh, I hope not. Otherwise, we're both getting old."

"In my line of work, there is no old. Only alive and dead."

"Damn, Kaiser, how depressing! And you wonder why I never call?"

Kaiser grinned, glad their rapport hadn't diminished over time. If it had, he wouldn't have revealed the real reason for his call. "So tell me, how's the corporate world?"

"Boring as hell. How about you? How's the . . . um . . . *concierge* business?"

"Lucrative."

"Even in a recession?"

"*Especially* in a recession."

"Good to know," Payne said, although he wasn't the least bit surprised.

"What about DJ? How's he doing?"

Payne glanced at Jones, who was sipping a beer while sitting nearby. "Right now he's working on his tan. I can put him on if you'd like."

"Actually," Kaiser said, "can I speak to both of you at once? That might be easier."

"Not a problem. Let me put you on hold and call his cell. We can do one of those *ménage à call* things."

"Excuse me?"

"You know, a three-way call."

Kaiser laughed at the term. "Now, that's funny. I'll have to remember that."

"Trust me, they're hard to forget," Payne joked as he put Kaiser on hold.

Jones looked at him, confused. "So, what did he want?"

Payne shrugged. "I don't know yet. He wants to talk to both of us."

"About what?"

"No idea. But he seems in good spirits. I doubt it's anything major."

"Bet you a buck that someone died."

Payne smiled. "A whole dollar? Are you sure you can afford that?"

"Fine! Let's make it a hundred. That way I can use *your* money to pay off all the bets I lost on your swim. I think there's some justice in that."

"Let's see if I got this straight: You're using gambling to settle your gambling debts? Sounds foolproof to me."

Jones feigned indignation. "Give me a break, Jon. It's not like I need an intervention. In fact, I'll bet you twenty bucks I don't have a gambling problem."

Payne laughed as he dialed Jones's number. "Just answer your phone so we can talk to Kaiser. I'm curious about his call."

A moment later, the three of them were catching up on old times.

Kaiser said, "If I remember correctly, the last time we met was before your trip to Greece. It seems your journey paid off handsomely."

"Yeah," Jones said from a boat named after that adventure, "you could say that."

While helping an American student stranded in Russia, Payne and Jones had found themselves tangled in a global conspiracy that involved assassins, Spartans, and several dead monks. At the heart of their adventure were a lost relic from Ancient Greece and more treasure than anyone could spend in a lifetime. Although they'd discovered it, Payne and Jones weren't allowed to claim it as their own due to government intervention and international law. However, the countries involved gave them a finder's fee that had more digits than a sheikh had wives.

Needless to say, it made headlines around the world.

"Looking back on it," Kaiser asked, "which was more thrilling: hunting for the treasure or getting the reward?"

"The hunt," Payne blurted. "Definitely the hunt. No question about it."

Jones argued from his chair. "Easy for you to say. You were rich already."

Payne smiled. "That's a very good point."

"Does that mean you disagree?" Kaiser wondered.

"Not really," Jones admitted. "I simply like mocking Jon."

"In other words, you loved the hunt, too?"

Jones nodded. "You could say that."

"Great! I'm glad to hear it."

Payne paused in thought, wondering where this was

headed. "Okay, Kaiser. Enough with the foreplay. What's going on?"

"Yeah," Jones said, "did someone die?"

"Did someone *die*?" Kaiser echoed. "Why would you ask that?"

"No real reason. Just a hunch."

"Well," he said, searching for an appropriate response, "someone *did* die, but his death was fortuitous."

"Not for *him*," Payne observed.

"True, but it was for *us*."

Jones grinned in victory. "I couldn't agree more."

Kaiser sensed he was missing something—perhaps an inside joke—but didn't take the time to ask. He knew a fortune might be at stake, and the clock was already ticking. "Out of curiosity, have either of you been to Munich?"

"Munich?" they asked in unison.

"Yes. The capital of Bavaria."

Payne shook his head. "Can't say that I have."

"Me neither."

Kaiser continued. "It's a wonderful city, perhaps my favorite in all of Germany. There's an interesting mix of old and new, and the *weisswurst* is simply delicious."

"The *what worst*?" Jones said.

"The *weisswurst*," Kaiser repeated. "It's white sausage. A Bavarian specialty."

Payne and Jones tried not to laugh, which took a lot of effort from them. The last time they had dined with Kaiser, he had spent half the meal professing his love of sausage. The man had dozens of rivals in central Europe, yet the odds were pretty good a heart attack would kill him before one of his adversaries could. And in between bites of meat, he had admitted as much.

"Before you start listing ingredients and cooking times, I'd like to back up a little bit. Tell us more about the guy who died," Payne demanded.

Kaiser answered cryptically. "I'd prefer not to mention any details over the phone. However, let me assure you that I wasn't involved in his death—if that's what you're wondering."

"And yet his death benefits *us*. I believe that's how you phrased it."

"Yes, I did. And yes, it does."

"Care to explain?" Payne asked.

"I'd love to, but not over the phone. For additional details, you need to come here."

"Where's *here*?" Jones wondered.

"*Munich*. I thought that was pretty clear."

Payne laughed. "Nothing about this conversation has been clear."

Kaiser considered the remark, then nodded. "Perhaps not. But I assure you there's a reason for my caution. The fewer people who know about this, the better."

"Well, you're doing a great job. Because we've been chatting for five minutes, and neither of us has any idea what you're talking about."

Kaiser paused, searching for a different angle. "Jon, do you trust me? If so, come to Munich. I promise it will be worth your time."

Payne shook his head. "Actually, Kaiser, it's *you* who needs to trust *us*. If you're not willing to give us some basics, there's no way we're getting involved. So far, all we know is someone died and you love *weisswurst*. And that's not a lot to go on."

Sensing some tension, Jones reentered the conversation. "Speaking of *weisswurst*, leave it to Germans to invent a white sausage. What kind of racist bullshit is that?"

Kaiser laughed. Softly at first, and then much louder. After a while, it became apparent that he wasn't laughing at Jones. He was laughing at himself. "You're right, Jon. Obviously, you're right. I called you out of the blue and asked for too much trust in return. If the roles had been reversed, I would have bucked as well."

Kaiser took a deep breath, hoping to start anew. "Tell me, what would you like to know?"

"Let's start with the basics. Why did you call us?"

"Why? Because you're the only guys I know who have experience in this field."

"Really? What field is that?"

Kaiser smiled as he answered. "Buried treasure."

5

✤

SUNDAY, SEPTEMBER 19
Munich, Germany

Payne and Jones didn't see themselves as treasure hunters. They really didn't. But thanks to the fortune they had discovered in Greece and a few recent adventures, the world viewed them that way—whether they liked it or not. In truth, neither of them had a background in history, archaeology, or any related field, but they made up for their deficiencies in other ways. Both men were highly trained operatives, extremely intelligent, and always looking for a challenge.

To them, the promise of a new mission was the ultimate bait.

To sweeten the deal, Kaiser had chartered a luxury jet for their nine-hour flight to Germany. Because of the six-hour time difference, the Gulfstream V left a private terminal in Pittsburgh just before midnight and arrived in Munich at 2:50 P.M. All things considered, the trip was a pleasant one. Payne and Jones slept comfortably in reclining leather chairs. They spent the rest of the time playing cards and watching movies on a giant plasma screen. A fully stocked refrigerator, filled with an assortment of snacks and gourmet foods, kept them fed. Sports drinks and bottled water kept them hydrated. Over the years, they had been on enough missions to perfect the art of traveling. They knew when to eat, when to sleep, and what they needed to bring. Like expectant mothers, they even kept travel bags by their doors, just in case they were forced to leave in the middle of the night and didn't have time to pack.

Of course, pregnant women rarely packed ammo.

Despite the luxury jet and the lure of treasure, Payne and Jones had played hard to get until Kaiser brought out his secret weapon—the pageantry of the world's largest fair. As luck would have it, Oktoberfest had started the day before and would continue through October 3. Held annually in Munich, the sixteen-day festival would attract more than six million people, many of whom would eat too much and drink even more. The duo had always wanted to attend but had never made the arrangements. With Kaiser's connections in Germany and his generous offer to foot their bill, Payne and Jones realized this was the perfect time to go.

The meeting came first, then two days of celebrating.

What could possibly go wrong?

Kaiser greeted them inside a private hangar near Munich Airport. He was wearing a T-shirt, blue jeans, and a brown leather jacket—the same clothes he always wore. Nothing about his appearance really stood out, and nothing about him seemed menacing. In his mid-fifties, he had slicked-back gray hair and bushy eyebrows that dangled above his dark eyes. When he talked, he smiled a lot, like a friendly neighbor or a local merchant who cared about his customers.

And the truth was he actually did.

A decade earlier, when Payne and Jones had met Kaiser for the first time, they figured his kindness was just an act. That he was being nice to them in order to get their business. But over time, they realized that wasn't the case. Kaiser was a good guy, a gracious guy, who was very good at his job. He didn't lie, or steal, or sell drugs. He didn't rip people off. He made his money by acquiring hard-to-find items and selling them at a fair price. To military personnel stationed in Germany, Kaiser wasn't a criminal; he was a businessman. Nothing more, nothing less.

Then again, every once in a while, Payne and Jones would hear stories about Kaiser that were less than flattering. Mostly they involved suppliers who tried to con him, or buyers who went against their word. In those situations, Kaiser abandoned his cordial persona and handled the offenders in an appropriate fashion. He liked to refer to it as "street justice." Once Payne and Jones had asked him about a violent rumor, but Kaiser wouldn't confirm or deny anything, obviously enjoying his reputation. Then he told them something they would never forget.

Never mistake kindness for weakness.

To this day, it was still one of their favorite sayings.

. . .

"How was the flight?" Kaiser asked as he shook Payne's hand.

"Wonderful. Thanks for the royal treatment."

"Nothing but the best for you two."

Jones gave Kaiser a friendly hug. "Not to be rude, but are you sure you can afford it?"

Kaiser looked at him, confused. "Why would you ask that?"

"Because you've been wearing the same clothes for the past ten years. Don't they have malls over here?" Jones glanced at Payne. "We need to take him shopping."

Kaiser laughed, enjoying the good-natured teasing. "I'll have you know I bought a new T-shirt just last year. I'm good to go for the rest of the decade."

Jones argued. "Come on, man. A guy in your business should have some style. We need to get you a shiny suit and some fancy jewelry, like a gangster. Maybe even a fedora."

Payne shook his head, embarrassed. "Please ignore him. It was a long flight, and he's overcaffeinated. Just let him run around the airfield for twenty minutes, and he'll be fine."

Kaiser smiled. "I wish we had the time, but we're on a tight schedule. If we don't leave now, we won't get to the site before dark."

"The site? What site?" Payne asked, still unsure what Kaiser had found and what was expected of them. "Now that we're here, I was hoping you'd fill in some blanks."

"I'd be happy to," Kaiser said as he picked up Payne's bag. "Once we're airborne."

"Airborne?"

Kaiser started to walk across the hangar. "Didn't I mention that on the phone?"

Payne hustled after him. "You didn't mention *anything* on the phone."

"Really? I could've sworn that I did."

Payne caught up to him and grabbed his arm. "Hold up, Kaiser. We need to talk."

Kaiser turned, smiling. "About what?"

"Listen, I appreciate your enthusiasm and understand the time constraints, but we're not getting on another plane until you tell us where we're going."

"Not a plane," he countered, "a helicopter."

"Cool," Jones blurted as he caught up to them. "I love choppers. Can I drive?"

Kaiser shook his head. "Sorry, we have a pilot."

"Then I call shotgun. You can't see shit from the backseat."

Payne gave him a dirty look. "Hold up. You're not bothered by this?"

"Actually, now that you mention it, I *am* bothered by this." Jones handed his bag to Kaiser, who gladly accepted it. "I figure, if he's carrying your bag, he should carry mine, too."

Payne growled. "That's not what I was talking about."

"Really? Then what's bugging you?"

"We don't know where we're going or what we're involved in."

Jones sighed, trying to get under Payne's skin. "Fine! Be that way! Kaiser's trying to surprise us, and you're determined to ruin everything."

Jones spun toward Kaiser, who was trying not to laugh. "Is the site in Germany?"

"Yes," he answered.

"Is the site secure?"

"Yes."

"Can we bring weapons?"

"If you'd like."

"Will we need them?"

"Probably not."

"Are we dressed appropriately?"

Kaiser inspected their clothes. Both men were wearing cargo pants, long-sleeved shirts, and comfortable shoes. Perfect for where they were going. "Yes."

"What about snacks?"

"Yes, there's food at the site."

Jones threw his arm around Payne's shoulder and squeezed. "Come on, Jon. The man has *snacks*. How bad can it be?"

6

Garmisch-Partenkirchen, Germany
(59 miles southwest of Munich)

Garmisch and Partenkirchen were separate towns for more than a thousand years, until Adolf Hitler forced them to combine prior to hosting the 1936 Winter Olympics. Located near the Austrian border, the picturesque town of nearly thirty thousand people sits near two of the largest mountains in Germany: the Zugspitze and the Leutasch Dreitorspitze.

The helicopter circled above the valley for a few minutes, giving Payne and Jones an aerial view of the landscape before it touched down in a green pasture southwest of town. A lush forest, filled with tall pines and rugged trails, started at the edge of the meadow, as if God had run out of grass and had been forced to change the terrain at that very spot. In a span of less than ten feet, the topography went from flat and grassy to steep and rocky.

Although the sun was shining and the weather was pleasant, Payne and Jones had spent enough time in the mountains of Afghanistan to understand how drastically altitude could affect the weather. It was sixty-eight degrees where the chopper had landed, yet the peak above them was covered in snow. Depending on the length of their hike, they knew the temperature could drop significantly—especially after dark.

Jones swore under his breath, not thrilled with the possibilities. Despite years of training and hundreds of missions, there were few things he hated more than cold. And Payne knew it.

"Looks *frigid* up there. I hope you packed your mittens," he taunted.

Jones swore again, this time a little louder.

"What was it that you said earlier? *The man has snacks. How bad can it be?*" Payne asked in a mocking tone. "Well, I guess you're about to find out."

Unhappy with the turn of events, Jones was ready to unleash a string of four-letter words, but Kaiser cut him off before he had a chance. "The sun goes down around seven—even sooner where we're headed. The trees choke out the light."

Payne nodded in understanding. "Then we better get moving."

Kaiser pulled a cargo bag from the belly of the chopper. "I've got flashlights and basic supplies. Everything else is at the site."

"How far away?"

"Maybe thirty minutes."

"Not a problem," Payne said as he studied the forest. Starting at the edge of the meadow, a narrow path snaked its way up the hillside until it disappeared in the trees. "Out of curiosity, who owns this field?"

Kaiser walked toward him. "Why do you ask?"

"Why? Because we just landed a helicopter on it. Plus, if we need to haul something off the mountain, we'll need to bring in a truck."

"Don't worry. It's taken care of."

"Meaning?"

Kaiser smiled. "Meaning, it's taken care of. Seriously, Jon, you need to relax. All I need you to do is figure out what we're dealing with."

Even though Kaiser had kept his word and filled in some details during their trip from Munich, Payne wasn't comfortable with his role as a consultant. Normally, he was the man in charge of the mission, not the one with all the questions.

"Sorry," Payne said, "force of habit."

"No need to apologize. Or worry. I'm telling you, Jon, this will be easy. You'll be drinking beer at Oktoberfest before you know it."

Payne forced a smile, hoping he was right. "Sounds good to me."

"It's about freaking time," snapped Jones as he brushed past them and headed toward the trail. "The longer we wait, the colder it gets."

Confused, Kaiser looked to Payne for an explanation. "What's his problem?"

"Unfortunately, there are too many to name."

. . .

All things considered, the hike was a simple one. The weather was mild, the ground was dry, and the path was well defined. Someone had marked the way with chalk, placing an X on trees in order to highlight the route. Every once in a while, there would be a circle or a square, or an arrow pointing to the left or right, but Kaiser explained they were "dummy signs" meant to confuse intruders. Payne and Jones weren't sure who would follow symbols in the middle of the woods—unless Robert Langdon was in town—but they took it in stride. Until they knew what had been discovered, they weren't sure how much caution was necessary.

"We're almost there," Kaiser assured them. He reached into his bag and pulled out a two-way radio equipped with GPS. "I have to let them know we're approaching."

"And if you don't?" Payne asked.

"They'll shoot us," he explained.

Jones, who was leading the way, stopped instantly. "Good to know."

Kaiser powered on the unit, then mumbled several words in German. A few seconds later, a short response crackled through the speaker.

Kaiser nodded in understanding. "Okay, we're clear. It's just up ahead."

But Jones refused to move. "That's okay. I'll wait."

"For what?" Kaiser wondered.

"For a white guy to take the lead."

"You're such a racist," Payne said as he walked past

Jones. For as long as they had been friends, race had never been an issue, so they felt comfortable teasing each other about the subject. In their friendship, very few things were off-limits.

"Maybe so," Jones mumbled, "but my black ass is still alive."

"Because you're a coward. A racist coward."

"A coward?" Jones hustled to catch up with his best friend. "Did you just call me a coward? I swear, if I wasn't so damn scared of you, I'd punch you in the face."

Payne was going to tease him some more until he spotted something in the trees. Instinctively, he froze and threw a clinched fist into the air. In the military, it meant to stop and shut up because a threat had been detected. Jones saw the sign and instantly obeyed. No questions, no debate. No sound of any kind. During his career, the signal had saved his life many times. He wasn't about to challenge it now.

"What's wrong?" Kaiser asked.

Jones turned and signaled for him to be quiet. A moment later, Payne pointed to the right, letting them know where danger was lurking. Jones nodded and calmly pulled a gun from his belt. The Sig Sauer had been tucked underneath his shirt at the small of his back. From the front of the group, Payne did the same, drawing his weapon with a steady hand.

One moment they were joking around. The next, they were ready to kill.

As if someone had flipped a switch.

"Where are your men?" Payne asked as he dropped into a crouch.

"Up ahead, guarding the site."

"All of them?"

"I don't know," Kaiser admitted.

"Get on your radio and find out."

"But I just talked to—"

Payne cut him off. "Do you *like* your men? If so, get a head count."

"But—"

"Listen," Payne explained. "If I send DJ into the woods, he's going to take out anyone he sees. And trust me when I say this—he's very good at what he does."

"I'm like a ninja," Jones assured him.

"Therefore, for the sake of your men, *please* ask them where they are. Otherwise, this is going to get messy."

Kaiser nodded, concerned and exhilarated at the exact same time. He had heard stories about the duo, but had never seen them in action until that moment. Needless to say, he was impressed by their performance. "No problem. I'll call them right now."

Kaiser turned on the radio and started whispering in German. His message was longer than before, and a lot more urgent. So was the response from the guards. About halfway through, a smile surfaced on Kaiser's lips.

"It's okay," he said, breathing a sigh of relief. "Richter was just taking a piss."

"A piss?" Jones lowered his weapon. "That piss almost cost him his dick."

"I'll be sure to tell him."

Despite the explanation, Payne remained on high alert—

unable to fully relax until he got more details from Kaiser. "Who are these guys?"

Kaiser frowned. "Why do you ask?"

"Why? Because they're armed, and I know nothing about them."

"Fair enough," he said. "They're men I've used before. Men I trust."

"And their backgrounds?"

"German."

"Yeah, I figured that out on my own."

"What's wrong?" Jones asked.

"Nothing's wrong," Payne said, forcing a smile. "I just wanted to know who we're dealing with. Better safe than sorry. Right?"

Jones stared at him, trying to read his expression. "And you're cool?"

Payne nodded, ever so slowly. "Yeah, I'm cool."

"Great!" Kaiser exclaimed. "Then what are we waiting for? We're almost there."

7

❖

While approaching the site, Payne and Jones kept their heads on a swivel. Not only because armed guards were watching their every move, but because the duo still didn't know what Kaiser had discovered in this desolate stretch of woods. Or exactly why they had been summoned.

For the past twenty-four hours, Kaiser had been less than generous with the details, keeping information to himself for security reasons. Or so he claimed. At first, they were willing to let it slide because of their history with Kaiser. They trusted him and knew he wouldn't have flown them to Germany for something trivial or illegal. But the longer the mysteries lingered, the longer he kept them in the dark about their role, the more suspicious they became.

"Ten o'clock," Payne whispered to Jones. "Behind the fallen rocks."

Jones glanced in that direction and nodded. Although Kaiser's men were dressed in woodland camouflage—a mixture of greens, browns, and black that was perfect for this terrain—Payne and Jones had spotted four guards in less than a minute. An amazing feat in dim light.

"Unbelievable," Kaiser gushed. "You found them all."

"Not yet," Payne said. He pointed to the hillside that overlooked the site. "Twelve o'clock, on the ledge. There's a bird's nest up there."

"Bird's nest" was military slang for an elevated sniper position.

"Nice spot," Jones said. "Good protection, wide field of fire. And high enough to take a nap without the other guards knowing. That's where I'd set up, with a camouflage Snuggie."

Kaiser studied the rock face. "Sorry. I forgot about him."

"Somehow I doubt that. But if you did, it makes me wonder," Payne said.

"About what?"

"What else you've forgotten to tell us."

Kaiser grimaced when he heard the tone of Payne's voice. Usually playful, it was now tinged with distrust. "*Forgotten*? Nothing about the site. *Omitted*? Plenty. But I promise, there's a method to my madness. Once you see what we've discovered, you'll understand why I brought you here. Not only that, you're going to thank me for my discretion."

Payne stared at him. "Who's *we*?"

Kaiser blinked a few times. "Excuse me?"

"You said *we* discovered the site. Whom were you talking about?"

"Come on, Jon. Did you really think I found this place on my own? Look at my stomach. See the way the fat hangs over my belt? Do I look like I climb mountains in my free time?"

"Not unless they're made of sausage," Jones teased.

Payne rolled his eyes. "In that case, who found it?"

"A friend of the deceased."

"And when did you get involved?"

Kaiser explained. "As luck should have it, I was notified right after the site was discovered. Due to the embarrassing nature of the hunter's death—getting crushed by a flying pig—a colleague of mine was paid good money to move the corpse to a secondary location, one that would be more dignified. He made it look like the hunter had died in a fall."

"This colleague of yours. Is he your partner?"

Kaiser shook his head. "Thankfully, my colleague owed me several favors, so I traded them for the rights to the site. Personally, I think it was a bargain."

"Do you trust this guy?" Payne asked.

"Not completely, but I have enough dirt on him to guarantee his silence."

Payne agreed. "Sometimes that's better than trust."

Kaiser read between the lines, trying to remain calm. "Listen, I understand your frustration. I truly do. You've come all this way, and I've been stonewalling you the entire time. But I promise, that's about to change. Give me five minutes—just five more minutes. That's all I need. After that, everything will make sense. My secrecy, your involvement, *everything*!"

"It'd better, or we're leaving," Payne warned.

Kaiser smiled, hoping to lighten the mood. "Trust me, Jon. What you're about to see will convince you to stay. I guarantee it."

Payne glanced at his watch and noted the time. More than twenty-four hours had passed since Kaiser's initial call. Since then, he and Jones had traveled nearly forty-five hundred miles from Pittsburgh to Munich to Garmisch-Partenkirchen. And now, under the vigilant watch of five armed guards, the duo had followed a smuggler up the side of Zugspitze, yet they didn't know why. In many ways, it was exhilarating.

"You've got five minutes. Lead the way."

Kaiser did as he was told, leading them into the natural cul-de-sac where the boar had been killed. The area didn't seem special in any way, except for the large hole in the forest floor. For safety's sake, the perimeter had been marked with several wooden posts and a bright yellow rope. With a buffer zone of ten feet, the rope formed a semicircle with the rock face on the far side of the hole.

"What do you think?" Kaiser asked.

Jones crouched and examined the boundary. "I like the rope. Is this nylon?"

"I meant about the site."

Payne scrunched his face. "This is the site?"

"Technically, it's the entrance to the site, but what do you think?"

Payne paused, searching for words. "It looks like a hole."

"Well, it is a hole. But a hole in what?"

Payne guessed. "The ground."

Kaiser shook his head. "Actually, it's a hole in the roof."

Jones stood, confused. "The roof of what?"

"A secret bunker," Kaiser replied. "As far as I can tell, the ground collapsed from the weight of the pig. I'm telling you, it's a massive sucker. At least six hundred pounds."

Jones whistled. "That's a big pig."

"Unfortunately, you'll get to see it—and smell it. It's way too big to lift by hand. We'll need a winch to move all that meat."

Jones grinned. "I dated a girl who said the same thing about me."

Kaiser ignored the comment. "Obviously, I can get you anything you need for the site. But extra equipment means extra workers. And at this stage of the game, I felt privacy was more important."

Payne smiled. "Same old Kaiser. Still loving your privacy."

Kaiser corrected him. "Not *my* privacy, *your* privacy. I'm doing this for *you*."

"For *me*?" Payne asked.

"For all of you."

Although he wanted Kaiser to explain himself, Payne figured it would be a waste of time. Why settle for an ambiguous response when they were *this* close to learning the truth? On multiple occasions, Kaiser had said everything would make sense once they saw the contents of the site. So it seemed foolish to ask any more questions.

They were standing ten feet from the entrance to the site.

It was time to climb inside.

8

❈

D ue to the instability of the terrain, the fifteen-foot extension ladder did not lean against the sides of the hole. Instead, the ladder was attached to scaffolding on the floor of the bunker. The last thing they wanted was for the ground to open any wider and swallow another victim.

"Coming down," Kaiser yelled as his feet clanked on the aluminum steps. At the bottom, he was greeted by a sixth guard, who was positioned underground just in case intruders slipped past everyone else and tried to raid the site.

"You're next," Payne said to Jones. "I'm fifty pounds heavier and the ground is unstable."

Jones nodded and carefully approached the opening. As he did, his heart pounded in his chest. Not from fear of the unknown but from the promising possibilities. The last time he had felt this way was in Greece, right before they had found the treasure that had changed his life forever. Until then he had been making a decent living, running a detective agency out of free office space at the Payne Industries Building. A solid life, for sure, but not nearly as exciting as he had hoped it would be. Then again, compared to his time with the MANIACs, what could possibly compete? In many ways, he felt like a star athlete who had been forced to retire during the prime of his career. No matter what he did to stay near the game—coaching, scouting, or broadcasting—the thrill just wasn't the same as it had been in his former life.

But moments like this came close.

Grabbing the ladder with his right hand, Jones stretched his left leg over the opening and placed his foot on the metal step. A moment later, his second foot followed. As it did, the top of the ladder rattled and swayed. Not enough to be dangerous, but more than enough to get his attention. While waiting for the ladder to settle, Jones peered into the dark void below. A single beam of light danced underneath him, revealing nothing but a glimpse of the bunker's floor. It looked old and dusty, like a pharaoh's tomb.

"Hurry up," Payne urged. "It's getting darker by the minute."

"Trust me, Jon, it doesn't matter. It's like a black hole down there."

"Speaking of black a-holes, what are you waiting for?"

Jones smiled. "I'm waiting for the ladder to settle."

Payne rolled his eyes. "And you wonder why I normally go first."

"You know, if I were you, I'd want to stay on my good side."

"Why's that?"

"I'll be invisible in the dark."

"Great! We can play Marco Polo without closing our eyes," Payne teased, referring to the children's game. "Now, hurry the fuck up and climb down the ladder."

Jones laughed as he started his descent. When he reached the bottom, he pulled out his flashlight and flicked it on. Thirty seconds later, Payne was standing next to him, doing the same thing. Suddenly, the room around them came into view.

At first glance, nothing about it seemed remarkable. Eleven feet long and twenty feet wide, the chamber's walls and floor were made of white concrete. Over the years, cracks had formed in two of the walls, allowing moisture to seep in. The tiny fissures were surrounded by patches of lime-green mildew that appeared to move in the light. Like something from science fiction. Like something from outer space. On closer examination, Jones realized it was simply an optical illusion—light refracting off different surfaces—yet the effect was still creepy.

"Take a look at this," Payne said from the other side of the room.

Jones whirled and spotted him behind the scaffolding. He was crouched down, examining a large object wrapped in a plastic sheet. "What is it?"

"The murder weapon."

"The what?" Jones asked, confused. A few steps later,

he noticed the face of the dead boar. It was pressed against the plastic, its bloodstained tusks poking through. "Holy balls! Look at that thing. It's huge!"

"It's the biggest boar I've ever seen."

Jones knelt next to it and patted its side. Even though it was wrapped in plastic, the scent of death lingered in the air. Grabbing one of its tusks, he said, "This little piggy had roast beef."

Payne smiled. "No wonder the other piggy had none. This one ate the whole cow."

Jones laughed. "Hey, Kaiser, is this why we're here? To see the nursery rhyme pig? If so, we're a little late. No way Hogzilla is going to market. He's a little too ripe."

"Actually," Kaiser said from the far corner, "I brought you down here for this."

Payne stood. "For what?"

"For the other room."

Jones stood, too. "There's another room?"

Kaiser nodded, and then twisted a small handle in the wall. Made of metal, the recessed lever had been painted white to conceal its existence. Intrigued, Payne and Jones shined their lights in the corner and watched in amazement as a door suddenly appeared in the concrete.

One moment, it looked solid. The next, there was a slight opening.

"How'd we miss that?" Jones whispered.

Payne shrugged and walked forward to examine it.

In a brightly lit space, the doorway would have been easy to spot. But years of dirt and mildew, coupled with the gloom of the underground lair, had obscured its presence. Not only to Payne and Jones, but to Kaiser, too. On his first visit, it had taken him an hour to notice it.

Kaiser said, "I'm pretty sure this back room was a bomb shelter."

"Why do you say that?" Payne asked.

"Feel this sucker. It's solid concrete. Doors like this are built for two reasons: safes and shelters. And since there isn't a lock, I'm guessing it's not a safe."

Payne knocked on the door, impressed. "What's back there?"

"A tunnel, then a room."

Payne glanced at the ladder to get his bearings. "Unless I'm mistaken, the tunnel goes underneath the rock face. That's the best place to build a bunker. Use the mountain instead of concrete. Much cheaper that way."

Kaiser leaned against the door, but it barely budged. "If you don't mind, can you give me a hand? This thing weighs a ton."

"No problem. I like helping the elderly."

Payne smiled and pushed the door with all of his strength. Slowly but surely, it swung open from left to right until it crashed into the tunnel wall behind it. Made of concrete and painted the same color as the first chamber, the arched corridor was nearly six feet wide and seven feet high, and it stretched twenty-two feet into the mountain. At the far end of the passageway, there was another thick door. In between, there was nothing but concrete and empty space.

No lights. No signs. No markings of any kind.

"Thanks," Jones said as he slipped past Payne. "I knew we brought you for a reason."

"Please, after you," he mumbled sarcastically. "Really, I insist."

Jones grinned in the dark as he took the lead. Guided by his flashlight, he studied the tunnel's construction as he moved toward the back room. "Notice anything about the walls?"

"Not really," Payne said. "Then again, you're blocking my view."

Jones answered his own query. "They're spotless. No mildew or cracks of any kind. Whoever built this section did a much better job. Then again, that makes sense if the next room is a bomb shelter—although I'm beginning to have some doubts."

"Why's that?" Kaiser asked from the rear.

"As far as I can tell, there's no ventilation."

Kaiser nodded. "Actually, you're right. Not a single vent anywhere. I checked."

Payne stopped and shined his flashlight at Kaiser. "No vents? There *have* to be vents. No vents means no air. No air means no people. Why build a bunker that can't hold people?"

Kaiser smiled cryptically. "You're about to find out."

9

✺

Mitte District
Berlin, Germany

Hans Mueller grabbed the sharpest knife he could find and plunged it into the sausage. It hissed when its skin was pierced, grease oozing like lava onto the hot grill.

Watching closely, the man across the kitchen winced.

He knew this was a message, not a meal.

Born in India but a recent resident of Berlin, Asif Kapur had been invited to dinner through unconventional means. Two thugs had kicked in his front door and had dragged him out of his shower. At first, he had screamed and tried to fight back, but a swift kick to his groin and several layers of duct tape around his hands and mouth had put an end to that. Dripping wet and completely naked, Kapur was thrown into the trunk of a Mercedes and driven around the city for more than an hour. By the time they were done, he was shivering with fear.

That's when he was delivered to the restaurant.

Recently purchased by Mueller as a way to launder money, the complex was still being renovated. Over the past few decades, the entire neighborhood had received an extensive face-lift. Formerly a part of East Berlin, the borough of Mitte had been surrounded by the Berlin Wall on three sides. Although there had been some crossing points between East and West Berlin during the Cold War—the most famous being Checkpoint Charlie—Mitte wasn't a popular tourist destination until the wall came tumbling down in 1989. Since then, the area had experienced a renaissance. Galleries were built. Cafés were opened. And derelict houses were destroyed. After so many years of being an embarrassment, Mitte has reestablished itself as the heart of Berlin.

And Mueller hoped to take advantage of the influx of visitors.

"Tell me," he said without turning away from the grill, "do you know who I am?"

Kapur, still naked but no longer gagged, nodded in fear. "Yes, sir."

Mueller stabbed another sausage with the tip of the knife. "Do you know why you're here?"

Kapur gulped, his heart pounding in his throat. "Yes, sir."

"One more question," Mueller said as he turned off the flame and faced his guest for the very first time. "Do you enjoy curry?"

The topic caught Kapur off guard. "Excuse me?"

Wearing a white apron over his dress shirt and tie,

Mueller carried the platter of sausages across the kitchen and set it on a large butcher block. Made of maple, it sat in the center of the workspace and was partially covered with kitchen equipment. "It's a simple question, really. One I thought you could answer without much difficulty—especially considering your heritage. You are Indian, correct?"

Kapur nodded from the opposite side of the wood.

Mueller, a fit German in his forties with a military haircut and eyes as black as coal, glared at his guest. "I believe I asked you a question. If you're unwilling to answer me verbally, my men will gag you once again. Is that what you'd prefer?"

Kapur shook his head. "No, sir."

A smile returned to Mueller's face. "Good. You are Indian, correct?"

"Yes, sir."

Mueller stared at him, sizing him up. "Do you enjoy curry?"

Kapur nodded. "Yes, sir. Very much, sir."

Mueller leaned closer. "Do you like it . . . *spicy*?"

"Yes, sir. Very spicy."

Mueller considered Kapur's answer, then nodded his approval. "This restaurant, once the renovations are finished, will serve the finest currywurst in all of Germany. Are you familiar with the dish?"

"No, sir."

Mueller gasped in surprise. "You are an Indian living in Berlin, and you are not familiar with currywurst? How can this be?"

Kapur swallowed hard. "I haven't been here long. Only a month."

"A month," Mueller echoed, letting the words hang in the air like smoke from the grill. "You are correct. You have been here a month. One month exactly. One month to this very day."

Kapur nodded. He was very aware of the date. "Yes, sir."

Mueller took a deep breath and blew it out slowly, trying to control his rage. "Even so, you cannot go anywhere in this city without passing a currywurst stand every fifty feet. I am surprised that an Indian, such as yourself, did not smell the spice and stop for a taste of your homeland. To me, that's inconceivable. Tell me, are you a vegetarian?"

Kapur shook his head. "No, sir."

"Wonderful!" Mueller exclaimed as he jabbed one of the sausages with his knife. "Then allow me to make you a plate. Please don't take this the wrong way, but you are the only Indian I know. Personally, I feel it would be a wasted opportunity if I didn't get your opinion."

"Of course, sir. Whatever you want, sir."

Mueller reached to his right and grabbed a metal contraption that Kapur had never seen. It had a wide opening on top, a handle on the side, and several blades in the middle. "A woman named Herta Heuwer invented this dish way back in 1949. As you probably know, Berlin was in horrible shape after the war, and supplies were at a minimum. Herta had a street stand in the Charlottenburg district where she grilled pork wurst for construction workers rebuilding the city. One day she was given some ketchup, Worcestershire sauce, and curry powder from British soldiers and decided to make a sauce to pour over her wurst."

After sliding the sausage into the top of the machine, Mueller placed a dish underneath the contraption, then pulled the handle with a loud *thwack!* A second later, several bite-size pieces of sausage tumbled into the dish.

Mueller grinned with delight. "Currywurst was so popular with the workers that word spread around the city. Within two years, she was selling over ten thousand servings a week. Her recipe was so beloved she had it patented. To this day, there is still a plaque in Charlottenburg that marks the spot where her stand once stood."

Mueller momentarily turned his back in order to get his sauce from the stove. Kapur, who was still completely naked, eyed the knife on the butcher block but thought better of it. Even if he managed to stab Mueller, there was no way he'd get past the guards, who were watching him from the far side of the kitchen.

"Obviously," Mueller said as he grabbed the saucepan from the stove, "many chefs have tweaked Herta's recipe over the years. Nowadays there are all kinds of variations. Some are made with paprika. Some are made with onions. Some are made with tomato paste. As hard as this is to believe, over eight hundred million servings of currywurst are sold in Germany every year. Can you believe that number? Eight hundred million!"

"That's hard to believe, sir."

Mueller laughed. "But it's true! I read that fact at the Currywurst Museum that opened last year. Can you believe that? Currywurst is so popular in Berlin that it has its own museum. As soon as I heard about it, I knew I had to open a restaurant using my grandmother's secret recipe. Everyone who has eaten it swears it's the best they've ever had."

Kapur watched as Mueller drizzled some curry onto the sausage. Steam rose off the pieces as he did. "It smells delicious, sir."

Mueller set the plate in front of him. "Wait until you taste it! I'm telling you, your taste buds will dance and your sinuses will clear—if they haven't already."

Kapur eyed the meal skeptically. Even if it was the worst thing he had ever tasted, he planned on gushing over it like it had been the best. But much to his surprise, the curry-wurst was wonderful. Somehow the sausage and the curry, which seemed to have nothing in common, actually complemented each other's taste. "Sir, it's excellent! Truly excellent!"

Mueller beamed with pride. "See, I knew you would like it. Some people are hesitant to try new things, but not me. I'm always looking for something new."

Mueller walked around the butcher block and patted Kapur on his shoulder. The flesh-on-flesh contact sent a tremor through Kapur's body. "Take you, for example. A lot of people told me *not* to get involved with you. They said you couldn't be trusted to hold up your end of the bargain. But I disagreed with them. I said if wurst and curry could mesh together into something so delicious, then so could a German and an Indian. Don't you agree?"

Beads of perspiration formed on Kapur's forehead.

Whether it was from the spices or his nerves, he wasn't sure. "Yes, sir. I wholeheartedly agree."

Mueller grimaced as he grabbed the contraption. Its base squeaked softly as he pulled it across the wood. "Unfortunately, my Indian friend, your first payment was due one month after your arrival in Berlin, but according to my assistant, you have failed to hold up your end of the bargain. You have not paid a single euro."

"Yes, sir. I'm sorry, sir. But there's a—"

"Don't!" Mueller growled, all the compassion gone from his face. "Do *not* make excuses. In my business, there are no excuses. You promised your first payment on this day, and you failed to deliver. That leaves me with no choice. I *must* punish your betrayal, or others will follow your lead."

"But, sir! If you—"

Before he could utter another word, Kapur felt one of the guard's arms wrap around his throat. Instinctively, Kapur raised his bound hands and tried to fight him off— tried to gouge out his eyes or do anything he could do to loosen his grip—but it was the biggest mistake of his life. While Kapur was flailing and fighting for air, the other guard grabbed Kapur's penis and shoved it into the contraption.

Kapur's eyes doubled in size when he realized what was about to happen.

Meanwhile, Mueller smiled as he clutched the handle.

Thwack!

10

❈

Garmisch-Partenkirchen, Germany

The second door was identical to the first. Same weight. Same concrete. Same recessed handle. As if the bunker's architect had shopped at a buy-one-get-one-free sale before he had started the project—*whenever* that might have been. Without a trained historian, Payne and Jones had no idea how old the bunker was. Twenty years? Fifty years? More than a hundred?

They weren't sure but hoped the back room would provide some answers.

To prove his worth, Jones opened the heavy door without any help, a process that took twice as long as Payne's effort on the first door. Afterward, despite being out of breath, he stared at Payne and said, "Maybe we don't need your muscles after all."

"Sure you do," he replied. "I'll be the one who carries you out when you collapse."

"Thanks," Jones wheezed. "That'll be pretty soon."

Payne smiled and turned toward Kaiser, who was standing behind him in the tunnel. "If you don't mind, why don't you take the lead? Show us why we're here."

"I'd be happy to," Kaiser said as he squeezed past the duo. "Just so you know, none of my men have been back this far. What you're about to see is between us."

"How do you know?" Payne wondered.

"How? Because I trust my men," he said harshly. Then, as if he suddenly remembered whom he was talking to, Kaiser caught himself and grinned. "Plus, I told them there's going to be a lie-detector test once we leave Bavaria, and if any of them fail, they'll lose a limb."

Jones glanced at him, unsure if he was kidding. "How does that work? Do they pick a limb ahead of time, or do you spin a giant wheel of body parts if they fail?"

"Cross me someday and find out," Kaiser said with a wink.

Payne laughed, but Jones didn't—still not sure if Kaiser was joking.

"Anyway," Kaiser said, "let me show you what I found."

Following the beam of his flashlight, Kaiser led the duo into the back room. Roughly twenty feet long and thirty feet wide, its walls were made of the same concrete as the outer chamber. Besides the width and length, the main difference in the construction was the height of the ceiling, which was a mere seven feet tall. Standing six-foot-six in hiking shoes, Payne instinctively crouched until he was certain he could walk upright without banging his head.

After that, his focus shifted to the room's contents instead of the room itself.

Payne stared in fascination at the dozens of wooden crates of varying sizes that lined the back wall. They were stacked in neat rows, one on top of the other, like Lego blocks from another time. Until recently, the crates had been covered with long canvas tarps, which Kaiser had folded and stored along the left wall. Other than that, the rest of the room appeared empty.

Excited by the possibilities, Jones hustled toward the stacks with childlike enthusiasm. He shined his light on the first crate he came across, expecting it to be open and overflowing with valuables, but its lid was nailed shut. Undaunted, he dashed over to the next crate, which was slightly larger than the first one, and discovered it was sealed, too. The same with the next one, and the one after that. All of them appeared to be sealed.

Jones glanced over his shoulder, confused. "What's in the crates?"

Kaiser looked at him and shrugged. "I honestly don't know."

"You don't know?" Jones blurted.

Kaiser shook his head. "Nope."

"Hold up," Payne said, trying to understand. "You flew us four thousand miles on a private jet, but you don't know what's in any of these crates? Sorry, but I don't buy that for a second."

"Actually," Kaiser admitted, "I know what's in one. That's all it took."

"Which one?" Jones demanded.

Kaiser pointed toward a crate in the far right corner. It had been moved a few inches from those nearby, like a book pulled from a crowded shelf and then hastily returned. From where Jones was standing, the crate appeared to be sealed like the others. Upon closer inspection, he realized the lid had been placed on top but hadn't been reattached.

Jones turned and faced Kaiser. "Let me see if I got this straight. The contents of this box compelled you to fly us here overnight, but worried you so much you didn't open any of the others. . . . Please tell me it's not cursed."

Kaiser grimaced. "Define *cursed*."

Payne furrowed his brow. He had known Kaiser for more than a decade, and in all those years, he had never seen him act so strangely. Cautious, yes. But never bizarre.

"Listen," Payne said to him, "it's obvious there's something going on that we don't understand. Do you want to fill us in, or should we open the box and find out for ourselves?"

"Just open the box. We can talk when you're done."

Jones grinned in the darkness. "Can one of you hold my light?"

Payne nodded and stepped forward, hoping to get a closer look.

Measuring nearly four feet in height, width, and depth, the crate was made of vintage wood and free of exterior labels. Rope handles, common on boxes from yesteryear, dangled from its sides like elephant ears. Overall, the crate was in remarkable shape—completely free of cracks or scuff marks of any kind. Whoever had placed it there had done so with respect.

Using both hands, Jones removed the lid and placed it on a neighboring crate, careful not to damage either. With questions dancing in his head and adrenaline surging through his veins, he rushed back to Payne's side and they gazed into the box together.

At first glance, they were less than impressed. The crate's interior was equipped with seven strips of plywood that ran from left to right, forming eight vertical slots that extended to the bottom of the crate. All of the slots, which were roughly six inches wide, were filled with a mixture of hardwood panels and unframed canvases. Because of the darkness of the bunker and the depth of the slots, they had no idea what they were looking at until Jones removed one of the objects and held it in the beam of Payne's flashlight.

"Holy shit." Jones gasped as he stared at the oil on panel.

The Impressionist masterpiece depicted five sunflowers—three in a green vase and two more lying in front of the vase—painted against a royal blue background. The colors were so vibrant and the brushwork was so unmistakable that both of them recognized the artist.

"Is that a van Gogh?" Payne whispered to Jones.

Kaiser answered for him. "It's called *Still Life: Vase with Five Sunflowers*. Painted by Vincent van Gogh in August 1888, supposedly destroyed by fire in 1945."

With his heart pounding in his chest, Jones carefully returned it to its slot and pulled out another. This one was oil on canvas, depicting a man and a woman walking through a garden. Though not nearly as colorful as the first painting, the brushwork was just as distinctive.

Kaiser spoke again, his tone similar to that of an art expert in a museum. "*The Lovers: The Poet's Garden IV.* Painted by Vincent van Gogh in October 1888. Last seen in Germany in 1937."

A few seconds later, Jones pulled out another oil on canvas. The most colorful of the three, it depicted a painter on his way to work, walking down a bright gold path as he carried his art supplies. The background was filled with green and yellow fields and majestic blue mountains.

"*Painter on the Road to Tarascon,*" Kaiser announced. "Painted by Vincent van Gogh in August 1888, destroyed by fire in World War II."

Jones nodded and returned the painting to its slot. He was about to pull out another when Payne grabbed his arm and told him to wait.

"What's wrong?" Jones wondered.

Payne turned toward Kaiser. "Did you say it was destroyed in World War II?"

Kaiser nodded, wondering when they would catch on. "Yes, I did."

"And the first one?" Payne asked.

"Burned in 1945."

"What about the second?"

"Vanished from Germany in 1937."

"Shit," Payne mumbled as the dates fell into place. "Shit, shit, shit!"

Jones looked at him, confused. "What's wrong?"

Payne raised his voice, which echoed through the chamber. "What's wrong? I'll tell you what's wrong. Kaiser promised us treasure but brought us to a goddamned Nazi bunker."

Jones's eyes widened in surprise. "He *what*?"

"Think about the dates and where we are. All of this shit was looted in the war."

Jones glanced at Kaiser. "Please tell me he's wrong."

Kaiser shrugged. "I hope he is, but I honestly don't know."

Payne raised his voice even louder. "Oh, so that's how you're going to play it? You bring us to a Nazi bunker, filled with stolen artwork and who knows what else, and you're going to pretend like you're not sure? Son of a bitch, Kaiser! What in the hell were you thinking? Did you *really* think we'd want to get involved with this shit?"

Kaiser took a deep breath, trying to remain calm. "As a matter of fact, I did."

Payne laughed sarcastically. "Really? You honestly thought we'd want to get involved with Nazi loot? Why in the world would we do that?"

"To save a good friend of yours."

"To save you from what?" Payne growled.

"Actually," Kaiser said, "I'm not the friend who needs to be saved."

11

❧

The comment caught Payne completely off guard. For the past thirty seconds, he had been lecturing Kaiser about their involvement with a cache of stolen art in a Nazi bunker—only to discover that something else was going on. Something to do with one of Payne's friends.

Suddenly, their mission was a lot more urgent.

"What do you mean?" Payne said, trying to remain calm. "Who needs my help?"

"A close friend of yours," Kaiser assured him.

"Who?" he repeated, this time a little louder.

"Before we get to that—"

"Now!" Payne demanded, veins popping in his neck. "Tell me now, or I swear to God I'm going to—"

"Jon!" Jones shouted as he stepped in front of Payne. "You need to calm down."

"Excuse me?" Payne barked, towering over his best friend.

"You heard what I said. Calm the fuck *down*." Jones emphasized the word *down* by drawing it out for an extra beat. "We're on the same side here. There's no need for threats. Take a deep breath, and let Kaiser explain."

Payne followed his advice, trying to relax. Although he rarely lost his temper, it occasionally flared up whenever he felt lied to or deceived. Factor in a friend in danger, and his anger was easy to understand. "Who needs our help?"

Not wanting to be the messenger, Kaiser swiftly moved toward one of the crates. He raised the lid that Jones had removed a few minutes earlier so they could inspect the underside. "See for yourself. Look at the lid."

In the dim light, it was tough to see the mark inscribed on the lid. It wasn't until Jones stepped closer that he noticed a coat of arms on its underbelly, a symbol vaguely familiar to him. Branded into the wood several decades earlier, it depicted an eagle with sharp talons holding a sword in one foot and a scroll in the other. On its chest the bird wore a striped shield emblazoned with a smaller symbol. Upon closer inspection, he realized it was the letter *U*.

Suddenly, everything made sense to Jones.

Kaiser's deception, the half-truths, the total need for secrecy.

In a flash, Jones knew whom they were there to save.

"Son of a bitch," he mumbled under his breath.

Payne heard the comment. "What's wrong?"

Jones tapped on the symbol. "Do you recognize that?"

He shook his head. "No, should I?"

Jones nodded. "It's the Ulster family crest."

The name hit Payne like a sucker punch, temporarily leaving him stunned. "As in Petr Ulster? Are you sure?"

"Yeah, Jon, I'm positive. I've seen it on one of his rings."

"The stolen art belongs to his family?"

Off to the side, Kaiser nodded in confirmation. "As soon as I saw the symbol, I sealed the site and called you. I know how close you are with Petr. And I know what would happen if his family was ever linked to the Nazis. The Archives would be tarnished forever."

Built in Switzerland by Austrian philanthropist Conrad Ulster, the Ulster Archives was the most extensive private collection of documents and antiquities in the world.

Unlike most private collections, the main goal of the Archives wasn't to hoard artifacts. Instead, it strived to bridge the ever-growing schism that existed between scholars and connoisseurs. Typical big-city museums displayed 15 percent of their accumulated artifacts, meaning 85 percent of the world's finest relics were currently off-limits to the public. That number climbed even higher, closer to 90 percent, when personal collections were factored in.

Thankfully, the Ulster Foundation had vowed to correct the problem. Ever since the Archives had opened in the mid-1960s, it had promoted the radical concept of sharing. In order to gain admittance to the facility, a visitor had to bring something of value—such as an ancient object or unpublished research that might be useful to others. Whatever it was, it had to be approved in advance by the Archives' staff. If for some reason they deemed it unworthy, then admission to the facility was denied until a suitable replacement could be found.

It was their way to encourage sharing.

For the past decade, the Archives had been run by Petr Ulster, Conrad's grandson. He had befriended Payne and Jones a few years earlier while the duo was at the facility conducting research for one of their missions. During their stay, a group of religious zealots had tried to burn the Archives to the ground. Their goal had been to destroy a collection of ancient documents that threatened the foundation of the Catholic Church, including evidence about the True Cross. Fortunately, Payne and Jones managed to intervene, thwarting the attack and saving the facility from irreparable damage.

Now it appeared they would have to save the Archives again.

But this time from a self-inflicted wound.

Payne grabbed the lid and studied the Ulster family crest. A sword in one talon and a scroll in the other, it represented their role as guardians of history. "This has to be a mistake. Petr has done more for the preservation of history than anyone I know."

"Maybe so," Jones said. "Then again, who knows what his ancestors did?"

"But that's what doesn't make sense. Petr has told me

countless stories about his family, all of them positive. I can assure you, he reveres his grandfather as much as I revere mine."

Payne paused for a moment, replaying some of the details in his head.

During the early 1930s, Conrad Ulster had sensed the political instability in Austria and realized there was a good chance the Nazis would seize his prized collection. To protect himself and his artifacts, he smuggled his possessions across the Swiss border in railcars, using thin layers of coal to conceal them. Though he eventually planned to return to Austria after World War II, he fell in love with his new home in Küsendorf and decided to stay. When he died, he expressed his thanks to the people of Switzerland by donating his estate to his adopted hometown— provided that they keep his collection intact and his family in charge.

"I'm telling you, it doesn't make sense. Do you know why his grandfather built the Archives in Switzerland instead of his homeland? He was afraid Hitler was going to seize his collection. Does that sound like someone who was in bed with the Nazis?"

"No, it doesn't," admitted Kaiser, who had learned about Payne and Jones's close relationship with Petr Ulster through media accounts of the Greek treasure. "But that doesn't mean his grandfather was innocent."

Payne glared at him. "What do you mean by that?"

"I mean that was a horrible time filled with many regrettable acts. Tell me, what do you know about the end of World War II?"

"The good guys won," Jones cracked, trying to inject some levity.

"Yes, that's correct—if you were rooting for the Allied Forces. But here in Germany, some people might argue your point."

"True," Jones conceded.

Kaiser continued. "That being said, postwar Germany was an interesting place. Due to its unconditional surrender, the country was divided into four militarized zones: American, British, French, and Soviet. Most of the cities had been devastated by ground campaigns and Allied bombings, so the first order of business was to fix the infrastructure. One of the top priorities was clearing away all the rubble so supply trucks could get back on the roads. Since millions of German men had died in the war, most of this work was done by women and children, who were paid in food, not money."

Payne and Jones nodded, quite familiar with the realities of war.

"In 1945, an economic condition known as hyperinflation swept through this country like a plague. In the year after the war, prices rose a dramatic eighty-five percent, leaving most German citizens in desperate straits. During this time, many of the so-called good guys—the Americans, the Brits, the French, and so on—capitalized on the situation, doing things in this country that even I find despicable."

"Such as?" Payne asked.

"Buying babies, running sweatshops, trading food for sex. Basically, doing whatever they could to take advantage of the Germans—including poverty-stricken Jews who were struggling to put their lives back together. I'm telling you, some of the postwar stories I've heard about this place make the Wild West seem tame."

"What does that have to do with these crates?" Payne asked.

Kaiser answered. "For a span of about sixteen years—starting in 1933 when Hitler was named chancellor of Germany until 1949 when the American, British, and French zones combined to form West Germany—artwork was the most profitable sector of the European black market. And trust me when I tell you, these deals weren't limited to Nazis and criminals. It was common in all levels of society, including the upper crust. People were so desperate for money they were willing to sell family heirlooms at bargain-basement prices. I'm talking priceless paintings for pennies on the dollar. Technically speaking, the sales weren't illegal, but . . ."

Payne nodded in understanding. "It was a sleazy way to obtain art."

Kaiser pointed at the crates. "For all we know, Petr's family did nothing wrong. They might've obtained all of this art for a fair price on the open market."

"But you don't think that's the case," Payne said.

Kaiser shook his head. "If I did, I wouldn't have called you."

12

Psychologically speaking, it didn't take an expert to figure out why Payne was so loyal to his friends. His parents had died in a car accident during his formative years, and since neither of them had siblings, Payne had no aunts, uncles, or cousins to comfort him. If not for his paternal grandfather, Payne would have been placed in the foster-care system, as his other grandparents had died before the accident. Actually, they had died before he was born.

During his entire lifetime, Payne had met three relatives.

Now all of them were dead.

Payne was more than an orphan. His entire family was gone.

One of the main reasons Payne had joined the military was to be a part of something. To know that others had his back and he had theirs. It had given him a sense of purpose, a sense of belonging. And when he had been forced to give that up to take over Payne Industries after his grandfather's death, he found himself clinging to the only "family" he had left. He would go to any length to protect his friends, like a mother guarding her young. Occasionally, he took it a bit too far. It was an issue he was aware of, one that had plagued him for years.

One that had led to his earlier outburst.

"Just so you know," he told Kaiser, "I'm sorry."

"For what?" Kaiser asked.

"For everything. My yelling, my suspicions, my threats. I shouldn't have acted that way. I hope you can forgive me."

"Of course I forgive you. I gave you every right to be paranoid. I realize I kept you in the dark for a very long time, but like I said earlier, there was a method to my madness. If word got out about this bunker, it would destroy Petr. And me, too."

Payne furrowed his brow. "You? How could it destroy you?"

"You know what I do for a living. In my line of work, I'm forced to bend laws all the time. The last thing I need is for the German government to be snooping around my life. Seriously, if word *ever* got out that I had anything to do with a Nazi cache—if that's what this is—then I'd be fucked forever."

"And if it isn't?" Jones asked.

"That depends."

"On what?" Payne wondered.

"On what's in the crates," Kaiser said, smiling. "If we crack them open and they're filled with items that can't be traced to a rightful owner, then in my opinion, the stuff belongs to me. Finders keepers, you know?"

Payne didn't have a problem with that. "And the items that *can* be traced?"

Kaiser shrugged. "Whatever you and Petr decide is fine. All I ask is that you keep my name out of it. Seriously, I don't want to be linked to Nazi loot in any way. Agreed?"

"Agreed," Payne said as he shook Kaiser's hand. "Not to pry, but I'm sensing this is a sore subject for you. Did you lose a loved one to the Nazis, or . . . ?"

Kaiser winced. "Damn, Jon, how old do you think I am?"

"Don't take it personally. Jon sucks at math," Jones teased.

Payne nodded. "I even need my fingers to count to one. Here, let me show you."

Then he flipped off Jones for making the comment.

Kaiser smiled but didn't laugh, the gravity of the topic still weighing on his mind. "What can I say? Everyone has their boundaries, even men like me. Over the years, I've had plenty of chances to sell Nazi plunder—for *serious* money—but my conscience wouldn't let me. Who knows? Maybe I've been in Germany a little too long. I must be turning native."

The comment confused Payne. "Meaning?"

Kaiser stared at him. "Were you ever stationed here?"

Payne shook his head. "Passed through, but never stayed."

Kaiser nodded, as if Payne's confusion should have tipped him off. "Outsiders find this hard to believe, but ninety-nine percent of all Germans are embarrassed by their homeland's role in World War II. Actually, I take that back. *Embarrassed* doesn't even begin to describe it. Humiliated, ashamed, horrified, mortified—you get the idea. I'm talking about Germans who weren't even alive during that era, yet they carry around the guilt like a stain on their DNA. Sure, I might be an American, but I've lived in this country long enough to recognize their pain. And out of respect to my German friends, I refuse to profit from Nazi loot."

"Is there a big market for that stuff?" Payne asked.

"Sadly, yes," Kaiser admitted. "Then again, I know people who will sell *anything*—including their daughters' virginity."

"Damn. That's harsh," Jones interjected.

Kaiser nodded. "Obviously, I refuse to deal with such lowlifes, but our paths still cross from time to time. And when they do, it's rarely pretty. Truth be told, men like that are another reason I didn't tell you about this bunker until you were here. If word ever leaked to one of those men, this mountain would be a war zone before morning."

Petr Ulster, a round man with a thick brown beard that covered his multiple chins, was napping in his office at the Ulster Archives. Sprawled on a comfortable leather couch, he snored loudly as he clutched an Italian book called *Il trono di Dio* to his chest. A passionate academic, Ulster tried to follow the example of inventor Thomas Edison, who took power naps during the course of the day in order to forgo sleep at night. Unfortunately, due to Ulster's love of gourmet food and his passion for fine wine, it was rarely past midnight when he crawled into bed with a full belly and a slight buzz. The intent was there, but not the conditioning.

The ringing of Ulster's private line pulled him from his sleep. Few people had his private number, and those that did called infrequently—not because he wasn't loved and admired, but because everyone assumed he was busy.

Intrigued by the call, Ulster rushed to his desk. "Hello, this is Petr."

"Hey, Petr, it's Jonathon Payne."

Ulster beamed. Even though he was in his mid-forties, he came across as boylike because of the twinkle in his eye and his zest for life. "Jonathon, my boy, what a pleasant surprise! How are things in the States?"

Sitting on a log near the entrance to the site, Payne grimaced at his unpleasant task. Telling Ulster bad news would be like kicking a puppy. How could he hurt someone so warm and cuddly? "The States are great. Then again, I'm not in the States."

Ulster took the phone from his desk and returned to his couch. It groaned from his bulk as he sank into its cushions. "You're not? Where are you, then?"

"I'm in Germany."

"Was machst du in Deutschland?" he said fluently.

"Excuse me?"

Ulster grinned at Payne's confusion. "I said, what are you doing in Germany? Wait! Let me guess. You and David went to Oktoberfest! Am I right? Have you been drinking?"

"I wish I was. It would make this conversation a little less painful."

For the first time, Ulster recognized the tension in Payne's voice. "Tell me, is everything all right? You sound rather glum. Do you need bail money?"

Payne glanced over his shoulder, making sure no guards were around. Obviously, they knew about the bunker, but according to Kaiser, they didn't know anything about the crates. Lowering his voice to a whisper, Payne said, "Petr, are you alone?"

"Am I alone? Why do you care if I'm alone? Wait, just a moment. You aren't at Oktoberfest, are you?"

"No, Petr, I'm not."

Ulster gasped. "Good heavens! Are you on a *mission*?"

"Something like that."

Ulster grinned with delight. Over the past few years, Payne and Jones had used his expertise on topics ranging from the crucifixion of Christ to the prophecies of Nostradamus. And Ulster had loved every minute—even the times he had feared for his life. Running from gunmen while carrying scrolls and artifacts made him feel like an overweight Indiana Jones. "Tell me, my boy, what do you need? Just make a wish and I shall grant it."

Payne exhaled as his blood pressure spiked.

The next few minutes would be brutal.

13

❊

Ulster's flight from the Archives was a short one, less than two hundred miles to the German city with the twenty-one-letter name. Long before they could see it, Payne and Jones heard the roar of the helicopter as it soared over the Alps and swooped into the valley like an angry hawk. Standing near the foot of the hiking trail, they shielded their eyes as the chopper landed fifty feet in front of them, its downdraft kicking up dirt and debris from the surrounding field.

The night before, Ulster had been nearly despondent after hearing the potentially devastating news about his grandfather. He realized that if Conrad had conspired with the Third Reich, it would cause irreparable damage to the Archives and the Ulster family name. Three generations of hard work and goodwill burned to a crisp like the Nazis used to burn books. In a flash, Ulster would be persona non grata in the world of academia, an outcast in the only field he ever cared about—even though he had done nothing wrong. Suddenly, every object at the Archives would be questioned. Not only individuals but entire governments would crawl out of the woodwork, claiming to be the rightful owners of every scroll, painting, and artifact in his family's collection. Lawsuits would fill his days and anxiety would ravage his nights, a life of kindness and generosity torn asunder by sins that had been committed long before he was even born.

Unless, of course, they could prove his grandfather's innocence.

As the rotors on the chopper slowed, Payne and Jones rushed forward, eager to comfort their friend. The grass, still glistening with dew, stained their shoes and the cuffs on their cargo pants as they hustled across the field. Unsure of what to expect, they were greeted by a smiling Ulster, who practically leapt out of the cockpit to give both of them a hug.

"It's so wonderful to see you. Simply wonderful!" Ulster exclaimed.

The duo exchanged worried glances, afraid he'd had a nervous breakdown during the night. Or, at the very least, had finished a few too many cocktails during his flight.

"You seem, um, chipper. . . . Have you been drinking?" Jones asked.

Ulster roared with laughter. "Nothing stronger than coffee. Although I must admit I was tempted to drown my sorrows after your call."

"Not *my* call. *His* call. If you're going to shoot the messenger, shoot Jon."

Ulster grinned and patted Payne on his shoulder. "Don't worry, my boy, you are safe from repercussions. In fact, my respect for you has never been greater. Only a true friend would have made that call."

Jones winced at the comment. "For the record, *I* wanted to call you, but *he* wouldn't let me. What can I say? He's selfish that way."

Ulster smiled. "Rest assured, David. I appreciate you equally."

"Glad to hear it," Jones said, basking in the praise.

Strangely, Payne had remained silent during the entire conversation, struggling to reconcile the cheerful Ulster who stood before him with the depressed one he had been expecting. Obviously, something had changed in the last twelve hours, but he didn't know what.

"Petr," Payne said delicately, "please don't take this the wrong way, because the last thing I want to do is ruin your mood. But why are you so cheerful?"

"Aren't I always?" Ulster asked with a twinkle in his eye.

"Normally, yes. But you weren't last night. In fact, you were devastated."

"Maybe so, but I'm better now. After we spoke, I had an epiphany."

"Really?" Jones cracked. "I smoked one of those things in Amsterdam. Couldn't feel my teeth for a week."

Payne ignored the joke, focusing on Ulster. "An epiphany about what?"

"About something you told me."

"Care to be more specific?"

Ulster smiled. "If it's okay with you, can I explain once we're there? In case you haven't noticed, my body wasn't built for hiking. And I'd like to get there before Christmas."

Moving at Ulster's slothlike pace, it took them twice as long to reach the bunker as it had the day before. Despite the cool morning air and the shade from the trees, Ulster was oozing so much sweat when they reached the site that he had to wring out his shirt. Thankfully, he had packed some extra clothes with the rest of his supplies—which included a laptop, a digital camera, and a tool kit filled with archaeological equipment—and was able to change his shirt before he thanked Kaiser, whom he had never met before, with a massive bear hug.

After helping Ulster down the ladder, Payne led him to the back chamber where the crates had been stored for several decades. As a historian, Ulster viewed the site differently than did Payne and Jones. Growing up near Germany, Ulster had toured dozens of Nazi bunkers over the years, so he knew what to expect and what didn't belong.

At first glance, one important element was missing.

Ulster said, "Where are the swastikas? There should be swastikas."

"Sorry," Jones joked. "We didn't have time to decorate."

Ulster moved about the room, studying the walls. "The Nazis were big proponents of symbolism. They marked everything they got their hands on. Obviously, the swastika was their main symbol, but they had many others. The *Reichsadler* was a black eagle. The *Wolfsangel*, or wolf's hook, came from the Black Forest. And the SS insignia looked like two side-by-side lightning bolts. If this place was built by the Nazis, they would have branded it in some way."

Kaiser shook his head. "I found nothing like that."

"I'm glad. We don't want to find any Nazi symbols."

"What about the crates? Wouldn't they be marked?"

"Without a doubt. Like I said, they branded everything—including people."

The comment hung in the air like a black cloud, nearly as palpable as the stench from the outer chamber. Even though Payne, Jones, and Kaiser had served in the military, none of them could fully comprehend the death and destruction of World War II. It had swept across Europe like a deadly wave, leaving absolute destruction in its wake.

"So," Payne said, trying to lighten the mood, "tell us about your epiphany."

Ulster smiled. "I was wondering when you'd bring that up. Fortunately, this is the perfect time to discuss it. Please, if you don't mind, can you show me the open crate?"

Payne walked into the right corner and held his flashlight above the van Gogh crate. During the night, the lid had been closed to protect the paintings inside. "It's this one here."

Ulster reached into his pocket and pulled out a pair of XXL latex gloves that he had to stretch and pull over his chubby fingers. When he was done, he looked like a surgeon ready to operate. "When you told me about this crate, I initially panicked. Not only was I familiar with the paintings, but I knew all of them had been lost during World War II."

Ulster paused for a moment while he opened the crate. Just as Payne had promised, the underbelly of the lid had been marked with the Ulster coat of arms. Even though he had been expecting to see it in the bunker, its presence still took his breath away.

Jones cleared his throat. "Go on."

Ulster blinked a few times. "Wait, where was I?"

"You were talking about the paintings."

Ulster handed the lid to Jones, then thumbed through the canvases in the crate. "Late last night, once I had a chance to ruminate a bit, I realized something crucial about one painting in particular."

"Which one?" Kaiser wondered.

Ulster pulled out the masterpiece and held it in the air. As he did, he admired its beauty. "*Still Life: Vase with Five Sunflowers*. Painted by Vincent van Gogh in August 1888."

Kaiser nodded. That matched the information he had learned from one of his sources. "Supposedly, it was destroyed by fire in an air raid way back in 1945."

"That is true," Ulster admitted. "But you've omitted the most important part of the story—at least as it pertains to my family. Where did this bombing occur?"

Kaiser shrugged. "I have absolutely no idea."

Ulster grinned. "Ashiya, Japan."

Payne furrowed his brow. "Did you say *Japan*?"

Ulster nodded. "Owned by a Japanese industrialist."

"If that's the case, how did the Nazis get their hands on it?"

Ulster grinned even wider. "Who said they did?"

14

❁

Silence filled the back chamber as they waited for Ulster's explanation, each of them wondering how a painting from Japan, believed to be destroyed in World War II, had ended up in a secret bunker in Bavaria. Anxious to clear his grandfather's name, Ulster explained.

"Even though Germany and Japan were Axis powers, their relationship was based on a common enemy and little else. Other than a few diplomats stationed near Tokyo, there weren't many Nazis in the Far East. Ground troops were far more valuable in Europe."

Payne, who had a great understanding of the war from his Naval Academy education, nodded in agreement. "Japan wanted to control the Pacific. Germany wanted to conquer everything else. Their alliance was one of convenience, nothing more."

"If that's the case, how did the painting end up here?" Kaiser asked.

Ulster returned the masterpiece to the crate before he answered. "Toward the end of the war, Japan was repeatedly warned about an Allied superweapon, capable of wiping out an entire city in a single blast. Fearing the destruction of their most important treasures, members of the Japanese upper class scrambled to protect their assets. Those who doubted the rumors hid their heirlooms in basements and bank vaults, more concerned about invading troops than atomic bombs. But those who believed the stories about the bomb made arrangements with men like my grandfather who were willing to protect their treasures until after the war."

Payne grimaced. "Why didn't you mention that last night?"

"Why? Because I didn't have any proof. Over the years, I've heard dozens of stories about my grandfather's escape to Switzerland in the early 1930s. I know he returned to northern Austria and southern Germany a few years later and helped many of his friends get to safety, leading them through the Alps to evade Nazi patrols. According to my father, the people who made the journey weren't allowed to bring anything with them except the most basic supplies. Everything else—heirlooms, artwork, jewelry—was stashed before they left."

Ulster glanced around the bunker, wondering how something so large had been built without detection. "That's what this place was for. To protect the treasures that were left behind."

Payne rubbed his eyes, still not understanding Ulster's happiness. As far as he could tell, they still faced a major uphill battle to clear his family's name. "Please forgive my skepticism, but where's your proof? Right now all we have is a crate filled with artwork that may or may not have been looted by your grandfather and fifty other crates filled with God knows what. Obviously, I'm on your side and willing to give your family the benefit of the doubt, but the rest of the world is going to require a lot more evidence than a few anecdotes from the war."

Ulster smiled, hoping to ease his concerns. "I couldn't agree more."

"Really? Then why are you so damn happy?"

"As I mentioned earlier, I lacked tangible evidence at the time of your call, but things have since changed. Fearing the worst, I spent the entire night going through my grandfather's papers, searching for anything that had to do with Japan. Early this morning, about an hour before my departure, I stumbled across a folder filled with correspondence from the rightful owner of the van Gogh. Suffice it to say, my grandfather was named legal guardian of the painting way back in 1945, and he figured out a way to smuggle it overseas. Once my lawyers sort through all of the paperwork, we will formally return the painting to Japan."

"Hold up," Payne growled. "That doesn't make any sense. Why would someone smuggle a work of art *into* Nazi Germany? That's the dumbest thing I've ever heard."

Ulster laughed. "I thought the same thing until I read

through the correspondence. Toward the end of the war, most Japanese shipping lanes were blocked by Allied troops, so there was very little getting in or out of the country. That is, except for a distribution channel from Tokyo to Munich that was controlled by the Nazis. Apparently, this was how German diplomats and their supplies were ferried back and forth between Europe and the Far East. I'm not sure who thought of it—whether it was my grandfather or the man who owned the van Gogh—but they forged Nazi paperwork and used their route to get the painting out of Japan."

"That's awesome," said Jones, who loved hearing stories about the war, especially when the Nazis were made to look like fools. "What happened then?"

"If you look at a map, this bunker was built between Munich and the Austrian border. If I had to guess, my grandfather didn't want to subject the artifacts to an arduous trip across the Alps, so he stored them here. Sadly, he must've passed away before he had the chance to retrieve them."

Kaiser pointed toward the open crate. "What do you know about the other van Goghs? Did you find their paperwork, too?"

"To be honest, I didn't have time to look. The paperwork from Japan stood out to me because it was so different from all the others. Once I get back to the Archives, I'm sure I'll find documentation for all of the other artifacts—now that I know what to search for."

"And what if you don't?" Payne asked.

A look of determination filled Ulster's face. "If I don't, I'll use every source I have to track down the names of the rightful owners. Thanks to my grandfather, all of these artifacts survived the war. The least I can do is honor his memory and finish what he started."

Driving a black SUV with German plates, the man pulled onto the grass near the side of the road and rolled down his tinted window. For the fourth day in a row, a helicopter had landed in the open field near the base of Zugspitze, the peak that towered above Garmisch-Partenkirchen. But unlike all of the previous trips, this time the chopper had arrived from the south.

More curious than alarmed, he grabbed the binoculars from his passenger seat and studied the strange scene at the foot of the mountain. No people. No trucks. No movement of any kind. Just a luxury helicopter sitting in the middle of a pasture, less than twenty feet from an unmarked trail. During ski season, he was used to the über-wealthy flying into town to enjoy the Olympic-quality ski slopes, but he had never seen this much activity in September.

Obviously, something unusual was going on.

But he didn't know what.

Zooming in on the tail number, he hoped to determine the helicopter's country of origin. From his time in the military, he knew every rotorcraft registered in Germany started with the letter *D*, followed by a hyphen and four additional letters. Yet this designation was different. Not only did two letters (*HB*) precede the hyphen, but three letters followed it. Although the two-three structure was fairly common around the world, he didn't recognize the first two letters.

"HB," he mumbled to himself. "Where in the hell is HB?"

After jotting the five-letter code into his notebook, he pulled out his phone and called an associate who worked in customs at Berlin Tegel Airport, the second-largest international airport in Germany. His friend had access to the aircraft registration database and was willing to look up tail numbers for the promise of a free beer. All things considered, it was money well spent. For the price of the first round, he would learn the name and address of the helicopter's owner. From there, he would be able to determine if this situation was worth pursuing.

That is, if this was even a *situation*.

Because right now it was just a helicopter in a field.

15

❧

Halogen lights, powered by a portable generator that purred in the outer chamber, lit the back room like the afternoon sun. Within seconds, the temperature started to rise in the confined space. Not wanting to sweat like Ulster on their hike up the mountain, Payne removed his long-sleeved shirt and threw it into the corner, anxious to begin the next phase of their journey.

Using its rope handles, Jones and Kaiser carried a three-foot-square crate to the center of the room, where Payne waited with a crowbar. Muscles bulging against his undershirt, Payne slid the bar under the lid and popped it open with a mere flick of his wrists.

The feel of iron in his hands and the rumble of a distant motor reminded him of his teenage years in Pittsburgh. While most of his friends earned money by cutting grass or working the roller coasters at Kennywood Park, he had spent his summers slaving away in the brutal heat of his family's factories. According to his grandfather, what better way to learn the business than from the bottom up? He was picked on by all the union workers, his shifts so long and grueling it made his plebe year at the Academy seem easy by comparison.

Yet looking back on it, he wouldn't have changed a thing.

Those summers had hardened him like steel.

Tossing the crowbar aside, Payne eased his fingers under the lid and carefully removed it. Similar to the van Gogh crate, the underbelly of the lid had been branded with the Ulster family crest. The guardian eagle looked particularly fierce in the glow of the halogen lights, as if the bird was furious about being sealed inside a box for more than sixty years. But none of the men—not even Ulster himself—cared about the coat of arms. Instead, their attention was focused solely on the contents of the crate. Eager to glimpse what was inside, the four of them crowded around the box like hungry orphans opening their only present on Christmas morning. Expecting to find famous paintings or fancy jewelry, they were crushed to discover a crate filled with nothing but old books and a stack of documents, everything written in German.

To Jones, it was the equivalent of receiving an ugly reindeer sweater instead of the video game system he had been hoping for. "What the fuck? We flew all the way from America, and this box is filled with homework."

Payne and Kaiser said nothing, but they were thinking the same thing.

Meanwhile, Ulster bent over the crate, hoping to determine why these items had been stored in a protective bunker since World War II. Still wearing his latex gloves, he picked up the first object that caught his eye—a decorative, leather-bound journal embossed with Conrad Ulster's initials—and flipped through its weathered pages. Having spent most of the night going through his grandfather's papers, Ulster instantly recognized the handwriting.

"What is it?" Payne wondered.

Ulster shrugged as he scanned the text for clues. "Obviously, I've never seen it before, but it definitely belonged to my grandfather. I think it's some kind of daily log."

Payne stared at Ulster. "Like a diary?"

"Somewhat, but not really."

"Well, that narrows it down," Jones cracked.

Ulster glanced up at them to explain. "It has the structure of a diary—dozens of dated entries over a period of two or three years—yet it's lacking personal reflection of any kind. Instead, it's filled with a series of clinical observations, as if he was systematically searching for something in the surrounding hills. Unfortunately, I don't know what he was looking for because most of his entries appear to be written in code."

Jones took a guess. "Maybe he was looking for Hogzilla. I bet that fucker was alive back then. Probably got that big by eating Nazis."

Payne rolled his eyes. "Why do you say stuff like that?"

Jones shrugged. "I get bored easily. Plus, I like pissing you off."

"Well, it's working."

He grinned. "I can tell."

Payne took a deep breath, trying to remember why Jones was his best friend. At that particular moment, nothing came to mind. "If you're *that* bored, why don't you go and open the next crate? The sooner we know what we're dealing with, the better."

"But do so carefully. There's no telling what's down here," Ulster pleaded.

"Don't worry, I'll be gentle," Jones assured him as he walked toward the back corner. "And unlike some people I know, I won't have to take off my shirt to use a crowbar."

Payne glanced at Kaiser. "Please do me a favor and help him out. The only physical labor he's performed all year involved Internet porn and a box of tissues."

"I heard that," Jones yelled from the back of the room.

Fighting a smile, Payne apologized to Ulster. "Anyway, what were you saying?"

"If you give me a while, I might be able to put the code into some kind of context based on the other documents in this crate. But for all I know, it might be a total waste of time. He could have been charting Nazi patrols or planning a future escape."

"It's not a waste of time."

"I meant in terms of finding additional treasure."

"Listen," Payne said as he crouched next to Ulster, "as far as I'm concerned, protecting your family name is the number one priority here. Do whatever you need to do. If that means digging through this crate and looking for information, you have my blessing."

Ulster stared at the journal in his hands. For as long as he could remember, he had hoped to discover a detailed account of his grandfather's exploits during World War II. Over the years, he had heard many rumors from secondary sources, but nothing had been supported by fact. Now, after all this time, he might have found the mother lode. As far as his family was concerned, the book in his hand was far more valuable than a crate filled with van Goghs.

"Maybe for a little while," Ulster said sheepishly. "But please let me know if you need my assistance. I'll be happy to answer any questions, particularly involving my grandfather."

"Jon," Jones called from the back of the room.

Payne signaled for him to wait. He would be there shortly. "The same goes for you. If you need anything, just let me know. Remember, we're here for you, not for the treasure."

"Jon," Jones called a little bit louder. "You should see this."

Payne growled in frustration. "In a minute. I'm talking to Petr."

Ulster shooed him away. "Go! Tend to David. He needs you more than I. For the time being, I have everything I need: a box of books and my grandfather's journal. I couldn't be happier."

Payne smiled, glad that everything had worked out for Ulster. He knew how much time and energy Ulster had put into the Archives and realized how quickly it would have fallen apart if his grandfather had conspired with the Nazis. Thankfully, that did not seem to be the case. Now Payne could shift his focus to the rest of the crates. If, as they expected, the crates were filled with heirlooms that had been hidden from the Nazis, Payne would love nothing more than to return them to the rightful owners. That simple act would make his entire year.

"Jon!" Jones yelled. "You need to see this *now.*"

Still annoyed by Jones's earlier behavior, Payne was tempted to make him wait another few minutes out of spite, but the urgency in his friend's voice told him it was important.

"What's wrong?" Payne grumbled.

Jones said nothing. He simply handed the lid that had been pried off the third crate to Payne, who immediately recognized that it was different. Unlike the first two, the underbelly of this lid did not have the Ulster family crest. Instead, the ancient wood had been branded with an elaborate black swan. Its wings were spread wide, its neck twisted to the side as if it was looking for a predator that might be gaining on it.

Kaiser whispered. "Remember what Petr said. The Nazis marked *everything.* Admittedly, I've never seen this symbol before, but what if this was one of theirs?"

Payne glanced over his shoulder, paranoid. The last thing he wanted to do was ruin Ulster's mood, unless it was completely necessary. "What if it was? For all we know, Conrad found one of their crates and used it to store his belongings. Remember, a war was going on. Supplies were in high demand. People used everything they could get their hands on."

"Trust me, it's not that simple," Jones assured him.

"It's not? How can you be so sure?"

Jones grimaced and pointed toward the crate. "Go see for yourself."

16

❊

Although his journey was a short one, every step that Payne took was filled with dread, as if he were a convicted felon heading toward the gallows. Time seemed to slow as he approached the crate, giving him a chance to envision all of the horrendous possibilities that might be inside. He realized the contents had spooked Jones and Kaiser, two men who didn't spook easily.

Still, he hadn't been expecting anything like this.

The crate was packed with several rows of gold bars that glowed like the legendary city of El Dorado, thanks to the bright light of the halogen lamps. Each bar weighed five thousand grams (approximately eleven pounds) and had been carefully stamped with the elaborate swan symbol that had been branded onto the lid. Payne had no idea what or whom the swan represented, but it was pretty obvious that money hadn't been a problem—at least until the gold had disappeared.

"Shit," Payne mumbled under his breath. "This isn't good."

"No, it's not," Jones whispered. "Not good at all."

During their time in the MANIACs, they had discovered thirty crates of gold bars in a bunker outside of Baghdad. The treasure, plundered from a royal palace, had been hidden by an Iraqi diplomat who had tried, in vain, to smuggle it across the border. Realizing the roads were patrolled by American troops, he had buried the cache in the desert, planning to return a few years later after tensions had calmed. But much to the diplomat's chagrin, Payne and Jones had uncovered the bunker before the Iraqi had a chance to claim his plunder.

In retrospect, it was the first treasure the duo had ever found.

Payne grabbed one of the bars from the crate. It felt like a brick in his hand. Using his body to shield it from Ulster, he flipped it over and searched for additional markings but saw none. "What do you know about Nazi gold?"

Jones whispered. "Do you want facts or myths?"

"Both."

"In simple terms, Nazi Germany financed its war effort by looting its victims. Most of the assets were stored in regional depositories that were heavily guarded. When the Nazis needed a large influx of currency, they cashed in the gold at dozens of financial institutions in Europe—including the Vatican Bank and the Franciscan Order. That is, if you believe the civil suits filed by Holocaust survivors."

Jones made sure Ulster wasn't listening before he continued. "Now, this is where things get complicated. After the war, most of these accounts miraculously disappeared. I'm talking *here today, gone tomorrow*. Some people believe the gold was stolen by the upper class and hidden in vaults, much like the gold we found in Iraq. Others speculate that only the paperwork was destroyed, that the depositories themselves are still out there waiting to be found. Personally, I'm not sure what to believe. If I had to guess, I'd say it's a combination of the two. Some gold was stolen, and the rest got lost in the shuffle."

Payne held up the bar. "What about *this* gold?"

Jones struggled for words, not wanting to condemn a man he had never met—especially the grandfather of one of his friends. "For the time being, the best thing we can do is figure out the meaning of the swan. For all we know, it might be something innocuous, like the crest of one of the families that Conrad smuggled out of the country. Maybe he was storing this gold for them."

"And if he wasn't?" Kaiser asked, worried about the repercussions.

"If he wasn't, we'll have some tough choices to make," Jones said.

Payne glanced at Ulster, who was so focused on his grandfather's journal that he was oblivious to everything going on in the back of the room. "As much as I hate to do this, I have to ask Petr about the swan. He knows more about history than the three of us combined. It would be foolish to leave him out of the loop just to spare his feelings."

Jones grimaced at the task. "Do you want me to join you?"

Payne shook his head. Things would go smoother if he did it alone. "While I talk to Petr, open some more crates. Hopefully, you'll find something that explains the gold."

"Such as?"

"A receipt would be nice. Preferably one without a swastika."

Jones leaned closer. "I know people who could forge one."

"So do I," Kaiser admitted.

Payne winced at the suggestion. "Guys, I was kidding. We're *not* forging a receipt."

"Of course not," Jones said in a less-than-convincing tone. "Wouldn't even think of it."

Kaiser didn't blink or smile. "I was serious."

Back when Kaiser was starting his operation, one of the first people he hired was a world-class forger who specialized in visas and passports. Not only was he an expert on ink, paper, and handwriting, but he also had a unique perspective since he used to be a border guard at the Berlin Wall and knew what he had looked for. In recent years, the forger's son had entered the family business, but unlike his father, he specialized in artwork and older documents.

Payne smirked. He was quite familiar with Kaiser's services. "Although I appreciate the offer, both of us know that's not the best way to go."

"I never said it was. I'm just letting you know it's an option."

"Thanks, but no thanks," Payne said, trying to distance himself from the topic. "But if you think of something legal, be sure to let us know."

Mueller's assistant answered the encrypted satellite phone in the front seat of the Mercedes-Benz limousine. The custom-built car had more safety features than the Popemobile. Armor-plated doors, bulletproof, nonsplinter, multilayered windows, a fuel-tank safety system, run-flat tires, and a remote starting system that could be activated from a distance of three hundred meters—just in case an explosive device had been wired to the ignition. To some, equipment like this would be overkill. But in Mueller's line of work, it was essential.

He made enemies every day, and most of them were criminals.

Gazing at the Binnenalster, one of two artificial lakes in Hamburg, Mueller sipped his morning coffee in the back of the limo while pondering his hectic schedule. Rarely awake before noon since most of his business was done at night, he wasn't in the mood to speak to anyone except the arms dealer he was about to meet in the park. If all went well, Mueller would make seven figures before lunch.

"Sir," said his assistant over the intercom system, "there's a call for you."

Annoyed by the interruption, Mueller jabbed the button. "Who is it?"

"It's Krueger. He has news from Bavaria."

Mueller nodded his approval. Krueger was a trusted

worker who wouldn't call unless it was important. "Fine. Give him to me."

With a flip of a switch, the soundproof partition behind the front seat was lowered. After handing the phone to his boss, the assistant raised the partition to its original position.

Mueller spoke to Krueger in German. "Yes?"

"My apologies, sir. Sorry to disturb you so early."

"What is it?"

"Over the past few days, I've noticed some unusual activity in Garmisch-Partenkirchen. The type of activity that might interest you."

"Define *unusual*."

"Helicopters, sir. Both coming and going to the foot of Zugspitze."

Mueller stroked his chin in thought. "Probably just a lost hiker. Nothing to be alarmed about."

Krueger demurely disagreed. "I thought the same thing at first, but this morning's chopper was more luxurious than the others. Just to be safe, I ran its tail number."

"And?"

"It's definitely not a rescue craft. This helicopter arrived from Switzerland."

"Switzerland?" Mueller's interest was piqued. "Did you learn the name of the owner?"

Krueger nodded. "The chopper belongs to Petr Ulster."

"Ulster?" he said, trying to place the name. "Why is that so familiar?"

Krueger smiled. "Because he owns the Ulster Archives."

17

Wanting to learn as much about the swan symbol as possible, Payne showed Ulster the back of the lid instead of one of the gold bars. He figured it would be less shocking that way. But as soon as Ulster saw the symbol, he snapped to attention.

"Where did you find this?" Ulster demanded.

"Why? Do you recognize it?"

"Of course I recognize it. It's the black swan!"

Payne furrowed his brow. "Which is?"

"Which is *this*!" Ulster said as he repeatedly tapped the lid.

"Yeah, I kind of figured that out. I meant, what does it represent?"

"Please, help me to my feet."

Payne grabbed his hand and easily yanked him up.

"Now, where did you find this? Show me at once!"

"About that," Payne said, reluctant to break the potentially bad news. "I should prepare you for what you're about to see. You're not going to like it."

"I'm not?"

Payne shook his head. "Nope."

Ulster lowered his voice to a whisper. "Is the crate filled with treasure?"

Payne nodded. "Dozens of gold bars."

Ulster whooped with glee. "Brilliant! Just brilliant! I knew the rumors were true!"

Payne blinked a few times. "Rumors? What rumors? About your grandfather?"

"My grandfather?" Ulster asked, confused. "Of course not! I'm talking about Ludwig."

"*Ludwig*? Who in the hell is *Ludwig*? I thought your grandfather's name was Conrad."

"My grandfather's name *was* Conrad. But I'm talking about Ludwig!"

Payne shook his head, completely baffled. Not only about Ulster's excitement, but also about Ludwig—whoever that was. "Hold up! Tell me what you're talking about."

"In a moment. First, show me where you found this."

Payne led Ulster to the crate of gold, where they were greeted by Jones and Kaiser. Having heard the commotion on the other side of the chamber, Jones was ready to console Ulster, but one look at his face told him it wasn't necessary. Ulster was far from distraught.

"It's beautiful!" Ulster grabbed one of the bars and held it up to the light. His smile gleamed as he ran his fingers over the stamp. "And look! It has the mark of the swan!"

Payne met his gaze and shrugged. The term meant nothing to him.

Undeterred, Ulster glanced at Jones and Kaiser, expecting to see a glint of recognition in their eyes. But they stared at him like he was speaking a foreign language.

Ulster continued. "Don't you know what this is? It's an explanation!"

"An explanation?" Payne asked.

Ulster nodded. "An explanation of my grandfather's journal."

Payne grimaced, getting more and more confused. "Speaking of explanations . . ."

"Yes, of course, how silly of me! Here I am rambling on and on about the black swan, yet it's painfully obvious that none of you know what I'm talking about." Ulster pointed at Jones. "Although I must admit, I thought *you* might get the reference."

Jones winced. "Why? Because I'm black?"

Ulster blushed at the insinuation. "Good heavens, no! I meant because you're a history buff, not because you're, um . . ."

"Relax, Petr! I was just teasing."

Ulster breathed a sigh of relief. "Thank goodness! I thought perhaps I had offended you."

"Of course not," said Jones, who had a history of teasing everyone. "To answer your question, I'm not familiar with the black swan."

Ulster turned toward Kaiser. "What about you? You've lived in Germany for a while now. In all that time, you've never heard of the black swan?"

"Nope."

"What about the Swan King?"

Kaiser shook his head. "Sorry. I've been busy."

Ulster sighed in frustration. "Perhaps it's an American thing. Because children in Europe are taught about the Swan King in primary school."

Jones raised his voice. "Wait! Now you're making fun of America?"

Payne rolled his eyes. This was going nowhere. "DJ, please shut the hell up and let Petr talk. You know damn well he wasn't insulting you. Or America."

Jones grinned a devious grin. "Sorry, Petr. What were you saying?"

Ulster gathered his thoughts, trying to figure out where to begin. Known for his attention to detail and his tendency to digress, he started at the beginning, hoping to give them enough background information for them to understand. "When Napoleon abolished the Holy Roman Empire in 1806, Bavaria officially became a kingdom, and Maximilian I was named its king. For the next eighty years, the crown passed from father to son until it was placed on the eighteen-year-old head of Ludwig II, a handsome lad who was ill-prepared for the title."

Payne recognized the name. "You mentioned Ludwig earlier."

Ulster nodded. "Known as the Swan King, Ludwig is best remembered for the elaborate stone castles that he built throughout Bavaria—including the legendary Neuschwanstein. The castle is so scenic and grand, it inspired Walt Disney's design of Sleeping Beauty's castle at Disneyland. If you haven't seen Neuschwanstein, you should arrange a tour before you return to the States. It truly is remarkable."

Familiar with Ulster's habit of getting off track, Payne steered the conversation back to Ludwig. "How did he get the nickname?"

"Due to his obsession with Lohengrin, a famous character from German folklore who was known as the Swan Knight. If you are familiar with Arthurian legend, you might recognize the name. Lohengrin was the son of Percival, one of the Knights of the Round Table who pursued the Holy Grail. Over the centuries, Lohengrin's tale has taken many forms and has been translated into many languages. Still, the basic details remain the same. Lohengrin is sent to rescue a maiden in a far-off land, a journey he makes in a cockleshell boat pulled by a magical swan."

Jones frowned. "Did you say a cockleshell boat pulled by a magic swan? Pardon me for saying so, but that's the gayest thing I've ever heard. And that includes Jon's ringtone."

Payne rolled his eyes, but he didn't dignify the comment with a response.

Meanwhile, Ulster used the off-color remark as a teaching moment. "I realize you meant it as a joke, but history tells us that Ludwig was one of the most flamboyant rulers of all time. In fact, Ludwig often dressed up in a Swan Knight costume and pranced around the halls of his castle while listening to opera."

Jones, who was a smart-ass, not antigay, tried to bite his tongue but simply couldn't. "Sorry, fellas, I just changed my mind. *That's* the gayest thing I've ever heard."

"Regardless," Ulster said, "the costume helps explain why he was called the Swan King. Strangely, the majestic creatures had fascinated him even before he had heard of the Swan Knight. As a small child, he used to draw pictures of swans in his notebooks and on his schoolwork. Later in life, when he ruled Bavaria, he sealed his correspondence with a swan and a cross, a reference to Lohengrin and the Holy Grail. Even his personal crest had a swan on it. I'm telling you, it was an obsession."

Payne pointed to the symbol on the lid. "Is this his personal crest?"

Ulster shook his head and lowered his voice. "No, the symbol that you're holding is known as the black swan, and its history is far more mysterious. Unlike his personal crest, which is celebrated in history books and museums across Germany, the black swan is kept in the shadows, a dark reminder of Ludwig's final days as king. If you believe the rumors—and most historians do—the symbol in your hands is the reason for Ludwig's murder."

18

❀

Born in 1845, Ludwig II was the eldest son of King Maximilian II of Bavaria and Princess Marie of Prussia. His parents had wanted to name him Otto, but Ludwig I, the deposed king of Bavaria, who was known for his eccentric behavior, insisted his grandson be named after him since they shared a birthday. In time, Ludwig II would be renowned for his own eccentricities.

As a small child, Ludwig despised ugliness. If approached by an unattractive servant, he would cry and refuse to look at the employee. His father tried to change his ways, assigning several ugly servants to wait on the petulant boy, but when his behavior became a phobia, Ludwig's staff was made up of the most attractive servants they could find.

Embarrassed by his son's unusual ways, King Maximilian had little interest in him except in regard to his training and schooling. For that, he hired private tutors. Realizing that Ludwig would someday be king, Maximilian subjected the crown prince to a demanding regimen of education and exercise, which some experts believe amplified the odd behavior that had already taken root. Still, as bad as his relationship was with his father, Ludwig was even further detached from his mother, whom he coldly referred to as "my predecessor's consort."

Not surprisingly, it was a term rarely seen on Mother's Day cards.

Despite his abhorrent behavior behind the scenes, the Bavarian public fell in love with Ludwig at his father's funeral—his first public appearance as king. As a handsome, well-spoken eighteen-year-old, he performed so admirably at the memorial service that word of his composure spread across Europe. Before long, Ludwig was more than a monarch; he was a pop-culture icon whose public appearances and passion for the arts were even more celebrated than his politics.

One of his first acts as king was to summon composer Richard Wagner to the Royal Palace. Three years earlier, Ludwig had been deeply moved while watching *Lohengrin*—Wagner's opera about the Swan Knight, the Holy Grail, and a mysterious castle—and had become obsessed with the production. Now that Ludwig was finally in charge of the kingdom, he had the opportunity to reward the composer for all the joy he had brought into his life. Wagner, who was on the run from various creditors, happily accepted the invitation to Munich. The two of them got along so well that Ludwig offered to settle

Wagner's considerable debts and agreed to finance several of his operas with money from the royal coffers.

For a young king barely into his reign, it was a careless mistake.

A mistake he would repeat again and again until he was marked for death.

Payne stared at the black swan symbol on the back of the lid and wondered how it had led to the king's death. "Ludwig was murdered?"

Ulster answered. "Officially, no. But logically, yes."

"What does that mean?"

"It means there was a cover-up of the grandest proportion."

Payne glanced at his watch. He sensed a long story coming on. "Explain."

Ulster beamed. He loved sharing his knowledge. "Ludwig was killed in Berg, less than a hundred miles from here. Though I don't remember an exact date, I'm fairly certain the year was 1886. Obviously, back then, forensic science was far from sophisticated. Still, the conclusions that the police reached on that night were downright laughable."

"In what way?" Jones asked.

"Allow me to paint the scene. Ludwig, who wasn't officially the king at the time of his death since he had been deposed a few days before, decided to take a stroll with his psychiatrist along the shore of Lake Starnberg. When they didn't return for supper, palace guards conducted a search and found them dead, floating in the nearby shallows.

Now, as far as I'm concerned, it doesn't take a trained crim-
inologist to examine these facts and presume the possibility of foul play. Nevertheless, the authorities ruled
otherwise. With nothing but a cursory investigation, conducted under a cloak of darkness, Ludwig's death was officially ruled a suicide. Furthermore, the doctor's death
was labeled an accidental drowning. They claimed the
doctor went into the lake to save Ludwig and lost his life
in the process."

"How deep was the water?" Payne asked.

"Roughly knee high."

Jones laughed. "Were they hobbits? If not, how do you
drown in two feet of water?"

"Good question. Which is why the coroner decided to
perform an autopsy—even though the new regime had no
intention of changing their official ruling."

"And what did he find?" Jones asked.

"There was no water in Ludwig's lungs, so the odds are
pretty good he didn't drown. Meanwhile, the doctor—I
believe his name was Gudden—wasn't so lucky. He had a
fractured skull and several scratches on his face, possibly
the result of a struggle. But unlike Ludwig, the doctor's
lungs *were* filled with water. That means he probably
drowned."

Payne scratched his head. "If Ludwig didn't drown,
how did he die?"

Ulster shrugged. "Poison is a possibility since no injuries were found, but no one knows for sure, because the
proper tests weren't allowed. The new regime wanted to

distance itself from Ludwig, and the quickest way to accomplish that would be a convenient suicide."

"So they killed the king?" Jones asked.

"As I mentioned, Ludwig wasn't *officially* the king at the time of his death. A few days prior, the Bavarian government had organized a medical commission to declare Ludwig insane. This gave them the authority to remove him from power. Amazingly, the doctor who had the final say in the matter had never met Ludwig before his ruling. Instead, he based his decision on conjecture and hearsay, not a personal examination."

"I'm not positive," Jones cracked, "but I think that goes against the Hippocratic oath."

"Don't worry, David. The doctor ultimately got punished for his sins."

"How? Did they revoke his license?"

"Actually, they revoked his life. He was murdered next to Ludwig."

Jones smirked. "Really? It was the same doctor?"

Kaiser laughed at the irony. "Karma's a bitch, ain't it?"

"More importantly," Ulster concluded, "it was the perfect way for the new regime to tie up loose ends. What's that expression? 'Killing two birds with one stone'? Not only did they kill the rightful king, but they murdered the man who had effectively ended his reign."

Payne rubbed his neck in thought, trying to remember how they had gotten onto this topic to begin with. That was the trouble with Petr Ulster. He knew so much and his stories were filled with so many details that it was tough to separate the wheat from the chaff. Thankfully, on this occasion, Ulster's "bird" metaphor helped to jump-start Payne's memory.

"Speaking of birds, what does the black swan have to do with this?"

Ulster grinned, as if he suddenly remembered the point he had been trying to make. "During the course of his twenty-two-year reign, Ludwig quickly burned through his family's fortune. Whether donating large sums of money to the arts or giving lavish gifts to peasants he had met during his travels, Ludwig lived an extravagant life, one filled with luxury and indulgence. After a while, his spending was so out of control—particularly in the realm of architecture—that his advisors begged him to stop. They feared personal bankruptcy. But the eccentric king lived in a dreamworld, one in which his wishes were granted. As I mentioned earlier, Neuschwanstein is Ludwig's most famous castle, a Romanesque fortress that looks like it was pulled off the pages of a fairy tale, yet it was far from his most ambitious project. During a ten-year span, Ludwig built or planned over a dozen castles, including a few that would have made Neuschwanstein look like a cottage."

"Go on," Payne said, still waiting for his answer.

"Toward the end of his reign, Ludwig started borrowing money from royal families across Europe. Not to pay back the fourteen million marks that he already owed, but to continue moving forward with his personal projects. Dreading the reaction of his finance ministers, Ludwig considered firing his entire cabinet and replacing them with yes-men. Ultimately, he decided a mass firing would be attacked by the media, and the last thing he wanted to do was to lose the adulation of his citizens. So he opted to go in a different direction. Desperately broke but unwilling to stop his spending, he hatched a plan to find money from other sources. And let me assure you, it was crazier than Ludwig himself."

Payne arched an eyebrow. "What was the plan?"

Ulster grinned. "He created the black swan."

19

❦

To this day, Ludwig is beloved throughout Bavaria. They still refer to him as *unser kini*, which means "our king" in the Bavarian dialect. Ironically, Ludwig wasn't a people person. He was a borderline recluse who spent most of his time in seclusion, whether that was at his home in the Alps or at one of his many palaces.

By most accounts, Ludwig was a strange man whose odd behavior slowly worsened over time. Whether he was insane or eccentric at the time of his death depended on who was asked. Early in his reign, his conduct was considered peculiar but relatively harmless. For instance, his hair had to be curled every morning or he wouldn't enjoy his food—even if his favorite meal was served. A lover of animals, Ludwig once invited his favorite gray mare to dinner and insisted her food be served in the dining hall on the palace's finest crockery. Not surprisingly, the horse ate the meal, then proceeded to smash everything to bits.

As early as 1868—less than five years into his reign—Ludwig had become nocturnal. This wouldn't have been an issue if he had worked the late shift at a factory, but it was problematic as king. On most days, he woke up at 7 P.M., had lunch at midnight, and enjoyed dinner around daybreak. When he was in Munich—a city he despised because he hated politics and felt like he was under a microscope at all times—he spent many nights riding in circles at the Court Riding School. He picked a random city where he would rather be (for example, Berlin), then he calculated how many laps he had to ride in order to cover the equivalent distance. While imagining the journey, he would often stop at the halfway point to enjoy a picnic. Then he would pack everything up and continue riding until he reached his imaginary destination.

As a well-known pacifist, Ludwig was considered one of the worst military leaders in history. He referred to his officers as "clipped hedgehog heads," and when he saw a tired sentry outside of his residence, he would order a sofa brought out to him. Despite his aversion to war, Ludwig thought he looked exceptionally handsome in his military uniform, so he wore it often. When he did, he liked having imaginary conversations with famous generals.

Unfortunately, this type of behavior became more common toward the end. A strong believer in reincarnation, Ludwig once signed a letter "Louis" and added "of our fifth reign," possibly believing he used to be the king of

France. Sometimes his servants would enter the dining hall and hear him having imaginary conversations with members of the French Court. His admiration of Marie Antoinette was so extreme he had a statue of her placed on one of his terraces. Anytime he passed it, he would take off his hat and gently stroke her cheek. On occasion, he also liked to dress up as Louis XIV, who was known for his exaggerated walking style. In an attempt to imitate him, Ludwig would throw his leg out as far as he could reach, and then he would slam his foot down as if squashing a bug. He would repeat this process again and again, his footsteps echoing in the palace as he moved across the floor like a spastic giraffe.

Nevertheless, in spite of his antics, his enemies wouldn't have acted so decisively if Ludwig's biggest sin had been his eccentricities. As peculiar as he was, his behavior probably would have been overlooked since it had never threatened the future of Bavaria.

But everything changed when he created the black swan.

Ulster explained. "One of the reasons that Ludwig was such a popular ruler was that he never used government funds to build any of his castles. Instead, he drained his family fortune, spending hundreds of millions of dollars on his projects. Ironically, even though it wasn't his intent, Ludwig's indulgence actually stimulated the Bavarian economy. Not only did he create thousands of jobs for laborers, but his money slowly trickled throughout the region, one peasant at a time. For many years, the only group that had a valid complaint about Ludwig's spending habits was his family. After all, he was wasting their inheritance. But as luck should have it, he had only one sibling—his younger brother Otto—and he was even crazier than Ludwig."

"Yeah," Jones joked, "how lucky can one guy get?"

Ulster instantly regretted his choice of words. "Obviously, I didn't mean he was blessed to have a crazy sibling. I meant lucky in terms of the hereditary monarchy. If Otto, his next of kin and potential successor, had been the least bit ambitious, he would have fought for Ludwig's crown much earlier. And if he had won it, he would have controlled the purse strings. However, since Otto had been declared insane in 1875—well before Ludwig had gone into debt and started borrowing large piles of money from outside sources—there was no one willing to challenge his authority. Not until he went too far."

"Let me guess," Payne said. "You're talking about the black swan."

Ulster nodded. "When the royal coffers began to run dry, Ludwig tried to raise funds for his projects through legal means. He asked the Bavarian finance minister to arrange a loan of seven and a half million marks from a consortium of German banks, which temporarily kept him afloat. But Ludwig realized the money wouldn't last for long, especially at the rate he was spending it. With that in mind, he went to the drawing board—*literally* went to the drawing board with a quill and ink—and designed the black swan. As you can see, Ludwig was a talented artist.

He figured if he was going to start an organization, he might as well have some fun with it."

Payne glanced at the symbol on the lid. Admittedly, it did have a certain flair. "What type of organization are you talking about?"

"The secret kind."

"Meaning?"

"Meaning he didn't want people to know about it."

Payne growled softly. "Believe it or not, I know what *secret* means. I meant, what was the function of the organization?"

"Sorry," Ulster said, blushing. He was so excited about the discovery, he was rambling more than usual. "Ludwig's goal was to acquire funds through illicit means."

Kaiser laughed. "He became a thief? That's awesome!"

Jones was tempted to tease Kaiser, then thought better of it.

Ulster shook his head. "Not a thief per se. More like the head of a new syndicate. Ludwig hatched a series of crazy schemes, then recruited his most loyal followers to carry them out. Unfortunately, most of his men realized that Ludwig was bonkers, so they only pretended to follow his orders—often with comic results."

"Such as?" Jones asked.

Ulster thought of a good example. "After being turned down for a loan by a Rothschild bank, Ludwig decided to steal the money instead. Realizing that his men might be recognized in Munich, he sent a group of his servants to Frankfurt to rob a bank there. Not soldiers, mind you, but *servants*—cooks, butlers, stable boys, and the like. Obviously, these men had no intention of robbing a bank, but all of them wanted a free vacation. With that in mind, the group went to Frankfurt for a few days, where they spent plenty of the king's money. Eventually, they returned home empty-handed. When asked about their lack of success, they claimed they had been *this* close to finishing the job but a last-minute glitch had prevented it."

Payne, Jones, and Kaiser laughed. It sounded like the plot of a bad movie.

"So," Payne guessed, "the government caught wind of these crazy schemes and decided to remove Ludwig before he did irreparable damage to the crown."

"Actually, no. The servants didn't want to be punished— or ruin a good thing—so most of these stories didn't surface until long after Ludwig had been murdered."

"Really? Then what got him in trouble?" Payne asked.

Ulster pointed at the gold. "Rumors about the black swan."

20

✤

Unlike some historians who refused to offer an opinion about anything until every fact had been collected and studied ad nauseam, Ulster tended to develop theories on the fly. Sometimes that resulted in a rambling monologue that went on forever, but Payne and Jones had been around him enough to understand his process. For Ulster, talking about the subject matter was the key. As he painted the scene for others, pieces of the puzzle fell into place in his own mind.

"Nine months before his murder," Ulster explained, "Ludwig summoned the best horsemen in his kingdom to Linderhof—one of his castles—and asked them to deliver a series of letters across Europe. To escape detection, the riders were sent on their journeys in the dead of night. According to a witness who worked in the stables, each of the documents had been sealed in advance, and each had been stamped with an elaborate black swan. Other than that, not much is known about their mysterious quest. No one knows what the letters said, where they were sent, or if they were actually delivered."

"Why didn't someone ask the riders?" Payne asked.

"Why? Because the riders never returned."

"None of them?"

Ulster shook his head. "No one knows if they were shot, captured, or ordered to stay away."

"That's bizarre," Jones said. He was familiar with Ludwig and his castles, but he had never heard about the black swan.

"Trust me," Ulster assured them, "it gets even stranger. The very next night, Ludwig disappeared—simply vanished without a trace for roughly thirty-six hours. No one knew if he was kidnapped, killed, or lost in the nearby woods. Obviously, it was a scary time for his advisors. Not wanting to start a panic and not wanting to give his opposition any ammunition, they decided to keep things quiet until they figured out where he was. Slowly but surely, they began to understand what had happened. In the middle of the night, Ludwig had snuck out of Linderhof—past a team of armed guards—and departed for Schachen, a small palace less than five miles from here. For some reason, he wanted to be left alone for a week."

Ulster paused to gather his thoughts. "Once he was found, his advisors were relieved. With Ludwig on vacation, they could spin his departure any way they wanted. At least until rumors started to spread about the midnight horsemen and the mysterious letters. Worried that Ludwig had hatched another crazy scheme, they decided to pay him a surprise visit to see what he was plotting. When they got there, he was covered in dirt—like he had been working in the fields all day. They asked him what he had been doing, but he refused to say."

"Any theories?" Payne asked.

"Not until you showed me the crate of gold with the black swan symbol. Now, if I had to guess, I'd say Ludwig got dirty while visiting this bunker."

Payne furrowed his brow. "How is that possible? I thought you said your grandfather built this bunker in the 1930s?"

Ulster shook his head. "Actually, Jonathon, I said my grandfather *used* this bunker. I never said he *built* it. Considering all the Nazi activity in these parts, there's no way he could have built something like this without detection. No, if I had to speculate, I'd say Ludwig commissioned its construction in 1886, and my grandfather found it fifty years later."

To make his point, Ulster held up his grandfather's journal. "Remember earlier when I said the black swan was an explanation? At the time, I meant it in terms of this book, but . . ." He paused, still coming to grips with a theory. "On further reflection, the black swan explains a lot more than that. Actually, it explains just about everything."

"Everything?" Payne asked.

Ulster nodded. "Imagine a set of directions with no starting point. No matter how many turns you make, you can never reach your destination because you don't know where to begin. In many ways, that's how I felt before you showed me that symbol. Similar to the Rosetta stone, which helped linguists decipher the hieroglyphics, the black swan gave me the context I was lacking when I first entered this bunker. Suddenly, I see things in a different light."

"Wonderful," Payne said dryly. "Hopefully, that means you'll be able to address some of the questions that you still haven't answered."

"Such as?"

"Why did Ludwig build this bunker?"

Ulster pointed at the crates. "To hide his treasure."

Kaiser interrupted. "What treasure? I thought he was broke."

"So did his creditors," Ulster said, laughing. "At the time of his death, Ludwig was more than fourteen million marks in debt. Creditors were lining up at his door, demanding to be paid. In fact, the company that supplied water and fuel to his castles actually took him to court over nonpayment. According to several sources, it was the biggest embarrassment of Ludwig's life."

"What's your point?" Payne asked.

Ulster grabbed one of the gold bars for emphasis. "If Ludwig had this much gold lying around, why didn't he spend it and avoid all that humiliation?"

Jones took a guess. "Because he was nuts."

"Or," Ulster countered, "the rumors about the black swan were true."

"What rumors?" Payne demanded. "You keep mentioning rumors."

Ulster smiled, relishing the opportunity to explain. "According to legend, Ludwig sent the mysterious letters—known as the black swan letters—to aristocrats throughout Europe, asking for their support in a secret project that he was working on. At the time of his death, Ludwig's reputation was far better in foreign countries than in Bavaria, so there is a good chance that his letters would have carried a lot of weight. From the look of this gold and all these crates, a lot of people took the bait."

Kaiser laughed. "Let me see if I got this straight. The king of Bavaria was running a Ponzi scheme on the richest people in Europe? That's hilarious!"

Ulster shrugged. "Actually, no one knows if he was scamming people out of their money or if he was looking for investors in a *legitimate* project. The truth is he was killed before his plot was revealed. In theory, the Bavarian government wouldn't have been pleased with either result—whether he was swindling the rich or hoarding money while refusing to pay his bills. Either way, Bavaria was going to be embarrassed by Ludwig's actions. That's why he was eliminated."

"Allegedly," Payne stressed. "Or was there proof?"

Ulster shook his head. "As I mentioned earlier, all of this—his murder, his secret plan, his disappearance—is pure speculation. The only tangible evidence ever discovered regarding the black swan was a series of Ludwig's sketches and a few snippets in his diary about a secret organization. Everything else is a mixture of rumors, hearsay, and conjecture."

"Until today," Payne said.

Ulster beamed as he stared at his grandfather's journal. "Yes. Until today."

"So," Kaiser said, anxious to open the other crates, "what's the next step? Can we dive right in, or do you have to do some kind of archaeology shit?"

"About that," Ulster said, "I'm afraid I might have some bad news for you. From the looks of these crates, I'm not sure you're going to find anything of value."

Kaiser laughed and snatched the gold bar from Ulster. "I don't know about you, but gold has plenty of value to me. What does this thing weigh? Ten, twelve pounds? This crate alone will buy me an island."

Jones looked offended. "Just a second! I pried off the damn lid. What's my cut?"

"Don't worry, man. You can use my beach."

Ulster cleared his throat, suddenly nervous. He wasn't used to dealing with men like Kaiser and wasn't sure how he would react to bad news. "Actually, that's not what I meant. If my theory is correct, there's a very good chance that most of these crates are worthless."

"Worthless?" Kaiser blurted. "Why would they be worthless?"

Ulster ignored the question. Instead, he searched through the stacks—kicking a few crates, shaking another— until he found three that met his needs. "If you don't mind, can you open these for me? They will illustrate my point."

"Sure," Kaiser said as he grabbed the crowbar.

"Actually," Ulster told him, "tools won't be necessary. The crates aren't sealed."

"Why not?" he asked.

"Remove the lid and find out."

Intrigued, Payne and Jones moved closer as Kaiser pulled off the first lid. Much to their surprise, the crate was completely empty.

Ulster tapped on another. "Now this one."

Kaiser did what he was told, but it was empty as well.

"And this one."

Same thing. The crate was empty.

Ulster motioned toward the stacks. "Unfortunately, I have a feeling most of them will be empty. Otherwise, my grandfather wouldn't have stacked them like this."

Payne grimaced. "Your grandfather? How do you know they were his crates?"

"Simple. Look at the wood."

"What's wrong with the wood?" Kaiser demanded.

"Nothing. And that's the problem." Ulster ran his hand over one of the empty crates. "No nicks, no cracks, no scuffs of any kind. Much different than Ludwig's crate, which was weathered and worn, but quite similar to the crate with my family's crest. I noticed that earlier, but it didn't make sense until now. If I had to guess, most of these crates were assembled here in anticipation of my grandfather's next discovery."

Jones glanced at the crates. "Which was?"

Ulster shrugged. "I honestly don't know what he was searching for. Perhaps his journal will give us a clue, perhaps not. However, based on the size of this bunker and the dozens of crates that fill this chamber, he was preparing for something huge."

21

✤

Over the next hour, Payne, Jones, and Kaiser opened every crate in the bunker while Ulster studied his grandfather's notes on the other side of the room. To everyone's disappointment, Ulster's theory about the crates was proven correct: Most of them were empty. The few that had something to offer were filled with family heirlooms—personal items that would be returned to the rightful owners—but nothing came close to the van Gogh crate or Ludwig's gold.

"I'm sorry," Kaiser said after they opened the final one.

"For what?" Payne asked.

"For wasting your time."

Payne wiped the sweat off his brow. "What are you talking about? You didn't waste our time. This was kind of fun—in a chain gang kind of way."

Jones took a gulp of water. "Speak for yourself. My

back is killing me, and I got a blister on my thumb the size of a dumpling. I hope our host has insurance."

Kaiser smiled. "Just grab some gold and we'll call it even."

Jones considered the offer. "It's a pleasure doing business with you."

"In all seriousness," Payne said to Kaiser, "we appreciated the heads-up. Obviously, things didn't work out the way we had hoped—"

"That's an understatement," Jones mumbled.

"—but we managed to protect Petr's reputation. And that's good enough for us."

Jones cleared his throat loudly, the sound echoing through the room.

Payne stared at him. "What?"

"Aren't you forgetting something?"

"I don't think so . . . Am I?"

Jones sighed in disappointment. He had always been better with details than Payne. "Please forgive my former captain. The mind starts to go at his age."

"What are you talking about? You're older than I am!" Payne grumbled.

Jones ignored the comment. "What Jon *meant* to say was this: Although we were thrilled to protect the Ulster family name, we'll still gladly accept the free trip to Oktoberfest."

Payne paused in thought. "Actually, he's right. That *is* what I meant to say."

Kaiser laughed at their antics. "Don't worry, fellas. I'll keep my word. You'll still get two days at Oktoberfest. If all goes well, you'll be in the beer gardens before dinner."

"Unless . . ." Ulster called from the far side of the room.

All three of them turned toward Ulster, who was sitting on an empty crate with his back against the bunker wall. In his hands, he held his grandfather's journal.

"Unless what?" Payne asked.

"Unless you want to retrieve the treasure that was destined for these crates."

Jones stepped forward. "What are you talking about?"

Ulster rocked back and forth a few times in order to generate enough momentum to stand up. "While you gentlemen have been searching through the crates, I've been conducting a search of my own—one that has been a tad more fruitful than yours. According to my grandfather's notes, his biggest problem wasn't *finding* Ludwig's treasure. It was *retrieving* it."

Silence filled the room as they considered Ulster's words.

A few seconds passed before Kaiser spoke. "What do you mean?"

Ulster grinned. "I had a feeling that would get your attention."

"Well, you have it. Now explain."

"As I mentioned earlier, Bavaria was swarming with Nazis during the 1930s. This area in particular was under high alert because of the 1936 Winter Olympics, which were held in the valley below. As a matter of fact, this mountain was actually used for some of the skiing events.

Because of all the extra security, my grandfather was forced to abandon his pursuit of Ludwig's treasure shortly after finding this bunker. From the looks of things, he had a pretty good idea where the treasure was hidden, but he wasn't able to retrieve it thanks to World War II."

"Fucking Hitler! Always screwing things up," Jones joked.

"What are you saying? You know where the treasure is?" Kaiser demanded.

Ulster lowered his voice. "According to my grandfather, Ludwig hid a secret document in his *Gartenhaus* that would reveal the location of the treasure."

Jones winced. "One time, when Jon and I were crossing the Afghan border, I had to hide a document in *my Gartenhaus*, and—"

Kaiser cut him off. "*Gartenhaus* means 'garden house' in German, *not* what you were about to describe."

"Thank goodness," Jones cracked. "Because I got a paper cut when I pulled it out."

Payne rolled his eyes. Sometimes his best friend didn't know when to stop joking around. "Petr, are you familiar with any place that would fit your grandfather's description?"

Ulster replied. "Off the top of my head, I can think of three possible locations. One would be good news. One would be tolerable news. The third would be truly dreadful."

"Let's start with the good," Kaiser suggested. "That is, if you guys are interested."

Payne answered before Jones had a chance to make

another joke. "We've come this far. What's another few hours? Besides, Oktoberfest goes on for two more weeks."

Ulster grinned. He loved working with Payne and Jones. "In my opinion, the King's House on Schachen would be the best news for us. It's a small castle on top of Schachen, a peak about five miles from here. As I mentioned earlier, this is where Ludwig went when he disappeared for thirty-six hours—the night after he sent the mysterious letters."

"The place where his advisors found him covered in dirt?" Payne asked, trying to remember the details from Ulster's long-winded story.

Ulster nodded. "Even though it looks more like a hunting lodge than an actual castle, it is adjacent to Alpengarten auf dem Schachen—a small botanical garden that is open to the public."

"A house by a garden. Makes sense to me," Payne said.

"This would be the best news for a variety of reasons. First of all, it's close by, meaning we could be there in less than an hour. Secondly, it's on top of a desolate peak. Without a helicopter, the only way to get there is an arduous four-hour hike. Since most people don't have one, I tend to think we'd have the run of the place."

Kaiser nodded in agreement. It sounded ideal to him.

"If it isn't there, what's the 'tolerable' location you mentioned?" Jones asked.

Ulster replied. "That would be Linderhof Palace, the only one of Ludwig's castles that he saw completed before his death. If you recall, that is where his horsemen departed from on their mysterious quest. In addition, that is where he returned after spending time on Schachen."

Kaiser gave it some thought. "What's troubling about the Linderhof?"

"The grounds alone are over a hundred and twenty-five acres. That's a large area to search. In addition, the palace is filled with valuable artwork. Because of that, the crowds are big and security is high."

"Crowds can be good in certain scenarios," Payne suggested. "But you're probably right. This doesn't sound like the kind of place where we'll have much freedom to move around."

Ulster shook his head. "And yet the Linderhof would be *much* better than the final option, a place called the Winter Garden. Ludwig built it on top of the roof of the north wing of the Munich Residenz, which was the former royal palace of the Bavarian monarchs. It is the largest palace in all of Germany and gets thousands of visitors every day. The complex contains ten courtyards and more than a hundred and thirty rooms, most of them massive in scale. One of the grandest is the treasury, which holds everything from the house jewels of the Wittelsbach dynasty to a collection of royal crowns, including some from the first millennium."

Kaiser pondered the security. "That doesn't sound good."

"Actually," Payne said, "it doesn't matter how many guards are in the treasury. This document *isn't* in the treasury. If it's already been discovered, Petr would have heard of it."

"That is true," Ulster claimed. "Unfortunately, the treasury would be a lot easier to explore than the garden itself. Like everything Ludwig built, the Winter Garden was stunning. Inside of a massive greenhouse was a man-made lake, a Himalayan mountain scene, Indian huts, a rainbow machine, and tropical plants from around the world. The servants who lived in the rooms underneath the lake had to sleep under umbrellas because of all the dripping water. I've seen pictures of the garden, and I'm telling you, it was remarkable. Like an indoor jungle."

Payne focused on one word in particular. *"Was?"*

Ulster nodded. "The Winter Garden was demolished right after the king's death. Its weight was so great it actually bent the beams in the palace walls."

Jones sighed at the news. He was hoping to see the place. "You're right: Option three sucks. It's tough to explore something that's no longer there."

"Let's be honest," Payne said. "None of these options are great. I mean, we're talking about three castles that have been toured by millions of people. Do you really think we're going to stroll in and spot something that everyone else has missed in the last one hundred and twenty years?"

"Of course not," Ulster said as he held up his grandfather's journal. "Thankfully, we have a lot more to go on than good, old-fashioned luck. We actually have a detailed set of instructions. All we have to do is find the starting line, and this journal will do the rest."

It took a few seconds for the comment to sink in. Once it did, Payne shook his head in disbelief. Leave it to Ulster to wait so long before he revealed something so vital to the group. One of these days, Payne was going to have to teach Ulster how to start off with the most important news before he went off on his tangents—just in case Ulster died of old age before he finished his background information.

Payne laughed to himself. "In that case, what are we waiting for? Let's go find Ludwig's treasure."

22

❦

Mount Schachen
Bavaria, Germany

I n Kaiser's world, there were very few guarantees when it came to money. Deals frequently collapsed at the last minute. Longtime associates often tried to screw him for table scraps. And rivals always looked for opportunities to steal his clients or get him in trouble with the police.

Being in the business for as long as he had, Kaiser had learned many lessons along the way. One of the most important was the danger of greed. Early in his career, he had lost plenty of money because of his recklessness. Like a gambler who refused to pocket his winnings, Kaiser used to take too many risks when the smart play was to walk away. But all of that changed a few years ago when he lost millions of dollars' worth of merchandise in a warehouse fire. Instead of selling the goods to a trusted customer who had offered a fair price, Kaiser had tried to leverage a better deal for himself by negotiating with an unsavory character from the Russian mafia. The whole thing fell apart when the two clients found out about each other. To this day, Kaiser still didn't know which of them had torched his warehouse—although he assumed it was the Russian—but from that point on, he decided to minimize his risks whenever he could.

With that in mind, Kaiser skipped the next leg of the journey to protect his discovery. While Payne, Jones, and Ulster flew to the top of Mount Schachen and searched for the location of Ludwig's treasure, Kaiser made travel arrangements for the gold they had already found.

Known as the Königshaus am Schachen in German, the King's House on Schachen took three years to build (1869–1872) because all of the supplies had to be carted up the mountain. A lover of the outdoors, Ludwig chose this site for the spectacular views of the surrounding peaks and for its isolation. Thousands of feet above civilization, the two-story Alpine cottage was Ludwig's sanctuary anytime he wanted to escape the politics and prying eyes of Munich. Up here among the clouds, he used to fantasize about starting his own kingdom across the sea, a modern-day Camelot where he would build the most spectacular castle the world had ever seen.

As the pilot circled the ridgeline looking for a place to land, Payne and Jones stared out the chopper's windows, both men filled with disappointment. After hearing so many stories about Ludwig's opulence, they were expecting the cottage to rival the Taj Mahal. Instead, they saw a plain, wooden structure that looked like a hunting lodge.

Jones spoke into his headset. "If that's the outhouse, where's the King's House?"

"I'm afraid you're looking at it," Ulster replied from the front seat. "But don't let the exterior fool you. The interior is far more lavish."

"That's not saying much, because the outside looks like a shed."

Payne cracked a smile. "A shed with a hell of a view."

"Good point," Jones admitted.

"If we flew a little higher, you could see Austria. We're just north of its border," Ulster said as he stared at Mount Dreitorspitze of the Wetterstein Mountains.

"Isn't that kind of stupid?" Payne asked out of the blue.

Ulster turned in his seat. "What are you referring to?"

Payne answered. "The placement of this cabin. I mean, if I'm a Bavarian general, there's no way in hell I'd let Ludwig build a house this close to a foreign border. Look at the surrounding peaks. This area is indefensible."

Jones nodded in agreement. "Jon makes a valid point. Set a few explosives on the top of that ridge, and the resulting landslide would have wiped out the king."

"Not only that," Payne said, "but if the Austrians had wanted to kidnap Ludwig, they could have done so with ease. What do you think, DJ? Three, maybe four men at most?"

In less than a second, Jones ran through several scenarios in his head. When it came to planning missions, he was a strategic genius—the type of guy who played chess when everyone else was playing checkers. "Give me four men and a cloudy night, and I could've nabbed more than Ludwig. I could've stolen his house, too."

Payne laughed. "Actually, that sounds kind of fun. Let's do that instead of Oktoberfest."

"Petr," Jones said with a straight face, "can we borrow your helicopter tonight? I promise we'll pay for gas."

The Swiss pilot, who had heard the entire conversation through his headphones, glanced at Ulster. Tension filled the pilot's face. "Sir?"

Ulster patted him on the shoulder. "Relax, Baptiste. They're only kidding."

Ulster paused, then glanced back at Payne and Jones. "You *are* kidding, aren't you?"

To minimize attention—which was tough to do in a helicopter—the pilot landed on top of a rocky plateau approximately two hundred yards below the King's House. A grass-covered hill that looked like a backdrop for *The Sound of Music* separated them from the cottage.

As they strolled up the meadow toward the main entrance, Payne focused on a cluster of buildings in the valley behind the King's House. Their light gray roofs blended perfectly with the surrounding rock face, minimizing their presence in the Alpine scenery.

Payne pointed at the compound. "What's over there?"

"That's the Schachenhaus restaurant," Ulster answered without even looking. "In addition, there are several guest cabins for those inclined to spend the night."

"People do that?" Jones asked as he shivered in his long-sleeved shirt. It was fifteen degrees colder than it had been when he boarded the chopper a few minutes earlier.

Ulster grinned. "For most people, it's a lengthy hike to reach this site. After a four-hour climb, I'd be tempted to stay myself."

"But it's cold up here," Jones complained.

"Hardly!" Ulster said, laughing. To prove his point, he took a deep breath and exhaled it slowly. "Smell that mountain air! It reminds me of Küsendorf."

"Really?" Jones mumbled to himself. "It reminds me of Siberia."

Familiar with Jones's hatred of the cold, Payne decided to change the topic before Jones started to bitch. Because once that started, it was hard to stop.

"So," Payne said to Ulster, "tell us more about the *Gartenhaus*. It would probably be helpful if we knew what we were looking for."

Ulster nodded in agreement. "According to my grandfather, Ludwig used a riddle to conceal the location. All we have to do is solve it, and we should be able to find the document."

Payne smiled. "You make it sound so easy."

"Well, I don't know about easy, but I think we have a decent—"

Jones interrupted him. "What's the riddle?"

Ulster laughed at his oversight. "Yes! That would be helpful, wouldn't it? Obviously, the original version was written in Bavarian—or some kind of Austro-Bavarian dialect—which my grandfather eventually translated into Austrian German. That's the language he spoke prior to moving to Switzerland. Later in life, he—"

"Petr!" Jones blurted. "You're giving me a headache. Just tell us the riddle."

Ulster blushed. "Sorry, David. I'm just excited."

Jones immediately felt guilty and softened his tone. "And we're excited, too. We really are. But we can't help if you don't tell us the riddle."

Ulster nodded in understanding. Most of the time they humored him and let him ramble on and on, but even a long-winded historian like Ulster realized that some situations called for brevity. And this was one of those times. Without any further introduction or additional background information, he honored their request and revealed the riddle.

"Where would a swan go on his journey home?"

23

❈

Garmisch-Partenkirchen, Germany

Krueger couldn't believe his luck. First the surprising appearance of Petr Ulster, and now *this*. Obviously, something significant was going on, and it was his job to figure out what. After three years of doing small jobs for Hans Mueller, he hoped this would be his ticket out.

Not that Krueger hated the Oberbayern region of Germany—it certainly had its charm. But ever since he had left the 10th Armored Division of the German Army, he had always wanted to work in a larger city. Perhaps Frankfurt or Berlin. Or even Cologne. At this point, anything would be better than a seasonal town like Garmisch-Partenkirchen. The only time he saw local action was during the winter months when the big spenders rolled into town for skiing and Mueller needed extra protection to conduct business meetings on the slopes.

Other than that, Krueger was forced to fend for himself for six months a year. He ran a small crew of his own—mostly ex-military types—that specialized in break-ins and broken legs. Occasionally, when they were desperate for cash, they would steal a few cars and sell them to an Austrian associate who took them across the border before they were even reported missing. The money paid their rent for a few months and bought them plenty of beer, but in the grand scheme of things, Krueger realized the risks he took were never worth the reward.

For the past several weeks, Krueger had been looking for a way to make a name for himself, a way to get noticed by Mueller or one of his top lieutenants. He had considered all types of jobs, including a bank heist in Düsseldorf, an art theft in Stuttgart, and a kidnapping in Dresden. Amazingly, during all of his legwork and advance planning, he had never expected a once-in-a-lifetime opportunity to surface in his own backyard. And yet he was staring at it through his binoculars.

If he pulled this off, he'd be a legend overnight.

Kaiser's plan was simple: Get the gold off the mountain as quickly as possible.

Once it was safely on its way to one of his secured facilities, Kaiser would worry about the van Gogh crate and all the other heirlooms that Ulster wanted to transport to the Archives for documentation. After that, Kaiser didn't care what happened to the items—whether Ulster returned them to the rightful owners, donated them to a museum, or sold everything on eBay. As long as no one mentioned the gold or his involvement to the authorities, Kaiser would walk away with the biggest score of his life, the type of payday that would allow him to retire.

He could practically taste the piña coladas already.

As for Ludwig's mythical treasure, it sounded like more trouble than it was worth—especially to someone who shunned the spotlight like he did. If Payne and Jones found something of value, Kaiser would gladly take his share, as long as it could be handled far from the public eye. The last thing he needed was his name and picture in every newspaper around the world. That's what had happened to Payne and Jones when they found the Greek treasure, and they had been struggling with the attention ever since.

For a man like Kaiser, that type of notoriety would be a death sentence.

No, as far as he was concerned, he was more than willing to sell the gold and retire with a brand-new Ferrari. Or twelve.

Krueger gasped when he saw Kaiser's face through his binoculars. Not only was Petr Ulster involved, but so was Mueller's biggest rival. Could this get any better?

In the world of smuggling, Kaiser was the king.

And Mueller sought his crown.

If Krueger played his cards right, he would be set for life.

Within minutes, he had summoned his local crew.

Within the hour, they were dressed in camouflage and ready for battle. None of them knew the numbers they faced or the prize they were fighting for, but they trusted Krueger's leadership and feared Mueller's wrath.

For henchmen, that was all the motivation they needed.

Using two-way radios for communication, they entered the woods in pairs. Two men went to the left, and two men went to the right. Meanwhile, Krueger stayed near the base of the mountain. His job was to call the shots while keeping his eye on the helicopter that was parked near the path. Earlier there had been two choppers in the field, but one of them—carrying Ulster, his pilot, and two others—had flown up the mountain before Krueger's crew had arrived.

As far as he was concerned, the timing was perfect.

Suddenly, there were four fewer men to worry about.

And Kaiser had stayed behind.

The crate of gold was far too heavy to carry up the ladder by hand. To hoist that much weight, a series of pulleys had to be rigged outside of the bunker. While two of Kaiser's men fiddled with the equipment, the other three stayed hidden in the trees, keeping a close eye on the site.

Initially, Kaiser had considered carrying the gold out one bar at a time and repacking the crate outside. It certainly would have been quicker than building a winch. He had already made two trips on the off-road utility vehicle that had hauled most of their supplies—one to the chopper to retrieve a tool kit and a second trip to arrange the truck that would take the gold to his warehouse. But after giving it some thought, Kaiser had decided the extra time was worth it if it prevented his men from knowing what was inside the crate. Even though he trusted them, the sight of that much gold could do strange things to a man's psyche. And the last thing he wanted was a setback of any kind, especially with this much money at stake.

"How much longer?" Kaiser asked his men.

One of them answered. "Five minutes at most."

"Before you haul up the crate, put some extra nails in the lid. It's a bumpy ride down the mountain, and I don't want it popping open en route."

"Yes, sir."

Kaiser stared at the device they were building. It didn't look sturdy to him. "Actually, before you even touch the crate, I want you to test this contraption out."

"On what, sir?"

"On Hogzilla. If it can handle the pig, it can handle the crate."

As far as Krueger was concerned, the biggest stroke of luck had occurred during his early-morning call to Mueller. At the end of their conversation, Krueger had asked Mueller how often he wanted to be updated on the situation, and Mueller had told him that he was heading into an important meeting and didn't want to be disturbed for the next several hours.

Mueller had even used the phrase "no matter what."

At the time, it didn't seem important since the odds

were pretty slim that anything significant would happen before lunch. After all, Ulster had arrived that morning, and the other chopper had been around all weekend. Krueger had assumed this would drag on all day.

Of course, Kaiser's presence was a game changer.

Normally, Krueger would have been required to notify Mueller, who would have taken control and flown in an outside crew to make sure things were handled properly. If Krueger was lucky, he would have been given a finder's fee and a pat on the back. Certainly not a new position in the organization. But thanks to Mueller's explicit instruction, Krueger could handle the situation however he saw fit.

And in his mind, that meant two things.

A gun in his hand and a bullet in Kaiser's brain.

24

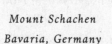

Mount Schachen
Bavaria, Germany

A s they walked up the meadow toward the King's House, Payne repeated the riddle to make sure he had heard it correctly. "Where would a swan go on his journey home?"

Ulster nodded. "Any thoughts?"

"Yeah," Jones cracked, "Ludwig liked swans *way* too much."

"I told you he was obsessed."

"I know you did, but I think it's weird. I mean, swans don't even taste good. You know how people say most things taste like chicken? Well, swans don't. They taste like shit."

Ulster laughed in agreement. As a gourmand, he had tasted swan on multiple occasions but had never enjoyed the bird. To him, the meat was stringy and tough, and had a fishy aftertaste—even when it was covered in gravy. "Hopefully, you didn't partake in England."

Jones shook his head. "Why's that?"

"Because every swan in England is the sovereign property of the Queen. Until last century, killing one was a treasonable offense."

"The Queen owns *every* swan? How does she remember their names?"

Ulster ignored the question. "Technically, she owns every unmarked swan in the United Kingdom except the swans of Orkney, which is an archipelago in northern Scotland. According to an old Udal Viking law, Orkney swans are the property of the island's residents."

Payne glanced at Ulster. "And what does this have to do with Ludwig?"

"Nothing," he admitted. "I just thought it was interesting."

"Well, for the time being, maybe it would be best if we focused on Ludwig instead of the Vikings. You know, since we just flew up the mountain to visit his house."

"Yes, of course. I apologize for my rambling. Let us focus on the riddle."

Payne asked, "How do you want to handle this? Do you want to walk the grounds, looking for possibilities? Or do you want to brainstorm the answer to the riddle and go from there?"

Ulster gazed at the house. "Which would you prefer?"

"You tell me. You're the historian."

"Personally, I think it would be best if we determined the solution before we scurried around the site. However,

I'm not sure that is feasible. Obviously, I've given the riddle some thought, and the most logical answer is a swan's nest. That's where a swan would go on its journey home. After all, that's where cygnets are hatched."

Payne furrowed his brow. "What's a cygnet?"

"That's the technical name of a baby swan."

Payne shrugged. "If you say so. I don't know much about swans."

"Neither do I," Jones admitted. "But a swan's nest is his home."

Ulster sighed. "Unfortunately, that means we can probably rule out 'nest' as the answer. By definition, a riddle is a puzzle in the form of a question. If the obvious answer were the solution, it wouldn't technically be a riddle. It would merely be a question."

Jones blinked a few times. "Believe it or not, that actually made sense."

Payne stayed focused. "If it isn't a nest, what could it be?"

Ulster considered other possibilities. "I guess it could be a body of water. After all, most swans build their nests along the shore. Perhaps Ludwig had a favorite spot in mind."

Payne turned and studied the grounds that surrounded the King's House. Because of the steep slope of the peak, melting snow flowed down the mountain and collected in natural ravines. "If that's the case, we're in the wrong place—unless there's a hidden lake around here."

Ulster shook his head. "Not that I know of, but we can certainly ask."

Jones reentered the conversation. "I know you're going to think I'm joking, but is Swan Lake a real place?"

As little as Payne knew about swans, he knew even less about ballets and classical music. "I don't know. Is it?"

Ulster answered. "That's an interesting question. Geographically speaking, there isn't a modern lake in Germany that goes by that name. However, the story of *Swan Lake* is based on an ancient German legend. Who knows? Perhaps there used to be a Swan Lake in Bavaria that is now called something else."

"I'll tell you who would know: a man obsessed with swans," Jones said.

Payne nodded. "Good point."

Ulster continued. "Speaking of *Swan Lake*, did you know the main character in the ballet was actually modeled after Ludwig? Tchaikovsky, the Russian composer who created this classic in 1875, was fascinated with Ludwig's life and followed it from afar. In many ways, the two of them were quite similar. Both were sexually confused dreamers who escaped reality by venturing into dreamworlds. Tchaikovsky had his music, and Ludwig had his castles."

Jones asked, "Did they ever meet?"

Ulster shook his head. "Not that I'm aware of."

"But the ballet was written before Ludwig's death?"

Ulster nodded. "Roughly ten years prior."

Jones pondered the timeline. "I know Russia and Germany weren't exactly allies, but I would think a music lover like Ludwig would have been familiar with the production."

"Undoubtedly."

"Perhaps he even recognized bits of himself in the main character?"

"Probably."

Jones gave it some thought. "If that's the case, do you think the riddle could have something to do with the ballet? Could there be a clue in there?"

Ulster shrugged. "Maybe."

"Just to be safe," Jones said, "can you explain the basic plot? I honestly can't remember what *Swan Lake* is about."

Payne groaned. He felt a lecture coming on. "But please keep it short."

Ulster promised to be concise. "The story of *Swan Lake* is centered on Prince Siegfried, who is notified before his twenty-first birthday that his marriage will soon be arranged. Dreading his future responsibilities, he heads to the woods, where he stumbles across an enchanted lake that is filled with many swans. Much to his surprise, one of the swans has a crown on its head. As the sun sets, the swan turns into the most beautiful woman he has ever seen. Her name is Odette, and she's the Swan Queen. She tells the prince that over the years an evil sorcerer has turned many girls into swans. The lake itself was formed by the tears of crying parents. She also informs him that the spell can only be broken if a man pledges his heart to her. Head over heels in love, the prince is about to confess his true feelings when the sorcerer takes Odette from the prince's arms and whisks her away."

"Is that it?" Payne asked, hopeful.

"For the first two acts. I still have two more to go."

"I thought you said you were going to be concise."

Ulster smiled. "For me, that was concise. Keep in mind, this is typically a three-hour production. I just covered half of it in thirty seconds."

Payne nodded his appreciation. "Go on."

"The very next day, the prince is shown several prospective brides at his birthday gala. One of them is Odile, the daughter of the sorcerer, who has been made to look like Odette through a magic spell. Captivated by her beauty, the prince confesses his love to the impostor, an act witnessed by Odette from a nearby window. Brokenhearted, she runs toward the woods crying. As she does, the prince catches a glimpse of her and realizes his error. Eventually, he catches up to Odette at Swan Lake and explains his mistake. As she accepts the prince's apology, the sorcerer arrives and tells him that he must keep his promise to marry his daughter. The prince says he would rather die with Odette than marry Odile. To prove his point, he grabs Odette's hand and they jump into the lake together, where they promptly drown. But thanks to his actions, the magic spell is broken and all of the other swans turn back into girls."

Jones interrupted him. "Wait a second! You're telling me the character based on Ludwig drowns in a lake and, ten years later, Ludwig dies in a lake, too? *That's* some freaky shit!"

"Actually," Ulster said, "I'm not quite finished yet. There's more drowning still to come."

"Really?"

Ulster smiled. "Angered by the two deaths, the girls

force the sorcerer and his daughter into the lake and watch them drown. The ballet ends as the spirits of the prince and Odette ascend into the heavens above Swan Lake."

Jones waited for a few seconds, unsure. "Are you done now?"

Ulster nodded. "I am."

"That's some freaky shit, too!" Jones blurted.

"How so?" Payne asked.

"Weren't you listening?"

"Barely."

Normally, Payne was the serious one and Jones was joking around. All it took was one story about a ballet for their roles to be reversed.

Jones smiled at the irony. "Don't you get it? The sorcerer behind the deception drowned in the same lake as the prince—just like the doctor behind the deception drowned in the same lake as Ludwig. That can't be a coincidence."

Payne grunted. "You're right. That does seem suspicious."

Ulster shrugged his broad shoulders. "Honestly, I don't know if Ludwig's murder was staged to mimic the ballet or not, but the story of Siegfried and Odette helped establish Ludwig's nickname as the Swan King."

"How so?" Payne asked.

"If they hadn't been killed, Siegfried and the Swan Queen would have been married, which would have made him the Swan King. And, as I mentioned, the character of Siegfried was based on Ludwig, so . . ."

Payne nodded in understanding. "Throw in Ludwig's obsessions with swans and that Swan Knight character that you told us about earlier, and the nickname stuck."

"He was also called the Dream King, the Fairytale King, and Mad King Ludwig, but the Swan King is used most often."

Payne paused for a moment to consider everything he had learned. *Swan Lake*, one of the most famous ballets in history, was connected to Ludwig. The black swan logo had been designed by Ludwig. And the riddle about the swan had been written by Ludwig. Yet as far as Payne could tell, they still had no idea where a swan would go on his journey home.

Or what they would find if they figured it out.

25

✤

From a distance, the King's House on Schachen resembled a hunting lodge on top of a scenic crest. Painted beige and dark brown, the wooden post-and-infill structure was two stories in the center but only half as tall on the left and the right, as if additional rooms had been added at the last minute. To Payne, the house looked like two capital *L*s, stapled back to back. It certainly wasn't the worst design he had ever seen, yet it seemed out of place in the dreamworld that Ludwig had created for himself. Why build a house instead of a castle?

"Remember," Ulster said as if reading Payne's mind, "the interior is far more luxurious than the exterior. Don't be fooled by the outside."

"Your friend is correct," said a feminine voice from the top of the hill. "The rough outer shell protects the pearl within."

"Petr," said Jones as he searched for the source, "the house is talking."

"And listening," she replied, her voice slightly tinged with a German accent.

Jones grabbed Ulster's arm. "Petr, I'm scared. . . . Hold me."

Payne laughed and pointed out her location. A series of decorative wooden beams ran from the top of the house's sharply peaked roof to the banister of the second-floor veranda. The mystery woman was standing underneath the overhang, partially hidden in the shadows. Though he couldn't see her face, her naturally blond hair and fair complexion had given her away.

"How often do you scare tourists?" he called out as he walked up the hillside.

"Only when they scare us first. We thought there was an avalanche," she said.

Payne kept walking, still unable to see her face because of the shadows. "Why did you think that?"

"Why?" she said sharply. "Because most people walk here."

"Uh-oh," Jones whispered. "We pissed off the house."

Payne told Jones and Ulster to stay put, then he focused his attention on her. "Sorry about the helicopter. We parked down below to minimize the noise. I hope you can forgive us."

"That depends."

"On what?"

"On the reason you didn't hike here like everyone else."

When Payne reached the top of the hill, he could finally

see who he was talking to. Dressed in jeans and a dark sweater, the pretty blonde stared at him, her emotions partially concealed by the long hair that danced across her face in the crisp mountain breeze. In a well-practiced move, she casually grabbed her hair with one hand and slid a band off her wrist with the other. A few seconds later, a blond ponytail dangled back and forth behind her head.

"I'm still waiting," she said impatiently.

As Payne walked closer, he noticed several small things about her—the freckles on her nose, the way her jeans hugged her hips, the curves underneath her sweater. But most importantly, he noticed a twinkle in her light blue eyes. It let him know that she was sassy, not angry.

"I'm waiting, too," he shot back.

She stared at him. "For what?"

"For you to say hello. Or isn't that ritual observed up here?"

"Hello," she said sarcastically. "Now answer my question. Why didn't you hike here?"

"Hello to you, too," he said, ignoring her question. "My name's Jon. What's yours?"

She sighed. "Heidi."

He stuck out his hand. "Nice to meet you, Heidi. I like what you've done with the place. When did you move in?"

But instead of shaking his hand, she stared at it coldly. "Sorry, Jon. No more kindness from me until you answer my question. Why didn't you hike here like everyone else?"

He lowered his voice to a whisper. "Can you keep a secret?"

"Depends on the secret."

Payne pointed back toward Jones and Ulster. "I'm not going to name any names, but one of my friends is *slightly* out of shape. To be perfectly blunt, we didn't know if his heart could handle a four-hour hike, so we convinced him to fly instead."

She peeked around Payne—since he was too tall to glance over—and studied his friends. It didn't take long to figure out which one he was talking about. "What if he wasn't here?"

"You mean, if he was dead?"

"No!" she gasped. "If he wasn't with you, would *you* have made the hike?"

"Come on, Heidi. What do you think?"

Now it was her turn to check him out.

Starting with his feet, she noticed his hiking boots. They were worn and caked with dirt. His muscular legs stretched his cargo pants to their limit, yet somehow the seams didn't burst. Earlier, she had noticed his hand when he had attempted to shake hers. It wasn't the hand of a workingman—the nails were too clean and his fingers were free of calluses—but she had noticed some scars near his knuckles. Clearly, he had been in a few fights over the years, and judging by his size, he had probably won most of them. For some reason, she found that quality—the willingness to fight for something—very attractive in a man.

She patted him on the arm. "If I had to guess, I'd say no."

"No?" he said, laughing.

"You're too big to hike. I'm guessing a guy like you has no stamina."

"Trust me, Heidi. I have size *and* stamina."

She ignored the innuendo. "Why are you here?"

"To see the house. Why are you so mean?"

"Not mean, *protective*. Big difference."

"Not to the person you're yelling at."

"Trust me, I'm not yelling. If I were yelling, you'd know."

"In other words, you're a screamer?"

This time, Heidi smiled. "Does this approach work often?"

"What approach is that?"

"Your whole flirty-comment thing."

"First of all, my *thing* isn't flirting. If it was flirting, you'd know. Secondly, you're the one who started it. My friends and I were having a personal conversation and you butted in."

She poked him in his chest. "Only because *you* shook the mountain."

"With our talking?"

"With your helicopter," she snapped. "Tell me, do you know why King Ludwig chose this remote location for his house?"

"Because he wanted to get away."

"From what?"

"Civilization."

"Do you know why?"

"Not really," he admitted.

She explained. "Because up here, Ludwig could look down on the world instead of the world looking down on him."

Payne smiled, impressed. "That's pretty deep. Did you just make that up?"

She stared at him, trying to figure out if he was being sarcastic. Eventually, she decided he wasn't. "As a matter of fact, I did."

"You're pretty passionate about this place. How long have you worked here?"

"Since June. That's when we opened for the season."

"And before that?"

"Ludwig's other castles: Linderhof, Neuschwanstein, and the Munich Residenz."

"Are you a student?"

She laughed at the question. "I'm too old to be a student."

"Maybe for high school. But there's no age limit on learning."

"Now look who's deep."

Payne smiled. "If you're not a student, what are you? A tour guide?"

"Something like that. I work for the Bavarian Palace Department. We oversee all the castles and royal properties in Bavaria. My area of interest is Ludwig Friedrich Wilhelm von Wittelsbach, but most people call him Ludwig."

Payne laughed. "That's because most people can't remember Ludwig Friedrich von blah blah blah—or whatever you said."

She smiled, revealing a perfect set of white teeth. "So, why are you here? From your accent, I would say you're from, um . . . Ohio?"

He shook his head. "Western Pennsylvania."

"Oh, well. I was close."

"And based on your diction and mild accent, I'd say you were born in Germany but went to school in the States."

She nodded, impressed. "Big *and* smart. Now I'm doubly curious about your presence here. Are you a fan of Ludwig?"

"Honestly, no. But my plump friend is." Payne turned and signaled for Jones and Ulster to join them by the house. "We're just keeping him out of trouble."

She watched Ulster as he waddled up the hill. Despite gasping for air, he had a smile on his face the entire time. "Yeah, he seems like a troublemaker."

"Don't let his cheerfulness fool you. The guy is a tiger."

"What about your other friend? Is he a tiger, too?"

Payne grinned, relishing the opportunity to make fun of his best friend. "No, he's a different species altogether. If I had to sum him up, I'd say he's part pit bull, part jackass."

26

✤

After a brief introduction—in which they avoided the real reason for their trip—Heidi grabbed Ulster by the elbow and led him toward the entrance of the King's House.

"Jon said you're a fan of Ludwig. Have you been here before?" she asked.

Ulster shook his head. "No, my dear, I haven't. Over the years, I've been tempted to stop on multiple occasions, but the length of the hike and the short tourist season have always made it difficult."

Heidi nodded in understanding. Public tours started in June and ended at the beginning of October. After that, the house was closed until the following spring because of snow and ice in the Alps and treacherous footing on the hiking trails. "Personally, I think you came at the perfect time. Summer tourists are long gone, and the cool weather keeps most hikers away until early afternoon. Other than a few people who stayed the night at the lodge, the house is empty."

"Wonderful!" Ulster exclaimed. "Does that mean you can show us around?"

She glanced over her shoulder and smiled at Payne. "I'd be happy to—as long as Jon doesn't mind being stuck with me for a while. He thinks I'm mean."

Ulster patted her hand. "Well, I think you're fabulous, and that's all that matters."

Heidi led them to the covered porch, where she stopped outside the main door. "Before we go inside, let me tell you some general information about this site. If you start getting bored, please let me know and I'll gladly skip ahead."

Jones whispered to Payne. "I wish Petr had the same policy."

Payne smiled and nodded.

Heidi started her lecture. "We are standing 5,628 feet above Garmisch-Partenkirchen and 7,951 feet above sea level. The mountain directly behind you is called the Partenkirchen Dreitorspitze. Standing 8,638 feet tall, it is the fourth-tallest peak in Germany and part of the Wetterstein mountain range that forms a natural border with Austria to the south."

Payne, Jones, and Ulster turned and stared at the Dreitorspitze. It loomed over them like a gray tidal wave, as if the smallest breeze would send it crashing down with so much force that the King's House would be turned into kindling.

Heidi continued. "The chalet was built from 1869

through 1872. Ludwig and his guests reached it on horse-drawn carriages or sleighs, depending on the time of year. The lone route up the mountain was called the König-sweg. In English, that means the King's Road."

"How did they get supplies up here?" Jones asked.

"The same way. Everything was hauled by horses."

"Even water?"

She shook her head. "Water is one of the few things they didn't haul. Because of the large amounts of precipitation, they built a cistern to collect and store the melted snow to use throughout the year."

"Really?" Jones said, trying to get the information they needed to solve the riddle. "I thought I heard there was a freshwater lake up here. Somewhere Ludwig liked to go."

She shook her head again. "Perhaps you're thinking of one of his other homes. There was a freshwater lake near Schloss Hohenschwanstein. He stayed there as a child with his parents."

Payne's ears perked up when he heard "schwan" in the middle of the word. "What does that name mean in English?"

"Schloss Hohenschwanstein? It means 'high swan stone castle.' Later in life, Ludwig stayed there for several years while he was overseeing the construction of Neuschwanstein. It's adjacent to the lake as well." She glanced at Payne, anticipating his next question. "And before you ask, Neuschwanstein means 'new swan stone.'"

"Thanks for reading my mind," Payne said.

Heidi smiled and opened the door. "Now, if you'll follow me . . ."

Payne and Jones lingered on the porch for a few extra seconds as Ulster went inside.

Jones whispered. "That's two homes with 'swan' in the name. Either one could be the answer to the riddle. If so, we're screwed. How are we going to find a document in a castle?"

"Remember, the answer to the riddle is only half of the equation. First we find the *Gartenhaus*, then we solve the riddle. Not the other way around."

"Crap! I forgot about the *Gartenhaus*. All of these clues are confusing."

"That's why pirates made treasure maps. They were too drunk to remember clues."

Jones glanced at his watch. "Speaking of drunk, we could leave right now and be shit-faced by lunch. Just say the word and we're off to Oktoberfest."

Payne stared at him, trying to gauge if he was serious. "What's your problem? Normally, you're the one twisting my arm to fly halfway around the world to do stuff like this, not the other way around. Is something wrong?"

Jones blew on his hands and rubbed them together. "Besides the temperature?"

"Yeah, princess, besides the temperature."

Jones shrugged. "I don't know. I guess I'm just not feeling it. When I saw all of those crates, I thought we were onto something. Now I'm not so sure."

Payne patted him on the shoulder. "Do me a favor and hang in there a little bit longer. Don't ask me why, but I have a feeling that things are about to change."

"In what way?" Jones asked as he opened the door.

Payne took a deep breath before he stepped inside the house. "Honestly? I don't know. But I can smell it in the air. Something big is going to happen."

Schneider, one of Kaiser's guards, spotted movement on the slope but decided not to call it in until he knew what he was dealing with. The woods were filled with animals of all shapes and sizes, and his colleagues had given him a hard time when he had sounded the alarm a few days earlier and it had turned out to be a deer. And not even a big deer. It was small and cuddly and looked like Bambi. Ever since then, his friends had called him "Aesop"—the Greek storyteller who had created the fable about the boy who cried wolf in the mid-sixth century B.C.

Needless to say, he didn't find it as funny as they did.

Positioned a quarter mile from the site, Schneider crouched behind a thick beech tree and waited. Whatever was heading his way was heavy. He could hear twigs snapping and leaves rustling as it moved. In some ways he hoped it was a boar. He had seen Hogzilla in the bunker and was amazed by its size. Something that big running across the forest floor would be a sight to behold—and something he could tell his wife. She knew he had been working a job near Munich for the past week, but nothing else. In many ways, it was similar to his former career in the armed forces. Whenever he had called home, he was allowed to tell her personal things—how he was feeling, what he had for dinner, and so on—but nothing that would reveal his location or jeopardize the success of his mission.

But spotting a pig the size of a Volkswagen?

As far as he was concerned, he could talk about that all night without getting into trouble.

Unfortunately for Schneider, the giant boar didn't materialize. Instead, he spotted a man, wearing bright-orange camouflage, heading his way.

"Shit," he mumbled as he pushed the button on his radio. "Sir, I've got a situation."

A few seconds passed before Kaiser responded. He was positioned near the bunker, watching his men assemble the equipment. "What's wrong, Aesop? Is Bambi back?"

"No, sir. A hunter, carrying a Remington 750."

Kaiser swore under his breath. A few more minutes and they would have been ready to test the winch. Twenty more minutes and the gold would have been on its way down the mountain. "Where are you?"

Schneider looked at his GPS unit and radioed his coordinates.

Kaiser wrote them down. "Can you handle this, or do you need help?"

Schneider shook his head. The last thing he needed was for his friends to bail him out. If that happened, he'd never hear the end of it. "No, sir. I got this."

"Good," Kaiser said. "Stick with the script and you'll be fine."

"Yes, sir."

"And Schneider? Call me when you're done."

27

❖

Other than a few royal touches—like an up-holstered toilet seat and an intricate wooden chandelier—the five rooms on the ground floor of the King's House were spectacularly unimpressive. Simple wood paneling, made from Swiss pine, covered the walls, and most of the furnishings were plain and anti-quated. Jones was so underwhelmed by the décor he compared it to a granny house, the type of place that had more cats than furniture.

His opinion instantly changed the moment they walked upstairs. Named the Türkische Saal by Ludwig, the opulent room filled the entire second floor and was protected by a velvet rope. Payne, Jones, and Ulster crowded against it, gawking at the room for more than thirty seconds before Heidi stepped over the rope and started her lecture from the right corner of the room.

"This is the Turkish Hall, which was inspired by *One*

Thousand and One Nights, a collection of folktales from the Islamic Golden Age that included 'Ali Baba and the Forty Thieves,' 'The Seven Voyages of Sinbad the Sailor,' and 'Aladdin's Wonderful Lamp.' In English, the story collection is often called *Arabian Nights*."

Heidi walked to the edge of the colorful Oriental rug that covered the wooden floor. Besides the periphery of the room, the only part of the floor that wasn't covered was the very center. A giant hole had been cut in the rug so it could be slipped over a large golden fountain that looked like it belonged in a hotel lobby instead of a Swiss chalet. The sound of its trickling water could be heard throughout the hall.

She continued. "This is where Ludwig threw elaborate birthday parties for himself, all with an Arabian Nights theme. Sometimes his servants sat on the floor smoking hookah pipes, while others played Arabian music or pranced around in the nude. Meanwhile, Ludwig lounged on the luxurious couches that line the walls, often wearing outfits from Arabia."

She moved deeper into the room, careful not to step on the rug as she pointed out a series of golden vases that were nearly as tall as she was. Each of them was stuffed with colorful arrangements that resembled tiny palm trees. "From where you are standing, it's probably difficult to see what these are made of. Instead of using flowers, which would have to be hauled halfway up the mountain, the king used peacock feathers. Aren't they just lovely?"

Ulster nodded, then raised his hand as if he were on a high school field trip and needed permission to speak.

Heidi looked at him and smiled. "Did you have a question?"

Ulster shook his head. "Actually, my dear, I was hoping for a favor."

"A favor? What kind of favor?"

He glanced over his shoulder, paranoid. "Normally, I wouldn't think to impose, but considering the scant crowd and my passion for the subject matter, I was wondering if I could remove my footwear and tiptoe across the room for a closer look."

She winced, unsure. "I don't know . . ."

He raised his hand again, this time to swear the truth. "I promise my socks are clean."

She giggled at Ulster's enthusiasm. He was like a little kid. "Fine, but if we hear anyone coming, you have to hustle behind the rope. I could get in a lot of trouble."

"I'll be careful, I promise," Ulster assured her as he dropped to the floor to remove his boots.

Meanwhile, Payne backed up toward the stairs. "Don't worry, Heidi. I'll stand guard. If I hear anything, I'll let you know."

"Thanks, Jon. I'd appreciate that."

"See how that works? When you're nice, I'm nice," Payne teased.

Heidi smiled. "I'm not the least bit surprised. My dog is like that, too."

Jones laughed loudly. "Jon is like a dog. That's funny."

"Not as funny as the animal he compared you to," she insisted.

Jones stopped laughing. "He said what now?"

Heidi winked at Payne, who was slightly embarrassed. "Actually, I better stay out of it. I'll let you guys discuss it among yourselves."

Jones looked at him, serious. "You think I'm an animal?"

"Heidi," Payne said, hoping to change the topic, "before you run off, can I ask you a question about the room?"

"Sure," she said, grinning ear to ear.

"You said Ludwig used peacock feathers because he didn't want to haul fresh flowers up the mountain. Why didn't he get them out of the garden?"

"What garden?" she asked.

"Isn't there a famous garden up here?"

"Oh, you mean the Alpengarten auf dem Schachen."

"Gesundheit," Jones cracked.

Payne ignored him. "If you say so."

She explained. "The Alpengarten auf dem Schachen is an Alpine garden maintained by a botanical society from Munich. The garden has over a thousand types of exotic plants from as far away as the Himalayas."

Payne nodded. It was the garden that Ulster had mentioned earlier, the one that led him to believe that this house might be the *Gartenhaus* that Ludwig had referred to in his notes. "Why didn't they get the flowers from there? Isn't it close by?"

"It's real close, but it wasn't built until *after* Ludwig's death. Don't quote me on this, but I think it was built around 1900. I can find out a specific date if you'd like."

He shook his head. "Nope, that isn't necessary."

"You got that right," Jones whispered to Payne. "No garden means no dice. We're looking in the wrong place."

Schneider stepped out from behind the beech tree and stared at the man walking toward him. In his hands, Schneider held a Heckler & Koch G36, a German 5.56mm assault rifle. It was the preferred weapon of the Bundeswehr, the unified armed forces of Germany.

"Halt!" Schneider ordered in German.

Weber, one of Krueger's men, stopped and threw his hands in the air.

"What are you doing here?" Schneider demanded.

"I'm hunting deer," Weber lied. "Have you seen any?"

Schneider ignored the question. "You have entered a restricted area. You must turn back immediately, or I am authorized to place you under arrest."

"For what? I have the proper license to hunt," Weber claimed.

"Not for here, you don't."

"Why? What's going on? Is everything all right?"

"Everything is fine. We are merely conducting military drills on the mountain. This area is restricted because it isn't safe for civilians."

Weber cleared his throat and spit on the ground. "It isn't safe for you, either. Not with hunters roaming around."

Schneider raised his weapon. "Sir, don't make me use force! I'm asking you to *leave*."

Weber grinned. "But I don't want to leave. I want to stay."

"Sir, if I call for backup, you'll be sor—"

Before another word could be said, Weber's partner emerged from a clump of trees behind Schneider and slit his throat, using a nine-inch hunting knife with a serrated edge.

Blood gushed from Schneider's neck as he gurgled and slumped to the ground. As he fell, he squeezed his trigger and fired several wild shots from his G36. Although he didn't hit his targets, the sound of automatic gunfire and the strafing of the nearby trees echoed through the mountain air like warning drums in a primitive culture. The sound was so loud and distinct it could be heard inside the bunker and as far away as Mount Schachen.

Within seconds, a firefight had erupted in the Bavarian Alps.

Within minutes, Payne and Jones would enter the fray.

28

❈

Payne and Jones were standing on the front porch of the King's House, waiting for Ulster to put on his shoes and join them downstairs, when they heard the distant chatter of gunfire. To experienced soldiers, the sound was unmistakable—like a musical instrument to a symphony conductor. In a heartbeat, they knew Kaiser's men were under attack.

Jones sprinted to the helicopter while Payne pulled the Sig Sauer from his belt and opened the front door. "Petr! Stay here! Kaiser's in trouble."

"What do you mean?" Ulster yelled from upstairs.

"We're taking the chopper! Stay here until we come back!"

"What's wrong?" Heidi shouted from the Turkish Hall.

Wearing only one shoe, Ulster nearly stumbled down

the steps as he tried to get more information. "What kind of trou—"

Payne cut him off. "Stay here! Keep an eye on Heidi!"

"Of course," Ulster said while holding his shoe. "But—"

"Now lock this door!"

Payne slammed it shut and leapt off the porch. By the time he landed, Ulster and Heidi were already gone from his thoughts. For the next few minutes, the only thing that mattered was getting to the bunker as quickly as possible. Not to protect the gold or the van Gogh crate, but because lives were on the line and he could save them.

Jones reached the helicopter thirty seconds before Payne and ordered the pilot to start the engine. Baptiste, who took orders only from Ulster, was going to argue— until he saw the gun in Jones's hand. Baptiste swallowed hard and started flipping switches.

As the engine whirred to life, Jones coolly searched the back compartment for equipment but found nothing of value. "Do you have a rope?" he yelled.

"For what?" Baptiste shouted.

"Our exit."

He turned in his seat and stared at Jones. "Your *what*?"

"Our exit. You can't land where we're going. We're gonna have to jump."

Baptiste laughed. "You're joking, right?"

Jones flashed his gun. "Does it look like I'm joking?"

"You're going to jump out of my chopper?"

"Only if you have a rope."

Baptiste pointed to the other side. "Try over there."

Jones scurried around the back and opened the far hatch. Inside was a wicker basket. It was stuffed with a loaf of French bread, a hunk of cheese, two salamis, an assortment of fresh fruit, a bottle of wine, and a red-and-white checkered tablecloth. "What the hell is this?"

"A picnic," Baptiste said.

"A *picnic*? Why did you pack a fucking picnic?"

Baptiste shrugged. "Petr gets hungry."

Jones slammed the hatch in frustration. "My friend is going to die unless you have a rope. Do you have one or not?"

"Next compartment back."

Jones flung it open and grabbed a large coil of black rope. Made with sure-grip synthetic fibers, the low-stretch rope was perfect for rappelling. One end was already equipped with a sturdy metal clasp that could be attached to the chopper's floor. "How long is this?"

"About a hundred feet."

Jones pulled out the coil, which weighed over fifty pounds, and tossed it onto the backseat. Then he searched the compartment for additional equipment, anything that could help them get to the ground in one piece. "What about gloves? Or belts? Or harnesses?"

Baptiste shook his head. "This isn't a rescue chopper."

Payne arrived in time to hear the comment. "Well, it is today."

Jones pointed to the hook in the center of the floor, which Payne could reach while standing outside the chopper. "Attach the clasp. I'm almost ready."

Payne did as he was told, then hopped into the back. As he did, he could hear Jones rummaging through the hatch on the other side. "What are you looking for?"

"A snack," Jones shouted.

Payne cupped his ear and leaned in closer. "A what?"

Grinning from ear to ear, Jones hopped into the chopper. He held his gun in one hand and the picnic basket in the other. Payne stared at him like he was crazy.

Jones grinned even wider. "Don't worry. I have an idea."

"What kind of idea?"

"I'll tell you when it's time to jump."

Krueger cursed when he heard the gunfire. Obviously, something had gone wrong with his plan, because his men had been told to avoid interaction at all costs. Their job had been simple. Spy on Kaiser, figure out what he was doing, then report back to Krueger so he could coordinate their attack. His men weren't supposed to confront Kaiser or do anything that might attract attention. This was supposed to be a surveillance mission. Nothing else.

From his position at the bottom of the mountain, Krueger called his men on the radio. "What happened?" he growled in German.

One of his men responded. "We were spotted by a guard with an assault rifle. We managed to take him out quietly."

"Did you say *quietly*? There was nothing quiet about it! I could hear it down here!"

"Blame the guard, not us. We used a blade. He used a gun. He got off a few rounds when he fell to the ground."

Krueger took a deep breath, trying to remain calm. "Did anyone get hit?"

"No, sir."

"What are we up against?"

"Too early to tell, sir. But so far we're winning."

Krueger shook his head. His men were so shortsighted. "Winning?"

"Yes, sir. They're down one man, and we're up one gun. This G36 is a serious weapon."

"Maybe so, but we lost the best weapon of all—the element of surprise."

His goon grunted. He couldn't care less. "What do you want us to do?"

"Find Kaiser and send me his coordinates. I'm on my way."

The bunker was positioned near the base of a cliff and surrounded by ancient beech trees that were a lot taller than their rope was long. Hoping to survive their descent, Payne and Jones searched for a clearing near the site, somewhere they could land safely when they rappelled out of the chopper. The best they could find was a grove of fir trees approximately a quarter mile from the bunker. Not only were the evergreens significantly shorter than the beeches, but they hoped the fallen pine needles underneath the trees would cushion their fall. Due to the slope of the mountain, they realized they would have to hit the ground and roll, or risk breaking a leg.

Fighting strong gusts of wind, Baptiste held the chopper in place just over the tops of the trees. To make sure the weld would hold his weight, Payne yanked on the hook with all of his strength before Jones tossed the coil of rope over the side. Both of them watched it unravel until the far end disappeared into the thick blanket of branches.

"Did it hit bottom?" Payne asked.

Jones shrugged. "Can't tell for sure, but I think it's close."

Payne nodded. It wouldn't be the first time they had jumped blindly from a chopper. Then again, a picnic basket was something new. "Do you mind telling me what that's for?"

Jones plucked a grape from its stem and popped it in his mouth. "Here's what we're facing: No gloves, no belts, no harnesses. Rough wind, blind drop, unknown enemy. I don't know about you, but I'd like to lose as little skin as possible."

Payne stared at his hands. They'd be torn to shreds in a fast descent. And if he took the drop slowly, his palms would survive intact but he'd be an easy target for several seconds as he dangled from the chopper. "What's the solution?"

Jones grabbed two salamis and handed one to Payne. "We use these."

Payne stared at the cured meat. It was nine inches long

and sealed in a rough casing. For the life of him, he had no idea what his friend meant. "Excuse me?"

Jones reached into his cargo pants and pulled out his knife. With a flick of his wrist the blade popped open, and he plunged the sharp tip into the top of the salami. As Payne watched, Jones cut the meat vertically, making a nine-inch incision that went halfway into the salami. When he was done, he held it up so Payne could understand what he had in mind.

"We wrap the salami around the rope like a bun around a hot dog. This casing is hard and coarse. Our hands should be fine as the meat gets torn to shreds."

"And if the casing doesn't hold?" Payne asked.

Jones shrugged as he traded salamis with Payne and went to work on the other one. "We hope the branches break our fall."

Payne stared at him. "You're serious, aren't you?"

He nodded. "I'd rather fall fast than dangle slow. Too many unknowns."

Payne searched the basket for alternatives. "What about the tablecloth? We can cut it in strips and wrap it around our hands."

Jones shook his head. "Our fingers would get filleted. Cut right to the bone."

Payne grimaced. He had seen that happen to one of his men, and his hands never fully recovered. "You realize this is crazy."

Jones laughed at the danger. "That's what makes it fun."

29

✵

Garmisch-Partenkirchen, Germany

The United States Special Operations Command
(SOCOM) is headquartered at MacDill Air Force
Base in Tampa, Florida. It oversees the various
special operations units of the U.S. Armed Forces and the
U.S. intelligence community. The concept of a unified
command sprouted from the disastrous rescue attempt of
hostages at the American embassy in Iran in 1980. The
ensuing investigation noted a lack of interservice cooperation and the breakdown of a clear chain of command as
significant factors in the mission's failure.

Seven years later, SOCOM was officially activated.

The main goal of SOCOM is to coordinate the efforts
of the different branches of the Armed Forces whenever
joint missions are conducted. Each branch has a Special
Operations Command that is capable of running its own
missions, but when different Special Operations Forces

(Green Berets, Navy SEALs, Rangers, etc.) need to work together on a mission, SOCOM takes control of the operation—for example, Operation Desert Storm and Operation Iraqi Freedom.

In addition, SOCOM conducts several missions of its own, which are run by the Joint Special Operations Command (JSOC). These Special Mission Units (SMUs) perform highly classified activities, such as personnel recovery, counterguerrilla sabotage, unconventional warfare, psychological operations, and counterterrorism. So far, only three SMUs have been publicly disclosed: the Army's 1st Special Forces Operational Detachment (Delta Force), the Navy's Special Warfare Development Group (DEVGRU), and the Air Force's 24th Special Tactics Squadron (AFSTS). One of the SMUs that is still classified is the MANIACs.

Composed of the top soldiers from the Marines, Army, Navy, Intelligence, Air Force, and Coast Guard, the MANIACs are a military all-star team, assembled from a small list of candidates who passed the most stringent selection process and training in the world. One of the most important skills the soldiers learned was the art of improvisation. Without it, they wouldn't last long behind enemy lines, where weapons and equipment were scarce. To survive, they were forced to make do with whatever they could find, whether that was picking a lock with a paper clip or making an explosive out of household chemicals. Not only did this skill require ingenuity, but it also required guts. Otherwise, new ideas would never be tested in the field.

During his time in the MANIACs, Payne had used a grapefruit as a silencer, stalled a car with a tube sock, and killed a man with a stapler, but he had never used salami for anything except sandwiches. Of course, that didn't mean it wouldn't work. It simply meant that one of them had to be a guinea pig. Normally, that burden would fall on Payne, who preferred to lead by example. But in this situation, Jones insisted on going first.

"My idea, my glory," Jones shouted over the wind and the roar of the rotor. "Plus, your ass is so fat you might snap the rope."

Payne watched closely as Jones clamped the salami around the rope and stepped onto the skid tube, which was attached to the chopper's wheels. "See you soon."

Jones took a deep breath, then leaned back on the skid more than a hundred feet above the ground. As he did, he focused on his grip. If this didn't work, he knew his hands would never be the same, and neither would his life. Jones was brave, not stupid. He realized if his idea failed, there was a damn good chance he was going to die— either from the fall or from the gunmen down below who would pounce upon him like cheetahs on an injured gazelle.

And yet Jones remained unfazed.

Compared to the things he had faced in the MANI-ACs, this was less dangerous than bungee jumping. Sure, something could go wrong, but he wasn't about to let it ruin his fun. With a smile on his face, Jones launched himself backward and yelled, "Geronimo!"

A second later, he was falling toward the forest.

As expected, the salami ripped to shreds as Jones clutched the casing on his way to the forest floor. In his wake, tiny chunks of meat clung to the rope like a used piece of dental floss. Of course, Jones didn't notice anything above him as he zipped past the trees, since he was far more concerned with his landing. Clamping the rope with his legs and boots, Jones eased to a stop just before he reached the end of the rope, which dangled ten feet above the ground.

Wasting no time, Jones released his grip and dropped to the slope. He minimized his impact by tumbling once, then scampered behind the nearest tree, where he pulled his gun and secured the area for his partner's arrival. Unfortunately, Payne's trip didn't go quite as smoothly. Whether it was the remnants of Jones's salami on the rope, Payne's extra weight, or a combination of the two, Payne struggled to control his pace on his descent. He used his legs and boots, just like he had been taught, but the pregreased line minimized friction. Whereas Jones was able to stop before he reached the end of the rope, Payne didn't have that luxury.

One moment, Jones was scouting the area for enemy troops. The next, Payne was tumbling past him like a boulder rolling down the mountain—a grunting and groaning boulder. When he finally came to a stop, Jones rushed to his side, worried that his friend was dead.

"Are you okay?" Jones demanded.

Sprawled on his back and covered in pine needles, Payne blinked a few times before his head was clear. Once he regained his focus, he brought his hands near his face and stared at his fingers. "I'll be damned. The salami worked."

Jones breathed a sigh of relief. "Told you so."

Payne sat up and nodded. "Landing was a little rough, but . . ."

"Mine was worse," Jones lied. "Tumbled right into a tree."

"Really? Are you all right?"

Jones groaned for effect. "I think I'll make it. But I'll feel a lot better once we know what we're up against."

Payne wobbled slightly as he stood. "Communications?"

Jones shook his head. "No signal on my cell phone."

Payne rubbed his eyes, then looked up at the surrounding trees. The forest was so thick he could barely see sunlight. "Which way to the bunker?"

Jones pointed diagonally up the slope. "That way."

"How far?"

Jones stared at Payne, slightly concerned. Normally, his sense of distance and direction were impeccable. "Are you *sure* you're okay?"

"I'll be fine once we're moving. I need to clear some cobwebs."

Jones tried to examine Payne's eyes. "Cobwebs? Or a concussion?"

Payne pushed him away and pulled out his Sig Sauer. He had played some of his best football games at the Naval Academy with fuzzy vision and bells ringing in his ears. He wasn't about to stop for some cobwebs. "Come on! We're wasting time. Let's get moving."

Jones relented. "Fine! But I'm in charge until you can recite the alphabet backwards."

"Hell, I couldn't do that *before* I jumped."

Even though Kaiser cared about the welfare of his men, he wasn't about to grab a rifle and charge toward the gunfire. He was paying them for protection, not the other way around.

"What's your status?" Kaiser asked from the relative safety of the cul-de-sac. He had been tempted to hide inside the bunker until the mountain was secure, but his two-way radio was ineffective down there and he wanted to call the shots. "Schneider, can you hear me?"

Silence filled the line, as it had for the past few minutes.

Kaiser cursed to himself. Based on Schneider's last transmission and the gunfire that followed, they had to assume that he was dead. If so, what had happened?

And more important, who had killed him?

Kaiser had plenty of enemies, but how did they find him in the woods above Garmisch-Partenkirchen? Had one of his men betrayed him? Or had the leak come from somewhere else? For the time being, it didn't matter. The only thing he cared about was getting off the mountain. Preferably with the gold in tow, but not if it meant his life.

Because in Kaiser's world, he had more to worry about than gunmen.

He also had to evade the police.

30

✳

Gunfire came in sporadic bursts, a mixture of shotgun blasts and automatic fire from somewhere near the bunker. Leading the charge, Jones used the noise as a beacon, zeroing in on the firefight without stopping to check his GPS or studying the symbols that Kaiser's men had marked on the trees. Of course, Jones didn't have much of a choice while running at top speed. The sun could barely be seen through the trees—which was how the neighboring Black Forest had received its name—so Jones relied on his ears just as much as his eyes.

Despite his height and muscular frame, Payne kept pace with the wiry Jones, who darted under branches and leapt over logs like a deer escaping a forest fire. One of the things that had made Payne a star on the football field was his rare combination of speed and strength. Not only was he faster than most people, he was also much stronger. Mix in his toughness, athleticism, and discipline, and a world-class athlete had emerged. If not for his sense of duty, Payne would have made millions as a pro football player. Instead, he honed his skills in the military and became one of the best soldiers the world had ever seen.

Although Payne and Jones were retired from the MANIACs, the top brass at the Pentagon still spoke their names with reverence and contacted them for their expertise.

Over the next few minutes, they would display their skills.

A wave of gunfire forced them to scramble for cover. Jones slid to a stop behind a fallen tree while Payne ducked behind a nearby boulder. Both men struggled to breathe, the thin air and steep slope wreaking havoc on their lungs. The bunker was less than a hundred yards away, but it wasn't visible from their position. With no communications, they didn't know if Kaiser was alive or dead—or what they were facing. Three men? Five men? Maybe even ten?

To survive, surveillance would be essential.

Payne scanned the surrounding trees, searching for colors and shapes that didn't belong. Nothing seemed out of place. "Where did those shots come from?"

"Somewhere up ahead. Couldn't tell where."

Payne rubbed some dirt on his face and clothes, trying to blend in. "What's our move?"

"Get Kaiser. Go home."

"Easier said than done."

Jones nodded as he studied the terrain. Without communications, they had to worry about enemy bullets *and* friendly fire. Especially from the sniper positioned in the bird's nest above the bunker. If he had a "loose trigger"— that is, if he lacked shot discipline—there was a damn good chance he would shoot every unidentified target that moved. And since most snipers were proficient up to a mile away, Payne and Jones were well within his kill zone.

"The sniper worries me," Jones admitted. "He doesn't know we're back in play."

"I was thinking the same thing."

Jones peeked over the fallen tree and stared at the rocky crag above the cul-de-sac. It could only be accessed from above. "Either we get a radio, or we go for the nest."

Payne considered their options. "What about both?"

"Both?"

"I go for Kaiser, you go for the nest."

Jones glanced at him. "You want to split up?"

"Don't worry, we can still be friends."

"I meant, do you think that's wise?"

"I don't see why not."

Jones explained his position. "If we reach Kaiser, we can use his radio to talk to the sniper. Why risk a trip up the cliff?"

"Why? Because I want *you* in the nest, not some asshole I don't trust. I know what *you* can do with a rifle."

"Oh, why didn't you say so? What did you have in mind?"

Payne grinned. "I'll lure them out, and you pick them off."

· · · ·

With a sniper watching over him and calling out potential threats, Kaiser was more confident than he should have been—especially in the rugged environment near the bunker. Telescopic sights were quite effective on long-distance shots, but they couldn't see through trees. And since branches and leaves blocked out the sun, there were plenty of places for gunmen to hide.

"How's it look?" Kaiser asked as he roamed toward the front of the cul-de-sac and crouched behind a gray boulder that was covered with green moss. "Anything?"

"Looks clear," the sniper answered.

Kaiser leaned against the rock in thought. One of his men was presumed dead; the others were in the woods searching for the enemy. Unfortunately, he didn't know who the enemy was or what they were after, but he had to assume they were gunning for him. As far as he knew, his own men didn't even know what they had discovered in the bunker, so the odds were pretty good the gunmen weren't after the gold or the van Gogh crate. They were there for him.

Kaiser had heard the initial shots. They had been fired ten minutes earlier and had continued in intermittent bursts. First to the north, then to the east, and then to the west. According to his men, the enemy had scattered like roaches, which effectively forced Kaiser's hand. If the enemy had gone one way or the other, Kaiser would have used the off-road utility vehicle to escape. But since he didn't know where they were, Kaiser knew he couldn't risk it.

He had to stay put until a route was clear.

Armed with a Remington 750, one of Krueger's goons spotted Kaiser behind the boulder. Every once in a while, Kaiser would peek above the rock like a prairie dog looking for hawks, and when he did, the goon tried to line up the perfect shot before his target disappeared.

This went on for nearly three minutes.

Up, then down. Up, then down. Up, then down.

Each time, the goon was close to pulling the trigger when Kaiser lowered his head to safety. Eventually, the goon became so frustrated by his futility that he vowed not to blink or breathe until Kaiser popped back up. And the instant he did, the goon was going to fire.

As Payne moved into position in the woods, Jones sprinted to the right of the cul-de-sac, then veered back toward the cliff that overlooked the bunker. To reach the bird's nest without ropes and harnesses, he had to climb the hill from the side while avoiding possible gunfire.

To Jones, it sounded like fun.

With gun in hand, he charged up the steep slope, careful not to trip on the roots that jutted from the trail like fossilized snakes. Arms pumping and knees churning, Jones slipped more than once when his footing gave way, but he never fell. Each time he quickly regained his balance and continued his journey forward until he reached the top.

Breathing deeply, Jones eyed the treacherous path in front of him. Partially hidden by the foliage, it was more than eighty feet above the sharp rocks below. Roughly halfway across the cliff, which cut horizontally across the rock face, there was an access point for the bird's nest. To reach it, he would have to lower himself onto a narrow ridge by holding on to the trunk of a tree. If his hand slipped or his foot missed, there was a very good chance he would fall to his death, but Jones ignored the possibility. Instead, he focused on what would happen if he *didn't* take the risk: Payne would be exposed in the field as he tried to rescue Kaiser.

With that in mind, Jones continued his journey forward.

For the fourth time in the past five minutes, Kaiser peeked his head above the boulder.

This time he was greeted by a rifle blast.

When Krueger's goon pulled the trigger on his Remington 750, the firing pin struck the primer in the .243 Winchester cartridge. The impact produced a tiny spark that ignited the gunpowder in the sealed chamber. A split second later, the gases from the burning powder forced the projectile down the 22-inch barrel and sent it screaming toward its intended target at a velocity of over 3,000 feet per second.

Frequently used for large game like wild hogs and black bears, the bullet struck the boulder a few inches from Kaiser's head and ricocheted wildly. Unfortunately, the force of the impact was so great that it shattered the top of the rock. The resulting shards erupted in Kaiser's face, tearing through the soft flesh of his left cheek and causing significant damage to his eye.

Dazed from the blow and howling in pain, Kaiser made a foolish blunder. Instead of dropping to the ground where he would have been protected by the boulder and the sniper, he tried to retreat to the bunker, a distance of nearly thirty feet. With his hand against his face, blood poured through the gaps between his fingers as he sprinted toward the entrance.

Stunned by Kaiser's decision to run, the goon wasn't prepared to hit a moving target. Barely taking the time to aim, he fired again. This time he missed by several inches.

It was a mistake he wouldn't make again.

The sound of the second blast fueled Kaiser's panic. In the military, he had been a supply sergeant, not a member of the infantry, so he wasn't used to firefights. Outside of a shooting range, he hadn't fired a gun in nearly a decade, and the last time someone had taken a shot at him was in an urban environment, not in the middle of the woods. Back then, he had escaped in his Mercedes. Out here, he had to do it on foot.

Halfway to the bunker, Kaiser realized his mistake—and it had been a big one. With a gunman trying to kill him, he wouldn't have time to use the ladder. Instead, he would be forced to leap through the narrow hole while

running at top speed. Making matters worse, he wasn't
sure what was going to greet him at the bottom of the
bunker. His men had been working on a pulley system
when the first shots had been fired, so there was a very
good chance he was going to land on some kind of equipment, whether that was a toolbox or part of the winch.

Then again, that sounded much better than the alter-
native.

Because if he stopped to use the ladder, he was fucked.

31

❉

When it came to math, Kaiser was a genius. It was one of the reasons he was great at his job. Whereas most of his rivals used calculators to determine their prices, Kaiser was able to do complex equations in his head. In a fraction of a second, he was able to crunch several numbers—the street value of his goods, the cost of shipping, the risk involved, and about twenty other variables—and figure out the true worth of a deal. His speed and accuracy were so renowned, his customers rarely haggled for a better price because they knew Kaiser couldn't be fooled.

Unfortunately, the math skills that had made Kaiser so much money over the years weren't very effective when he was running for his life and screaming in pain. If they had been, he would have known that the diameter of the hole was far too narrow to leap through while sprinting at top speed. And yet when Kaiser left his feet, he thought his body would slip cleanly through the gap and he would land safely inside the bunker.

But he was wrong. And it wasn't even close.

Making matters worse, the goon pulled his trigger about the same time Kaiser went airborne. This led to a series of traumatic events that ravaged Kaiser's body in several different ways. In a span of about two seconds, the gunman's bullet hit Kaiser in the center of his back, just before he slammed stomach-first into the far side of the hole. From the force of the impact, his torso lurched forward and he smashed his already damaged face into the hard ground, knocking out some teeth in the process.

Unconscious from the blow, Kaiser slumped backward through the hole and crashed awkwardly onto the equipment that littered the bunker's floor. When he landed, his left leg was pinned underneath him at a severe angle, so much so that he ruptured his patellar tendon and tore every major ligament in his left knee with a sickening snap.

The sound was so loud that it echoed through the chamber.

Although the goon couldn't see the fall or hear the snap from his position in the trees, he knew Kaiser had been seriously injured during the chain of events. No one—not even a soldier half Kaiser's age—could have survived everything that he had gone through without suffering several devastating injuries. In fact, the goon was so confident that Kaiser was unconscious and defenseless at the bottom of the hole that he rushed forward to finish the job.

And as he did, the goon smiled in triumph.

Payne heard the rifle blasts and zeroed in on the sound. As far as he could tell, the weapon had been fired somewhere near the bunker.

Wasting no time, Payne hustled through the foliage, trying to make as little noise as possible. Despite his size, Payne was able to move with great stealth, an ability that was often compared to the Apache warriors of the Old West, who were able to stalk their enemies without being heard. Genetically speaking, Payne knew his relatives had come from central Europe, not the American Southwest, yet he took it as a great compliment since the Apache were considered one of the fiercest tribes in Native American history.

When he reached the edge of the clearing near the cul-de-sac, Payne spotted a man wearing green-and-brown camouflage. He was holding a rifle in his hand and moving slowly toward the entrance to the bunker. From his current position, Payne couldn't see the man's face. Then again, even if he could, he realized he didn't know what most of Kaiser's men looked like. Sure, he had spotted all of them in the woods when he had first arrived at the site, but that had been done from long distance. Truth be told, he couldn't have identified any of them in a police lineup.

Obviously, that was a major problem when looking for targets.

Not wanting to kill a friendly, Payne decided to creep closer.

The goon stopped a few feet short of the hole and carefully peeked over the edge. Until that moment, he didn't know what he would see. Perhaps a crevasse or a natural spring. Maybe even a grave. He certainly hadn't been expecting a bunker. The instant he saw the concrete floor, he knew he had made an important discovery, something he had to report at once.

From his jacket pocket, the goon pulled a two-way radio and called Krueger, who was still making his way up the slope.

"Come in," the goon whispered in German.

A few seconds passed before Krueger replied. "What's wrong?"

"I found something big."

"What is it?"

"Some kind of building."

Krueger paused. "Did you say *building*?"

The goon nodded. "It's underground, like a cave or something."

"You mean a bunker?"

"Yeah! A bunker. A very old bunker."

"How old?" Krueger demanded.

"I don't know. I haven't gone in yet."

"Why not?"

"Because it's a *bunker*. I'm not going down there without backup. I shot some guy and he fell inside. I have no idea if he's dead or alive."

"Give me the coordinates. I'll be there soon."

Payne couldn't speak German, so he had no idea what had been discussed during the brief radio conversation. However, based on the goon's reaction when he peered into the bunker, Payne could tell that he hadn't been there before and wasn't one of Kaiser's men.

That meant he needed to die.

From his current distance, Payne figured he had a ninety-nine percent chance of a killshot with his Sig Sauer. The problem was the noise it would make when he fired his weapon. Sometimes noise was a good thing. It could lure the enemy to a particular spot, where they could be eliminated by an explosive or a well-placed sniper. Originally, that had been the plan he had discussed with Jones. Lure the enemy to the cul-de-sac, then mow them down.

Unfortunately, a major part of the equation was missing.

He needed Kaiser's radio to coordinate the attack.

Without it, Payne couldn't risk attracting any attention to the area—especially one where he would be pinned against a cliff with no way to escape. Furthermore, if Kaiser was hiding in the nearby woods, there was a decent chance the advancing troops might spot him during their charge toward the bunker, and if that happened, Payne probably couldn't save him.

For the time being, the noise just wasn't worth the risk.

Of course, Payne knew many ways to kill quietly.

The goon leaned forward, hoping to see the man he had shot in the back, wondering if he was dead or if he would require another blast from the Remington. Just to be safe, he raised the tip of his rifle and pointed it in the hole, looking forward to pulling his trigger one more time.

A few seconds later, the goon was a goner.

Moving with incredible stealth, Payne sprinted across the clearing and grabbed the goon around his neck before he knew someone was behind him. Without hesitation or remorse, Payne twisted the goon's head so hard and at such an awkward angle that the vertebrae in his neck popped like corn in a microwave. Instantly, he became deadweight in Payne's arms.

But just to be sure, Payne twisted his head the other way—even harder.

Not wanting to leave the body in plain sight, Payne inched forward and was ready to dump it down the hole when he noticed a battered figure on the concrete floor beneath him. At first glance, he couldn't tell who was unconscious in the shadows of the bunker, but once his eyes adjusted to the dim light, he gasped in horror.

The bloodied man was Kaiser.

32

✳

After using a tree to lower himself to the access trail, Jones glanced into the cul-de-sac below and spotted a hulking shadow gliding across the clearing toward an unsuspecting target. Jones had been on enough missions with Payne to recognize his stride and his tactics, and knew the man near the hole would soon be dead.

A broken neck later, Jones was right.

Strangely, during the ten seconds of action, the sniper didn't take a shot even though he had more than enough time to shoot the man by the bunker. In Jones's mind, that meant one of three things: Kaiser's sniper was working with the enemy, he had been killed and replaced, or he was a reluctant shooter. Jones hoped for number three, but prepared for one and two by raising his weapon and picking up his pace along the narrow path.

The bird's nest was up ahead, and Jones could see the sniper. He was lying on his stomach, perfectly still, just as a sniper should be. Leaves and branches provided adequate cover, especially for an unwary intruder, but to an experienced soldier like Jones, who used to hunt snipers for a living, the shooter stood out like a neon sign.

Looking through his scope, the sniper eyed his target in the crosshairs. Someone as big as Payne would be tough to miss with a DSR-1, a bolt-action sniper rifle that was used by the GSG 9, the elite counterterrorism unit of the German Federal Police. Loaded with a five-round magazine of .308 Winchester cartridges, the DSR-1 had an expected accuracy of within .20 inches from a distance of a hundred yards.

"Don't even think about it," Jones growled as he aimed at the sniper, who was ten feet away. "Let go of your rifle and put your hands behind your head."

Not wanting to die, the sniper cursed to himself and did as he was told. The instant he released the DSR-1, which was supported by a bipod for maximum stability, the barrel tilted skyward. For the time being, it was no longer a threat to Payne or anyone else.

"Now *slowly* turn on your side and look at me."

Once again, the sniper followed orders. Only this time, his reaction was much different. As soon as he saw Jones, recognition flashed across his face and he breathed a huge sigh of relief. "Thank God!"

Jones stared at him. "For what?"

"For *you*," he said in perfect English. "You're one of Kaiser's friends."

"You know me?"

The sniper nodded. "You flew in yesterday. You and the big guy."

"What big guy?" Jones asked him, still trying to decide whom the sniper was working for.

He tilted his head to the right. "The guy down there."

"The one you were about to shoot?"

"What? I wasn't going to shoot *anyone*! I swear! I was using my scope to identify him. That's all! I didn't even know you guys had returned."

"From where?"

"How should I know? Kaiser never tells us anything! All I know is three of you left this morning. The big guy, the black guy, and the fat guy. But I don't know where you went!"

Jones scowled for effect. "Which one am I?"

"What?" he said, as his voice squeaked. "You're, um, the . . ."

"Never mind."

"Can I put my hands down?"

"Not yet. Why didn't you shoot the guy near the bunker?"

"What?" he asked, confused.

"You had plenty of time to kill him but didn't take the shot. I want to know why."

"Why? Because I watched him kill Kaiser. After that, I didn't know if I should keep fighting or I should run away. Why keep shooting if I won't get paid?"

Jones's face flushed in anger. "Kaiser's dead?"

He nodded. "The guy shot him in the back and he fell

in the hole. That's what the guy was staring at when your friend killed him."

Jones glanced below. Payne was no longer there. "Where's your radio?"

"It's in my pocket."

"Get on your knees and hand it to me slowly."

The sniper did as he was told, then waited for further instructions. "Now what?"

"Now you have a decision to make, the most important decision of your life." To emphasize how serious he was, Jones took a step closer as he continued to point his gun at the sniper's face. "You fight with us, or you jump from the cliff. Your choice."

Instead of using the ladder, Payne leapt into the bunker and rushed to Kaiser's side. Lying on the floor, he was unconscious and bleeding heavily from his mouth and face. His eye was dangling from its socket. His left knee was torn to shreds. But he was still breathing.

Experienced in basic field medicine, Payne knew his first order of business was getting his patient away from potential danger, so he carefully dragged Kaiser into the back passageway. From there, he turned on a flashlight and went through his mental checklist for trauma victims. Instructors at the Academy had taught him the "A, B, C, D, E" approach to field medicine. Clear *airway*. Check *breathing*. Check *circulation*. Determine *disabilities*. And *expose* all wounds.

Breathing was fine. Pulse was steady. The patient was

unconscious, so Payne couldn't check for movement in his limbs. But he could search Kaiser for bullet holes.

Using a pocketknife, he gently cut Kaiser's shirt open and was relieved to find top-of-the-line, hard-plated body armor—the kind worn by presidents and mafia dons, not security guards. Of course, in Kaiser's business, it made sense to have the best. And in this case it probably saved his life, because rifle blasts tend to cut through soft vests like rocks through a window.

Just then, Payne heard a muffled voice coming from the outer room near the bunker entrance. He instantly sprang to his feet and crept to the edge of the passageway, where he listened patiently. No footsteps. No movement. No breathing of any kind. Only a muffled voice that sounded suspiciously familiar.

"Come in. Over."

Payne peeked around the corner and spotted Kaiser's radio on the floor, close to where he had fallen. Although he doubted it was a trap, Payne grabbed the radio as fast as he could, then dashed back to the passageway before he answered Jones's call. "Where are you?"

Static filled the line.

Payne repeated his question. "Where are you? Over."

Still nothing. Not even a squeak.

Suddenly, Kaiser's condition made a lot more sense. His radio didn't work in the bunker, so he was forced to run things from outside. Which ultimately exposed him to gunfire.

Wasting no time, Payne moved forward until Jones heard his question.

"I'm in the nest. Where are you?"

"Tending to our friend," Payne said, not wanting to broadcast Kaiser's name.

"He's alive?"

"Unconscious, but stable."

Jones breathed a sigh of relief. "Good to hear."

"What about you?"

"Conscious and angry. I'm ready to fuck some boys up."

Payne smiled. "What are you working with?"

"A DSR-1. Standard optics. Plenty of ammo."

"How many teammates?"

"One down, four in play."

"Who are we facing?"

"Don't know, don't care."

"You say that *now*. You'll change your mind when the cops show up."

Jones nodded. "Good point."

"Out of curiosity, what's the penalty for justifiable homicide in this country?"

"For you, nothing. For me, they lynch me in Berlin."

Payne laughed at the comment, realizing that Jones was joking. The two of them had spent a lot of time in Germany—mostly shuttling in and out of American military bases on their way to foreign missions—and had never experienced any racial problems. If anything, German people went out of their way to prove Nazism was a thing of the past. "Don't take this the wrong way, but right now I'm more concerned about our friend than I am about you."

"First, you want to split up, and now *this*. I'm starting to reevaluate our friendship."

Payne ignored him. "Where's the sniper that you replaced? Is he nearby?"

"Why? Do you want his phone number?"

"Actually, I need his help."

"With what?"

"Our escape."

"Yours and his, or yours and mine?"

"All of the above."

Jones smiled. "In that case, I'll let you talk to him."

Ulster's confusion worked to his advantage for the first ten minutes or so. The truth was he honestly didn't know why Payne and Jones had sprinted out of the King's House on Schachen in such a hurry or why they thought his life was in danger. All they had told him was to lock the door and keep an eye on Heidi until they returned. Obviously, something big was going on, but he didn't know what it was since he hadn't heard the gunshots near the bunker while he was touring the interior of the house.

Unfortunately for Ulster, Heidi was twice as confused and three times as feisty. Hoping to get as much information as possible, she peppered him with question after question—about Payne and Jones, the real reason they were in Bavaria, and everything else she could think of—which put a man like Ulster in an uncomfortable situation. He was an educator at heart, someone who enjoyed sharing his knowledge with the rest of the world, as could be seen from his life's work. At first, he answered her questions openly and honestly, because he really didn't know where Payne and Jones had gone, but after that, she touched on some topics he knew he shouldn't talk about. He tried to change the subject and tried to bite his tongue, especially when the spotlight focused on Ludwig, but she eventually wore him down.

After that, Ulster was putty in her hands.

33

✤

The guy's name was Collins. Until his arrival in Garmisch-Partenkirchen, he had never been a sniper but had volunteered for the position because he thought it would be a lot easier than hiking in the woods all day. For the past two years, he had worked for Kaiser, mostly doing security but occasionally doing grunt work. Like most people in the criminal world, his loyalty only went so far. In their business, the main motivation was money.

Payne used that knowledge to his advantage. "Have you been paid yet?"

Collins answered over the radio. "No."

"Would you like a big raise?"

"What do I have to do?"

"Simple. Help me get your boss to safety."

"He's still alive?" Collins asked.

"Alive but unconscious. I need help moving him."

"To where?"

"His ATV."

"Then what?"

"You tell us. Any contingency plans?"

Collins gave it some thought. If he risked his life and Kaiser survived, he would get a huge bonus and a possible bump in the organization. Both sounded good to him. "If the cops showed up, we were supposed to—"

"Shut up!" Payne ordered. "Not on the radio! *Never* on the radio! Someone might be listening. Tell my partner instead. If he likes it, I'll like it. Then we'll go from there."

Collins glanced at Jones, who was studying the surrounding tree line with the rifle's scope. If anyone threatened the bunker, Jones would take him out.

"What's the plan?" Jones asked as he continued to search for targets.

Collins explained. "If the cops showed up, we were supposed to meet at the southern end of the gorge."

"What gorge?"

"The Partnach Gorge. It's halfway between the bunker and the city. There's a clearing on the far end where the chopper can pick us up."

"Then what?"

"We fly to Austria. It's just over the mountains."

Jones liked its simplicity. "Sounds good to me. Can I speak to him?"

"Who?"

"The pilot."

"Why do you want to talk to him?"

"Because the plan *sucks* if he doesn't show up."

Collins nodded in agreement. "He's on a different channel."

"And what about your girlfriends? Will they know what to do?"

"Just say the word, and they'll meet us there."

Ten minutes later, Payne and Collins were in the cul-de-sac attaching a metal cable to the back of Kaiser's ATV. The goal was to lift four crates—the van Goghs, the gold, Conrad Ulster's books and papers, and the family heirlooms stored during the war—with the pulley system and load them into the off-road trailer before Payne carried Kaiser up the ladder. Then they would strap him to the top of the crates and haul everything to the rendezvous site.

Because of the extra payload—and Payne's desire to evacuate all the men at once—two choppers would be needed. To accommodate them, Jones ordered the pilot to fly up the mountain to the King's House on Schachen and tell Baptiste to meet them at the far end of the gorge. If things went smoothly, the choppers would swoop in, pick them up, and then fly them across the border where they could get Kaiser the medical care he needed at a private facility. Meanwhile, Ulster's chopper would continue on to Switzerland, where he would protect the cargo at the Archives until Kaiser was healthy enough to travel.

"Can you drive this thing?" Payne asked as he double-checked the cable.

Collins nodded. "I drove it up the slope on day one."

"Carrying what?"

"Most of our gear and some of the men."

"You any good?"

"At what?"

"Driving ATVs."

"Yes, sir. I take them hunting all the time."

Payne stood. "In that case, you're hired. You drive, and I'll feed the crates through the hole. Do you think you can handle that?"

"Yes, sir. Piece of cake."

"Don't get cocky, Collins. If you fuck up, my partner will shoot you."

Collins gulped hard, then started the engine as Payne hustled to the bunker. Per military tradition, he loved busting the balls of his subordinates. It used to be one of his biggest joys in life, but he was forced to curtail his habit when he took control of his grandfather's business. During his first week on the job, he had teased one of his assistants—a mild rebuke without profanity—and made her cry. Obviously, she had overreacted, but he felt so bad about the episode that he had censored his comments in the workplace ever since. It was one of the reasons that he teased Jones about everything. He knew his best friend wouldn't cry.

"Are we clear?" Payne asked from the bunker entrance.

"Clear," Jones said, still searching for targets.

"Then let's roll."

As Collins inched the ATV forward, Payne steadied the van Gogh crate from his position on the bunker floor.

More cumbersome than heavy, the crate was slowly hauled to the surface as Payne supported it from underneath, just in case the cable snapped or the bottom of the crate broke. Step by step, he climbed the ladder until the cargo reached the top. A few minutes later, all four crates were in the open-air trailer, ready to be towed down the mountain.

Following the GPS coordinates he had received from his goon, Krueger ordered his men to converge on the site. He didn't know what type of bunker Kaiser had discovered in the middle of the woods, but if the Ulster Archives were involved, it had to be significant.

The first man to get there was Zimmermann. From two hundred feet away, he could hear the roar of the ATV. He didn't know what was making the noise, but he knew it was close. Unsure of what to do, he called Krueger on his radio. "I can hear an engine, sir."

"What kind of engine?" Krueger demanded.

"It sounds like a jeep or some kind of off-road vehicle."

"Can you see it?"

"Not from where I'm hiding."

"What about Braun? Do you see Braun?"

"No, sir. No sign of him."

Krueger grimaced. "I haven't heard from him since he found the site."

"Me neither. Do you want me to search for him?"

"Negative. He can fend for himself."

"Then what should I do?"

Krueger stared at his GPS. He was still a few minutes away. "Investigate the site, then report back to me. I want to know what we're dealing with."

Made with a heavy-duty, all-steel frame, the trailer had a durable mesh floor for drainage and four flotation tires for the extra-rough terrain. Collins watched as Payne carried Kaiser out of the bunker and placed him on top of the crates. Working as quickly as they could, they used stretch cords with hooks to strap Kaiser to the crates and guard-rails so he wouldn't slide off during his journey down the mountain.

As they strapped down his injured leg, Kaiser started to groan. It was his first sign of consciousness since Payne had found him on the bunker floor. "Where am I?"

Payne rushed to his side. "Hey, man, how are you feeling?"

"Horrible," he moaned, barely able to speak. Gauze and tape from a first-aid kit had been wrapped around his head, holding his injured eye in its socket.

"I was kind of hoping you wouldn't wake up."

"Thanks," he lisped because of his broken teeth. "I love you, too."

Payne laughed and patted him on his shoulder. "Obviously, I wanted you to wake up *eventually*. But I was hoping it would be later."

Kaiser opened his good eye. "Why?"

"We need to haul you off the mountain. I'm afraid it's going to be bumpy."

He tried to swallow. "Where are you taking me?"

"To the gorge. Your pilot is going to meet us on the far end. Is that okay with you?"

He nodded slightly. "Where's the . . . stuff?"

Payne smiled. Even in his current condition, Kaiser was protective of his discovery. As always, his main concern was the bottom line. "Don't worry, I strapped you to the crate. I figured you wouldn't want to leave it behind."

Satisfied with the answer, Kaiser closed his eye and drifted away.

34

❦

Zimmermann heard bits and pieces of the conversation from his hiding spot near the cul-de-sac. Following orders, he updated Krueger on the information.

"I saw three men at the site," he whispered into his radio. "One of them is badly hurt. They just strapped him to four crates in the back of a trailer."

Krueger responded. "What kind of crates?"

"Wooden. Medium-sized. Rope handles."

"What's inside?"

"I'm not sure, but they look really old."

"Anything else?"

Zimmermann hesitated. "Maybe."

"What is it?" Krueger snapped, not in the mood for games.

"I think I know where they're going."

"Where?"

"One of them mentioned the gorge. He said a pilot would—"

Before Zimmermann could say another word, his head erupted in a fountain of pink mist, thanks to the perfectly placed shot from Jones's DSR-1 rifle. After passing through his medulla oblongata—dubbed the "apricot" by snipers, it was the part of the brain that controlled involuntary movement and ensured an instant kill—the bullet blew out Zimmermann's teeth and struck the radio that he was holding against his mouth. A split second later, a mixture of blood, bone, and technology covered the forest floor, as if Jones had just shot the Terminator.

But unlike the infamous cyborg, Zimmermann wouldn't be coming back.

Thunder roared from the bird's nest, high above the cul-de-sac. The rifle blast was so deafening it echoed throughout the Garmisch-Partenkirchen valley.

Like a sprinter bursting from his starting blocks, Payne reacted instantly, grabbing Collins and throwing him behind the trailer before diving to safety. Whereas most people took several seconds to process violent stimuli, years of training had taught Payne how to shrug off the confusion that followed an unexpected surge of adrenaline and focus on the mission at hand.

Pulling his gun from his belt, Payne crouched next to the crates, his eyes scanning the surrounding trees for possible gunmen. As he did, he realized Kaiser was unprotected, strapped to the top of the crates like a dead animal. Thankfully, he was unconscious and lying perfectly still. To most intruders, he would look like a corpse instead of a potential target, so Payne left him alone instead of cutting him free.

"Status?" Payne whispered into his radio.

Focused on more urgent matters, Jones didn't reply right away. "One down, approximately fifty feet to the north . . . Still searching for hostiles."

"Keep me posted."

Twenty seconds passed before he spoke again. "Looks clear."

"You sure?"

Jones paused. "Not really."

Payne didn't smile. "Let me know when you're *sure*."

"Ain't gonna happen. Forest is too thick. Too many blind spots."

"Recommendation?"

"The sooner you roll, the better."

Payne nodded in agreement. Not only was he worried about a team of gunmen attacking the site, it was only a matter of time before the authorities arrived. "Will you be joining us?"

"Eventually, but not right away."

"Gotta take a piss?"

"Gotta cook Hogzilla."

The moment Payne and Jones joined a Special Mission Unit, their fingerprints were permanently classified by order of the Joint Special Operations Command. This protected their identities when they were running top-secret missions for SOCOM, such as counterterrorism, unconventional warfare, or personnel recovery. But sometimes, classified fingerprints weren't enough. Occasionally, they were forced to take drastic steps in order to cover their tracks—whether that was to destroy physical evidence (security videos, bullet casings, etc.) or to conceal the identities of local contacts, people who would be killed or arrested if their involvement was detected.

When done properly, it was quite effective.

And a whole lot of fun.

Normally, the thought of setting a fire in the woods would have been dismissed as overkill, but after weighing the pros and cons, Jones realized he didn't have much of a choice. If he wanted to keep Kaiser and Ulster out of trouble, he had to torch the bunker before the cops had a chance to investigate it. He reasoned the concrete walls and the lack of ventilation would keep the blaze from spreading to the nearby vegetation, yet it would burn long enough to destroy all the evidence that could be used against them. As an added bonus, he knew the sight of black smoke billowing from the trees would be a wonderful distraction during their escape attempt. When the authorities rushed to put out the fire, the choppers could land undetected in the gorge.

It was a win-win in his mind.

While Jones watched over them, Payne and Collins cleaned the site by dumping everything they could find into the bunker. This included camping supplies, the winch-and-pulley system, and both dead goons. Curious about their identities, Payne searched their pockets and found their wallets—a sure sign they weren't trained professionals. After memorizing their names and addresses, he threw their wallets in the hole, then started his journey to the rendezvous point.

Once the ATV and trailer were safely on their way, Jones hustled down the slope and tossed the rifle into the bunker, where it would burn with everything else. Next to the entrance, Jones found the two items that he would use to set the blaze. Payne had stacked them neatly by the ladder, as if he were leaving gifts underneath a Christmas tree.

One was the emergency fuel can for the ATV.

The other was a box of waterproof matches.

Let the pig roast begin.

Even though Krueger was smart, it didn't take a genius to figure out what had happened to Zimmermann. He had stopped talking at roughly the same time as the rifle blast. After that, no additional shots were fired. Repeated attempts to get him on the radio were fruitless.

Obviously, they had taken him out.

Much like the other goon before him.

No longer in such a hurry to investigate the bunker, Krueger replayed the conversation with Zimmermann in his head. What did he say before he was shot? Something about a pilot meeting Kaiser at the gorge? Considering the density of the forest and the slope of the mountain,

Krueger knew the far end of the ravine was the closet spot a helicopter could land.

All things considered, it was a good place for a rendezvous.

But a better place for an ambush.

35

✤

Partnach Gorge
Bavaria, Germany

Located on the Zugspitze, the highest peak in the Bavarian Alps, the Schneeferner is a glacier that formed during the Little Ice Age, an extended period of cooling that ended in the mid-nineteenth century. Since that time, the glacier has been gradually melting. Slowly at first, but now at an alarming rate. To protect the ice in the summer months, local workers lay down more than sixty thousand square meters of reflective tarps, hoping to shield the glacier from the sun.

Unfortunately, the tarps can't stop global warming.

As the ice continues to melt, the water trickles down the mountain in tranquil streams that eventually run together to form the Partnach River. For most of its voyage, the Partnach is a peaceful waterway. It meanders at a casual pace, as if it is trying to see all of the sights in the Bavarian countryside before it flows through the middle of

Garmisch-Partenkirchen, where it divides the city into two separate villages: Garmisch to the west and Partenkirchen to the east. However, during one particular stretch of its journey, the waterway changes drastically, morphing from a gentle, rolling brook into a nasty, roaring river.

The Partnach Gorge, or Partnachklamm, is a natural channel that was created over time by the force of rushing water. For a span of 2,305 feet, the Partnach River surges through a narrow limestone canyon, its walls soaring to the height of 262 feet. Along the way, dozens of waterfalls fill the air with spray, moistening the moss-covered cliffs and cooling the thousands of tourists that explore the gorge every year. Since 1912, when the gorge was declared a natural monument, a series of tunnels has been carved into the limestone on one side of the river. Originally used by hunters and lumberjacks to reach the mountains above, the sloping path allows hikers to duck behind waterfalls and stroll next to raging rapids with minimal risk.

Of course, the danger would be much higher today.

When bullets filled the air like mist.

As Collins drove the ATV toward the gorge, Payne jogged behind the trailer. Occasionally, he dashed into the woods when he spotted something that bothered him—whether that was a flash of color that didn't belong or a glimpse of movement in the nearby trees—but he always came back to the rugged trail where he could watch over his injured friend.

In Payne's mind, Kaiser was the number one priority.

Forced to move at a sluggish pace because of the terrain, they had been traveling for nearly fifteen minutes when Collins slowed the ATV to a gradual halt. Not a quick, jolting stop that screamed of panic, but a calm, leisurely stop that whispered confusion. Hoping to get a better view of the situation, Payne hopped on the back of the trailer and quickly spotted the problem. Fifty feet ahead, there was a rustic intersection, a place where two hiking paths came together. Payne's trail was going east and west; the other was going north and south. Unfamiliar with the territory, Payne told Collins to stay put as he ran ahead to investigate a large display case that had been posted at the junction for confused hikers.

Thirty seconds later, Payne was cursing loudly.

Inside the glass case was a detailed map of the area, written in German and English. It showed everything—ski slopes, mountain peaks, major roads, museums, theaters, hotels, restaurants, and the best places to park. Of course, none of that mattered to Payne, since he was desperately trying to get out of town, not looking to enjoy his stay. The only thing he cared about was getting through the gorge as quickly as possible.

But everything changed when he studied the map.

Using the butt of his gun, Payne smashed the case open and ripped the map off the corkboard inside. Then he stomped back toward Collins, anger punctuating his every step.

"What's wrong?" Collins asked.

Payne shoved the map against Collins's chest. "Where's the chopper going to land?"

"What?"

"Where's the chopper going to land?" he asked again.

"By the entrance to the gorge," Collins said.

"Really?" Payne growled, his voice dripping with sarcasm. "And how are we going to get there? I'd love for you to show me!"

Collins knew something was wrong, but he didn't know how dreadful the situation was until he glanced at the map. There were several photos of area attractions, including a picture of the narrow trail that ran through the gorge. It was barely wide enough for two people; there was no way it could handle an ATV and a trailer. "Shit. We won't fit."

"Exactly! So why in the hell did you choose the gorge as the rendezvous point?"

"I didn't," Collins argued. "It was Kaiser's plan, not mine. And in his defense, he thought we'd be escaping on foot, not on an ATV."

Payne took a deep breath and nodded. It was a valid point. As an apology, he patted Collins on the shoulder and grunted. He knew it wasn't Collins's fault. He was simply frustrated by an oversight that could have led to their demise. And since Kaiser was currently unconscious, Payne had lashed out at the first person he encountered. That just happened to be Collins.

"What'd I miss?" someone said from behind.

Payne whirled and raised his gun in one fluid motion,

like a gunfighter from the Wild West. Thankfully, he didn't squeeze his trigger or else he would have killed his best friend.

"What the fuck?" Jones shouted, not the least bit amused. "If you want to get rid of me, just say the word. I'll go to Oktoberfest alone."

"Sorry," Payne said. "I'm having a bad day."

"Not as bad as mine, if you had shot my ass."

"I wasn't aiming for your ass. I was aiming for your heart."

"Oh," Jones mocked, "now I feel *much* better."

Payne turned and pointed at the map. "We have a problem."

"Yeah, I thought I detected a disturbance in the Force."

Payne ignored the *Star Wars* reference. "You know that expression, *you can't get there from here*? Well, we're facing it right now."

"Wonderful," said Jones as he snatched the map from Collins's grasp. "It looks like I arrived at the perfect time. I love rescuing damsels."

When it came to planning missions, Jones was a brilliant strategist. He had received the highest score in the history of the Air Force Academy's MSAE (Military Strategy Acumen Examination) and had organized hundreds of operations with the MANIACs. He had a way of seeing things several steps ahead, like a chess master.

"Out of curiosity, who chose the gorge?" Jones asked.

Payne moaned. "Kaiser."

"Before or after he was knocked out?"

Payne wasn't in the mood for games. "Do you see something or not?"

"Relax! Would I be messing with you if I didn't have a solution?"

"Yes."

Jones smiled. "You're probably right. However, as luck should have it, I actually know how we're going to get this stuff to the rendezvous point."

"The trailer won't fit through the gorge," Collins volunteered.

Jones stared at him. "Did I say you could speak?"

Collins dropped his chin to his chest, embarrassed.

Jones winked at Payne, who tried not to laugh. No matter the gravity of the situation, they liked busting balls. "Anyway, what was I talking about?"

"Reaching the rendezvous point."

Jones nodded and pointed at their location on the map. "Here's the problem. We're just east of the Partnach River. According to this, there's no way to cross the water until we get near the gorge. That means we can't escape to the west. Unfortunately, the east is out, too, because of the fire I just set. It's only a matter of time before Johnny Law comes running."

"That leaves north and south," Payne said.

"Obviously, the south is out because of the mountains. I mean, this is a sweet-ass ATV, but it's not climbing the Alps."

"Agreed."

"So we have to go north."

Payne nodded. "I figured as much, but how?"

Jones moved his finger on the map. "We take this into town."

Payne leaned closer and studied the yellow icon, which looked like a tiny train. "What the hell is *that*?"

"The Eckbauerbahn."

"Which is?"

"A cableway. It runs from the peak of Eckbauer to the Olympic stadium. Which, from the looks of things, is right next to the rendezvous point."

Payne rolled his eyes. "You want to take a ski lift into town?"

"It's not a ski lift. It's a *cableway*. Big difference."

"Really? How so?"

Jones smiled. "We don't have to wear skis."

36

❖

Krueger realized this was the opportunity he had been waiting for since he had joined Mueller's organization three years earlier. It was his chance to prove that he was a major player, not a two-bit thug who couldn't be trusted with big-money deals or serious projects.

This was his chance to make an impression.

Realizing the importance of the situation, Krueger decided to cash in a favor he had been holding on to since he had left the 10th Armored Division of the German Army. One of his best friends in the division, a violent man named Krause, had been accused of a brutal armed robbery, a crime he had committed. However, because of sworn testimony by Krueger that the two of them had been together at the time of the crime (and because of a lack of physical evidence), charges against Krause were eventually dropped. As a show of appreciation, Krause told Krueger that he owed him a gigantic favor—no matter what it was or when he needed it.

Well, that time was now.

From his hiding place near the southern end of the gorge, Krueger called Krause, who lived in the small town of Griesen, which was approximately ten miles to the west of Garmisch-Partenkirchen. The two areas were connected by the Bundesstraße 23, a scenic German highway that was known as the B 23.

Krause answered in German. "How are you, my friend?"

Krueger didn't have time for small talk. "Where are you?"

"I'm at home. Why?"

"It's time."

"For what?"

"The favor."

Krause nodded. He knew this day would eventually come, and he was fully prepared to pay his debt. After all, his friend had kept him from spending the majority of his life in jail. "What do you need me to do?"

Krueger explained the situation, coloring the facts to suit his needs. "A group of armed men just attacked my crew in the woods above Garmisch. Two of my friends are dead, and the others are missing. I overheard some of the gunmen. They said a chopper will be meeting them on the northern side of the Partnach Gorge, somewhere close to the ski stadium. I'm heading there now, but they have a head start. I need someone to run interference until I arrive."

"What kind of interference?"

"The kind you're good at."

"Let me see if I got this straight. If I drive to Garmisch and stop that chopper, my debt is *completely* forgiven? No more holding it over my head?"

Krueger promised. "If you stop the chopper, we're finally square."

Krause smiled. "In that case, I'll be there in ten minutes."

Prior to reaching a fork in the path, Payne and Jones reconnected with three of Kaiser's men, who were waiting near the southern end of the gorge. For the past thirty minutes, they had been running through the woods, hunting for the gunmen who had killed Schneider. Unfortunately, their effort had been unsuccessful, which left two goons (or more) unaccounted for.

With so much at stake, Payne took a few minutes to address their situation, using the map to highlight a few trouble spots and to pinpoint where the choppers would be landing. Now that they were talking face-to-face, he could discuss every aspect of their mission without risk.

Payne explained. "The instant we hit the main path, we're going to start encountering tourists, and it's only going to get worse as we get closer to town. With that in mind, we need something to quell potential panic. Personally, I like the cover story that you guys have been using—we're German soldiers who have been conducting military drills in the mountains. That would explain our weapons, equipment, and Kaiser's condition. He simply got hurt during a training exercise. Out of curiosity, how many of you guys speak German?"

All four of Kaiser's men—Collins, Huber, Lange, and Richter—raised their hands. Unbeknownst to Payne, it was a requirement for Kaiser's security detail.

"Really?" Payne said. "Well, I guess that makes me the class idiot, because I can't."

"You'll get no argument from me," Jones cracked.

Payne ignored him. "To make our cover story believable, one of you will have to take charge if we're stopped along the way—whether that's by a tourist, a tour guide, or a cop. Simply tell them there was a training accident, and we're rushing our man to a medevac chopper that is waiting for us. That should prevent them from summoning the authorities."

Jones continued from there. "It will also help us at the Eckbauerbahn. In order to load these crates into the gondolas, we'll need the operators to stop the cableway for a few minutes. If they want to know why we can't leave the crates behind, tell them they're filled with explosives. That should spook them enough to get their full cooperation."

Payne smiled. "We'll also need them to stop the cableway at the bottom so we can unload the payload before it gets whisked back up the mountain. To make sure that doesn't happen, we'll put someone in the first gondola who can hop out and explain the situation. Obviously, it would be great if there's a cart or truck for us to borrow, but we can't count on that. Which means there's a chance we'll have to carry everything to the choppers ourselves."

Jones pointed at the trailer. "I've labeled the crates two through five, based on priority. If we're forced to carry our payload, that's the order of importance. Two goes first; five goes last. Understand?"

Huber shook his head. "Why two through five? Why not one through four?"

"Why?" Jones asked. "Because *Kaiser* is priority number one. Not the crates, not your guns, not even yourselves. If Kaiser dies, this mission is a failure. Is that clear?"

They grunted and nodded tentatively.

But that wasn't good enough for Payne. Hoping to drive home the point, he used the same motivational technique he had used when he had recruited Collins. "Guys, it's pretty simple: If Kaiser dies, none of you will get paid. That means a week of hauling, and guarding, and sleeping in the woods for nothing. On the other hand, if you help him survive, I see a shitload of money headed your way. I'm talking about a one followed by a bunch of zeroes, just for doing your job. Is there some risk involved? Of course there is. But you knew that going in."

Payne took a moment to meet the gaze of every man, making each of them feel like they were the most important part of the team. "Before we proceed any further, I want you to answer a simple question for me. Your response will help me decide if you want to continue with this mission or if you want to quit, here and now."

Payne paused for effect. "Which sounds better to you: a huge pile of cash or unemployment? I know that sounds cold, but let's be honest—that's the choice you have to make."

Not surprisingly, everyone voted for the money.

"Good!" Payne applauded. "Now that everyone's on board, let's hand out some duties. Collins, you're in charge of the ATV. Your job is to get to the cableway as quickly as possible. That doesn't mean I want you to run over tourists. It simply means I want you to keep moving if you have the opportunity. If you're forced to stop, do not abandon the vehicle. You're the driver, not a foot soldier. We'll clear the path for you. Understand?"

Collins nodded. "Yes, sir."

Payne studied the other three men. Based on body language alone, he could tell Huber was higher on the totem pole than Lange or Richter. He pointed at him. "How's your German?"

"Flawless," Huber answered.

"Then you're our lead dog. You're setting the pace. If we come across a situation—tourists, guides, whatever—I want you to handle it peacefully. Is that clear?"

"Yes, sir."

Payne looked at Lange. "You're his understudy. If he gets delayed, you become the lead dog until he's able to resume his post. Our goal is to keep moving. Our excuse is Kaiser's health. If anyone questions our urgency, that's what you need to stress. He's our ticket to freedom."

"What about me?" Richter demanded. He was the largest of Kaiser's men, but looked the dumbest. For some reason, he perpetually had a look of puzzlement on his face.

"Don't worry," Payne assured him. "I have a special job for you. Probably the most important job of all. You're in charge of the trailer. If it gets stuck, I want you to free it. If the crates start to slide off, I want you to fix the straps. And if someone tries to examine the cargo, I want you to growl at them like a junkyard dog. Do you think you can handle that?"

Richter started barking. "I can do that like a champ!"

Payne fought the urge to smile. "Glad to hear it. Any questions?"

Huber raised his hand again. "What's your job?"

"I'm in charge of security. I'll keep an eye on the woods from the back. If I see any problems, I'll let you know A-SAP."

Huber pointed at Jones. "And what about you?"

Jones wiped his nose with his sleeve. "I'm the token black guy. If the cops show up, I'll make sure they chase me instead of you."

"Are you serious?" asked Richter.

Jones rolled his eyes. Some people had no sense of humor.

37

❁

Mount Schachen
Bavaria, Germany

Heidi didn't know what was going on, but she knew Ulster was hiding something. She could tell from the way he stammered every time she asked him a question about his visit to the King's House on Schachen. He had the same reaction when she asked him about Ludwig; even simple questions about his interest in the subject matter seemed to cause him a great deal of stress. First Ulster would blush, then he would stumble around like a politician trying to evade a scandal, then he would try to change the subject.

In many ways, she found his behavior endearing. He simply refused to lie and was willing to do just about anything to avoid it, including locking himself in Ludwig's private bathroom, where he had remained for nearly fifteen minutes. After a while, she realized she needed to change her approach. If Ulster wasn't willing to talk about his visit, maybe she could get him to talk about something else that would eventually get him to reveal small pieces of the puzzle.

But first, she had to lure him out.

"Take as long as you need," she said through the bathroom door. "I'm pretty tired, so I'm heading upstairs to the Turkish Hall. I'll be resting on one of the couches if you want to find me."

Ulster replied a few seconds later. "Is that permitted?"

"Is what permitted?"

"Sitting on Ludwig's furniture."

She fought her urge to smile. "I won't tell if you won't tell."

He opened the door a crack, just wide enough to make eye contact. "Rest assured, my dear. Your secret is safe with me."

A few minutes later, the two of them were reclining on the lavish couches that lined the walls of the opulent room. Ulster stared at the gold fountain in the middle of the hall, admiring its handcrafted beauty as water trickled from one level to the next until it splashed into the tiny pool on the bottom. The relaxing sound took him to another place, one far from the stress of his everyday life, which was why it had been installed there to begin with.

"I feel like a king," he said playfully.

"And I your queen," she replied.

Ulster laughed loudly. Even though he housed some of the most spectacular artifacts ever discovered, he never got to enjoy them in this fashion. He could touch them, and study them, and admire them all he wanted, but he couldn't lounge on them. To a historian, this was an extra-special treat—getting a taste of the life of the man he was researching. It gave him the context he normally lacked when he delved into the mysteries of the past.

Heidi noticed the satisfied smile on his face. She hoped that meant his guard was slipping. "Tell me more about yourself. What do you do for a living?"

Ulster put his hands behind his head and closed his eyes. "I run a small research facility in the mountains of Switzerland. It's called the Ulster Archives."

"Are you serious?"

"I never joke about research."

She slid closer to him on the couch. "Wait a minute! Are you Petr Ulster?"

He opened one eye. "I am indeed. Have you heard of me?"

She nodded enthusiastically. "I read a piece you wrote for *The Times*."

He opened his other eye. "Which one?"

"The one in London."

"No, my dear, I meant which *piece*. I've written several."

She smiled warmly. "It chronicled your recent trip to Greece, and all of the obstacles that you were forced to overcome. I never knew so much had to be done *after* a treasure was discovered."

He leaned forward and met her gaze. She seemed truly interested in the subject matter, which was a rarity for him. He hardly ever met fans outside of the world of academia. "It wasn't easy, I can assure you of that. Then again, certain problems were expected before I made my trip. Gold brings out the worst in people. Always has, always will."

"I bet you have thousands of stories."

"I certainly do, but most of them are boring."

She laughed. "I find that hard to believe."

He shook his head. "Trust me, my dear, my stories have put more people to sleep than late-night television. If you want excitement, you should talk to Jonathon and David. They are the *real* heroes of Greece. After all, they were the ones who found the treasure."

It took a few seconds for the information to sink in. When it did, she felt a jolt of adrenaline. "You mean Jon and DJ?"

"I do indeed."

"The guys who ran out of here?"

He nodded. "The very same."

"*They* discovered the Greek treasure?"

"And several other artifacts. They seem to have a nose for it."

Heidi thought back to her initial conversation with Payne and tried to recall what he had said about their trip to Mount Schachen. Very little, if she remembered correctly. He claimed they had flown up the mountain because of Ulster's weight and were there to keep him out of trouble. Yet ten minutes into their visit, they pulled out their weapons and abandoned Ulster, forcing him to fend for himself. Obviously, they were more concerned about someone else.

Or *something* else.

Maybe that was it. Maybe they were in Bavaria hunting for gold. After all, what had Ulster said about the duo? *They seem to have a nose for it.* Over the years, there had been a lot of speculation about Ludwig and his family fortune. Perhaps they were investigating some of the rumors? If so, maybe she could help their cause. As an employee of the Bavarian Palace Department, she had worked at Ludwig's other castles (Linderhof, Neuschwanstein, and the Munich Residenz) and knew many things about his life that couldn't be found in books. If she could help them find a long-lost treasure, it would be the thrill of her lifetime!

Then again, why would they turn to someone like her?

Ulster owned the best historical research facility in the world and had a vast network of contacts around the globe. If he needed assistance, he would call the Palace Department's headquarters in Munich or fly there himself. He certainly wouldn't team up with a glorified tour guide, even if she had a wealth of knowledge at her disposal. These guys had guns, and helicopters, and flew around the world looking for exotic treasures. The last thing they needed was someone like her getting in the way.

Unless, of course, she forced their hand.

In her spare time, Heidi loved playing cards. Her favorite game was Texas Hold'em, a variation of poker that was quite popular on television. The game consists of two cards being dealt facedown to each player before five community cards are placed on the table. As the community cards are revealed, players place bets on the outcome of the hand. By betting aggressively, players can trick their opponents into folding superior hands. By betting meekly, players with great cards can lure their opponents' money into the pot. The key, as far as Heidi was concerned, was the art of bluffing. When done correctly, it was tough to defeat.

And lucky for her, she was great at it.

38

❁

Partnach Gorge
Bavaria, Germany

N ear the southern end of the Partnach Gorge,
there was a major intersection where several hiking trails came together. Even though the paths
were labeled with codes and colors, it still took a while
for travelers to figure out which way they needed to go.
Paths that seemed to be heading one way often ended up
going another. Most of the time they went where geology
dictated, whether that was along the Partnach River or up
the side of a mountain. For hikers, this region was heaven.
They could spend hours crisscrossing the valley, switching
back and forth between easy paths and challenging trails
without venturing more than an hour from the city.

Anticipating some confusion, Payne made sure his men
knew they were supposed to follow the yellow sign with
the green arrow on the right. The path went toward Eckbauer, the small peak to the northeast. According to the

map, the trail zigged and zagged through the woods until it reached the Eckbauerbahn station, which sat on top of the summit. Although the elevation was listed at 4,035 feet, they wouldn't have much of a climb, since they were already more than three thousand feet above sea level. As long as the ATV kept chugging and the trailer kept rolling, Payne didn't expect any problems for well-conditioned soldiers.

A large group of hikers, all of them carrying rucksacks and walking sticks, clogged the intersection as the ATV approached its turn. Huber tried to seize control in German, ordering them out of the way for their medical emergency, but they stared at him like he was speaking in a foreign language. Which, of course, he was, since the hikers were from France. Upon seeing Huber's camouflage and 5.56mm assault rifle, a few of the Frenchmen panicked. Worried they had broken the law or had accidentally crossed the Austrian border, they threw their hands in the air and surrendered to the Germans like a scene from a World War II movie. Before long, all of them were crowding around the ATV, trying to figure out what they had done wrong.

Meanwhile, Collins did his best to keep moving. Lange rotated to the front of the pack and tried to clear enough space for the ATV and trailer to make the turn toward Eckbauer, but Lange's presence only added to the turmoil. Now there were two Germans with assault rifles yelling at the French, which made them twice as eager to surrender. Eventually, Collins had no choice. He had to stop the ATV or he was going to run over one of the hikers.

Payne heard the commotion from his position in the rear and came forward to investigate. It didn't take long to figure out there was a language barrier. Kaiser's men were speaking German and the hikers were speaking French. Neither group could understand the other. From his military experience, Payne knew English was the lingua franca—the bridge language for people who spoke different languages—for international business, science, technology, aviation, and diplomacy, so he decided to take charge of the situation.

Placing two fingers in his mouth, Payne unleashed a whistle that was so loud and authoritative that everyone shut up, including three Japanese hikers who were approaching the intersection from the opposite direction. Before he said a single word, Payne had everyone's undivided attention.

"Do any of you speak English?" he said calmly.

A middle-aged Frenchman, wearing a brightly colored bandanna over his long, gray hair, anointed himself spokesperson. "I speak English. Are we in trouble?"

Payne shook his head. "Not yet, but you will be unless you get off the path. We have a medical emergency, and we're trying to get into town."

"What kind of emergency?" said a voice from the back. A few seconds later, an older gentleman was pushing his way past his friends. "I'm a surgeon. Maybe I can help?"

Payne cursed under his breath. This was the last thing he needed. "Thanks, Doc, but no thanks. The patient is stable, and there's a chopper waiting for us in town. If you and your friends could just—"

"Is he conscious?" the surgeon demanded.

Payne stared at him coldly. "Not at the moment."

"Then how do you know he's stable?"

Payne quickly considered his options. He could stand there and argue with the doctor about Kaiser's health, or he could let the guy do his job as they continued toward the Eckbauerbahn. Ultimately, it was a no-brainer, since Kaiser's survival was his number one priority, and their cover story about a training accident would explain all of the injuries that the doctor would discover. "Fine! You can hop in the back, but you have to examine him while we're moving. We need to get to the chopper as soon as possible."

The surgeon nodded and hustled toward the trailer as the Frenchman with the bandanna explained what was happening to the non–English speakers in his group. Thrilled that they weren't being arrested, they started gathering their things and moving out of the way of the ATV when the first shot rang out from the woods. Fired from Krueger's gun, the bullet hit Collins just above his ear with so much force that it penetrated his skull and plowed into his temporal lobe. A moment later, he fell out of the ATV and slumped to the ground, dead.

Thanks to their training, Payne and Jones reacted a full second before anyone else. Payne fired his gun toward the sound of Krueger's blast, hoping to hit the gunman with a lucky shot, while Jones sprinted forward and jumped onto the driver's seat. Wasting no time, Jones cranked the accelerator on the ATV. In a cloud of dirt and stone, the vehicle rocketed forward into two unlucky Frenchmen, who got bowled over like drunken matadors. Thrown off balance by the abrupt movement of the trailer, the surgeon fell on top of Kaiser but managed to hold on to one of the straps or else he would have been trampled by his countrymen, who scattered at the intersection. One moment they were thankful for their freedom; the next they were shitting their pants and running for their lives.

Armed with assault rifles, Huber and Lange filled the woods with suppressive fire. The goal was to make the enemy scramble for cover while Jones escaped with the ATV. Their plan worked for nearly ten seconds, until Krueger's goons started firing from their hiding spot on the other side of the intersection. In a cruel twist of fate, one of them used the assault rifle they had taken from Schneider shortly after his throat had been slashed. Still stained with his blood, the Heckler & Koch G36 unleashed a hailstorm of automatic fire toward Schneider's friends. One shot caught Lange in the throat and another grazed his hip, while Huber remained unscathed. Risking his life, Huber grabbed Lange by the back of his shirt and pulled him into the nearby bushes as more shots whizzed overhead. Huber worked on him feverishly, trying to stop the geyser in Lange's neck, but it was all for naught. He died a short time later.

Realizing that no one was guarding Kaiser except for Jones, Huber darted through the trees and bushes until he found a narrow gap that allowed him to slip back onto the path toward Eckbauer. The ATV and trailer were still in sight, and the gunfire was now behind him. As far as he was concerned, he had made the right choice—even if that meant running from a fight.

With Collins and Lange dead, Jones driving, and Huber gone, Payne and Richter were left to deal with Krueger and his two goons. Based on shot patterns and geography, Payne figured out how many men they were facing and where they were located. Payne relayed this information to Richter, who was crouched behind a boulder about fifteen feet away, by using military hand signals. Despite the look of confusion that still plagued Richter's face, he nodded his head in understanding. Payne hoped that was the case, but since he was dealing with a man who had been barking at him less than ten minutes before, he wasn't overly confident.

Still, he reasoned, two guns were better than one.

Guns. The word triggered a thought in Payne's mind.

Until that moment, he had been using a Sig Sauer P228 to defend himself. It was the weapon of choice of many military agencies in the United States, but it had the stopping power of a slingshot when compared to the G36 assault rifles that Richter and one of Krueger's goons were firing. If he had a weapon like that in his hands, he could do some serious damage. Instead of hiding in the trees and playing charades, he could go on the offensive and end this bullshit once and for all, which was what MANIACs were trained to do.

But first, Payne had to acquire a rifle.

39

❖

Jones stopped the ATV about one hundred and fifty yards from the intersection, just past a thicket of trees that would temporarily shield the trailer. Glancing back, he saw the surgeon clinging to the cords that secured the crates in place, his fingers pale from clenching so tightly.

"Are you okay?" Jones asked as he hustled toward him.

The surgeon nodded and sat upright. "What was *that*?"

"*That* was an ambush. Obviously, someone was trying to kill you."

"*Me*? Why would anyone want to kill *me*?"

"I don't know. What did you do?"

The surgeon blinked a few times and tried to come up with an answer, which Jones found comical despite the situation. Normally, Jones would have messed with him even further, but he realized time was too valuable to waste.

"It's not important," Jones assured him. "What *is* important is your patient. The reason I saved your life was so you could save his. Don't worry. You can thank me later. For now, you need to focus on him and nothing else. Okay?"

The surgeon nodded, then turned his attention to Kaiser.

With a gun in his hand and an eye on the path, Jones pulled out his radio as the sound of automatic fire continued to roar in the distance. Although he felt guilty about abandoning Payne at the intersection, he knew he had made the right decision. He had rescued Kaiser, which was their number one priority, and had protected the cargo by driving the ATV out of harm's way. In the heat of battle, he had kept his composure and had done what he needed to do. It was a skill he had learned with Payne. During their time in the MANIACs, they had been taught to improvise behind enemy lines, since their missions rarely went as planned. Sometimes that meant using salami to slide down a rope; other times it meant taking over the duties of a fallen colleague. Ultimately, as long as they completed their missions, the Pentagon rarely questioned their methods or asked who did what. They cared only about success.

Of course, now that Kaiser and the cargo were temporarily safe, Jones's focus shifted back to everyone he had left behind. Success was important, but so was his best friend's survival. "Black Knight to White King. Can you hear me? Over."

There was fifteen seconds of silence before Jones heard a reply.

"I'm kind of busy," Payne said from his hiding spot in the bushes. "What's your status?"

"Hanging out. Chillin'. Working on my tan."

"How's our patient?"

"Safe. How's Collins?"

"Dead."

Jones had figured as much. "Do you need an extra gun?"

"Funny you should mention that. I'm working on that right now."

"Meaning?"

"I'll tell you later. For now, you're in charge of our patient. Get him to the chopper A-SAP. I'll take care of everything else."

"Hold up," Jones said tensely. He spotted a man in camouflage running up the path toward the ATV. Once he realized it was Huber, he slowly relaxed. "A pawn is heading my way. Do you want me to send him back?"

"That's a negative. I'm stuck with one already. I can't supervise two."

"Are you sure? Because—"

"Go!" Payne ordered. "Make sure you aren't followed. Take precautions."

Jones nodded in understanding. *Take precautions* was a coded message from Payne. It let him know that he could disable the cableway when he reached the bottom of the mountain because Payne was going to take another way down. Knowing his friend as well as he did, Jones was fairly confident that Payne's route would take him through the gorge.

It was the type of environment where he could work his magic.

Payne stared at the G36 assault rifle from his hiding spot in the trees. In some ways, he felt like a hungry fox eyeing a henhouse. He knew the risk was great, but so was the reward.

Even though the weapon was less than ten feet from his grasp, it would be tough to recover since it was strapped to Collins, who was lying dead near the intersection where they had been ambushed. It was an area surrounded by enemy troops. Making matters worse, Collins had fallen on top of the rifle when he had slumped out of the ATV. To recover it, Payne would have to grab more than the weapon. He would have to grab the corpse as well.

Over the years, Payne had been in enough battles to shrug off things like death. For better or worse, he had learned how to dehumanize his environment in order to survive. Otherwise, he wouldn't have stayed sane in such hellish conditions. To him, he wasn't killing people; he was merely shooting at targets. Nor was he risking his life on a daily basis; he was simply completing a mission. And when it came to grabbing the G36, he sure as hell wasn't stealing a dead man's gun. He was merely reacquiring an asset for the betterment of his squad.

"Are you ready?" Payne whispered to Richter.

Richter nodded from behind a large boulder.

"Are you sure? Because my ass is on the line."

Richter nodded again, this time more confidently.

Payne smiled and raised three fingers in the air. "Three, two, one, go!"

Working in unison, Richter fired several shots into the trees on the other side of the intersection while Payne burst from his hiding place and ran toward Collins. He knew the suppression fire would buy him some time, but he didn't know how much. He prayed it would be long enough to grab his fallen comrade and make it back to safety.

Sprinting as fast as he could, Payne reached Collins in less than two seconds. Experience had taught him how tricky it was to lift deadweight from the ground, so Payne made sure he had a good grip on the body before he dragged it back into the trees. From his knees, Payne plunged his arms under the dead man's armpits, then hooked his hands in front of the dead man's chest. When Payne stood, the corpse was facing away from him and most of its weight was draped on the crooks of Payne's elbows between his forearms and biceps, its skull resting on Payne's chest just below his chin. Wasting no time, Payne started to backpedal from the path. As he did, the dead man's heels dragged across the ground like two anchors skimming across a lake bed.

Krueger, who had killed Collins to begin with, watched this action unfold from his position near the entrance to the gorge. Although he had assumed the driver was dead, he didn't want to take any chances—especially since he had the opportunity to shoot two men with one bullet. If successful, it was the type of shot he could brag about for the rest of his life, an exploit that would impress the toughest of critics, even a grizzled criminal like Mueller. In Krueger's mind, that's what this mission was about, impressing his boss and moving up in the organization.

With a steady hand, Krueger raised his gun and fired a single round just before the two men disappeared from sight. The bullet exited the chamber with a mighty blast and whistled through the air toward its intended target. Branches scratched the back of Payne's neck at approximately the same time as the bullet's impact. It struck Collins in the sternum, just below the spot where Payne's hands were locked together around the dead man's chest. The impact was so close he felt the meaty thump in his fingers as he fell back into the trees. A few inches lower and the bullet would have ripped through Collins's gut and entered Payne's abdomen, bringing with it the type of bacteria that could have caused sepsis and possibly death. But thanks to Collins's rib cage, the bullet rattled harmlessly inside of the corpse as Payne tumbled safely to the ground.

Payne took a deep breath, then unhooked the black strap on the G36, which was slung over the dead man's shoulder. Weighing a little less than eight pounds, the Heckler & Koch assault rifle utilized NATO-standard 5.56mm cartridges and thirty-round magazines. To his delight, Payne found three extra thirty-round clips in Collins's pocket. He quickly stashed them in his cargo pants and prepared to make his move. Before he did, he eyed the fire selector just above the rifle's trigger. Made for the German military, it was labeled with three letters: *S*, *E*, and *F*.

S stood for *Sicherheit*, or "security."

E stood for *Einzelfeuer*, or "single fire."

F stood for *Feuerstoss*, or "continuous fire."

Payne grinned and cranked the selector to *F*. With his experience and 120 rounds to work with, he knew the *F* represented something more vulgar than automatic fire.

With this weapon in his hands, the enemy was fucked.

40

❧

Payne knew enough about the Partnach Gorge to view it as a promising escape route. The trail was downhill, narrow, and approximately a half-mile long. Protected by limestone cliffs and a raging river, he couldn't be outflanked or outmaneuvered. And if the goons tried to set up a barricade, Payne and Richter had enough firepower to blast their way through it.

In Payne's mind, the only drawback was the large number of hikers they were bound to encounter in the gorge. Families on vacation, tourists who didn't speak English, maybe even children on a field trip. Payne had a great deal of experience with urban warfare and trusted his shot selection. He knew the odds of his hitting an innocent bystander were pretty damn slim; he was that accurate when it came to shooting. Unfortunately, he wouldn't be the only one firing. If the ambush at the intersection was any indication, the enemy didn't give a damn about collateral damage. Either that or they had something against the French.

Payne studied the intersection, then turned his attention toward Richter. He was crouched behind the same large boulder as before, his rifle in his hands, the same confused look on his face. Thus far, he had proven himself to be an asset. He was strong, courageous, and just dumb enough not to question orders. Over the years, Payne had worked with a lot of men like Richter—the self-described "grunts" (**G**eneral, **R**eplaceable, **UNT**rained) who filled the infantry—and realized they were the backbone of the military. So much so that he went out of his way to show them respect, whether that was buying them beer or buying them *more* beer.

"You ever been to Oktoberfest?" Payne asked Richter.

"No, sir," he whispered back.

"Well, if we make it through this, you're going next week. My treat."

His eyes lit up. "Thank you, sir. I drink beer for breakfast."

Payne wasn't surprised. "What about the gorge? Ever been through the gorge?"

"No, sir."

"Me neither. But that's where we're headed. It's how we're getting to town."

"Yes, sir."

Payne stared at the intersection. He knew there was a gunman (Krueger) positioned near the entrance to the gorge. He was the assassin who had shot Collins twice.

First in the head, then in the chest. The other two goons were on the opposite side of the trail, nestled in a thicket of trees. So far they had been less than accurate with their shooting, despite being armed with two Remington 750s and a G36. To reach the path to the gorge, Payne and Richter would have to spray shots in both directions to minimize return fire while they made their escape. Since Payne was most concerned with the assassin they were running toward, he chose that target for himself. He assigned the other gunmen to Richter, explaining that only a few shots would be necessary to buy them some time. After that, the goal was to enter the gorge as quickly as possible.

Richter nodded in understanding, prepared to follow.

Once again, Payne counted down from three, but this time both of them burst from their hiding spots when he reached zero. For the next several seconds, shots flew in every direction. Payne shooting at Krueger, and Krueger shooting wildly while ducking for cover. Richter and the goons exchanging multiple shots, yet nothing getting hit except a few trees and one of the wooden signs at the intersection. By the time Payne and Richter reached the path that led to the gorge, there was a better chance they were going to get hit with flying splinters than by a bullet. Which was what Payne had been hoping for. He wasn't expecting to take out any targets with suppression fire—although that would have been a nice bonus. He was merely trying to get into the gorge unscathed.

Once inside, his objective would change. He would become a hunter.

Until then, his main goal was survival.

As they ran down the winding path toward the entrance, Payne spun and unleashed a quick burst of automatic fire, hoping to slow down the goons a little while longer. Blessed with speed and strength, Payne was a rarity among men, an athlete who ran with grace and agility in spite of his size. In a downhill sprint, he knew the odds were pretty good that no one was going to catch him on rough terrain, especially if they were burdened with equipment.

Unfortunately, the same couldn't be said about Richter, whose stride was hindered by his lack of coordination. If Payne was a thoroughbred, Richter was a plow horse. He was strong and dependable, yet not blessed with speed. Instead of running, Richter lumbered—his feet hitting the ground like heavy hooves, the sound echoing in the canyon. Payne realized that Richter needed as large a head start as possible, so he stopped on the path and fired a few more shots up the hill to buy him time. Then he turned and ran toward the gorge.

The entrance was marked by a wooden hut that had been there for years. Inside, an elderly man sat on a tiny stool, waiting to charge an admission fee. Hard of hearing and barely able to see, he didn't notice Richter as he rumbled past and ducked into the first tunnel. Nor did he hear the automatic fire from Payne's rifle or see him sprinting past a few seconds later. In fact, the first time he snapped out of his daze was when a screaming tourist jumped through the hut's window and hid behind the counter. More confused than scared, the old man looked down at the woman, who was cowering on the floor, and said, "That will be two euros."

Krueger and his goons ran past next. Although they were a few seconds behind, they were quite familiar with the gorge and knew there was plenty of time to catch up. The stone path curved constantly, weaving in and out of dark tunnels that had been carved into the limestone walls. The Partnach River, which flowed so close to the trail that hikers could touch the rapids, and the sheer height of the cliffs would prevent Kaiser's men from straying. Like everybody else, they'd be forced to stay on the narrow path, a path that tended to clog up at certain junctures. All Krueger had to do was stay close and wait for his opportunity to strike.

Huber jogged beside the trailer as Jones navigated the ATV through the twists and turns that led to the cableway. Once the path straightened out and started to climb the gentle slope of Mount Eckbauer, Huber jumped onto the back and positioned himself on one of the crates. From there, he watched the woods behind them with his rifle in his hands.

Built in 1956, the Eckbauerbahn stretched 7,020 feet and handled as many as 300 people per hour in each direction. Traveling along an inch-thick steel cable that was supported by 27 towers, the open-air gondolas offered a great view of the valley without the hike. During the descent, a scenic trip that took approximately 14 minutes, passengers dropped 1,640 feet from the top of the summit to the station below, zipping along at a speed of 8.3 feet per second.

"We're almost there," Jones called over his shoulder. "I'll pull right next to the station. When we stop, I'll need you to talk to the operator."

"Yes, sir," Huber replied.

The closer they got, the more people they passed along the way. Most of the hikers stopped and stared at the ATV, trying to figure out if these men were responsible for the gunshots they had heard, and whether or not they were dangerous. But Jones managed to ignore them. Used to far worse scrutiny when he had been deployed overseas—particularly in the turbulent streets of Baghdad—Jones kept driving without so much as a sideways glance. That didn't mean he didn't see the hikers, because he saw everything around him. It simply meant he didn't care. As long as they didn't pull out a camera and take his picture, they could stare all day.

The Eckbauerbahn station was housed in a two-story white building that resembled a rural church. Nestled beside several pine trees that towered above it, the simple structure was topped with a steep green roof that matched the color of the surrounding grass. Bisecting the lawn was a curved sidewalk that curled toward the left side of the building. Jones followed it around and parked the trailer next to a short flight of steps that led into the lobby.

Huber hustled inside and came out four minutes later. When he returned, he wasn't alone. Following him was a large pack of Austrian bodybuilders who had just ridden the cableway up from Garmisch-Partenkirchen. Dressed in muscle shirts and tight shorts, they had overheard Huber's description of the medical emergency and had offered to help.

Despite the thousands of Arnold Schwarzenegger jokes that floated through Jones's mind, he kept his tongue in check and politely accepted their offer. With arms the size of legs, the steroid club of Austria carried Kaiser in first, then came out for the cargo. The brute strength that these men possessed was nothing short of amazing. Even the crate filled with gold was handled by a single guy, who tossed it around like he had picked up a lunchbox.

Meanwhile, Huber climbed into the first gondola and started his journey down the mountain. He needed to reach the bottom before anyone else, so he could talk to the operator in the valley. After that, Kaiser was strapped into gondola number two and was accompanied by the doctor. The next four gondolas were filled with cargo, one crate in each, before Jones hopped into lucky number seven and was launched out of the station. Unless something strange happened, he knew they would complete their journey in fourteen minutes, which would give them plenty of time to reach the chopper before Payne exited the gorge.

If he exited the gorge.

41

❉

Payne had been in more firefights than Richter, Krueger, and the goons combined, but there were certain things that experience couldn't overcome, such as the inner workings of the human eye. After spending the past several minutes running and shooting in the bright sun, Payne found himself temporarily blind when he sprinted past the iron gate and into the first tunnel.

Carved into the limestone cliff, the narrow corridor lacked artificial lights of any kind. Other than a few beams of sunlight that leaked through a small gap cut into the rock, the passageway was completely dark. Payne skidded to a halt about ten feet inside, just before he slammed into a young couple who were walking hand in hand toward the exit. Unwilling to let go of each other's grasp, they had to turn their bodies sideways and lean against the handrail that had been installed in the jagged wall. Otherwise, Payne wouldn't have had enough room to pass.

The tunnel was *that* narrow.

Forced to temporarily rely on his other senses, Payne focused on the sounds that echoed in the darkness. The trickling of water. The giggling of children. The patter of footsteps. In a matter of seconds, he knew the tranquillity of the gorge would be replaced by the cacophony of war— the screaming, the crying, the gunfire—and it would be up to him to restore the calm. Thankfully, he had the expertise to finish the job quickly.

Just before he reached the gap in the rock, the tunnel turned to the right and stretched for more than a hundred feet through the limestone mountain. Along the way, large arches had been cut into the left-hand wall that offered intimate views of the Partnach River as it raged through the gorge. People of all ages crowded against the waist-high steel fence, which prevented them from falling into the water even as it splashed their feet and filled their ears with thunder.

With enough light to see, Payne sprinted across the uneven stone floor and caught a glimpse of Richter, who was nearly fifty feet ahead. For the time being, the presence of two large men with assault rifles running through the shadows hadn't made a large impression on the tourists, who were too enamored with the rapids to care about anything else. But Payne knew everything would change when a weapon was fired. Chaos would reign in the blink of an eye.

Hoping to keep the peace for as long as possible, Payne studied the terrain without slowing down. If he had been given advance surveillance of the tunnel, he would have positioned himself near the first turn and waited for his enemies to be blinded by the lack of light. As soon as they stopped in the darkness, he would have mowed them down with automatic fire, ending the drama in less than five seconds. Unfortunately, it was too late to go back now, not with his opponents so close behind. If they happened to beat Payne to that first turn, he would be the one stranded in the middle of the tunnel, not them. And all the tourists who were watching the rapids would get caught up in the cross fire.

To Payne, going back was too big of a risk.

Especially since he had other options.

For as long as Payne could remember, he preferred being the chaser instead of the chasee. Obviously, there were advantages to being in front during a foot pursuit, and if he had been stuck in the lead position, he would have made the most of it. But based on experience, he knew he was much more effective when attacking from behind. Not only did it match his aggressive personality, but it allowed him to use his stealth, which was an important part of his skill set. With that in mind, he looked for ways to let the enemy pass him in the gorge.

As Payne approached the last archway on the left, he noticed an absence of tourists near the steel fence. A rock formation, which jutted out from the side of the mountain and partially blocked the view of the water below, gave him the opportunity he was looking for. Wasting no time, Payne hopped the fence and slid back along the tiny ridge that lined the outside of the wall until he couldn't be seen from the corridor. After that, all he had to do was wait.

First, he heard Krueger rumble past the archway without slowing down. Then the lead goon did the same, his footsteps echoing as he ran. Realizing there was only one goon left, Payne moved into position to strike. As soon as the straggler passed, Payne sprang from his hiding place and landed on the goon's back like a cheetah bringing down a gazelle. In the tunnel, the only noises made—the sound of air being forced from the goon's lungs and the crack of the goon's neck as Payne twisted it viciously to the side—were drowned out by the roaring water.

Just like that, the goon was dead.

Worried about detection, Payne glanced in both directions and searched for any signs of trouble. To the north, Krueger and the other goon were still running at top speed. To the south, tourists continued to gawk at the gorge, completely unaware that death had just visited the shadows of the tunnel. Hoping to prevent their panic, Payne lifted the body and carried it over to the archway where he had launched his attack. He was thirty feet downstream from the closest hikers, who would find the corpse if he left it in the tunnel. If he dumped it, the authorities might not find it for days. To Payne, it wasn't a tough decision. With a mighty heave, he launched the body over the fence and watched it get sucked under the rapids.

After that, Payne turned and started chasing his next victim.

Over the next hundred feet, the corridor system changed dramatically. Instead of dark tunnels with periodic archways that offered views of the river, the entire left-hand wall had been carved away, leaving behind an open trail with a limestone roof hanging overhead. Sunlight from above reflected off the water below, filling the trail with natural light. Every nook and cranny seemed to glow, as if the rocks themselves were luminescent.

To keep tourists from falling into the water, two steel cables were threaded through sturdy posts that had been anchored into the limestone. The cables ran along the river's edge, curling gradually with the bend in the path as the water weaved its way toward the valley. Because of his size, Payne had to slow down when the trail narrowed or the roof dipped. Otherwise, he would have split his skull open on the jagged rocks above.

Despite this hindrance, Payne quickly made up ground.

Darting and ducking, bobbing and weaving, Payne closed the gap to less than twenty feet, yet the goon didn't know he was back there. Earlier, tourists had literally been in the dark when it came to the chase, but thanks to an abundance of light along the path, tourists now did everything possible to get out of their way—including straddling the steel cables while holding on for their lives. A Spaniard misjudged his leap as Krueger rushed toward him, and he fell waist-deep into the river. During a terrifying eight seconds, both of his flip-flops were ripped off his feet by the surging water, which was nature's way of saying people shouldn't wear flip-flops during a hike. Thankfully, his life was spared by Payne, who grabbed the man's arms and yanked him out of the water a moment before he was swept downriver.

"*Gracias,*" the Spaniard said, trembling.

Payne patted him on the back. "*De nada.*"

Then he started running again.

Realizing it was just a matter of time before a tourist was hurt or killed, Payne decided to increase his aggression. Instead of chasing the goon down, Payne would lure him to a section of the trail that could be exploited. If done correctly, Payne knew he could take him out with a single shot without putting anyone else at risk.

Actually, make that *two* shots.

The first would get him to stop. The second would end his life.

42

Mount Schachen
Bavaria, Germany

Heidi smiled when she thought about her initial conversation with Payne. He was charming, funny, and flirtatious—not to mention ruggedly handsome. If they had met in a coffee shop or in a bookstore, she would have been willing to chat with him all day. And when they chatted, she would have been open and honest about her life because that's the kind of woman she was.

On the other hand, if she had met him at a poker table, she would have lied her ass off from the moment they met because that was how the game was played. Afterward, she would have returned to her truthful ways, but during the give-and-take of competition, she would have used every trick in the book to ensure her success.

She planned to do the same thing here.

She would bluff to her advantage.

"May I ask you a question?" she said to Ulster, who had just finished a rambling dialogue about the history of the Archives while lounging on one of Ludwig's couches. "Jon said something to me when we first met, and it's been bothering me ever since."

"Of course, my dear. What did he say?"

"He said you guys were looking for some kind of treasure and needed my help."

Ulster sat upright. "He said *what*?"

With her best poker face, she continued her story. "He said you were looking for a secret treasure or something, and he wanted to ask me some questions about Ludwig."

"Wait a moment! When did he say *that*?"

"When he first came up to the house. You and DJ were still chatting on the slope, and Jon hustled over to introduce himself and apologize about noise from the helicopter. Remember?"

"I do indeed," said Ulster as he stood and started to pace. "Then what?"

"Then he asked about my job."

"And what did you say?"

"I told him I worked for the Bavarian Palace Department, and I've been . . ." She paused for a moment, letting the tension build.

He stared at her. "You've been what?"

"Maybe I should wait until Jon returns. I don't know why, but I feel like I'm doing something wrong here, like I'm going behind his back. Perhaps our discussion was supposed to be confidential."

Ulster rushed over to her side and patted her knee.

"Nonsense! I can assure you that isn't the case. Jonathon, David, and I are in this together. If he felt you could help our cause, perhaps you can. Tell me, my dear, what is your area of expertise?"

"Ludwig's palaces," she answered honestly. "Over the past few years, I've worked at Linderhof, Neuschwanstein, and the Munich Residenz. I know more about those buildings than Ludwig himself—mostly because they've done a lot of remodeling since his death."

Ulster laughed at her joke. He was a huge fan of historical humor. "What about his life? Are you familiar with his life?"

"If you're referring to Ludwig Friedrich Wilhelm von Wittelsbach, then the answer is yes. A famous historian once said, 'To understand a castle, you must understand the king.' Obviously, that's a difficult task with someone as complicated as Ludwig, but it's a passion of mine. I've spent the last few years studying his letters and journals and the books from his private library, trying to learn about his life. Eventually, I reached a point where I knew more about Ludwig than some of the men I've dated. I know that's pathetic, but it's the truth."

Ulster leaned back on the couch. "Tell me, my dear, do you know the name of the historian that you just quoted?"

She shook her head. "I'm sorry, Petr. I don't recall."

He smiled. "It was my grandfather, Conrad Ulster."

"Really?" Her voice cracked as she said it. She honestly didn't know. "Here I am going on and on like a pompous windbag, and I used your grandfather's quote as my thesis statement. I can't imagine what you think of me right now!"

He laughed. "Don't worry, my dear, I find you completely refreshing. During the past fifteen minutes, you praised my article in *The Times* and quoted my grandfather. Fifteen years and fifty pounds ago, I might have thought you were flirting with me!"

Heidi blushed, more embarrassed than a moment before.

Ulster continued. "Tell me, did Jonathon ask you any questions about Ludwig before he left? Perhaps we can figure out what part of our investigation you could assist."

She quickly replayed the conversation with Payne in her head. She hoped to find a nugget that would convince Ulster that she could be trusted with information about their trip to Bavaria. Unfortunately, the only questions she could recall were asked *after* Jones and Ulster had joined the discussion. Instead of saying nothing at all, she decided to use them to keep the ball rolling. "If you remember, DJ wanted to know about freshwater lakes that Ludwig might have visited around here. He seemed disappointed when I told him there were none. I thought maybe he was thinking about Schloss Hohenschwanstein, the castle Ludwig stayed at when Neuschwanstein was being built, since there was a large lake adjacent to the property, but that seemed to disappoint him even more."

"Yes, I remember."

"Then Jon asked me to translate the names of both

castles into English. His ears seemed to perk up when I mentioned 'high swan stone' and 'new swan stone.' Like that information was somehow important."

"Yes, my dear, I remember that, too."

"Then I said—"

Ulster interrupted her. "Actually, my dear, I was wondering if Jonathon asked you any questions that I *wasn't* privy to. Those are the ones that would be most helpful to our cause."

Heidi stared at him, intrigued. Even though she didn't know him very well, she knew Ulster was overly polite—one of the most well-mannered men she had ever met. Yet he had just cut her off in midsentence, right after she had mentioned the translation of the two names. In poker, whenever an opponent bet too quickly it usually meant he was hiding something. Suddenly, she wondered if Ulster's interruption was his way of changing the topic, much as locking himself in the bathroom was his way to avoid tough questions about his trip to Schachen.

"Let me think," she said, hoping to buy some time.

"Think away, my dear. I'm not going anywhere."

She leaned back on the couch and rubbed her eyes, trying to make sense of what she knew. "High swan stone" and "new swan stone" were simple translations. Anyone with a basic grasp of the German language could have done that for them, so it had to be something more than that. Okay, what led them to ask about the translations? The lake. They wanted to know about a lake that Ludwig might have visited on Mount Schachen. She told them there wasn't a lake around here, but there was a lake that Ludwig had visited on many occasions by the other castles.

Crap! She suddenly realized *they* weren't the ones who had brought up the castles; *she* had brought up the castles. Maybe she was wrong about their interest in the translation of the castles' names. Maybe she had misread their questions and Ulster's interruption, and turned them into an elaborate wild-goose chase, one that would end with a vast treasure. Of course, that would be appropriate considering the subject matter. After all, Ludwig had a history of taking boring tasks and turning them into whimsical adventures. Perhaps she was doing the same thing here.

Heidi opened her eyes and focused. Payne seemed interested in the word *swan*. She was well aware that one of Ludwig's many nicknames was the Swan King, but could there be another connection she was looking for?

If so, what did it have to do with a treasure?

A popular legend involved a series of mysterious letters—known as the black swan letters—that Ludwig had sent to aristocrats throughout Europe. With his royal coffers nearly dry, Ludwig reportedly asked for their support in order to finish a secret project he had been working on. Since his reputation was better in foreign countries than in Bavaria, it was assumed that many noblemen answered his call, and riches came flooding in.

Heidi had no way of knowing if the rumors were true, but if they were, there was a chance the money Ludwig had collected was still hidden somewhere, since he was murdered before he could spend it.

Could *that* be what they were looking for?

The infamous black swan treasure?

It would explain many of their questions and why Ulster had interrupted her right after she had mentioned the word *swan*. He was trying to shift her focus away from a key word.

Heidi smiled to herself. Obviously, none of this would hold up in a court of law, but in a game of poker, she had more than enough to work with. All she had to do was bluff a little more and see how her opponent reacted. So far, Ulster had shown an inability to lie, which was admirable in a friend but a serious problem in a game like this.

She glanced at him. "Now that I think about it, Jon did ask me something else. He wanted to know if I was familiar with the black swan."

Ulster tensed up. "And what did you say?"

"I told him I was quite familiar with the topic. I know all about the midnight letters, the mysterious project, and his massive treasure."

Ulster turned bright red. "Treasure?"

Heidi stared at him. She analyzed the color of his face, the crinkles around his eyes, and the way his hands trembled slightly. This was a man with a major tell. "I knew it!"

"Excuse me?"

"I knew it! I knew it! I knew it!"

"Knew *what*?"

"You're looking for his treasure! The black swan treasure!"

His face turned brighter. "I don't know what you *think* you know, but . . ."

She ignored his protest and continued her celebration by doing a small victory dance in the Turkish Hall, the same place where Ludwig used to prance around with his male servants.

Ulster sighed. "Bollocks!"

Heidi heard the word and couldn't help but laugh. It was probably the closest a man like Ulster ever came to swearing. Suddenly feeling guilty for her behavior, she collapsed on the couch next to him and patted his belly. "Don't worry, Petr. Your secret is safe with me."

"It is?" he asked, concerned.

"I promise, I won't tell a soul."

He glanced at her, hopeful. "You won't?"

She flashed a winning smile. "Not if you take me with you."

43

Partnach Gorge
Bavaria, Germany

Krueger didn't give a damn about bystanders. As far as he was concerned, collateral damage was an acceptable part of war, and that's what he was involved in: a goddamn war. Thus far, Kaiser's men had taken out half of his crew, which gave Krueger all the motivation he needed to be ruthless. If people got in his way, he was going to knock them to the ground, shove them into the river, or do whatever he had to do to complete his mission. If he failed, he knew Mueller would blame him, and that would be the end of Krueger's career. Maybe even his life.

Mueller was quite vindictive.

Despite his incentive to succeed, Krueger had been reluctant to fire his weapon during the early part of the chase because of a severe shortage of ammo. He had a few rounds in his clip, but not enough to take desperate shots while running—especially while navigating the upper section of the gorge where the narrow trail twisted in and out of tunnels. Farther up ahead, he knew the path widened and straightened. That's where he had planned to make his move.

But everything changed when he heard the gunshot.

Krueger slammed on his brakes and stared at Hahn, the goon directly behind him. While gasping for breath, he asked, "Where did that come from?"

Hahn gasped as well. "Back there somewhere."

Krueger stared at the short tunnel they had just run through. It had been cut through a narrow pillar of stone that jutted out like a peninsula into the river. "Where's Meyer?"

"He's behind me."

"When was the last time you saw him?"

Hahn shrugged. "I don't know. I've been following you the whole time."

Krueger cursed to himself. Suddenly, he had a tough decision to make. Continue forward with Hahn as an armed escort, or send Hahn back to check on the gunshot. Obviously, if Krueger had known all the facts—that Payne had killed Meyer near the entrance to the gorge and was simply setting them up—there wouldn't have been a dilemma. But since Krueger was in the dark about Meyer, he made his decision based on the survival of his crew. "You better go back and check on him. We need as many men as we can get to stop their chopper."

"Yes, sir."

"But before you go, give me the rifle."

Hahn stared at the G36 he had acquired from Schneider, right after slitting his throat. The rifle gave him a sense of comfort. "But, sir—"

"No buts!" Krueger growled. "There are two men ahead of us. I'll be damned if I'm going to face them with a handgun. Besides, you and Meyer can watch each other's backs for a while."

He reluctantly traded weapons with his boss. "Now what?"

"Now go! Check on Meyer before he's dead!"

Hahn nodded, then sprinted to the south, the opposite direction of where he had been heading. For the first few seconds, he felt completely discombobulated, as if everything in the world had been switched around in order to confuse him. Suddenly, the Partnach River was on his right and its water was surging toward him. His rifle was now a Glock. His boss was now behind him. And his current mission was to find his friend, not kill his enemy.

It was almost too much for his brain to handle.

Hoping to gather his thoughts, Hahn stopped inside the tunnel he had just run through—which was shorter and brighter than the earlier tunnels—and checked his weapon. The Glock 17, an Austrian-made pistol chambered in a 9×19mm Parabellum, was one of the most popular handguns in the world. Highly durable, it is a NATO-classified sidearm and is used by thousands of law-enforcement agencies around the globe. Unfortunately, the damn thing was useless without ammo, and a cursory check of the magazine revealed only three rounds to work with.

"*Scheiße!*" he grumbled in German.

Pissed at Krueger for putting him in this predicament, Hahn shoved the magazine back into the Glock and walked forward. He would curse out his boss later, after he rescued Meyer from whatever mess he had gotten himself into. Using caution, Hahn stared at the rocky terrain from the shadows of the tunnel. The trail ahead was fairly straight for twenty-five feet, then it curled back to the left. If Meyer was in trouble, that was probably where.

Suddenly, a thought dawned on him, one that would have come to him earlier if he hadn't been so confused. Why risk his ass when he could call Meyer instead?

Hahn pulled out his radio. "Come in, Meyer. Over."

Static filled the line for the next several seconds.

So Hahn tried again. "Come in, Meyer. What's your location?"

Once again, static hissed from the speaker.

Trying to improve reception, Hahn took a few steps forward, just beyond the edge of the tunnel. With an open sky above him, he hoped it would make enough of a difference that he would be able to talk to Meyer without having to risk his life.

Ironically, his caution led to his death.

From his perch above the tunnel entrance—where he had positioned himself on a narrow ledge—Payne waited until the goon was directly between him and the water. While leaning back against the rocks, he coolly lined up his shot and pulled the trigger. Fired at close range with a downward trajectory, the bullet tore through Hahn's skull and face with so much force that it ended up fragmenting against the rocks underneath the water's surface. A fountain of blood and brains splattered against the safety fence a moment before Hahn's body slumped to the path a few inches from his Glock and radio.

Wasting no time, Payne leapt from his perch and shoved the corpse into the Partnach, the same river that had swept away Meyer's remains. In death, the two goons were reunited in a watery grave. Of course, Payne couldn't have cared less about their reunion. When his adrenaline was flowing and his life was on the line, he didn't have time to think about what he had done. He was far too concerned with what he needed to do—like tucking the Glock into his belt and shoving the radio into his pocket. Both might come in handy somewhere down the line.

By Payne's calculation, there was only one target left: the man who had killed Collins near the intersection. Right now he was trapped between Payne and Richter in the middle of a steep gorge, yet Payne knew the shooter could still do some damage. So far, he had proven to be a pretty good shot. If he hunkered down in a crevice or inside a dark tunnel, he would be tough to root out in a short amount of time. That wouldn't be much of an issue for Richter since he could keep running to the rendezvous point, but it would be a major problem for Payne. He simply didn't have time to run back up the mountain.

To prevent that scenario, Payne wanted to trap the shooter in an open clearing, somewhere on the path where the guy couldn't take shelter. Unfortunately, the one man who could provide Payne with the advance surveillance he needed was currently running for his life. With no other options, Payne got on his radio and hoped for the best.

"Come in, Junkyard Dog. Can you hear me?"

Payne waited ten seconds before he tried again. "Junk-yard Dog, stop your running and answer me. I need your help. Over."

Several seconds ticked by as he waited for a response. Payne was about to try one last time when the silence was finally broken.

"Are you talking to me?" Richter asked.

Payne laughed to himself. In his excitement, he had forgotten whom he was dealing with. The truth was that most dogs were probably smarter than Richter. "Yeah, big guy, I'm talking to you. Are you somewhere safe?"

"Yes, sir. I stopped inside a tunnel."

"What's the path look like behind you?"

"Like dirt, sir."

Payne smirked. "I meant, describe the terrain. Straight, twisty, narrow . . . ?"

"Straight, sir. And pretty wide open. The canyon opens up farther ahead."

"Good, that's good. That's what we're looking for."

"For what, sir?"

Payne ignored the question. For one reason or another, Kaiser's men simply didn't understand the risks of radio transmissions. With the proper equipment, radio signals were very easy to intercept. "Do you see anyone headed your way?"

Richter peeked out of the tunnel. "Not right now, sir. No hikers or bad guys in sight. The path is all clear."

"And you're sure you're secure?"

"Yes, sir. I'm dug in real good."

"Then catch your breath and hold your position."

Richter nodded. "For how long, sir?"

Payne stared at the trail ahead. Based on Richter's slowness and Payne's speed, they were only a few minutes apart. "Stay there until you see me."

44

❖

As Payne sprinted along the narrow path, he felt as if he had been magically transported to a distant land, somewhere far away from central Europe. Gone were the pine trees and snowy peaks of the Alps, replaced by the moss-covered cliffs and roaring waterfalls of South America. Until that morning, Payne had never heard of the Partnach Gorge, but even if he had, he wouldn't have believed a canyon like this could exist in Germany.

The rain forest, maybe. But not Bavaria.

In retrospect, Payne could understand why a dreamer like Ludwig would have chosen this region to build his mountain lair. During the days, he could have hiked the scenic trails that seemed to go on forever, a wide variety of terrain and topography to fuel his imagination. At night, he could have returned to the peaceful solitude of Mount

Schachen, a place where he could pretend to be a knight, a swan, or a fire-breathing dragon without interference from advisors or whispers from onlookers.

In many ways, Payne could identify with the need to get away. Sometimes he found himself burdened by the huge responsibility of overseeing his grandfather's corporation, a job he didn't love but one he did out of familial obligation. In those situations, he shut out the world and stole some time for himself—whether that was going to the roof of the Payne Industries building, where he had installed a basketball court, or a nearby firing range. For an ex-athlete/soldier like Payne, shooting hoops and shooting bad guys were both ways to relieve stress.

Suddenly, the deceptive calm of the last minute ended in a burst of gunfire from somewhere around the next bend. Payne instantly recognized the sound; it came from a G36 assault rifle. A few seconds later, there was more automatic fire, this time a little bit closer. Payne cursed to himself as he picked up speed. Either Richter had left his position in the tunnel and was coming toward him, or the final gunman was armed with the G36 they had taken from Schneider. If it was the latter—and Payne assumed it was because Richter was obedient—everyone left standing was carrying a G36. In a confined space, all of that firepower could make things messy.

Sprinting around the corner, Payne spotted his prey less than thirty feet away. Krueger was running toward him, trying to get away from Richter, who was positioned in the tunnel ahead. Payne instantly skidded to a halt and hugged the rock face to his right before he unleashed a stream of bullets that tore into the path less than ten feet from Krueger. Not because Payne had missed, but because he wanted to question the guy and get some answers.

Stunned by his predicament, Krueger tried to stop way too quickly on the rocky trail. When he did, his feet slid out from under him. One second he was running for his life; the next he was skimming across the rocks on his ass, leaving chunks of cloth and skin behind. As he did, he accidentally squeezed the trigger on his G36, sending a torrent of bullets into the air, most of which struck the canyon on the other side of the river, far from Payne and Richter.

"Drop your weapon!" Payne shouted.

Too dazed to respond, Krueger remained flat on his back, trying to regain his senses. He blinked a few times and tried to sit up, but the sky was spinning way too much for him to do anything, so he simply lay back down.

Tactically speaking, a soldier has two options when an adversary is unresponsive to his commands. He can play it safe and monitor the situation from afar, or he can charge forward and eliminate the threat. Not surprisingly, Payne opted for the aggressive approach. He pulled out his radio and spoke to Richter, who was lingering in the tunnel on the far side of Krueger.

"Let's take him," Payne ordered.

In unison, both men hustled forward while staring at Krueger over the tips of their rifles. Payne got there first and viciously kicked the G36 out of his hands. It clanked on the rocky path near Richter, who picked it up and slung it over his shoulder.

"Should I search him?" Richter asked.

Payne shook his head. He didn't want Richter to get too close to Krueger. That was simply asking for trouble. "Hell, no! Let him keep whatever weapons he has. In fact, I hope he reaches for one. It'll give me an excuse to pull my trigger."

Richter backed away, just in case Payne opened fire.

Meanwhile, Payne's gaze never left Krueger, who was lying on the ground with his hands by his sides. Far from his pockets, they weren't viewed as a threat.

"Do you speak English?" Payne asked.

Krueger groaned but didn't answer.

Payne repeated himself in German. *"Sprechen sie Englisch?"*

Krueger took a deep breath. *"Ja."*

"Then answer me in English, you stupid Kraut!"

Until that moment, Payne had never used the word *Kraut* in his entire life, but he was quite familiar with its origin and hoped it would rile up his opponent enough to get him talking. A derogatory term for German soldiers, it became popular during World War I when British sailors learned their German counterparts ate large quantities of sauerkraut in order to battle scurvy. This practice was comparable to the Royal Navy's consumption of limes, which had earned them the nickname *Limey*, so they felt it was appropriate to belittle the Germans in a similar fashion.

"Yes," Krueger said as he sat up slowly, "I speak English."

Payne watched him closely. "If you twitch, you die."

Krueger used his arms to twist himself around onto his knees, then he placed his hands on top of his head. It was the universal position for surrender. "I understand."

"Wow, I get the feeling you've done that before. Is that a part of your training? Germans: surrendering to Americans since 1918."

Krueger sneered. "What do you want from me?"

"What do *I* want? No, Adolf, what do *you* want? You attacked us, in case you forgot. We were minding our business in the woods when you came along."

Krueger shook his head. "I did no such thing. I am man of peace."

"Yeah, a piece of shit."

"I am hiker, not fighter. I find gun in trees."

"Really? If that's the case, prove it to me. Show me your hands."

"What?"

Payne smiled. "I said, show . . . me . . . your . . . hands."

Krueger lifted his hands above his head. "Now what?"

"Now look at them! See all that blood? It came from *my* men. Do you understand what I'm saying? Their blood is on your hands."

Krueger glanced at his hands, confused. Despite a little grime, they were relatively clean. "Blood? I don't see blood on my hands."

Payne fired a single round through Krueger's right palm. "Look closer."

The German howled in agony as blood gushed from his hand, a painful and debilitating wound that would prevent him from firing a handgun for a very long time. To some, this act could be interpreted as sadistic. To Payne, it was justifiable. If anything, Krueger had gotten off easy for shooting Collins in the head. Then again, Payne was just warming up.

"What's your name?" Payne demanded.

"Krueger! Max Krueger!" he cried.

"Why did you attack us?"

"Kaiser. We saw Kaiser."

"Who do you work for?"

"No one!"

Payne repeated his question. "Come on, Max. Who do you work for?"

Krueger shook his head and refused to answer.

"Fine!" Payne growled. "Show me your feet!"

"What?" he wailed.

"You heard me, Max. I'm going to start with your feet and work my way up. And trust me, I'm *not* bluffing."

Krueger nodded in belief. "Mueller. His name is Hans Mueller."

"And who the fuck is—"

Before Payne could say another word, Richter raised his rifle and fired a single shot into the back of Krueger's head. Angled toward the river, the bullet went through his skull and continued forward until it hit the canyon wall on the other side of the water. Despite standing several feet away, Payne's face and clothes were spattered with blood.

This turn of events was so shocking to Payne, he raised his rifle and pointed it at Richter. Suddenly, he didn't know if he could trust the guy. "Drop your weapon!"

"What?" Richter said, confused.

"Drop your fucking weapon!"

Richter dropped his rifle, then lifted his hands above his head. The look on his face said he was confused. Less confused than Payne, but more confused than Krueger, who was now dead.

Payne stared at him. "What the fuck did you do? I was questioning the guy!"

"I know that, sir, but . . ."

"But *what*?"

"I was following orders."

"*Orders*? Whose fucking orders?"

"Kaiser's, sir."

"Kaiser's?" Payne glanced around like he was missing something. Had Richter snapped under pressure? "What the fuck are you talking about? Kaiser isn't here!"

"I know that, sir. But those were my orders."

"From when?"

"From the moment he hired me."

Payne stared at Richter. The oaf still had that dumb-ass look on his face. It had been there from the moment they had met. "You've got ten seconds to explain, then I start firing."

"Have you heard of Hans Mueller? He's Kaiser's biggest rival."

"Go on."

"Kaiser told us if Mueller's men ever interfered with one of our projects, we were supposed to shoot them immediately. *No questions asked*. So that's what I did. I shot him before you could ask him a question."

Payne's jaw dropped open. He was possibly staring at

the dumbest man in the world. "You've got to be shitting me!"

"No, sir. I'd never shit you. I swear to God, those were my orders."

Payne took a deep breath, stunned by Richter's stupidity. He honestly didn't know what to say to him. And even if he did, he was afraid it would be misinterpreted.

Richter frowned. "Did I do something wrong, sir?"

Payne sighed and pointed at the body. "If you think I'm cleaning that up, you're crazy. Search him for an ID, then dump him in the river. I need to wipe his brains off my face."

Richter smiled, relieved to be on his master's good side. If he had been a dog, he would have wagged his tail and licked Payne's shoe.

Taking no chances, Payne picked up the extra assault rifle and slung it over his shoulder. "On the way home, keep your weapon away from me at all times. Is that understood?"

"Yes, sir."

"I'm serious, Richter. If I even see your rifle, you're *not* going to Oktoberfest."

45

❖

The lower Eckbauerbahn station was a short walk from the Olympic ski stadium where Adolf Hitler opened the 1936 Winter Olympics, the first winter games in history to light the symbolic Olympic flame. Built to hold more than ten thousand spectators, the stadium had plenty of parking. On most days, the lots were filled with family cars and tour buses, not helicopters, so it was easy for Jones to spot the chopper on the far side of the lot as his gondola pulled into the station.

Huber greeted him on the concrete platform. He was trailed by a group of Japanese tourists, who were half the size of the Austrian bodybuilders from the upper station but more than eager to help. Jones grinned at the irony of the situation. Decades earlier, Conrad Ulster, an Austrian philanthropist, had teamed up with a Japanese industrialist to smuggle a van Gogh painting into Germany during World War II. Now the two countries were teaming up again to smuggle it back out, right past a sports stadium built by the Nazis. For Jones, the only thing that would make this better was if a couple of tanks rumbled by.

"What's the status on transportation?" Jones asked.

Huber answered. "The ski stadium has a giant plow that's never used in the summertime. It's like those ice machines for hockey rinks."

"You mean a Zamboni?"

"If you say so. I don't speak Italian."

"Actually, it's American. It's named after the guy who invented it."

Huber shrugged. "Anyhow, the cableway operator said the stadium has something for the ski jump that's parked in their maintenance garage. He called over there, and they're pulling it around for us. It should be here any minute."

"Is it big enough for Kaiser and the cargo?"

"According to him, yes. But I haven't seen it yet."

Jones glanced into the corner of the station. Kaiser was lying on a wooden bench, still being watched over by the French surgeon. "How's your boss?"

"Doc says he'll be fine. He keeps waking up, but he's loopy as all hell. Probably has a concussion or something."

"And the crates made it down okay?"

Huber nodded. "They didn't complain at all."

Jones smiled. "It sounds like everything is running smoothly. If it's okay with you, I'm going to run across the lot and talk to your pilot. Right now we're missing a chopper."

"No problem, sir. Things are under control."

Krause pulled into the parking lot and circled it twice, looking for security guards and potential witnesses. According to the digital clock on his car radio, he had completed the trip from Griesen to the ski stadium in a little less than thirty minutes. Not as fast as he had promised Krueger, but not too shabby considering the unexpected traffic on the Bundesstraße 23.

Thankfully, the helicopter was right where it was supposed to be. Parked on the far side of the lot, it sat in the middle of several empty spaces. The pilot, a middle-aged German with a military haircut and dark aviator sunglasses, stood beside the chopper like the cocky owner of a new Corvette. Every once in a while, he took a cloth out of his back pocket and removed a speck of dirt, whether real or imagined, from the side of his shiny toy. Whether the pilot was killing time or trying to impress tourists, his actions reminded Krause of his stint in the German Army. While Krueger and Krause were busting their humps over treacherous terrain, the pretty flyboys used to swoop into town and dazzle all the *fräuleins* in the local beer halls. No matter what he did or said, he simply couldn't compete with their tales of aerial assault.

To this day, he still harbored a grudge.

Earlier, when Krause had agreed to Krueger's terms on

the phone, he wasn't sure how he was going to prevent the helicopter from taking off, but one look at that Tom Cruise, Top Gun–wannabe motherfucker sealed the deal. Instead of damaging the chopper, he would damage the pilot, making sure that asshole never flew again.

Smiling to himself, Krause unlocked the stainless-steel case on his passenger seat. Inside was a Beretta 92FS, three magazine clips, and a custom-fitted sound suppressor. All five items were packed in soft-cell polyethylene, cut specifically to the dimensions of his gear. With a practiced hand, Krause pulled out the handgun, attached the silencer—just like he used to do before bank jobs and home invasions—and inserted a clip.

If all went well, Krause would be back in his car in less than five minutes. After that, he would go home and get drunk in celebration—his debt to Krueger finally paid.

While jogging to the chopper, Jones saw Krause get out of his car but thought nothing of it. No visible weapons. No fidgety behavior. No hat or mask to conceal his identity. The guy looked normal, like hundreds of other people in Garmisch-Partenkirchen, so Jones ignored him and focused his attention on the pilot. The two of them had spoken briefly on the radio, right after Jones had replaced Collins in the bird's nest above the bunker.

Jones said, "We'll be coming out shortly. Are you ready to go?"

The pilot nodded. "Just say the word, and I'll start her up."

"Wait until you see us coming. The less attention we draw, the better."

"Will do."

"Where's the other chopper?"

He shrugged. "I don't know. I flew up Mount Schachen like you told me to, and I spoke to the other pilot. What's his name—Bobby, Billy . . . ?"

"Baptiste," Jones said.

"That's the guy! Anyway, he said he couldn't leave until he got permission from Ulster, and he was somewhere inside the house. Everyone's got a boss, you know?"

"And?"

The pilot leaned against the chopper. "Then he hustled off to get permission. That's the last time I saw the guy. I wasn't about to wait for his ass. My boss was down here."

Jones quickly did some math in his head. If Payne and Richter, who were big physical specimens, survived the gorge, there was no way everyone could fit in the helicopter. On a short journey, the chopper could seat five. But on a trip across the Alps? Four would be pushing it, considering the size of the men. Right now there were six potential passengers (Payne, Jones, Kaiser, Huber, Richter, and the pilot), and that didn't include the crates or the weapons.

"We're screwed without the other chopper. No way we can make it out together." Jones explained the numbers, and the pilot agreed with his assessment. "As soon as Kaiser comes out, we'll load him and the cargo and get you out of here. Where are you headed?"

"To one of his warehouses in Austria. We can arrange medical from there."

"Sounds good. I'll stick around for the two in the gorge. If Baptiste shows up, we'll take the chopper out. If he doesn't, we'll improvise."

"What does that mean?"

Jones was about to explain when a glint of movement caught his eye. Glancing at the cockpit window, he spotted a man's reflection; someone was approaching him from behind. Jones turned at the same moment that Krause pulled out his gun. It had been tucked in the interior pocket of his windbreaker, which had prevented the pilot from seeing it until it was too late.

While Krause raised his Beretta and pulled the trigger, Jones dropped to his knee and fired a single shot from his Sig Sauer. The two bullets, fired at roughly the same time, passed each other in flight. Krause's shot hit the pilot in the center of his neck. It tore through his windpipe and spinal cord before it embedded itself in the side of the chopper. The pilot dropped instantly, skidding down the chopper door while leaving a trail of blood. Krause hit the ground a split second later with a bullet hole through the bridge of his nose.

Although both shots were highly effective, there was a major difference between the two weapons that had fired them. Krause's gun had a silencer that muffled the sound of his blast, whereas Jones's gun did not. The unmistakable sound of gunfire rippled across the parking lot and was heard by dozens of tourists. A moment earlier, they had been walking to the ski stadium. Now they were running for cover.

Huber heard the shot from his position outside the cableway. He had just loaded Kaiser into the back of a snow-cat, a fully tracked vehicle that was designed to groom ski trails and haul out injured skiers. It didn't move very fast, but it could climb a mountain of ice. Another two minutes and the cargo would have been loaded next to him, and he could have been on his way. Unfortunately, the gun blast on the other side of the parking lot had spooked his work-force before they could finish the job. The French surgeon ran first, which was understandable since the ambush at the intersection was still fresh in his mind, and was soon followed by the Japanese, who actually took a moment to bow in apology before they sprinted into the station.

Once they were gone, Huber was on the sidewalk alone. Just him and the four crates.

46

In close combat, elite soldiers are taught to check on the enemy before tending to their own. The rationale is simple: Threats need to be eliminated as soon as possible to prevent further casualties. With that in mind, Jones kicked the weapon out of Krause's hand and checked his pulse before he rushed back to the pilot's side. As suspected, both men were dead.

Jones cursed loudly, upset that he hadn't detected a problem sooner. Then again, there was only so much he could do against a faceless opponent with unknown motives. Spotting soldiers with rifles was one thing, but men with silencers was quite another. Suddenly, the game had changed. From this point forward, everyone would be treated as a threat.

"What happened?" Huber asked over the radio.

Jones spotted Huber near the cableway station, then replied via radio. "Some bastard in a windbreaker just killed your pilot."

"The pilot's *dead*? What do we do now?"

"Don't worry, I can fly this thing. But we need to leave A-SAP." Jones scanned the area for police. Because of his gunshot, the clock was ticking. "What's your status?"

"Our patient's loaded, but the cargo isn't."

"Why not?"

"You scared away my volunteers."

Jones pointed at the enclosed cabin of the snowcat. He could see someone cowering in the front seat. "Not everyone. What about your driver?"

"What driver?" The answer came to him a moment later. Jones was talking about the guy who had retrieved the snowcat from the ski stadium. "Oh shit! I forgot about him. I'm sure he'll be happy to help—especially if I ask nicely."

"Nicely, meanly, whatever it takes. You've got two minutes to load that thing."

"Yes, sir," Huber said.

"In the meantime, I'll clean this mess and start the bird. Call me if there's trouble."

Even though space was limited, Jones picked up the dead pilot and dumped him inside the chopper. As it was, two of Kaiser's men, Schneider and Collins, were left on the mountain because he didn't have time to deal with their bodies. Those were two major leads for the police to follow. There was no way he was going to leave a third.

Next he searched the pockets of the gunman but found nothing of value. After grabbing the Beretta, Jones dashed to where the guy had parked and snapped a photo of his license plate. If he'd had more time, he would have searched the car for the gunman's wallet or registration, but he knew a picture on his camera phone would have to suffice.

While heading back to the chopper, Jones heard a garbled transmission on his radio. He answered it immediately, expecting an issue at the cableway. "What's wrong?"

"Leav . . . will . . . ortly."

He turned toward the station and saw Huber loading a crate into the back of the snowcat. Obviously, it wasn't coming from him. "Please repeat."

". . . the gorge . . . shortly."

Jones smiled when he heard the word *gorge*. It was a message from Payne. "You're breaking up. Please repeat. Over."

Thirty seconds passed before Payne tried again. This time his transmission was much clearer. "We're leaving . . . gorge now. We'll be there shortly."

"Glad to hear it. How big is the guest list?"

"Two."

"Stay alert. A civilian just tried to take us out."

"Civilians in play. Check."

"See ya soon. Over and out."

Jones opened the door to the cockpit and was about to climb inside when he heard a loud rumble behind him. He turned and spotted the source of the sound. The snowcat with its tanklike tracks was pulling away from the station. Huber was standing in the back with his G36, surveying the parking lot like a gunner on an armored fighting vehicle.

Suddenly, Bavaria resembled Baghdad.

Minus the sand and those pesky terrorists.

Jones added to the tumult by starting the helicopter. The whooshing of the blades and the roar of the turbines fueled the adrenaline that surged through his body. A few years had passed since he had flown a chopper overseas, and that had been in Italy while trying to evade the Milanese police during his first archaeological mission. Less than twenty-four hours later, he and Payne toured the Ulster Archives for the very first time. Since then, Jones had logged hundreds of hours of flight time at military bases across the United States as part of an agreement he had reached with the Pentagon. He used their equipment, and they used him as a consultant.

With the helicopter ready to go, Jones hopped out of the cockpit and greeted Huber at the side door. The driver of the snowcat, a young man in his early twenties, parked the vehicle thirty feet away since he wasn't sure if it would fit under the chopper blades. Then he climbed out of the cabin and walked around back without having to be asked or threatened. Either the kid had a huge set of marbles, or he had been scared into submission at the cableway.

Huber leaned close and shouted into Jones's ear. "I heard your transmission. When our friends arrive, we're gonna be too heavy."

Jones shouted back. "That's not your problem. Load the chopper."

Huber nodded and hustled to get Kaiser.

From the parking lot, Jones could see Payne and Richter in the distance. They were hoofing it across a small courtyard that led to the Olympic ski stadium. By Jones's calculations, their journey had covered approximately two miles over harsh terrain. After all of that running, they deserved a lounge chair and a bottle of water, not a dose of bad news. Unfortunately, that's what Jones would greet them with. Because of weight restrictions, there wasn't room for them on the chopper. Even if they dumped the pilot, one of them would be left behind. Originally, Jones had planned to stick around with Payne, but that was no longer possible because of the pilot's death.

Payne and Richter were out of breath when they reached the chopper. While gasping for air, Payne pointed to the man, who was crumpled in a puddle of blood. "What happened?"

Jones answered. "He killed the pilot, so I took him out."

"Fair enough. Where's Petr?"

"Don't know. He never came back from Schachen."

"Did you try his radio?"

"He doesn't have one."

Payne shook his head. "I meant chopper to chopper."

"Didn't want to risk it. Too many ears."

"What's our status?"

"Bird's ready to fly, but we're too heavy."

"By how much?"

"Two men."

He took it in stride. "You flying?"

Jones shrugged. "I'm the only one who can."

Payne nodded and pointed at Huber, who was loading

the last crate into the chopper. "How's your guard? Is he any good?"

"Yeah, why?"

"If you're making me walk, we need to trade. I get Huber, you get Richter."

"Why?"

"Long story. I'll tell you later."

"Hold up! Is there something I should know?"

Payne nodded. "Keep Richter away from witnesses."

Jones waved Huber over to explain the situation. Suddenly, the downdraft around them increased, as did the roar of the turbines. Worried that something was wrong, Jones turned toward the cockpit and spotted the culprit fifty feet away. The extra wind and noise were coming from Ulster's helicopter, which was hovering nearby and preparing to land. The sound of its approach had been masked completely until it was almost on top of them.

Payne smiled when he saw the chopper. His escape just got a whole lot easier. "Where are we headed?"

Jones answered. "Some warehouse in Austria. Huber knows where."

"Then try to keep up."

"Not a problem."

Payne patted Huber on his shoulder. "You're with me. Richter stays with Kaiser."

"Yes, sir."

"Is everything loaded?"

"Yes, sir."

"Then follow me."

Payne led the way to the other chopper, where they were met by Ulster. As bubbly as ever, he greeted each of them with a hearty handshake.

"What took you so long?" Payne asked.

Ulster apologized. "Sorry about the delay. We ran into a small problem."

Payne slammed the hatch shut, then collapsed into one of the leather seats, where he planned on snoozing until they got to Austria. Compared to the belly of Kaiser's chopper, they would be flying in style. "A problem? What kind of problem?"

Before he could answer, Heidi waved at Payne from the front seat. "Hey, Jon."

Ulster smiled sheepishly. "A female problem."

47

❁

Even though Payne had enjoyed chatting with Heidi at the King's House on Schachen, he was noticeably upset by her presence in the chopper.

He growled at Ulster. "What in the hell is she doing here?"

Ulster lowered his eyes in shame. "I'm sorry, Jonathon. I had no choice."

"Of course you had a choice! You could have left her on the mountain."

Heidi spoke up. "Actually, no, he couldn't."

Payne glared at her. "Am I talking to you?"

Heidi glared back. "Well, you are *now*. Which is how it should have been all along. If you're mad at me, yell at me. Don't take it out on Petr."

Ulster shrugged but said nothing.

Payne lowered his voice to a whisper. "Petr, what is she doing here?"

Heidi heard the question and yelled over Ulster's shoulder. "You're doing it again! Talk to me, Jon. Not Petr."

Payne gently pushed Ulster back into his seat and focused his attention on Heidi. "Fine! I'll talk to you directly, since you're not giving me any other choice. Why in the hell are you on this chopper?"

"Why? Because I figured out what you're doing."

"Really? And what the hell is that?"

She smirked. "You're looking for the black swan treasure."

Payne took a deep breath and leaned back in his seat. After staying silent for a few seconds, he turned toward Huber, who was sitting next to him. Both of them were covered in blood and grime after spending the last hour fighting for their lives. "Can you believe this shit? She's yelling at me after everything we just went through. *This* is why I'm not married."

Huber shook his head. "Typical woman."

Heidi reacted instantly. The comment upset her so much she nearly jumped out of the front seat to get in Huber's face. The only things that kept her in place were her shoulder harness and the reprimand from Baptiste, who was trying to fly the chopper out of the valley.

Huber laughed at her behavior. "The defense rests."

She twisted in her seat and pointed at Huber. "I don't like you."

Huber shrugged and closed his eyes. "The feeling's mutual."

Then she pointed at Payne. "And I expected more from you."

He pointed at himself. "You expected more from *me*? What the hell does that mean?"

"You were so nice and sweet up at the house. Now you're acting like a jerk."

Payne took another deep breath, trying to calm the anger that was bubbling inside. Adrenaline from the battlefield was still flowing through his veins, making it difficult to control his emotions. It was one of the reasons the U.S. military had instituted a cool-down period before missions were debriefed. "Listen, I don't know what you said or did to con your way onto this chopper, but you don't know jack shit about what we're doing."

"Sure I do!" she snapped. "You're looking for a treasure, just like the one you found in Greece. Trust me, Jon, I know all about you, and David, and Petr. I know *everything*."

For Payne, that was the final straw. He simply couldn't take any more of her chirping. So he leapt out of his seat, pushed his way past Ulster, who was sitting in the middle row, and knelt in the aisle behind Heidi. From his position on the floor, he pointed at the blood on the front of his shirt. "You *think* you know everything, huh? Do you know about Collins? He was minding his own business, driving our ATV through the woods, when a gunman shot him in the side of the head. The bullet plowed through his skull and brain, killing him instantly."

She gulped at the description.

He pointed at a different stain. "Then there was Lange. Do you know about Lange? Ten seconds after Collins died, Lange was killed by automatic fire from an assault rifle. Hit him right in the throat. Good soldier, that Lange. He lost his life while trying to save ours."

"Hooah!" Huber said from the back.

"Then there was Schneider. Do you know what happened to Schneider? I'm going to guess you don't because *I* don't even know what happened to Schneider. One minute he was calling in a status report, the next he wasn't. Just like that, his radio went silent. Of course, we're assuming he's dead because his weapon was the one that killed Lange!"

Her face turned ashen as horror filled her eyes. "Why are you telling me this?"

"*Why?* Because you think this is a game. You *think* we're looking for a treasure! We're not looking for a fucking treasure. We're trying to leave Germany before someone else gets killed. And guess what? Since you managed to talk your way onto the escape chopper, you're coming with us—whether you want to or not."

She nodded but said nothing.

Payne was about to return to his seat when he thought of one final thing to say. When he spoke, his voice was much calmer than a moment before. "So you want to know why I'm angry and acting like a jerk? It's *not* because I hate you. It's because you talked your way into something that you knew nothing about. Now your life is in danger like the rest of ours. I wish that wasn't the case—I truly do. But those are the cards that we've been dealt, and we have no choice but to play them."

She grimaced at the poker analogy. Somehow it seemed fitting.

He pointed toward the rear of the chopper. "Now, unless you have something else to say, I'm going back there to decompress. After the morning I've had, I'm pretty sure I've earned it."

When Payne opened his eyes, the chopper was on the ground somewhere in Austria. He didn't know where and didn't really care as long as they were safe. Glancing out the open hatch, he saw Jones standing in the middle of a spacious hangar. Crates filled a third of the place, while the rest of it was empty. From the looks of things, they were in one of Kaiser's storage facilities.

Payne stood, and stretched, and felt like a new man. Although the loss of life had taken an emotional toll, it was the two-mile sprint that had wiped him out.

Jones saw him and approached. "Look who's back from the dead."

"How long was I out?"

"Unfortunately, you missed Christmas."

"Did you get me something nice?"

"A sweater made from reindeer fur. You'll love it!"

Payne smiled. "How's Kaiser doing?"

"He's okay. He's on his way to some private medical facility that's on retainer. Huber and Richter just left. They pulled out about five minutes ago."

"Why didn't you wake me?"

Jones laughed. "Why? Because I heard you had a hissy fit on the way here. Petr thought it might be best if we let you rest."

Payne shook his head. "Give me a break. I didn't have

a hissy fit. I gave an impassioned account of our current status. No more, no less."

"Like I said, a *hissy fit*!"

"Whatever."

Jones patted him on the back. "I have to admit, I was kind of surprised when I saw Heidi. That's a curveball I didn't expect."

"The question is, what do we do with her?"

Jones made sure no one else was listening. "I'll tell you what I'd like to do to her. That girl is gorgeous!"

"For the record, I said *with* her. I didn't say *to* her."

"With her, to her, in her, behind her—they're *all* prepositions. As long as she's having fun, what's the difference?"

Payne rolled his eyes. "Before you run to the store to buy whipped cream, don't you think we should clean up our mess first?"

"I thought I did that when I torched the bunker."

"Did you wipe down the ATV?"

Jones shook his head. "Nope."

"What about that guy you shot?"

"Which guy?"

"The one in the parking lot."

"What about him?"

"Did you get the slug from his head?"

"Nope. Not enough time."

"Which gun did you use?"

Jones grimaced. "My Sig."

"Like I said, we've got a mess to clean up."

"I guess you're right. What did you have in mind?"

Payne smiled. "Don't worry. I'll handle it."

48

❖

Kaiser's Warehouse
Innsbruck, Austria

After punching in the code to unlock his encrypted cell phone, Payne entered the phone number from memory. In his line of work, contact lists could get people killed.

His friend answered on the third ring. "This is Dial."

"Hey, Nick, it's Jonathon Payne."

Nick Dial leaned back in his office chair and grinned. He hadn't spoken to Payne in almost a month, which was normal for them since their hectic schedules got in the way of their friendship. Born in America but stationed in France, Dial ran the Homicide division at Interpol, the largest international crime-fighting organization in the world. His job was to coordinate the flow of information between police departments anytime a murder investigation crossed national boundaries. All told, he was in charge of 186 member countries, filled with billions of people and hundreds of languages.

Dial asked, "Are you calling to give me shit about your party?"

Payne laughed. Every year he sent Dial an invitation to his end-of-the-summer boat party, even though he knew Dial wouldn't be able to attend. The journey to Pittsburgh was a tad too long. "Come on, Nick. When was the last time I gave you shit about anything?"

"Let me think. When was the last time we talked?"

"Touché."

Dial smiled at his word choice. "Finally, a French word I can understand! I swear, I'd like this country a whole lot better if everyone spoke English."

"Hold up. You live in France and can't speak French?"

"I can speak it just fine. I simply prefer English."

"What about German? Can you speak German?"

"My German is okay, but not great. Why do you ask?"

"Because DJ and I are headed to Oktoberfest."

"Really? Wow, you two party a lot. When are you going?"

"We left Pittsburgh yesterday. We should be in Munich by the end of the week."

Dial pondered the timeline. Something didn't add up. "Please tell me you're not going by boat. If so, I've got some horrible news. Germany is *not* on the water."

Payne played along. "Are you positive? My instructors at the Naval Academy assured me it was. If you're right about this, the Pentagon has several invasion plans they have to change."

Dial laughed. "Glad I could help."

"Speaking of help, something big has come up. Do you have a few minutes to talk?"

"Of course. How sensitive is the information?"

"Very."

"In that case, let me call you from a secure line. Give me two minutes."

"Thanks, Nick. I appreciate it."

Payne hung up, dreading the conversation he was about to have. Over the years, Dial had tied up a lot of loose ends for Payne and Jones. Not because they were his friends or because they had saved his life in Greece while he was investigating the deaths of several monks—although those things didn't hurt. He did it because they were highly trained soldiers whose moral compasses often pointed them into sticky situations. They weren't afraid to get their hands dirty, and he was more than willing to clean up their mess. In fact, Dial had told them on multiple occasions that he wished he had the freedom to do the same thing as them, dispensing justice around the globe.

Regrettably, he spent most of his time in the office, not in the field.

One of the biggest misconceptions about Interpol was their role in stopping crime. They seldom sent agents to investigate a case. Instead, they used local offices called National Central Bureaus in the member countries. The NCBs monitored their territory and reported pertinent information to Interpol's headquarters in Lyon, France. From there, facts were entered into a central database that could be accessed via Interpol's computer network.

But sometimes that wasn't enough. Sometimes the head of a division (Drugs, Counterfeiting, Terrorism, etc.) was forced to take control of a case. Possibly to cut through red tape. Or to handle a border dispute. Or to deal with the international media. All of the things that Dial hated to do. In his line of work, the only thing that mattered to him was *justice*—righting a wrong in the fairest way possible. That was the creed he had lived by when he was an investigator, and it was the creed he followed in his head position at Interpol.

Unfortunately, Payne realized the mess in Bavaria was different from anything he had faced in recent years. Not because he and Jones had done something wrong—after all, they had been attacked by gunmen and simply fought back—but unlike previous cases, one of their allies was a well-known criminal whose involvement would put Dial in a difficult spot.

The question was: How would Dial react?

Payne sat on one of the wooden crates, trying to figure out what he could and couldn't say. His goal was to tell the truth about everything while omitting a few details. He wanted Dial to know what had happened in Bavaria without telling him too much about the bunker. Whether or not he could pull that off remained to be seen. It would depend on Dial's mood.

When his phone rang a few minutes later, the ringtone was no longer the Menudo song it had been in Pittsburgh. It had been replaced by a popular children's song called "Little Bunny Foo Foo," sung by a nursery school teacher who sounded a lot like Angela Lansbury.

Little Bunny Foo Foo,
Hopping through the forest
Scooping up the field mice
And boppin' 'em on the head.

Payne growled softly. When he figured out who was messing with his phone, he was going to bop them on the head—with the butt of a rifle.

"Fucking ringtones," mumbled Payne as he answered.

"*Ringtones*? You made me call you on a secure line to talk about *ringtones*? I thought this was important."

"Sorry, Nick, it's been a long day. DJ and I are lucky to be alive."

"What happened this time?"

Payne explained. "One of my contacts informed me about a possible discovery in the mountains of Germany, one with significant historical value. I notified Petr Ulster, who met us at the site early this morning. About three hours later, we were attacked by a hit squad."

"A hit squad?"

"Multiple gunmen, multiple weapons, no conversation. They simply opened fire."

"Was anybody killed?"

"Some of mine, all of theirs."

Dial groaned. "I'm assuming you're okay. What about DJ and Petr?"

"Both of them are fine."

"Where did this happen?"

"A town called Garmisch-Partenkirchen. It's near the Austrian border."

Dial nodded. "I'm familiar with it."

"They attacked us in the woods, about halfway up the mountain. After that, the battle spread all over the valley. It ended in town near the Olympic ski stadium. A man killed our chopper pilot as we were attempting to leave. We had no choice but to defend ourselves."

"Where are you now?"

"Not there."

Dial read between the lines. For some reason, Payne didn't want to answer. "Give me some numbers. How many suspects?"

"Six, possibly more. Like I said, the battle spread."

"Six confirmed dead?"

"Six of theirs, three of ours."

"But they ambushed you?"

Payne shrugged. "They struck first. We struck back."

Dial took notes, using a cryptic style of shorthand that only he could understand. "Who were these guys? Any ideas?"

"I can send you their names and addresses."

"Excuse me?"

"What can I say? The mountains are huge and filled with wolves. You'll be lucky to find the bodies. We had some time, so we grabbed their IDs. We figured it would help your cause."

"And yours."

Payne smiled. "The thought had crossed my mind."

"What about motivation? Did *that* cross your mind?"

"As a matter of fact, it did. Unfortunately, that's where things get messy."

Dial sighed. "Let me see if I got this straight: Nine bodies scattered across a mountain isn't messy, but their motivation is. Do I even want to know?"

"Trust me, I'd prefer not to tell you, because I'm not quite sure how you're going to react to it. But this is something you need to hear."

49

Payne tried to ease the sting of the information about Kaiser by framing it in the best possible way. "Back when DJ and I were in the military, we had contacts around the globe—people who gave us intelligence or sold us supplies when we were behind enemy lines. Some of them were the scum of the earth—the kind of guys that made your skin crawl—but some of them were pretty solid. Over the years, a few of them even became our friends."

"Where are you going with this?"

"One of those friends is the person who notified us about the possible discovery. He knew we had contacts in the world of antiquities and asked us to contact Petr on his behalf. After weighing the pros and cons, we decided to get involved despite his recent ventures."

Dial connected the dots. "In other words, he's a criminal."

"Yes."

"And you think the ambush has to do with him?"

"I know it does. One of the gunmen told me."

"He told you? Do I even want to know how you obtained this information?"

"Probably not."

"Yeah, you're right."

Payne smiled. So far the conversation had gone better than he had expected. Then again, he still hadn't mentioned the name of his contact. "Here's where things get tricky. The gunman gave me the name of his boss. Apparently, he has a major vendetta against my friend. I don't know all of the specifics, but it sounds like these two are bitter rivals."

"Why don't you ask your friend?"

"I can't. He was seriously hurt during the ambush."

"I'm sorry to hear that."

"Really?"

"Yes, *really*. You might find this hard to believe, but I've befriended a few criminals during my lifetime as well. Back when I was in the Bureau, I had a weekly dinner with this midlevel mafioso. He gave me info about his rivals while I gorged myself with the best pasta I ever ate in my life. After a while, a bond was forged—even though I knew what he did for a living."

"Then you know how it goes."

"Yes, I do. And yet, if I had seen him shoot a man, I would have arrested him. In my mind, there are certain lines that can't be crossed."

"In that case, I'm glad you didn't see me shoot anyone."

Dial smiled. "Let me ask you a question: What's the reason for your call? Clearly, you're telling me all of this for a reason. I'd love to know what it is."

"One of my friends was attacked, and three of his colleagues were killed in cold blood. I want to see the men responsible brought to justice."

"It sounds like you handled that already."

"As far as I know, the boss wasn't there. He's the one I really want."

Dial gave the situation some thought. "Okay, Jon, here's the problem. If you want me to go after the boss, you have to give me his name. After that, I'll track down his associates and rivals, which will lead me to the name of your friend. Is that something he really wants?"

"Trust me, he's already on your radar."

"Really? So he's a big fish?"

"You could say that."

"And his rival?"

"He's a big fish, too."

"Interesting."

"Listen," Payne said, "I didn't call you to be coy. I'm willing to tell you their names right now—as long as you enter one important fact into your database."

"What fact is that?"

"My friend and colleagues are innocent in this particular shooting. They were attacked, plain and simple. I'll vouch for it and so will DJ. Of course, we'd appreciate if you kept our names out of it. Just call us undercover assets, or something like that."

"If the evidence supports it, I'll gladly—"

"You're not hearing me, Nick. There is no evidence. This shooting went down in the middle of the woods. Sure, you might find some shell casings and some bodies, but there's no way in hell you're going to figure anything out without my testimony—especially after the fire."

Dial groaned. "What fire?"

Payne fibbed. "Those bastards torched the site."

"They *what*? Why did they do that?"

"I have no idea. Maybe you should ask them."

"I would if they were still alive."

Payne smiled. It was why he had been willing to stretch the truth. "So, what do you think? Our testimony for their names? Personally, I think it's a pretty sweet deal."

"For you."

"For everyone. Without my testimony, you won't have jack."

"Yeah, well, that remains to be seen."

"I'm telling you, Nick. My friend is innocent in today's events. He was hit early, and he's been unconscious ever since. Plus, you'll *love* the name of his rival. He's a serious player in Germany. I'm sure his name will cause some boners in Berlin."

Dial mulled his options. If Payne was painting an accurate picture of the crime scene, the name of a suspect would jump-start the local investigation and would do wonders with the German authorities. Anytime multiple people were killed in a tourist town, there was more to worry about than the loss of life. The local economy was also at stake—especially with ski season around the corner.

"Fine! Give me their names. But if I find out your friend

started this bullshit, I'm coming after him. Then I'm coming after you."

"Damn, Nick, I just got chills."

"I'm serious, Jon."

"I'm serious, too. You're a scary man!"

Dial couldn't help but laugh. "Give me their names before I change my mind."

"You got it. The man you're looking for is Hans Mueller. Have you heard of him?"

Dial nodded. "Of course I've heard of him. He's a major player in the world of smuggling. From what I've heard, he's one sick bastard. If you cross him, you're pretty much fucked."

"Which explains today's ambush. Like I said, he considers my friend his number one rival. Apparently, he's been trying to take him out for a while."

Dial gave it some thought. "Which means your friend is Kaiser."

Payne grew silent. "Damn."

"What can I say? I'm good at my job."

"Honestly, I'm glad you guessed it. Now I can tell him I didn't mention his name."

"Speaking of names, you promised me the names and addresses of Mueller's men. Do you have those with you?"

Payne shook his head. "DJ has them. I'll have him snap pictures of their IDs and send them to your office e-mail."

"That's fine, but make it quick. The sooner I have them, the better."

"No problem."

"Is there anything else? Or can I get the ball rolling?"

"Actually, there is one more thing. Probably the most important thing of all."

"Good Lord, what now?"

Payne laughed. "I wanted you to know we're still planning to go to Oktoberfest. If you can sneak away for a day, we'd love to get together. Believe it or not, DJ said he's buying."

Dial smiled at the thought. "DJ's buying? In that case, I'll see what I can do."

50

✣

Payne hung up as he strolled across the warehouse floor. Ulster and Heidi were nowhere to be seen, but Jones greeted him in the middle of the facility.

"How'd the call go?" Jones asked.

"Not bad at all."

"Is it my imagination, or did I hear 'Little Bunny Foo Foo'?"

Payne snapped at him. "Screw you."

"Screw *me*? What did I do?"

"What do you think you did? Quit messing with my phone."

Jones was surprised by the accusation. "Your phone? When could I have messed with your phone? Would that have been while I was driving the ATV from the ambush, or when I was hauling Kaiser down the mountain? Oh, I know! It was when I was flying the chopper here. Yeah, that's when I had time to mess with your phone."

Payne stared at him. It was obvious Jones was telling the truth. "Sorry, man, my bad. You're always messing with my stuff. I just assumed it was you."

"Well, it wasn't me."

"In that case, I feel bad about my revenge."

"Your revenge? What did you do?"

Payne smiled. "I invited Nick to Oktoberfest and told him you were buying."

Jones shrugged. "As far as revenge goes, that was pretty weak—especially since Kaiser's paying for our trip anyway."

Payne glanced around the warehouse. "Speaking of Kaiser, I think we should clear out of this place as soon as possible. There's no telling what he's storing here."

"I couldn't agree more. We already loaded the crates into Petr's chopper."

"All of them?"

Jones nodded. "Nothing against Richter and Huber, but I think the gold will be a lot safer at the Archives than it would be here. Besides, I think Petr wants to examine it closer. He's hoping it will provide some insight into Ludwig's treasure."

"And Heidi?"

"I don't know about Petr, but I'd love to examine her closer."

Payne rolled his eyes. "Yeah, yeah, yeah. You think she's attractive. How long are you going to keep this up?"

"With her, I'll keep it up all night!"

Payne started to walk away. "Let me know when you grow up."

"Says the man with 'Little Bunny Foo Foo' as his ring-tone."

Payne flipped him off and kept walking toward a small office in the back of the facility. He heard voices coming from the room. He assumed they belonged to Heidi and Ulster. The door was partially closed, so Payne knocked on it before he entered.

"Come in," Ulster said.

Heidi was sitting next to him on an upholstered couch that reeked of cigarettes. She had a bottle of water in one hand and a tissue in the other. From her bloodshot eyes and damp cheeks, it was obvious she had been crying, although she tried to cover it up. As soon as she saw Payne, she tucked the tissue into her pocket and wiped her cheeks with her sleeve.

"Are you all right?" Payne asked.

"I will be once I get something off my chest."

He folded his arms in front of him. "Go on."

"Sit down, if you'd like."

"That's okay. I'm fine right here."

She nodded in understanding. If she had been in his position, she probably would have acted in the same way. "This is hard for me, Jon. I mean, if you knew anything about me, you would know how tough this is for me to do. I don't like to admit this, but I come from a long line of ill-tempered, stubborn people. My parents were that way, and so were my grandparents—on both sides of my family.

You should hear us during the holidays. Either we're sulking in silence, or we're at each other's throats. There's no middle ground with my family."

She glanced at him, but he said nothing.

"Anyway, as hard as this is for me to say, I just wanted to tell you I'm sorry."

"For what?" he asked.

"For the way I acted on the chopper. For even being on the chopper. Everything you said was one hundred percent correct. I can understand why you got so mad."

He pointed at Ulster. "What about Petr?"

"What about him?"

"Did you apologize to Petr?"

She nodded. "I did. I told him I was sorry for tricking him into bringing me."

Ulster confirmed it. "Her apology was quite eloquent. It moved me to tears."

"Me, too," she admitted.

Payne pointed at them. "You're back on good terms?"

They looked at each other and nodded.

"Then I'm good, too." Payne turned to leave the office. "Chopper's leaving in five."

"Excuse me?" she blurted as she sprang off the couch.

He turned back and faced her. "What's wrong now?"

"What do you mean it's leaving in five?"

"Did I stutter? The chopper is leaving in five minutes. Please be on it."

"Where's it going?" she demanded.

"Switzerland."

"Switzerland? I'm not going to Switzerland."

Payne laughed. "Really?"

She folded her arms in front of her chest. "Yes, really."

"You're telling me you'd prefer to stay here? By yourself?"

She took a deep breath. "Yes."

Payne laughed louder. "You're such a hypocrite."

"A hypocrite? Why am I a hypocrite?"

"Unless I'm mistaken, didn't you just apologize for your temper and your stubbornness? Thirty seconds later, you're back to the same stubborn behavior."

"I'm not being stubborn. I'm being smart. Like you said, I have no business being on your chopper. I figure the sooner I get away from you, the safer I'll be."

"You still don't get it, do you?"

"Get what?"

"What you're mixed up in?"

"Apparently not."

Payne pointed at the couch. "Please, sit down."

"Why?"

"Why? Because I'm sick of arguing with you about every little thing. If this is going to work, all of us need to be on the same page. Personally, I'd rather hash it out now than fight with you all damn day. I just don't have the energy."

Heidi nodded and took a seat next to Ulster. "Okay."

Payne pulled up an office chair. "Tell me, do you know where you are?"

She shrugged. "Somewhere near Innsbruck."

He made a buzzer sound. "Sorry. Wrong answer."

"No, it's not. I recognized the city when we flew in."

"Actually, it's a wrong answer for a completely different reason. It's a wrong answer because your response could have gotten you killed."

"What? What do you mean?"

"I mean, the man who owns this warehouse would be furious over your response. If his guards had been smart, they would have blindfolded you so you wouldn't know the location of this place. But they were dumb, so now you're a threat to his whole organization."

"Whose organization?"

"A man you don't want to meet. Which is why I can't leave you here. For the time being, you're far safer with us than you would be alone—at least until I have a chance to talk to him."

Ulster nodded. "The Archives are protected by a team of armed guards around the clock. In addition, we recently installed a large panic room with enough food and water to last a month. If anyone comes looking for us, we'll be perfectly safe until November."

"Not that we're expecting trouble," Payne assured her. "In fact, I just got off the phone with my contact at Interpol. They're already hunting the man responsible for today's skirmish. With any luck, they'll have him in a day or two. After that, everything will be fine."

"Then what?" she demanded.

Prior to falling asleep on the flight to Austria, Payne had given the topic a lot of thought. If the violence in Bavaria had nothing to do with the contents of the bunker and everything to do with the gang war between Kaiser and Mueller, then the odds were pretty good that they could search for the treasure without any additional bloodshed. He'd still keep his guard up until he was back in America, but he figured as long as they stayed away from Garmisch-Partenkirchen, they didn't have a lot to worry about.

Payne said, "If you're up to it, I figured we could look for Ludwig's treasure. It would be a shame to stop our search because of a little ambush."

Her eyes lit up. "You mean it?"

"I don't see why not. From what Petr says, you're one of the leading experts in the field. Of course, you're the one who told him that, so who knows if it's true?"

She put her hand over her heart. "I swear it's true!"

"We'll find out soon enough. That is, if you'll be joining us."

She nodded enthusiastically. "Yes, I'll be joining you."

"In that case, you need to promise us something: no more games."

"I promise, Jon. No more games."

Payne stared at her. She seemed sincere. "I'm serious, Heidi. If we catch you in a lie or feel like you're manipulating us in any way, you'll lose our protection. Do you understand what that means?"

She gulped. "Yes, I understand."

Payne smiled. "Good. The chopper leaves in five."

51

✤

Küsendorf, Switzerland
(82 miles southeast of Bern)

The Ulster Archives were nestled against a sturdy outcropping of rock that shielded the wooden fortress from the Alpine winds that roared through the region during winter. Nut-brown timber made up the bulk of the chalet's framework and blended perfectly with the broad gables and deep overhangs of the roof. Square windows were cut into the front façade at regular intervals and were complemented by a triangular pane that had been carved under the structure's crown. A large picture window ran vertically through the middle of the chalet, giving people on the main staircase a spectacular view of the Lepontine Alps.

But Petr Ulster ignored the scenery as he trudged down the steps from the document vaults on the upper floors toward his private office. It was a journey he typically made several times a day, moving from room to room, helping researchers from around the world with their pursuit of historical data. Although he didn't consider himself an expert in any particular field, Ulster had a working knowledge of every significant historical subject from A to Z.

It was a skill set that served him well as curator of the facility.

Expecting to find his freshly showered guests in his office, Ulster was drawn toward the kitchen by the sound of laughter and the smell of freshly baked bread. Inside the spacious room, he saw Payne, Jones, and Heidi huddled around a plate of meats and cheeses. Standing next to them was Ulster's private chef, who was slicing a warm loaf while arguing with Jones.

"That isn't possible!" the chef blurted. "I don't believe you for a second."

Ulster looked at them, confused. "What isn't possible?"

Jones ignored the question. "I'm telling you, we jumped out of the helicopter while holding on to salami. We slid over a hundred feet, right into some trees."

Payne nodded. "If you don't believe us, ask Baptiste. He was flying."

The chef glanced at Ulster. "Sir, is that what happened?"

Ulster shrugged. "I don't know. I wasn't there. But it wouldn't surprise me. When the chopper landed to pick us up, Baptiste had to reel in a very long rope that smelled like fried salami. I thought I was imagining things, but perhaps not."

Jones laughed while patting Ulster on his belly. "Your

picnic basket saved some lives. Your stomach should be proud of its sacrifice."

Ulster grabbed a slice of bread. "In that case, I'll reward it."

Payne pointed at the food. "I hope you don't mind. We were waiting for you in your office, but we smelled the bread and couldn't resist. It's tough to think when you're hungry."

Ulster smiled. "Why do you think my office is so close to the kitchen?"

Once they had eaten, they went back to Ulster's office, where a research assistant had dropped off several books about Ludwig's life. All but one were written in German. The lone exception was a coffee-table book with English captions. It was filled with photographs of Ludwig's castles, including some taken during their construction.

Payne studied one of the pictures. "I wasn't expecting to see that."

"See what?" Ulster asked from his desk.

"Pictures of the building site."

"Why not?" Heidi asked as she peered over his shoulder. She instantly recognized the slim towers of Neuschwanstein underneath the scaffolding.

"When I think of castles, I think of ancient buildings that were built long before the age of photography. Then again, what do I know? We don't have many castles in America. We're too young of a country to have ancient ruins."

"Have you seen photographs of Abraham Lincoln?" she asked.

Payne nodded. "Several."

She walked around the couch and sat next to him. "They started building Neuschwanstein a few years *after* Lincoln's death—if that helps you understand the time period."

"Actually, it does."

Heidi tapped the photograph. "Ludwig built Neuschwanstein on the site of two medieval castles that had fallen into disrepair. To clear the way, they used explosives to blow up the old remains before they hauled everything away. The very next year, they laid the foundation stone of the new castle. The date was September 5, 1869."

Jones glanced at the book from the far end of the couch and noticed the date at the bottom of the page. Wondering if she had seen it or was quoting information from memory, he decided to test her expertise. "Who designed the castle?"

She looked at him. "An artist named Christian Jank. Believe it or not, he wasn't a trained architect. He was actually a stage designer for Richard Wagner's opera *Lohengrin*. Ludwig was so moved by Jank's artwork that he commissioned him to create several concepts of a dream castle. Ludwig selected a design that he liked, and the two of them worked on it together."

"Without an architect? That doesn't sound safe," Jones said.

She explained. "Ludwig eventually hired Eduard Riedel, a German architect who had restored Berg Castle for

Maximilian II, to make sure the plans were safe. However, Riedel was just the first of many. Over the next few years, a number of architects worked on the plans, including Georg von Dollmann and Julius Hofmann."

"Why so many architects?"

"Two reasons," she said. "One, because Ludwig was a control freak. He changed his mind all the time and every new draft required his personal approval. This was unbelievably frustrating for the architects, especially when Ludwig disappeared for days on one of his journeys. Sometimes construction stopped while they were waiting for his authorization."

"What was the other reason?" Payne asked.

"The construction took nearly twenty years. That's a long time to work with a crazy person."

Jones nodded in agreement. "I worked with Jon less than a decade, and it felt like *forever*. Twenty years would have killed me."

Payne smiled but said nothing.

"Sadly," she added, "that's one of the reasons it took so long to build the castle. Thirty people died during its construction—mostly because Ludwig was so demanding around self-imposed deadlines. Occasionally, when he made urgent changes to the designs, he had as many as three hundred workers at the site, working in shifts around the clock. They used to set up oil lamps on the scaffolding so they wouldn't have to stop at night."

"They must have hated him," Jones said.

She shook her head. "Despite the challenging conditions, the locals loved Ludwig because he was the biggest

employer in the region by a wide margin. Without
Neuschwanstein, many of the craftsmen would have been
out of work. That carried a lot of weight with them."

Payne glanced at her. "If I remember correctly, you said
Neuschwanstein means 'new swan stone' in English."

She stared at him, trying to read the emotions in his
eyes. But it was difficult. He was a much better poker
player than Ulster. "That's correct."

"What else can you tell us about the name?"

"That depends. What are you keeping from me?"

"What do you mean?"

She sighed, frustrated. "I mean, it's a simple translation
of three German words—*neu*, *schwan*, and *stein*. You
didn't need me to tell you that. Petr could have told you
the same thing. He speaks German, too."

"What's your point?" Payne demanded.

"My point is you asked me about the translation on
Schachen. When I explained it to you, your eyes lit up
when I mentioned the word *swan*. Then you huddled with
DJ to discuss it when I took Petr inside the house."

"And?"

"And I want to know why. Otherwise, I won't be much
help to your search. Not because I'll *refuse* to help you. I
simply won't be *able* to help."

Payne glanced around the room. First he looked at
Jones, who nodded his approval. Then he looked at Ulster,
who enthusiastically did the same. Finally, he looked at
Heidi, who was staring at him with her light blue eyes. He
didn't know her very well, but he was starting to understand how she had convinced Ulster to talk about Lud-

wig's treasure. She was smart, perceptive, and very observant. He was glad she was on their side.

Payne asked, "Are you familiar with Petr's grandfather?"

She nodded. "I unknowingly quoted him earlier today."

"Recently, we discovered some of Conrad's belongings. In one of his notebooks, he had written some clues that are supposed to lead us to Ludwig's treasure."

"What kind of clues?" she asked.

"The first one is a riddle that uses the word *swan*. That's why we keep asking you about Neuschwanstein. We thought maybe he hid the treasure there."

"I highly doubt it," she said.

"Why's that?" Jones asked.

"Because Ludwig was murdered before the building was finished."

Ulster questioned her from across the room. "Are you sure, my dear? Wasn't Ludwig staying there on the night of his arrest?"

She nodded. "Ludwig lived in the palace for a hundred and seventy-two days, but the castle was far from done. Only fourteen rooms were finished before his death. The rest of the building was filled with workers, struggling to complete the project. I highly doubt he would have hidden a treasure with so many witnesses around."

Payne agreed with her. "You're probably right."

Jones cursed. "I guess that means we should cross it off our list."

She stared at them. "Before you do, don't you think you should tell me the riddle? I know you guys don't fully

trust me, but didn't you say several clues needed to be
solved in order to locate the treasure? What's the harm in
telling me the first one? It's not like I'm going anywhere.
I'm stuck on a mountain in the middle of Switzerland."

Jones glanced at Payne. "She has a point."

Ulster nodded in agreement. "I concur."

Payne pointed at Ulster. "Conrad was your grandfather.
You should tell her, not me."

Ulster grinned with satisfaction. He was touched by the
gesture. "On the surface, the riddle seems fairly straight-
forward, but we haven't figured it out yet. We'd love a
fresh set of ears."

"What's the riddle?" she asked.

"Where would a swan go on his journey home?"

52

❦

Heidi closed her eyes and leaned back on the couch. Wearing a colorful ski sweater she had found in Ulster's guest closet and her initial pair of jeans, she whispered the riddle to herself, trying to decipher its meaning. After several seconds of this, her eyes popped open—only to realize that Payne, Jones, and Ulster were staring at her, patiently waiting for her response.

"Sorry," she said. "I've got nothing."

Jones mumbled to Payne. "Expert, my ass."

Heidi didn't hear his comment but quickly amended her statement. "Actually, let me take that back. I've got nothing *definitive*. Plenty of possibilities, but nothing definitive."

"How many possibilities?" Ulster asked.

"At least ten, maybe fifteen."

"Fifteen? We came up with less than five."

She stared at Ulster, who was sitting behind his desk. "As you know, Ludwig was fascinated with swans. They were an important part of his life from his childhood to his death. That's a whole lot of ground to cover. I only wish I had more information so I could narrow it down."

Payne, Jones, and Ulster exchanged a series of glances, much as they had done when they were deciding if Heidi was worthy of the riddle. This immediately got her thinking about their visit to the King's House and the questions they had asked up there.

"Just a second," she blurted. "Up on Mount Schachen, you were asking me about local lakes. Is that because of the riddle, or does that have to do with another clue?"

Jones answered. "That had to do with the riddle. We thought maybe there was a special lake up there where he watched swans."

She pointed at them, one at a time, when she spoke. "Then what was all that glancing back and forth that you just did? I've seen those looks before. You're hiding something."

Payne looked at her. "Will you stop doing that?"

"Doing what?"

"Reading our minds. It's really annoying."

She smiled. "Sorry. In case you haven't figured it out, I'm stubborn, ill tempered, and paranoid. I hit the genetic trifecta."

Jones leaned forward. "Don't apologize. Your genes look great to me."

She laughed and blushed slightly.

Jones whispered to Payne. "See what I did there? I

complimented her *genes*, but she's also wearing *jeans*. That's what they call 'repartee.'"

"If that's the French word for 'retarded,' I agree with you."

Heidi overheard the comment and snickered quietly. She tried to cover up her laughter by adjusting the band around her hair. A few seconds later, her blond ponytail was back in place and the grin was off her face.

"Anyway, where were we?" Payne asked.

"I was reading your mind," she said.

Payne smiled and nodded. "In addition to the riddle, Petr's grandfather also provided a hint about the treasure's location. In his journal, he described the hint as a starting point. It might give you the context you're looking for in order to solve the riddle."

She looked at Ulster. "What's the hint?"

"According to my grandfather, Ludwig hid a secret document inside his *Gartenhaus* that would help us find the treasure."

"His *Gartenhaus*?" She pondered the significance of the word. "Okay, now it makes sense."

"The riddle makes sense?" Payne asked.

She shook her head. "No, the reason you asked me about Ludwig and the Alpengarten auf dem Schachen makes sense. I wondered why you got upset when I told you the botanical garden was opened in the 1900s. Seriously, think of all the time you would have saved if you had just come clean with me from the very beginning."

Payne countered. "Probably less time than you've wasted with all your gloating. We get it: You're perceptive. Now use your ability for good, not evil. Tell us what the riddle means."

She smiled at Payne, enjoying their banter. They had been going at it since they had met on Schachen, verbally jousting about everything. After a while, she knew something was bound to happen. Either they would get into a huge fight, or they would rip each other's clothes off. She wasn't sure which, although she hoped for the latter. That sounded a lot more fun.

"Let me ask you a question," she said.

"What now?" Payne grumbled.

She pointed at Ulster. "Actually, I was talking to him."

"Oh," Payne said.

Ulster responded. "What is it, my dear?"

"Your grandfather—he wrote these clues in his journal?"

"That's correct."

"How was his handwriting?"

"His handwriting?" Ulster asked, confused.

"Was it easy to read, or were some of his words open to interpretation?"

"For the most part, his penmanship was exquisite. Why do you ask?"

"I was wondering how certain you were about the word *Gartenhaus*. Could you have misread that particular term?"

The leather-bound journal was sitting on the desk in front of him. Ulster flipped to the appropriate page and studied the word. "It says '*Gartenhaus.*' Clear as day."

"That's disappointing," she said, and sighed.

"Why is that?" Payne wondered.

"I was hoping it said something else. If it did, I'd know the answer to the riddle."

"Really?" Jones asked. "What word were you hoping for?"

"*Gartenlaube*. I wanted it to say '*Gartenlaube*.'"

"What does that mean in English?"

She looked at Jones. "It means 'garden arbor.'"

"That's pretty close to 'garden house.' Could it be that anyway?"

She shrugged. "I don't know. You tell me."

Payne looked at Ulster, who was searching the pages of the journal for additional clues. "Petr, after all the grief I've given you over the years about your long-winded stories, I can't believe I'm about to say this. Earlier today, I think I cut you off a little too early."

Ulster relished the moment. "Oh? Which time was that? Was it when we entered the bunker? Or when we opened the first crate? Or when we were talking about the black swan?"

Payne shook his head. "None of those."

"Then which instance are you referring to?"

"When we first landed on Schachen, you started telling DJ and me about the original language of the riddle. We begged you to skip the background information about the journal because we wanted to know the actual riddle. Do you remember that?"

"I do, indeed."

Payne continued. "I could be wrong, but didn't you say

something about the original version of the riddle being written in an ancient language that needed to be translated?"

"Actually," Ulster said, "it wasn't an ancient language at all. It was merely an older dialect, known as Austro-Bavarian. My grandfather then translated the riddle into Austrian German, which was the language he had spoken prior to moving to Switzerland. Once he took up residence here in Küsendorf, he started speaking Italian, which is the unofficial language of the canton of Ticino. Growing up, I had always found it strange since Küsendorf is such a German-sounding name. However, through some research of my own, I learned that this town was actually founded by a man with Polish ancestry who had the surname of Kuz—"

"Petr!" Payne shouted. "This is why we cut you off. Although everything you said about Küsendorf was riveting, it has nothing to do with our current conversation. Don't you see that?"

Ulster nodded. "I do now."

Payne took a deep breath, trying to remain calm. "If it's okay with you, I'd like to remain focused on your grandfather's journal."

"What about it?" Ulster asked.

"When your grandfather translated the riddle, could he have slightly altered the original meaning when he used Austrian-German words?"

Ulster nodded again. "It happens all the time—especially with unusual words or highly specific terms. Sometimes there isn't a perfect word in the new language, so a translator is forced to choose the closest possible replacement."

Heidi spoke up. "Could *Gartenhaus* have been substituted for *Gartenlaube*?"

"I don't see why not. Although their definitions are slightly different, their basic structures are remarkably similar, right down to the 'au' in the last syllable."

"So it's possible?"

"Yes, my dear, it's possible."

Heidi broke into a wide grin. "If that's the case, I know the answer to the riddle. I know where a swan goes for his journey home."

53

Hamburg–Berlin, Germany

During the two-hour car ride from his business meetings in Hamburg to his residence in Berlin, Hans Mueller reflected on the early-morning phone call he had received from Max Krueger, a devoted employee who wasn't known for hyperbole. Krueger had seemed truly excited about the appearance of Petr Ulster in Garmisch-Partenkirchen, yet several hours had passed without an update of any kind. With the day winding down, Mueller was curious.

From the backseat of his custom-built Mercedes limousine, Mueller flipped a switch that lowered the soundproof partition in front of him. "Have you heard from Krueger?"

His eager assistant responded. "No, sir, I haven't. But I assembled the information you requested on the Ulster Archives. Shall I send it to your laptop?"

Mueller nodded. "Then give Krueger a call. I'd love to

know what's going on down there. Garmisch isn't known for excitement—unless you're a skier."

The assistant laughed. "Yes, sir. I'll call at once. Would you like to speak to him?"

"Only if it's worth my time."

"I'll let you know."

Mueller nodded and flipped the switch to raise the partition. It was a third of the way up when he heard the deep voice of his muscular chauffeur, a man named Bosch, who spoke approximately once a week. If he had something to say, it was bound to be important. Mueller stared at his driver in the rearview mirror. "What's wrong?"

Bosch looked back at him. "Something happened in Garmisch."

Mueller lowered the partition. "What do you mean?"

"I was listening to the news while you were in your meeting. There was a shoot-out in Garmisch."

"A shoot-out? What kind of shoot-out?"

Bosch looked at him. "A bad one."

"How bad?"

"Multiple gunmen, several deaths."

"In *Garmisch*? Are you sure?"

"I'm certain. Someone was killed at the ski stadium."

"And the others?"

"In the mountains."

Mueller rubbed his chin in thought. According to Krueger, choppers had been flying in and out of Garmisch-Partenkirchen for the past week and had been landing in a field near the base of Zugspitze. One of the choppers, registered to the Ulster Archives, had arrived there early that morning, and now this? In Mueller's mind, it couldn't be a coincidence—not in a town where the last shoot-out had occurred in World War II.

His assistant turned around. He was holding an encrypted satellite phone against his ear. "Sir, it went straight to voice mail. Shall I leave a message for Krueger?"

Mueller shook his head. "No."

He quickly hung up. "Now what, sir?"

"Who do we know in Garmisch?"

"Krueger is our lead man. I wouldn't trust anyone else."

"What about the police? Who's our local contact?"

The assistant tried to come up with a name but couldn't because of the complex structure of the German police. Every state in Germany was responsible for operating its own force, which was then divided into a number of regional police authorities. The Bavarian State Police, known as the Bayerische Polizei, had ten such subdivisions. Krueger had many contacts within the Polizeipräsidium München, the force that protected the city of Munich, but Mueller's organization did so little business in Garmisch-Partenkirchen that his assistant wasn't even sure which regional authority was in charge of that section of Bavaria.

"I don't think we have a contact in Garmisch. Do you have a suggestion?"

"Call Munich. With so many dead, they might get involved."

"What about the SEK, sir?" It was an abbreviation for the Spezialeinsatzkommando, a special-response team that handled unusual cases, such as hostage situations and violent crimes. "I know they have a unit assigned to the Alps. Perhaps they're in charge of the mountains."

Mueller shrugged. He honestly didn't know. Most of his deals happened in major cities, not in the rugged terrain near the Austrian border. "Call whoever you want! Just find out what happened in Garmisch. And track down Krueger. I want to speak to him at once!"

He punctuated his statement by raising the partition, sealing himself from the commotion that was sure to follow in the front seat. While his assistant tracked down names and made a series of phone calls to their contacts all over Germany, Mueller could focus on the heart of the matter: Who was Petr Ulster, and what was he doing in Garmisch-Partenkirchen?

Although Mueller was familiar with the Ulster name, he didn't grasp the scope of the Ulster Archives until he viewed the file that had been sent to his laptop. The comprehensive dossier included videos about its history, newspaper articles on its collections, and thousands of pictures of its most famous treasures. Mueller had never cared much about art or artifacts, but that changed when he read that the estimated value of the Archives was more than a billion dollars. In his opinion, there was no way a man of Ulster's wealth (or weight) would fly to the nether regions of Bavaria to hike up a mountain unless he had found something extraordinary.

The question was, what?

Mueller spent the next fifteen minutes searching the Internet, trying to figure out what Ulster could have discovered that would have been worth his time. Historically speaking, there were a few possibilities in that part of Germany. Partenkirchen originated as the Roman town of Parthanum. It was founded on the trade route from Rome to Augsburg and was first mentioned in A.D. 257. Its main street, Ludwigstrasse, follows the original Roman road. More than a millennium later, the town flourished as a way station on a trade route to the Orient.

Perhaps he had located an old settlement? Or a ruin from Ancient Rome?

Or maybe something more recent, like relics from Castle Werdenfels?

Built in 1219 by Otto VII, Count of Andechs, the once mighty castle was now a ruin. Originally intended to guard a local military road, Werdenfels—which means "defense of the rock"—was turned into a palace of horrors when crop failures led to an outburst of witch hysteria. During the sixteenth century, the castle was used to hold, try, and execute those accused of witchcraft. Exact numbers aren't known, but hundreds were supposedly burned at the stake or garroted. By the mid-1700s, the castle was such an object of superstitious horror that most of it was torn down to prevent devil worship and matters of the occult.

Then again, things of that nature seemed to be beneath the lofty standards of the Ulster Archives—unless Ulster was trying to impress the *Twilight* crowd.

While searching for other possibilities, Mueller heard a beep on the car's intercom system. It meant someone in the front seat wanted to talk. He pushed the button to reply. "What is it?"

"I have news about Krueger."

Mueller lowered the partition. "What is it?"

His assistant spoke. "One of our police contacts in Munich just called. So far the authorities in Garmisch-Partenkirchen have identified two of the shooting victims. Neither one was Krueger, but both have significance to us."

"In what sense?"

"One of the men was *connected* to Krueger."

"How so?"

"He was listed as a known associate."

"Part of his local crew?"

The assistant shook his head. "They served together in the 10th Armored Division. When the victim—his name was Krause—was accused of armed robbery, Krueger gave him an alibi. The cops found it suspicious and noted it in both of their files."

"This Krause, where was he found?"

"He was shot at the ski stadium."

"Not on the mountain?"

"No, sir."

"Any witnesses?"

"Our contact doesn't know. He's still trying to find out."

Mueller nodded. "What about the other victim? Another friend of Krueger's?"

"I hope not, sir."

Mueller glared at him. He wasn't in the mood for games. "What does *that* mean?"

The assistant gulped. "Sorry, sir. As far as we know, he's not connected to Krueger. The guy's name was Collins.

He was found on a hiking trail above the Partnach Gorge. According to several witnesses, a small caravan of soldiers was ambushed at an intersection. Collins was one of the casualties."

"Collins was a soldier?"

"No, sir. He was a criminal dressed in camouflage."

"Camouflage? What was he doing?"

"I don't know, sir."

"What kind of criminal?"

"Collins was a hired thug."

Mueller stroked his chin. "But he *didn't* work for Krueger?"

"No, sir."

"Can we connect him to Ulster?"

"No, sir, we can't. But we *can* connect him to someone else."

"Who?"

"According to our source, Collins worked for Kaiser."

Fueled by a wave of anger, Mueller cursed for the next ten seconds. No one made his blood boil like Kaiser. More than competitors, they were rivals. Bitter, bloodthirsty rivals. In the world of smuggling, Kaiser was the old guard and Mueller was the new. As long as both were alive, neither could feel safe. "Collins worked for Kaiser? Was Kaiser there?"

"I don't know, sir."

"That's not good enough!" he shouted. "We need to know if Kaiser was there!"

The assistant nodded. "Sir, our source is checking. Unfortunately, the local police are overwhelmed at the moment. In addition to the shoot-out, there was a major fire on one of the mountains. Right now they're stretched pretty thin."

"A fire? What kind of fire? Was it connected to the shootings?"

"I don't know, sir. Our source doesn't know."

Mueller swore some more, this time in multiple languages. Something major was going on in Garmisch-Partenkirchen, and he was on the outside looking in. Unfortunately, because of the increased police presence in the region, he couldn't risk a visit himself. Instead, he'd have to work his network of contacts from his office in Berlin to find out what was going on.

If Kaiser and Ulster had a connection, he would find it. And then he would sever it.

54

✤

L inderhof Palace is located six miles west of the village of Ettal, not far from Ettal Abbey, a fourteenth-century Benedictine monastery that used to be a popular pilgrimage stop. From the window of Ulster's chopper, Payne and Jones could see the abbey's towering baroque dome in the distance. Covered in dew, it glistened in the early-morning sun.

Following Heidi's instructions, Baptiste landed the chopper in a large clearing on the east side of the Linderhof grounds. The gates didn't officially open until 9 A.M., but Heidi had called one of her friends on the security staff, who had given her permission to come an hour early since she had worked there for two years and was employed by the Bavarian Palace Department. The guard greeted her with a hug, then handed her the keys to a four-person golf cart that was parked nearby. Normally used to ferry elderly people around the spacious grounds, the cart would save them a lot of travel time as they made their way to the north end of the park.

Heidi and Ulster sat in the front seat while Payne and Jones sat in the back. As she drove, she provided some background information on the castle. "Ludwig was fascinated by the Palace of Versailles in France and copied many of its interior features, including the main staircase and the master bedroom. The exterior of the castle resembles Petit Trianon, a small château on the grounds of Versailles that was given to Marie Antoinette by King Louis XVI."

She followed a narrow, stone path through a thick grove of trees. When they emerged on the far side, they caught a quick glimpse of the castle, which was built at the bottom of a gently sloping valley. Much smaller than Payne had imagined, the marble building was less than a hundred feet in length. It was surrounded by several fountains, including one that shot water over seventy feet in the air. He was about to ask a question about the golden statue in its center, but before he had a chance, Heidi turned to the right and started driving north.

A moment later, the cart was swallowed by shadows when it entered the mouth of the longest arbor Payne had ever seen. Hundreds of arching metal poles had been planted into the ground, approximately one foot apart, on both sides of the steep path. The poles were connected by several horizontal rails, which formed a series of one-foot squares that functioned as a trellis. Over the years, dozens of trees had been trained to grow around the extensive framework. The resulting tunnel—a combination of vines, leaves, and branches—shielded them from the sun and blocked their view of water steps on their left that flowed toward the ornate castle behind them.

Ulster admired the vegetation. "Is this the *Gartenlaube* you mentioned?"

She nodded. "We entered it from the east. It arches all the way up to a music pavilion on top of the hill before it arches back down to the western side of the grounds. When viewed from the palace windows, the arbor looks like a green rainbow on the hillside."

Payne leaned forward. "And what does the arbor have to do with swans?"

"Nothing," she admitted as they reached a fork in the path.

"Then I'm confused. I thought *Gartenlaube* helped you solve the riddle?"

The arbor continued to arch gently around to the left, while an uncovered trail veered off to the right. This new trail went straight up the hill toward the north. She made the turn before she answered his question. "It did help me solve the riddle. Back in Ludwig's time, *Gartenlaube* had multiple meanings. Sometimes it meant 'garden arbor,' which is the literal translation of the term. But in the world of landscaping, it was a generic term for 'man-made garden.' If you think about it, that's what an arbor is: The trees and trellis were shaped by man."

"What's your point?" Payne asked.

"My point is simple," she said as she drove up the steep path. "There's more than one man-made garden on the

Linderhof grounds. The one we're going to was Ludwig's personal favorite. It's called the Venus Grotto."

"Does it have swans?" Jones wondered.

She smiled as she parked their cart next to a large rock formation that was covered in green moss. "The Venus Grotto has *everything*. I'm sure you'll be impressed."

Payne climbed out of his seat and stared at the spacious grounds. The approach of autumn had splashed the trees with a vibrant mix of colors. Everywhere he looked, he saw reds and yellows, oranges and gold, all mixed among a palette of greens. If the Venus Grotto was half as impressive as the leaves around him, he would be pleasantly surprised.

"Is it much of a hike?" Payne asked.

She shook her head. "Not at all."

"Then what are we waiting for?"

"I wanted to see if you would spot it."

"Spot what?"

"The secret entrance to the grotto."

He looked at her. "The *what*?"

"You heard me. The secret entrance to the grotto."

In unison, Payne, Jones, and Ulster turned toward the large mound behind them. Standing twelve feet in height, the rugged formation appeared to be a natural extension of the hillside. Weeds grew from the cracks in the gray rocks. Small trees sprang from the crevices. If they had walked past it, they wouldn't have given it a second thought. Everything about it looked like it belonged. Like it had been there since the dawn of time. Naturally curious, Jones tapped on one of the moss-covered stones to make sure it was real. Then he tapped on another. Payne and Ulster quickly followed suit, each of them hoping to find the entrance first.

Payne called over his shoulder. "If you're messing with us, I'm going to be pissed."

She laughed at his comment. "I swear, I'm not messing with you. There really is a secret entrance to the grotto. In fact, Ludwig designed several secret doors and passageways in his castles—not to mention a number of slick contraptions that catered to his dreamworld. Believe it or not, some of them were quite brilliant."

Payne glanced at her. "Such as?"

"When Ludwig was entertaining guests, he didn't want to be disturbed by servants. He felt they invaded his privacy and ruined the fantasies he was trying to create. Obviously, this was a major problem when he was throwing a dinner party with a lot of guests. No servants meant no food. So Ludwig designed a special dining room in the Linderhof that met his personal needs. The room featured a full-length table that could be lowered into the kitchen below. Down there, his servants could stock the table and raise it back up without being seen."

Payne smiled. "You've got to be kidding me."

"Trust me, that's nothing compared to what you'll see inside the grotto. That is, if you guys can find the way in. I thought one of you was supposed to be a detective?"

Jones, who was a licensed investigator, took the comment as a personal challenge. Less than thirty seconds later, he found a tiny metal handle embedded in the rock face. Without waiting for Heidi's permission, Jones yanked on the latch. A soft click could be heard in the center of the mound, followed by a loud rumble. Suddenly, the large boulder in the middle of the formation started to twist to the left. Unsure of what was happening, Jones jumped back and watched as the boulder turned on a center axis. The left side of the rock went in while the right side swiveled out. Once the rock stopped moving, Jones stared at the resulting fissure. It was seven feet tall and three feet wide. Beyond it, a narrow corridor stretched deep into the darkness.

Jones glanced back at the group. "I'm not sure, but I think I found it."

55

❀

Armed with flashlights, the foursome walked single file into the man-made cave at the northern end of the Linderhof grounds. Heidi led the way, followed by Jones, Ulster, and Payne. To ensure their privacy, Payne closed the door behind them. When the grounds were officially open, the narrow corridor would be awash with floor lights for the safety of the crowds. But that was later. For the moment, nothing was turned on.

"Watch your heads," Heidi called out from the front.

Fake stalactites dangled from the ceiling above as stalagmites rose from the floor, as if the group were passing through a sharp set of teeth. Payne wasn't sure where they were going or what they were about to see, but he sensed something great was lurking ahead. Outside, he'd had his doubts about this place until that giant boulder had twisted aside like something from a movie. *That* had changed everything. Suddenly, he felt like a little kid again, exploring one of the walk-through rides at Kennywood, the amusement park near Pittsburgh. All that was missing was the taste of cotton candy and the safety of his grandfather's hand.

"How old is this place?" Jones asked in the darkness.

Heidi answered as she opened the grotto's control panel, which was hidden behind a fake boulder. "It was finished in 1877. Workers installed a framework of steel girders and pillars. They covered them with cement, sometimes laid over canvas, then sculpted them into shape."

Payne shined his flashlight to the far left. At first glance, it looked like the ground was rippling. He assumed it was an optical illusion caused by his light until he heard the dripping of water. "What's out there? Is that a fountain?"

Heidi put her hand on the switch. "Nope. Something better."

"Like what?" he wondered.

Instead of answering, she started flipping switches. One by one, lights popped on throughout the grotto. Suddenly, the stalactites and stalagmites were bathed in blue light. Then the ceiling above them turned gold. An instant later, their pathway lit up like a ramp in a movie theater, followed by a series of recessed lights in a painted alcove. Finally, the ground to the left started to glow—blue at first, and then an alien green. It took a few seconds for Payne's eyes to adjust, but when they did, he was stunned by the sight. The entire time he had been walking in the darkness, he had been strolling beside an underground lake.

His mouth fell open. "Wow."

She turned off her flashlight and walked toward them. "I told you it was impressive."

Ulster nodded in agreement. "I've seen pictures of the grotto, but I never fully grasped how large it was until now. It is truly immense."

"Women have said the same thing about me," cracked Jones.

Heidi ignored him. "The Venus Grotto is the largest artificial cave in Europe. Everything you see in here—the rocks, the ceiling, *everything*—was made by man. The cave is two hundred seventy feet long and forty-two feet high. By comparison, the palace itself is only ninety-eight feet long."

Payne stared at the lake. At first, he had assumed it was shallow like the Pirates of the Caribbean ride at Disney World, but the longer he stared at the underwater lights, the more he could tell they weren't close to the surface. "How deep is the water?"

"In some places, it's ten feet deep."

Jones leaned against the safety railing that had been installed for tourists. He was struggling to comprehend the grotto's technology. "They built this place in the nineteenth century? When did they add the lights?"

"Believe it or not, they've been here since the grotto opened in 1877. Obviously, we've upgraded the technology over the years and made some repairs, but the basic look is the same. What you see is what Ludwig saw when he lived in Linderhof."

Payne shook his head in amazement. "I didn't even

know they had indoor electricity back then. I find it hard to believe they were able to do all of this in the 1800s."

"Back then, they used arc lamps—bulbs made of charcoal rods that had been invented fifty years earlier—to light the grotto. To change the color of the lights, they rotated a disk of colored glass and shined the bulbs through it. Sort of like a slide projector. Ludwig was actually able to program a sequence of lights—five sets of ten minutes each—in the order he wanted. In addition, he could shine the colors in unison, which projected a rainbow above the far alcove."

"How was it powered?" Jones asked.

"They used a primitive electromagnetic generator known as a dynamo. There were twenty-four of them in a machine shop about a hundred meters to the north. The power facility was one of the first of its kind in Europe."

Payne whistled softly. "I'll admit it, I'm impressed. This place is awesome."

She signaled for them to wait. "Hang on, I'm not quite done."

"There's more?" Jones asked.

She ducked behind the fake boulder. "Much more. Check this out."

With a flip of a switch, the water in the lake began to move. Slowly at first, and then more steadily. Before long, the entire lake was churning with waves. "Sometimes Ludwig wasn't satisfied with calm waters, so his designers installed a wave machine. This way, when his servants rowed him around the lake, he felt like he was facing the elements."

Payne laughed in amazement. "Un-friggin-believable!"

She called out from the control panel. "I thought you'd like that, but believe me, the best part is yet to come. If you don't mind, do me a favor and take a few steps forward on the path. I want you to have the best view for the finale."

Payne moved forward until she was satisfied.

"Okay, that's perfect! Prepare to be shocked."

He stood there, glancing around the grotto, wondering what was going to happen next. All of a sudden, he heard a soft rumble coming from the walls themselves. He glanced up and spotted a large opening in the rock face above him. The outer surface of the hole was glowing red, while the interior was light blue. Over the years, Payne had been involved in enough practical jokes to sense when one was being pulled on him. Luckily, he stepped aside a split second before water came roaring out of the spout, or else he would have been drenched by Ludwig's waterfall.

"Shoot!" she yelled from her position behind the boulder. "I almost got you!"

He stuck his hand into the water, imagining how cold it would have felt on his back. "You're lucky you didn't. Otherwise, you would have gone for a little swim."

She laughed as she headed his way. "That's not nice."

"Neither is luring someone under Niagara Falls."

She playfully punched his arm. "Oh, please! You can hear the water coming from a mile away. I didn't think it would actually get you."

He stared at her. "But you were *hoping* it did."

She giggled softly. "Maybe."

Jones listened to their banter and rolled his eyes. He didn't have the tolerance to listen to their flirting. "Sorry to bust up your honeymoon, but didn't you say something about swans?"

"Swans?" she asked.

"You know, the *riddle*. The reason we're here."

"The riddle!" she exclaimed. "Yes, of course, how silly of me! It's been a while since I've given a tour through the grotto. I guess I got caught up in the excitement."

Payne reassured her with a smile. "Don't worry about it."

Heidi took a moment to gather her thoughts, then pointed at a golden cockleshell boat that was near a colorful mural. It had been painted in a large alcove at the far end of the lake. The mural depicted a scene from Richard Wagner's *Tannhäuser* opera, one of Ludwig's favorites, and looked like it belonged in a museum, not an artificial cave. As the group walked closer to the painting, Heidi hustled over to the control panel and turned off the wave machine. Although it was an impressive special effect, it was rarely used during regular tours, because the "fake" waves eroded the artificial environment like "real" waves on a beach. Then she turned off the waterfall so they wouldn't have to shout above the roaring water.

"How much do you know about Lohengrin?" she asked.

Ulster answered for the group. "I know enough to fill a notebook, whereas they know the basics. I filled them in only yesterday."

Payne glanced at him. "You did? You better refresh my memory."

Ulster nodded. "Lohengrin was the son of Percival, one of the Knights of the Round Table. He was sent to rescue a maiden in a far-off land. Wagner wrote an opera about him."

Payne had a blank look on his face. "Go on."

"He made the journey in a cockleshell boat pulled by a magical swan."

Jones laughed at the description. "I remember that! Ludwig used to dress up in his costume and prance around the halls of his castle."

Payne finally remembered. "The Swan Knight."

"Yes!" Ulster exclaimed. "Ludwig was obsessed with him, which is why Ludwig is often called the Swan King. If you remember, Ludwig even sealed his mysterious correspondence with a black swan. Hence the black swan letters."

Jones grinned. "Ludwig going rogue."

"Actually," Heidi said, "if you believe the rumors, that's exactly what Ludwig did. He went rogue. Having bankrupted his personal fortune building places like this, he was forced to turn to outside sources to maintain his standard of living. The money he collected would have been the source of his mythical treasure."

Payne nodded. "Which leads us to the riddle."

Heidi pointed at the elaborate boat. It was elevated just above the waterline by a discreet metal stand to keep it in good shape. Painted gold and shaped like a giant cockleshell, the boat featured carved fish mounted near its base, wooden doves attached to the back of the shell, and several strings of dried flowers draped from its edges. Inside, there was a small padded bench and a single back pillow covered in red velvet. Two wooden oars were affixed to their stands.

She asked, "What's wrong with this boat?"

"Too many things to name," Jones cracked.

"I meant in terms of Ludwig."

Jones smiled. "In that case, not much. It fits him perfectly."

"I would agree with you, except for one tiny detail. Do you see it?"

Payne, Jones, and Ulster stared at the antique boat, trying to figure out what she was alluding to. At first glance, the boat seemed to fit Ludwig's lifestyle. It was ornate, whimsical, and somehow innocent—like something out of a child's dream. Even the carved figurehead, a naked cupid shooting his bow, seemed appropriate for a man of his ilk.

Sensing their confusion, Heidi gave them a hint to speed up their search. "Think about the boat in terms of the riddle. Where would a swan go on his journey home?"

A few seconds later, Payne figured it out.

56

❈

Payne grinned with pride when he solved the riddle. "That's really clever."

"What's really clever?" Jones asked.

"The riddle. We were thinking about it all wrong."

"Wait! You figured it out?"

Payne nodded. "Yep, I figured it out."

Jones turned toward him. "Well?"

"Well *what*? Figure it out for yourself."

Jones shook his head. "You're so full of shit! You don't know the answer."

Payne raised his right hand. "I swear to Ludwig, I figured it out. Like I said, we were thinking about it all wrong."

"In what sense?" Ulster asked.

"The swan isn't the one going home. So stop thinking

about nests and lakes. Think about it from a different perspective."

Heidi nodded her approval. Until that moment, she
wasn't sure if Payne had actually figured it out. "Jon's right.
The 'his' in the riddle does not refer to the swan. Someone
else is making the journey. Focus on the words: *Where
would a swan go on his journey home?*"

Jones was getting more and more confused by their
clues. "Wait! What are you talking about? Who's making
the damn journey?"

Ulster broke into a wide grin. Thanks to Heidi's hint,
he had figured it out. "Lohengrin! Lohengrin is making
the journey!"

Jones grimaced at the clue. "You mean the Swan Knight?
How in the hell am I supposed to know where he's going?
I'm not a travel agent!"

Payne laughed at Jones's frustration, since he was always
bragging about how much smarter he was than Payne.
"You don't have to know where the knight is going. That
doesn't matter. The question is, where would the swan go
on the knight's journey?"

"Don't ask me. I'd never take a bird on a fucking trip."

Payne and Ulster laughed so loud that tears formed in
their eyes.

Meanwhile, Heidi managed to bite her tongue and
stifle her laughter. Feeling bad for Jones, she put her hands
on his shoulders and gently turned him toward the boat.
While standing next to him, she simplified the riddle so he
could solve it. "Lohengrin used to travel in a cockleshell

boat pulled by a swan. In that scenario, where would the swan go?"

Jones shrugged. "In the front?"

"Exactly! The swan would go in the front, or else it couldn't pull the boat."

Jones, who was doing his best to ignore Payne and Ulster, pointed at the boat. "But I don't see a swan. I see a fat-ass cupid."

She nodded. "Which is the problem I mentioned earlier. Why would Ludwig build an exact replica of the Swan Knight's boat in his private grotto but omit the most important part? He *wouldn't*—unless the added feature was more important than a swan."

Suddenly excited, Jones turned toward Payne and smacked him in the back of the head. "Are you listening to this?"

Payne's laughter stopped immediately. "Listening to what?"

"I figured the riddle out *yesterday*, and you guys made fun of me."

Payne stared at him. "What are you talking about?"

Jones refreshed their memories. "Petr said Ludwig had hidden the secret document in his *Gartenhaus*, and I said I had done the same thing while crossing the Afghan border. Remember?"

Payne nodded. "What's your point?"

Always the showman, Jones used his hands to explain the process. "According to Heidi, Ludwig took his secret document and stuffed it right up cupid's *Gartenhaus*. Probably did it in the dark while listening to opera."

She blushed at his description. "I never said that."

"That's because you're a lady. But that's what you meant, right?"

"Not at all! I simply think the document is inside the cherub."

"Yeah," Jones said, still pleading his case, "which is what I said *yesterday*. The secret document is inside the cupid's—wink, wink—cherub."

Payne rolled his eyes at Jones's antics. His friend would do just about anything to avoid being wrong. "As far as I'm concerned, I don't care who solved the riddle. The only thing that matters is what happens next. How do we retrieve the document?"

Ulster made a suggestion. "Why don't we pull the boat over and examine it from shore?"

Heidi shook her head. "We can't. It's on a metal stand to keep it from rotting."

Ulster squatted and stared at the lake. For the first time, he realized the boat was being held just above the surface of the water. "Now I feel foolish. I didn't even notice the stand."

"No one does," she admitted.

Payne studied the lake. "How deep is the water out there?"

"Thigh-high at most. Back in Ludwig's day, he used to invite opera singers to perform on this side of the grotto. Once they arrived, he made them sing while standing in the water."

"Why is that?" Ulster wondered.

She pointed to the alcove at the far end of the lake. It

depicted a scene from one of Wagner's operas. "He used the mural as their backdrop. It helped set the mood for their performance."

Ulster chuckled. "He really was an interesting chap."

"Wasn't he? I've been a fan of his for a very long time."

Payne cleared his throat to get their attention. "As far as I'm concerned, we have two viable options. If you want, I can hop in the lake, rip cupid off the boat, and bring it to shore . . ."

She shuddered at the thought. "Or?"

"Or you can wade over there and examine it yourself."

She shook her head. "I vote for option three."

"Which is?"

She poked him in the chest. "You get in the water and I climb on your shoulders. Then you walk me over there like a trained hippopotamus."

Jones laughed. "I vote for that one."

Ulster nodded. "Me, too. It's the chivalrous thing to do."

"Screw chivalry. I want to see Jon treated like a hippo," Jones cracked.

Payne shrugged. He was more than willing to take one for the team. Before climbing into the lake, he took off his shoes and emptied his pockets. He set everything on the path near a fake stalagmite, then stepped over the safety rail where Heidi was waiting for him.

"How do you want to do this?" he asked.

"You step in, then I'll climb on," she replied.

Unsure of the water's depth, Payne sat on the stone ledge that surrounded the lake and slowly submerged his feet. The water was cold but bearable. The underwater lights and the reflection of the colorful mural on the rippling surface prevented him from seeing the bottom, but he sensed it wasn't very deep. Five seconds later, he was sure of it. He hopped in with both feet, and the water stopped just above his knees. "Now it's your turn. Climb aboard."

"Are you sure? The water's less than three feet deep. I can walk in that."

He pointed at the boat. "Even if you do, you're still going to need a lift to examine cupid. The front of the boat is taller than I am."

Jones glanced at his watch. "Come on, guys. We're pressed for time."

She nodded and climbed onto his shoulders. "Don't let me fall."

Payne wrapped his hands around her calves. "Don't worry, I got ya."

The boat was sitting ten feet away from the shore, a distance he could cover in a few long strides. On his third step, Payne felt the pinch of an electrical cable under his foot. He was startled by its presence. Until that moment, he hadn't even considered the possibility of electrocution. Now he couldn't get it out of his mind. The thought of being fried in an artificial lake wasn't a pleasant one. For an ex-soldier like Payne, it would be an embarrassing way to go.

"A little farther," she said as she reached for the statue. "Okay, stop!"

Although she had worked at Linderhof for two years,

this was the first time she had ever examined the wooden statue from close range. Approximately two feet in height, the cupid sat perched on the front lip of the boat. His right knee was bent up and his left leg was positioned down, as if he was struggling to balance himself on the choppy lake. He grasped a bow with his left hand and an arrow with his right. His head was tilted slightly in an effort to aim. On his back, he had a pair of wings and a full quiver of arrows. The craftsmanship was truly remarkable.

"What should I do?" she whispered.

Payne tried to look up at the statue. When he did, the back of his head dug into her stomach. It felt soft and firm at the exact same time. "Sorry, I can't see anything from down here. How is the statue attached?"

"What do you mean?"

"Was it nailed in place, or was it twisted on? Maybe you can unscrew it like a hood ornament."

She leaned in for a closer look. "I'm pretty sure it's glued. I think I see adhesive."

"Knock on it. Does it sound solid?"

Afraid to damage it, she put her ear against it and tapped on it softly. To her, it sounded like a wooden cookie jar. "It's hollow!"

Payne squeezed her calves in celebration. "Great! Now we're getting somewhere."

"Now what?" she demanded.

Jones called out from shore. "Look for a lever or a button."

She glanced back at him, confused. "What?"

"The boulder outside was held in place by a hidden latch. Maybe cupid has one, too."

She smiled. "Good idea. Ludwig loved his secrets."

The most obvious option was cupid's arrow, since it was aimed directly at her face. She grabbed it and tried to wiggle it, but the arrow held firm. Next she tried to twist his bow. Then she tried his arms and legs. All of them were secure. To examine the back of the statue, she asked Payne if he could move around to the far side of the boat. A few steps later, she was inspecting cupid's quiver, which was full of arrows. She went through them one at a time, checking to see if they moved in any way. Unfortunately, they were firmly attached.

"Now what?" she whispered to Payne. "There's nothing left to do."

He tried to look up but couldn't. "Tap on it again. Are you sure it's hollow?"

She knocked on it again. She could hear an echo inside. "I'm positive."

"Well," he said, "I hate to say it, but maybe this statue is like a piggy bank. You have to crack it open to get at the savings."

She shook her head. "I can't! I simply can't! If I'm wrong about what this is and there's nothing inside, I'll never forgive myself. This boat is beloved by Germany. I can't destroy it."

"Do you want me to?" he asked.

"No!" she exclaimed. "I don't want anyone to destroy it. Come on, guys! We must be missing something. Ludwig was a builder, not a destroyer. We're not supposed to break this! There has to be another option."

The next minute was filled with silence. During that time, each of them glanced around the grotto, wondering if they were looking in the right place for Ludwig's secret document. For all they knew, the swan riddle could have been pointing somewhere else. Perhaps the lake near Neuschwanstein, where Ludwig had fed the swans as a child, or the lake where he had been murdered. None of them had even considered that as a possibility. Maybe the treasure was hidden near Lake Starnberg, and Ludwig had been killed while trying to protect it.

Then again, there was another possibility that none of them were willing to accept. Maybe, just maybe, the treasure was like so many of the things in Ludwig's life.

Maybe it was just a fantasy.

57

❃

Berlin, Germany

Yesterday's meeting in Hamburg had clinched a seven-figure deal that Mueller had been working on for weeks, yet he didn't feel like celebrating when he got back to Berlin. No gourmet meals. No bottles of champagne. No whores or models. And all because of the news from Garmisch-Partenkirchen. *That* was the effect Kaiser had on his psyche. How could Mueller celebrate when his main rival was doing business in his backyard?

Short-tempered from a lack of sleep, Mueller walked down the marble staircase of his palatial estate and found his assistant waiting near the kitchen. Mueller, who was dressed in silk pajamas and a designer bathrobe, glared at him, letting the pissant know he shouldn't say a fucking word until he had grabbed his morning coffee. Mueller poured himself a mug, then took a seat in his breakfast nook. The view through his bulletproof windows did not brighten his mood. If anything, it made his mood worse since the sky outside was gray.

Stifling a yawn, Mueller took a sip of coffee. It was black, bitter, and steaming hot—just how he liked it. Maybe the day wouldn't be a total disaster after all.

"Come here," he growled.

His assistant approached the table with caution. He knew how volatile his boss could be and didn't want to provoke him. So he stood there, quiet, waiting for further instructions.

Mueller pointed to the chair across from him. "Sit."

He did what he was told, but remained silent.

"Now speak."

He opened a folder and glanced at his notes inside. "Here's the latest from Garmisch. Krueger's body showed up early this morning in the Partnach River. It was discovered in the gorge, not far from one of his associates'. Their bodies got hung up on some rocks and were discovered by the police."

"How did they die?"

"Krueger was shot at close range. The other man died from a broken neck. Autopsies are scheduled for later today. We'll know more then."

"What else?"

His assistant flipped through his paperwork. "They found another body near the ambush site. According to our police source, the victim was dressed in camouflage like the driver of the caravan. His name was Lange. He was a known associate of Kaiser's."

Mueller held up his hand and spread his fingers wide. "That makes *five*. Five dead gunmen, and we don't know what they were fighting over. Or do we? What's this caravan you keep talking about?"

He flipped to another page. "Multiple witnesses, including several employees at the Eckbauerbahn, reported a black man driving an off-road vehicle. He was hauling a soldier, four wooden crates, and an unconscious man, who was being treated by a French doctor. They used the cableway to get off the mountain."

Mueller stared at him like he was crazy. "They used a ski lift to escape?"

"According to witnesses, yes."

"Who the fuck does that?"

The assistant shrugged but said nothing.

"Does the ski lift go over the gorge?"

"No, sir. It's east of the gorge by a considerable distance. Here, take a look at this." He reached into his folder and pulled out a map of Garmisch-Partenkirchen. Several additions had been handwritten in colored ink. "I marked the ambush site, where the bodies were found, and the location of the cableway. As you can see, the violence was spread out."

Mueller stared at the map and tried to make sense of things. Two of Kaiser's men had been killed in the initial ambush, which had occurred on a hiking trail above the gorge. Afterward, the vehicle headed to the east, where its passengers had linked up with the cableway that took them to the Olympic ski stadium at the base of the mountain. Meanwhile, Krueger and his associate went in the opposite direction, perhaps trying to beat Kaiser's crew into town by using a shortcut through the gorge. A solid plan, especially if Krueger had someone waiting down below—which would explain the presence of Krueger's friend near the ski stadium. Of course, everything went to shit when Krueger and his associate were killed in the gorge. Without backup, Krueger's friend was killed as well, overpowered by the crew from the cableway.

As far as Mueller was concerned, all of that made perfect sense. The one thing that didn't, the one thing that still eluded him, was what had attracted Ulster and Kaiser to Garmisch-Partenkirchen in the first place. "What was in the crates?"

His assistant shrugged. "No one knows."

Mueller shoved the table forward, driving it into his assistant's stomach. "Obviously, *someone* knows, or there wouldn't have been a gunfight!"

The assistant nodded while trying to regain his breath. Once he did, he grabbed some napkins from a ceramic holder and cleaned up the coffee that had spilled on the table. Mueller watched him with a mixture of amusement and contempt, wondering how someone could take that much abuse without fighting back. If nothing else, his assistant was loyal.

Mueller waited until the mess was clean before he spoke again. "What else?"

His assistant glanced through his folder. "Krueger got me thinking. He tracked down the chopper's registration by using its tail number. That's how he discovered Ulster's involvement in the first place."

"So?" Mueller snapped.

"So," he said as he kept flipping pages, "I took it a step further. Most luxury helicopters are equipped with radio transceivers that are used to track the vehicle in case of theft. I gave Ulster's tail number to our police connection, who reported the chopper stolen. That automatically triggered its theft transceiver, a small device that emits an inaudible signal that can be detected by police tracking computers throughout Europe."

"And?"

"And the Bavarian State Police got a hit."

"Where?" Mueller demanded.

His assistant finally found the sheet he was looking for. "As of thirty minutes ago, Ulster's chopper had crossed the German-Austrian border."

"Shit! He's probably going back to Switzerland!"

"Actually, sir, the chopper was headed *into* Germany."

Mueller stared at him. "Ulster had left, but is coming back?"

"We don't know about Ulster, but his chopper was in Bavarian airspace as of thirty minutes ago. Our source said he would call us with updates."

Mueller smiled for the first time that morning. "Wonderful! Just wonderful! Good thinking on your part. I should have thought of that myself."

His assistant beamed. "Thank you, sir."

"What else do you have for me?"

"Our source mentioned another thing, although he wasn't sure if we would care. He said it was rather unusual for this type of case, so he thought he should mention it."

Mueller sipped his coffee. "What's that?"

"He said Interpol was actively involved in the case."

Mueller laughed. "Of course they're involved in the case! Those pricks follow me wherever I go, hoping I screw up in public so they can arrest me for jaywalking or some other nonsense. I'm sure they do the same thing with Kaiser."

"Actually, sir, our source wasn't surprised they were involved. He was surprised *why* they were involved. According to him, the Bavarian State Police were notified that two of the gunmen in the Garmisch shooting were undercover operatives working for an unknown agency."

Mueller winced. "You mean they were cops?"

"No, sir. If they were cops, the police would have notified Interpol—not the other way around."

"Not if they were Austrian cops. Maybe they tracked Kaiser's crew across the border. It's only a few miles away from Garmisch."

"You're right, sir. I guess that's a possibility. But . . ."

Mueller glared at him. "But what?"

"Our contact thinks otherwise because of the source of the information. It didn't come from a local agency. It came from Interpol headquarters."

58

❀

Linderhof, Germany

Jones wasn't the type of guy who stood on the sidelines. He got his thrills by being in the action, not by watching it. Frustrated by Heidi's lack of success, he kicked off his shoes and climbed into the artificial lake. The entire time, he mumbled under his breath. "They think they're so damn smart just because they solved a riddle about a bird. I figured out the goddamn boulder. I used a piece of meat to jump out of a chopper. I'm a licensed fuckin' detective. I'll be damned if I'm gonna be beat by a stupid cupid with a boat up its ass."

Payne grinned when Jones leapt into the water. He knew his friend better than anyone and was surprised it had taken him so long to hop in. "What are you doing?"

"What do you think I'm doing? I'm saving your ass!"

"But we don't need your help."

Jones trudged forward through the water. "It sure looks like you do."

Payne glanced up at Heidi and winked. "Believe it or not, I've had my head between a woman's thighs before. No complaints so far."

She blushed and playfully smacked his cheek.

Jones continued his rant. "While you guys are frolicking in the grotto, time is ticking away. The gates open at nine. We need to be out of here before the tourists arrive."

"And what are you going to do that she couldn't?" Payne asked.

Jones stopped near the side of the boat. Although the cockleshell was tall in the stern and the bow, it dipped down in the middle. The entire craft was supported just above the waterline by a metal stand. To see how sturdy it was, he grabbed the stand and pulled on it. "It's not a question of ability. It's a question of desire. I'm willing to do things that Heidi isn't."

She glared at him. "Such as?"

He smiled. "I'm willing to piss off Bavaria."

Without saying another word, Jones sprang out of the water and landed on his knees in the belly of the boat. It rocked from side to side on its stand, a combination of Jones's weight and the surge of water that followed his leap, but the boat held firm.

Heidi gasped in horror. "I can't believe you did that."

"And I can't believe you didn't," Jones argued. "It's a goddamn boat. Not a Fabergé egg. If you're gonna roll with us, you have to break some rules."

She looked down at Payne. "Jon?"

"Hey, don't look at me. I'm just a tamed hippo. You tell me where to go, and I take you there. Other than that, I'm staying out of this."

Heidi fumed, but there was nothing she could do. Jones was already in the boat, and he wasn't going to leave until he wanted to. "Fine! But be careful. This boat is an antique."

Jones flashed an evil grin. "Don't worry! I'm not going to break anything—unless I feel it's absolutely necessary."

She started to complain, but Payne assured her that he was kidding.

Meanwhile, Jones went to work on the statue. Not willing to trust Heidi's opinion, he put his ear against the cupid and knocked on it a few times. To him, it sounded hollow. Next, he took a minute to examine the cupid for a hidden seam. Ultimately, that was how he had found the secret entrance outside. He had spotted a crack next to the boulder and followed it to the latch. He figured the same method might work here. Using his flashlight for extra light, he studied the statue until he noticed a suspicious ridge just below the back of cupid's head.

Heidi saw his expression change. "Did you find something?"

"Maybe. There's a seam back here."

She leaned forward on Payne's shoulders. "I noticed that, too. I tried twisting his head and moving his quiver of arrows, but nothing happened."

Jones stared at the figure, trying to view it from Ludwig's perspective. Where would the infamous Swan King put a secret lever on a statue of cupid? A few seconds later, Jones was beaming like a lottery winner. "I think I got it."

"Got what?" Heidi demanded.

"The guy had a hard-on for swans."

"So?"

Jones studied the back of the statue. "What do swans and cupids have in common?"

Pushing gently, Jones applied downward pressure on the cupid's wings. Much to Heidi's surprise, they slid a few inches down its back. Inside the statue, a latch clicked into place, which opened a secret compartment between the cupid's head and his quiver of arrows.

She gasped with surprise.

Wasting no time, Jones lifted his flashlight and stared into the hollow center. He spotted a sealed envelope that had been folded into thirds. Much to his chagrin, his hand was too large to reach inside and grab it. "Son of a bitch!"

"What's wrong?" Ulster called from shore.

"There's something inside, but my hand is too big," Jones replied.

Payne made a suggestion. "Let Heidi try."

To prove her worth, she showed her hands to Jones. Her fingers were long and slender. Without tweezers or tongs, she was the group's best hope. "I promise I won't take all the credit."

Jones smiled. "Fine! But be careful. This boat's an antique."

She giggled at his comment, appreciating how he used

the very words she had spoken against her. "Okay, hippo, I need you to get me closer."

"Not a problem." Payne slid his hands down her calves and put them under her feet. From that position, he was able to boost her completely off his shoulders, much like a cheerleader being lifted in the air. "Is that better?"

"That's perfect! Now hold me steady." She reached inside the tiny compartment and clasped the envelope between two fingers. "Got it!"

Ulster shouted a warning. "Careful, my dear, it's liable to be brittle! There's no telling what a hundred years of moisture might have done to the parchment!"

She smiled at Jones. "Don't worry. I'm more gentle than DJ."

A few minutes later, all of them were huddling on shore, wondering what they had discovered. The envelope was made of high-quality paper. It had been sealed with black wax, then stamped with an elaborate swan. The emblem was identical to the black swan symbol that was on the crate of gold they had found in the bunker.

In Ulster's opinion, it was a very good sign.

As a historian, he was put in charge of the document. Initially, he had expressed an interest in taking it back to Küsendorf, where he could examine it in the climate-controlled environment of the Archives, but Payne and Jones laughed at him. There was no way in hell they were going to fly back to Switzerland to open the envelope. Even Heidi, who was a protector of all things Ludwig, agreed with them. She was far too excited to wait that long.

Despite his protests, Ulster was thrilled with their decision. Decades had passed since his grandfather had uncovered the path to Ludwig's treasure, a trail he had been unable to pursue because of World War II. In his mind, his family had waited long enough.

"Does anyone have a knife?" he asked.

Jones nodded and flicked open a switchblade. "Here you go."

Ulster grabbed the knife and prepared for surgery. Hoping to preserve the historic wax seal, he carefully slid the tip of the blade under the envelope's flap and sliced it open with a steady hand. When he was done, he studied the elaborate black swan with his flashlight. As far as he could tell, it appeared to be undamaged.

Ulster breathed a sigh of relief. "I think it survived."

Jones stared at him. "We're happy for the bird. Now get to the good stuff."

He nodded and gently pulled the lips of the envelope apart. Inside, there was a handwritten document. It was folded in half and yellowed with age. Not wanting to touch the paper with his bare hands, he turned the envelope upside down and tapped on it gently. The document fluttered out, landing on the fake boulder that served as his workstation.

A moment later, a second object emerged.

It landed with a soft clank.

59

In the dim light of the grotto, four sets of eyes focused on the object that had fallen from the envelope. Made of gold and carved by a craftsman, it was an ornamental key whose bow (or head) was in the shape of the black swan emblem. Surprised by their discovery, they didn't speak for several seconds. They just stared at it, imagining the treasures it might unlock.

Jones was the first to snap out of his daze. He snatched the key off the fake boulder and studied it with the beam of his flashlight. Starting near the tip, there was a message engraved on the side of the key. "I'll be damned. There's an inscription."

Heidi gasped. "Really? What does it say?"

Jones struggled to read it. "I'm not sure, but I think it says . . . *Made in China*."

"Are you serious?" she demanded.

Jones laughed at her. "No, I'm not serious! The damn thing's written in German, so it could say *anything*. But you should have seen your faces. Priceless!"

Payne cracked a smile. He had fallen for it, too. "I admit it, you had us going. But if you don't mind, can you give the key to Petr so he can examine it? The clock is ticking."

Jones kept laughing. "Sure, no problem."

Ulster grabbed the key and translated the inscription in his head. When he was done, he explained it to the group. "Thankfully, David was incorrect on two major points. First of all, the message was written in Bavarian, *not* German. This is good news, since Bavarian was the language of Ludwig. Secondly, there was no mention of China in the key's inscription."

Jones smiled. "Sorry, my bad."

Heidi waited with anticipation. "So, what does it say?"

Ulster lowered his voice. *"He who holds the key gets to wear the crown."*

"Crown? What crown?" she demanded.

Ulster shrugged. "Honestly, my dear, I'm really not sure. Perhaps my grandfather made a notation in his journal. If you give me a moment, I'd be happy to check."

Payne pointed at the document. "Or you could just read that."

Ulster blushed. "Yes, of course, how silly of me! Sometimes I get distracted. Like a toddler, I tend to focus on the shiniest toy in the room, not the one in front of me."

Jones snatched the key out of Ulster's hand. "In that case, why don't I hold this for you? Personally, I think I'd look pretty damn good with a crown."

Payne rolled his eyes. "Speaking of childish behavior."

Ulster chuckled at the comment, then refocused his attention on the document. Unsure of its age or fragility, he used the unsharpened side of the switchblade to unfold the paper on his makeshift workstation. Within seconds, he knew what he was looking at. "It's a map."

Payne and Jones exchanged knowing glances. The last time they had found a map they were on a fishing boat, piloted by a hard-drinking Finn, near the city of Saint Petersburg, Russia. The map eventually resulted in their wildly successful trip to Greece.

Jones cracked, "I'll buy the vodka. You call Jarkko. We'll find the treasure in no time."

Heidi ignored the comment. "A map of what?"

"Capri," Ulster said with certainty. "The Isle of Capri."

Standing across from Ulster, Payne glanced at the document. Although everything was upside down from his perspective and written in a foreign language, he quickly recognized the shape of the Tyrrhenian Sea and the Gulf of Naples. "The one in Italy?"

Ulster nodded. "Indeed."

Jones grunted at the news. "I was joking about Jarkko, but maybe we *should* give him a call. He hangs out near there this time of year. And he's always looking for a paycheck."

Heidi remained focused on the document. "Where is it pointing?"

Ulster studied the hand-drawn map, looking for a giant X that marked the spot. When no symbols turned up, he searched for objects that seemed out of place. A minute passed before he found a possibility. "I'm not sure, but I think it's pointing to the northwest coast."

"Why do you say that?" Jones wondered.

"Everything is written in Bavarian except for one item that is labeled in Italian. It says 'Grotta Azzurra.'"

"What does that mean?" Payne asked.

Heidi's face lit up. "The Blue Grotto."

Payne stared at her. "Are you familiar with it?"

She nodded, obviously excited. "The Blue Grotto is a famous sea cave in Capri. Sunlight passes through an underwater cavern that reflects the light into the cave. It makes the whole cavern glow an eerie shade of blue. Ludwig was fascinated by its beauty."

Payne sensed there was more information to come. "And?"

She smiled. "And Ludwig built a replica in this grotto."

Ulster laughed with delight. "Can you show us where?"

Heidi led the way, followed by Payne, Jones, and Ulster. They hustled to the landing near the artificial waterfall, which had been turned off for several minutes. With a grin on her face, she told them to stay put while she headed for the hidden control panel.

Payne objected. "Not this shit again."

"No tricks, I promise."

"Then what are you doing?"

She started flipping switches. "Obviously, there's no sunlight down here. In order to reproduce the Blue Grotto, the builders had to install a special light under the water. Keep your eyes on the sea cave on the far side of the lake."

"Where's the sea cave?" Jones asked a split second before an alcove on the opposite side of the lake turned a brilliant shade of light blue. "Never mind."

To produce the effect, a stone archway had been built just above the surface of the water. The curved gap between the stone and lake was so narrow that Jones had assumed it was a shadow on the base of the wall instead of an opening. But now that the blue light was on, he was able to see the arched gap above the water.

Heidi reappeared beside them. "Pretty, isn't it?"

Payne nodded. "Believe it or not, I think I've seen pictures of the actual cave. As soon as you turned on the light, the image popped into my mind."

"I'm not surprised. It really is quite famous. And the designers did a wonderful job."

Jones stared across the lake. It looked vaguely familiar to him, too. "That's all well and good, but what are we supposed to do now?"

She shrugged. "I have no idea."

Payne turned to Ulster for advice. "What do you think?"

Ulster paused in thought. After a few seconds of analysis, he broke into a wide grin. "I hate to say it, but I think the hippo should get back into the water."

Payne cracked a smile. He wasn't used to being teased by Ulster. "That's strange. I don't remember seeing you in the water earlier."

Ulster laughed and patted his own belly. "Touché."

"Seriously, do you think there might be something back there?"

"Obviously, I'm far from certain, but I think it would be foolish not to check. After all, we are a long way from home."

Payne nodded in agreement. "How big is the cave? Any idea?"

Heidi answered. "I honestly don't know. I've never been back there before. But the one in Capri is huge. The only thing that's small is the opening. To enter the Grotta Azzurra, people have to lie flat on their backs in rowboats or else they would bump their heads on the entrance. But once inside, it expands into a massive cavern."

Payne studied the gap on the far side of the lake. It was much more narrow than the one in Italy. So much so, a toy boat would struggle to pass underneath the stone archway, let alone a rowboat. Then again, that might have been done on purpose. If it were too inviting, it might have attracted too many unwanted guests.

Payne hopped into the water. "Screw it! I'll take a look."

Jones followed his lead. "Me, too."

The instant Jones hit the water, Heidi remembered the object he was carrying in his grasp. "Please be careful with the key! Try not to get it wet."

He laughed at the anxiety in her voice. She sounded like a first-time mom. "Heidi, you've got to relax. The key is shaped like a swan. A little water won't kill it."

60

With flashlights in their hands, Payne and Jones trudged through the chilly water of the lake while Heidi and Ulster rooted them on. For Payne, his journey had come full circle. Everything had started with a phone call while he was exploring the depths of the Ohio River. Now he was back in the water, hoping to find a secret treasure in the heart of the Blue Grotto. All things considered, searching for gold was a lot more exciting than finding a bottle opener.

As they passed the front end of the cockleshell boat, the water was barely up to their knees. After that, the lake bed started to slope away—much like a swimming pool near the deep end. Heidi had warned them of the possibility. She knew the lake had a depth of ten feet in certain parts; unfortunately, she wasn't quite sure *where* since she had never been in the water. In some ways, Payne and

Jones were glad they didn't know. It only added to their excitement.

By the time they reached the entrance to the Blue Grotto, Jones had to stand on his tiptoes or else the water would have been up to his eyes. Meanwhile, Payne had the luxury of an extra six inches. Although his height allowed him to stay comfortably above water level, it forced him to duck his head as he passed under the stone archway that led to the cove.

Lit by colored lights, the ceiling in the cavern glowed a magical shade of blue. But the lamps were so bright it actually prevented them from seeing clearly.

Payne called toward the shore. "Please cut the lights in here."

Heidi disappeared behind the control panel and flipped the switch. The Blue Grotto quickly turned dark. "Is that better?"

"Much," he shouted as he turned on his flashlight.

Jones rubbed his eyes, trying to get them to adjust. Wherever he looked, he saw light blue splotches. "Is it just me, or do you see Smurfs?"

"Seeing them is one thing. If they start to talk, we have problems."

Jones stared at him. "Holy crap. You look like that chick from *Avatar*."

Payne laughed. "If you touch my tail, you're a dead man."

Jones rubbed his eyes some more and hoped for the best. Slowly but surely, he became acclimated to the darkness. Once he did, he flipped on his flashlight and headed deeper into the grotto, where Payne was examining the ceiling. "What are we looking for?"

"Anything that doesn't belong."

"Like my black ass in a lake?"

Payne smiled. "That would qualify."

Unlike the spacious Grotta Azzurra in Capri, the cavern was relatively small. Approximately twelve feet in width and length, the Blue Grotto's most dominant feature was a giant stalagmite near the rear wall that towered five feet above the surface of the water. At first glance, Payne assumed the stalagmite concealed one of the roof's support beams, but that notion disappeared when he shined his light on the vaulted ceiling and realized there was seven feet of clearance above the top of the stalagmite. That meant the two of them weren't connected.

Payne called over his shoulder. "Take a look at this."

"At what?" Jones said as he tiptoed closer.

"This rock. It doesn't look right."

"That's because it's fake."

Payne thumped on it. "I mean its shape. It looks like a volcano."

"Knowing Ludwig, it *is* a volcano. If you piss off Heidi, she'll turn on the lava."

"I'm serious."

"Me, too. That girl's a firecracker."

Running his hand over the rough texture of the cement, Payne moved to his right and studied the stalagmite with the beam of his flashlight. His interest soared when he spotted a series of notches, cut vertically into the cement. They started well below the surface of the water and continued up its side. "I think I found something."

Jones looked at him. "Like what?"

Payne handed him his light. "Here, hold this."

"What did you find?"

"A ladder."

"Really?"

Instead of explaining, Payne placed his right foot in one of the notches and propelled himself out of the water. He quickly wrapped his arms around the stalagmite to steady his balance, then placed his left foot in the next notch and climbed higher. A few seconds later, he was sitting on top of the fake rock. Unlike the stalagmites they had seen near the shore, the top of this one was flat like a plateau. "Throw me my flashlight."

Jones tossed it up to him. "Is there room for me?"

Payne shined his light behind the stalagmite and realized there was a narrow ledge between the stalagmite and the rear wall of the grotto where both of them could stand. It was just above the surface of the lake. Payne shuffled into position, then reached down and helped Jones out of the water. Dripping wet and slightly out of breath, they studied the top of the rock—which was just below eye level—and spotted a circular seam that looked like a hatch. It was six inches from the outer edge of the rock and sealed tight. They tried to wedge their fingers into the gap, but it was far too narrow.

Payne glanced at him. "Suggestions?"

"A crowbar might work."

"Do you have one?"

"Nope."

"Then let's cross that off the list. While we're at it, let's eliminate Plan B."

During their years as MANIACs, "Plan B" often meant using C-4 and a remote detonator. Here, that wasn't an option.

Jones frowned. "Too bad. I always liked Plan B."

Payne knocked on top of the stalagmite. Although it was coated with cement, it sounded metallic—like the hatch on a submarine. For all he knew, it could have been an access panel to a mechanical floor underneath the grotto, a place where drainage pipes had been laid and colored lights could be fixed. Yet something about its placement told him otherwise. Boats couldn't enter the cove because of the stone archway, and due to the depth of the water, workers would have had a difficult time bringing in tools and supplies. In Payne's mind, the only reason to put a tunnel back here was to hide it from the rest of the world, and the only reason to do that was if it led somewhere important. What had Heidi said earlier? *Ludwig loved his secrets.*

Well, whatever was hidden back here was bound to be a doozy.

Payne glanced at Jones. "Start looking for levers or buttons. I'm heading to shore to talk to Petr and Heidi. Maybe they missed something on the map."

"Good idea."

Not wanting to jump into the water because of the presence of underwater lights, Payne hopped on top of the plateau and draped his legs over the side until he felt one of the stone notches with his toes. Once his feet were in place, he started his climb down, one foot at a time. As his face passed the highest notch on the stalagmite, his eyes widened with surprise. He quickly used his left hand to steady himself before he climbed back up.

"What's wrong?" Jones wondered.

"Nothing's wrong. I think I found a handle."

"Where?"

"It's in one of the steps."

Wasting no time, Payne threw his legs in front of him and flipped over on his stomach. This allowed him to hang his upper torso over the edge of the plateau and examine the interior of the notch with his flashlight. As he suspected, a small handle that activated the locking mechanism inside the stalagmite had been concealed in the notch. Although he wasn't quite sure how it worked—or *if* it would work—he realized he shouldn't be on top of the hatch when he gave the handle a tug. A few seconds later, he was hanging from the side of the stalagmite and pulling on the handle.

Payne heard a creak, then a whir, as a series of internal gears rotated into place. It was soon followed by a pop and a clank as the hatch sprang open. The entire process took less than three seconds. When it was done, the edge of the hatch closest to Payne was only a few inches above the outer rim of the plateau, but that was more than enough space for him to insert his hand and lift the hatch on its hinges until it was perpendicular to the lake.

Jones watched the proceedings from the nearby ledge. He immediately leaned forward and shined his flashlight into the center of the stalagmite, hoping to see a pot of gold or a treasure chest filled with jewels. Instead, he saw a series of rusty iron steps. They had been mounted into the side of a cement tunnel that went deep into the earth, far beyond the beam of his flashlight.

"Great," he mumbled. "We found a sewer."

Payne stared into the abyss. To him, it looked promising. Who knew what Ludwig had hidden underneath the grounds of Linderhof? "Stay here if you want. I'm going in."

"I wouldn't recommend it."

"Why's that?"

Jones pointed out the rusty steps. "Bare feet and rust don't mix. When was the last time you had a tetanus shot?"

Payne conceded the point. "Agreed. I planned on going back to shore anyway. I have a feeling our friends will want to join us."

61

✤

Payne and Jones returned to the hatch a few minutes later. This time, they were joined by Heidi and Ulster, who willingly braved the deep waters of the grotto for a chance to explore the secret passageway. Before they left shore, Heidi stashed their personal belongings and Ludwig's map behind a fake boulder, far from the tourist path. They figured it would be safer back there than in the lake and the unknown environment of the tunnel.

With a flashlight clenched in his teeth, Payne entered the stalagmite first. He slowly climbed down the ladder, testing the sturdiness of every step before he shifted his weight to the next one. By the time he reached the bottom of the steps—a distance of nearly thirty feet—he was covered in cobwebs and a wide variety of spiders. He calmly brushed them aside, then took the light out of his mouth to study his surroundings.

An arched tunnel ran uphill from left to right. It was made of cement and looked similar to the passageway he had just climbed through. Payne shined his light in both directions, hoping to see where the tunnel led, but the path curved out of sight.

Jones called down the shaft. "Are we clear?"

"Yeah," Payne said. "You're clear."

Although the trio didn't know what to expect or what they might find, they climbed down the ladder with a spring in their step. Heidi reached the bottom first. She was followed by Ulster, whose bulk gave him some trouble in the shaft, and Jones, who lowered the hatch but didn't close it completely in case there wasn't another way out.

Heidi shined her light downhill to the left. "What is this place?"

Payne shrugged. "I was about to ask you the same thing."

"Honestly, I have no idea. I never knew it was here."

"Any rumors about secret passageways?"

She glanced uphill to the right, trying to regain her bearings. "All of his castles have secret passageways: Neuschwanstein, Herrenchiemsee, Linderhof. I thought we had found all of them during the past century or two. I guess I was wrong."

While they were talking, Jones studied the composition of the tunnel itself. There was something oddly familiar about its color and design. He ran his fingertips across the concrete surface, trying to get in touch with the memory that eluded him. A few seconds passed before he figured it out.

"I'll be damned," he said, laughing.

"Is something wrong?" Ulster asked.

Jones knocked on the wall. "I was trying to remember where I've seen concrete like this before. Then it dawned on me. It's the same color and texture as the bunker."

Ulster considered the possibility. "Actually, that stands to reason. Ludwig could have used the same builders and materials for both projects. As I mentioned yesterday, the bunker is less than fifteen miles from Linderhof. It wouldn't surprise me if the bunker and tunnel were completed in the same year."

Payne overheard the end of their conversation. "Speaking of tunnels, let's figure out where this one goes. Does anyone have a preference, or should we flip a coin?"

Jones, who was blessed with an impeccable sense of direction, clarified their options. "In case you're wondering, the castle is to the left. I'm not sure if the tunnel goes that far, but the castle is definitely that way."

Payne pointed uphill. "In that case, let's go to the right. I have a pretty good idea where it leads, but I want to test my theory."

Jones laughed. "You have a theory? About what?"

Payne started walking. "About something Petr said."

Ulster hustled after him. "Wait! What did I say?"

Payne glanced over his shoulder to make sure everyone was following. Just to be safe, he signaled for Jones to bring up the rear. "Yesterday, you told us a story about Ludwig's disappearance from Linderhof. You said he vanished without a trace for thirty-six hours."

Ulster nodded. "It occurred the night after he sent the black swan letters. His advisors eventually found him at his house in Schachen."

"Covered in dirt," Jones added from the back.

Ulster grinned. "I'm glad you guys were listening!"

"We're *always* listening," Jones assured him. "We're often *bored*, but still . . ."

Payne tried not to laugh. "Anyway, as a former soldier, the thing that bothered me the most about your story was the negligence of the palace guards. How in the hell could an overweight king like Ludwig sneak past all of them without being seen? At first, I thought maybe he dressed up in one of his elaborate costumes, but then I remembered this happened in the middle of the night. The guards were bound to check anyone who passed through the castle gates."

Jones cleared his throat. "Are you getting to a theory?"

"As a matter of fact, I am." Payne spotted the end of the tunnel. It was less than thirty feet ahead of them. "My guess is he didn't go through the castle gates. My guess is he took this tunnel under the castle wall. That's why none of the guards saw him leave."

"And why was he so dirty?" Ulster wondered.

Payne guessed. "If he escaped through the grotto, he had to jump into the water to reach the secret hatch. That means he would have been soaking wet when he left this tunnel and hit the nearby woods. Dirt would have stuck to him like lint to a sweater."

"Where did he go?" Heidi asked.

Payne laughed. "How should I know? You're the expert, not me. But if I had to guess, I'd say he was meeting with one of his co-conspirators—someone he didn't want to be seen with. Otherwise, why go through all of this trouble?"

Ulster offered a possibility. "Unless, of course, he did this sort of thing all the time. After all, Ludwig was nocturnal and a tad bit crazy. Who knows what he liked to do after dark?"

"Or *who* he liked to do," Jones cracked.

"Either way," Payne said, "he could've used this tunnel to get away."

Heidi challenged him. "You seem pretty confident for a tourist."

As they walked forward, Payne shined his light on the wall that ended the tunnel. An iron ladder, which had been attached to the concrete, disappeared in the darkness of the vertical shaft. "Who knows? I could be wrong about everything. Maybe this is a mechanical tunnel that leads to all those generators you told us about. If you'd like, I'd be more than happy to bet on the answer. Care to wager your share of the treasure? That is, *if* there's a treasure."

She shook her head. "Not a chance."

"In other words, you think I'm right."

"No," she said with a giggle. "Well, *maybe*."

When they reached the end of the tunnel, he examined the shaft above him. It looked identical to the one from the grotto, except it was half the height—a fact he had expected since they had been walking uphill the entire time. "I guess we'll find out soon enough."

"Should I light your way?" she asked.

He nodded. "Thanks. That would help."

Payne put his flashlight in his pocket and started his climb through all the spiderwebs that had collected in the shaft over the years. In certain parts of the world—especially warm-weather locations, where some spiders were deadly—he would have taken more precautions, but he didn't have much to fear in Germany, so he simply brushed the webs aside as he climbed. Meanwhile, Heidi watched this from the tunnel floor and nearly went into convulsions. Few things in life freaked her out more than spiders, and it was obvious. Jones quickly recognized her fear and was tempted to tickle the back of her neck, but decided against it. In the long run, he figured his amusement wouldn't be worth the physical damage she'd inflict on him.

A few seconds later, Payne reached the top of the steps and studied the hatch. Attached to its center was a circular handle that resembled the mechanism on a submarine door. He could loosen or tighten the lock by spinning the handle one way or the other. To make things easier, a lever had been mounted on the right side of the wheel—probably to help Ludwig open the door while he was hanging from the steps.

"Be careful," Jones teased. "For all we know, it might

open on the highway. I'd hate to see a truck take off your head."

Payne grabbed the lever. "Somehow I doubt that's going to happen."

"If it does, can I have your house?"

Payne smiled and yanked on the handle. First there was a hiss, then a clank, and then the hatch popped open. A burst of fresh air came rushing into the shaft, which caused the remnants of the spiderwebs to dance in the breeze.

Heidi felt the wind. "Where does it go?"

"Be patient! I don't know yet."

With thoughts of trucks still fresh in his mind, Payne pushed it open slowly. One inch. Then two. Then five. Then ten. The more he opened it, the more sunlight leaked into the shaft. Before long, flashlights weren't needed below, and Payne's theory was proven correct. "Just as I thought. We're in the woods beyond the castle's grounds."

Ulster called up to him. "How was the hatch concealed?"

"Good question. Let me check." Payne climbed out of the shaft and examined the outside of the hatch. A moment later, his smiling face appeared above the shaft. "You're not going to believe this. It was sculpted to look like a tree stump. The damn thing's pretty realistic. I wouldn't have given it a second glance."

Heidi stared up at him. "Can I take a look?"

Payne nodded. "All of you can. But let's make this quick. I have a feeling the other end of the tunnel is going to be even better."

62

❖

andy Raskin sat in his windowless office, surrounded by next-generation computers and paper-thin digital screens that would be the envy of every hacker in the world. Unfortunately, due to his classified position at the Pentagon, he wasn't allowed to mention anything about his work or equipment to most of his friends. As far as they knew, he was nothing more than a low-level programmer, working a dead-end job in the world's largest office building—because that's what he was required to tell them. But in reality, he was a high-tech maestro, able to track down just about anything in the world of cyberspace.

As a computer researcher at the Pentagon, Raskin was privy to many of the government's biggest secrets, a mountain of classified data that was there for the taking if someone knew how to access it. His job was to make sure the latest information got into the right hands at the right time. And he was great at it. Over the years, Payne and Jones had used his services on many occasions, and that had eventually led to a friendship.

An infamous workaholic who consumed enough caffeine on a typical workday to jump-start a car battery, Raskin often pretended he didn't have time for Payne and Jones or their bimonthly favors. But the truth was he admired them greatly and would do just about anything to help. In fact, one of his biggest joys in life was living vicariously through them—whether that was during their time with the MANIACs or their recent adventures around the globe. Sometimes, especially when he was bored at work, he would tap into the GPS on their phones and try to figure out what they were doing. Then he would determine if he could assist them in any way.

For some, it would be considered stalking.

For Raskin, it was a perk of his job.

Over the past forty-eight hours, he had checked their location on several occasions. At first they were in Garmisch-Partenkirchen. Then Innsbruck. Then Küsendorf. Now back in Bavaria. Not surprisingly, when he cross-referenced their GPS data with his countless databases, he discovered a pile of bodies and no arrest warrants.

Obviously, Payne and Jones had remembered their training.

In a twisted kind of way, it made him proud to be an American.

Raskin considered giving them a call to see if he could

help, but he decided to do a little more research before
he offered. Based on their brief stop in Küsendorf, he
knew the Ulster Archives were involved. That meant whatever they were doing was historical in nature. Curious
about the Archives' latest projects, Raskin entered Petr
Ulster's name into his classified search engine and got an
immediate hit. Ulster's personal helicopter had been reported stolen earlier that day.

Raskin laughed at his screen. "What are you guys up to
now?"

After inspecting the fake tree stump, they returned to the
tunnel as an energized group. None of them knew what
they were going to find in the opposite direction, but they
sensed it would be significant. Payne closed and sealed the
hatch, then led them on their journey.

Whether it was the downhill slope of the tunnel or the
adrenaline surging through their veins, their stride and
pace increased significantly. Even Ulster, who tended to
lumber along like a water buffalo, managed to stay on
Payne's heels. Before they knew it, they were passing the
shaft to the grotto and covering new ground.

Jones spoke from the back. "Based on the angle of this
tunnel, we're heading directly toward the castle. I bet
we're underneath that trail we took from the arbor to the
secret entrance."

Heidi shook her head in amazement. "How do you do
that?"

"Do what?" he asked.

"Figure out which direction we're walking underground?"

Jones shrugged. "It's a gift."

She glanced over her shoulder. "I'm serious."

"I am, too. I have a great internal compass. I just *know* which way we're going. You can blindfold me, drug me, and spin me around. When I wake up, I'll know which way is north."

Payne defended him. "Believe it or not, he's telling the truth. We once did that to him at a bachelor party. He woke up in the back of a van in Tijuana but knew how to get to Canada."

She laughed. "That's impressive."

Jones waved off the compliment. "Actually, it was pretty easy. It was the middle of the afternoon, so I whipped out my sundial. Trust me, that thing casts a shadow like a sequoia."

She didn't miss a beat. "And yet it's not nearly as big as your ego."

Jones couldn't help but laugh. "You know what? You're pretty cool for a white girl. I vote we don't kill you at the end of this mission."

Ulster chuckled. "Me, too."

Payne looked back at her. "I'm still undecided."

She gave him a playful shove. "It doesn't matter. Majority wins."

"Fine! We'll let you live, but you have to buy us dinner. This is your homeland, after all. It's the least you should do for your guests."

She smiled at him. "Only if you return the favor when I visit the States."

"When is that?" Payne wondered.

"That depends. When are you going to invite me?"

Payne flirted back. "I guess that depends on *what* I have for dinner."

She blushed and bit her lip but didn't respond—even though she wanted to.

After a lengthy pause, Ulster cleared his throat. "May I change the subject?"

"Please," she said, relieved.

"Speaking of compasses," Ulster said, completely oblivious to all the flirting that had been going on, "my moral compass is spinning out of control right now and I'm not sure what to do. May I pose a dilemma to the group?"

Payne shined his flashlight in the tunnel in front of them. As far as he could tell, there was nothing on the horizon. No hatches, no intersections, no secret rooms. Nothing but a concrete tunnel that sloped downhill and curved out of sight. Based on his earlier view of the castle grounds from the window of the chopper, he guessed there was at least three hundred yards between the fake tree stump and the castle itself. Ultimately, if that's where the tunnel was leading, they still had plenty of time to kill. "What's bugging you?"

Ulster swallowed hard. "For argument's sake, let's say we discover a massive treasure at the end of this tunnel. If that happens, what are your intentions?"

"What do you mean?" Payne asked.

Ulster explained his concern. "We're assuming Ludwig

designed this tunnel for one purpose or another, which means we're technically on castle grounds. I'd like to know what we intend to do if we discover a treasure."

Jones laughed. "Do you even have to ask?"

"I guess so, because that's what I'm doing right now."

"Personally," Payne said, "I don't think there's a dilemma. We're on castle grounds, so the treasure belongs to the estate. We're not going to try to steal it."

"Do you mean it?" Ulster demanded.

"Of course I mean it! We're not thieves."

Ulster breathed a sigh of relief. "Oh, thank heavens! You had me worried there for a while when you wagered your share of the treasure. I thought perhaps you were serious."

Jones shook his head in mock disgust. "Damn, Petr, I thought you knew us better than that. Did you really think we'd try to steal it?"

"I *hoped* you wouldn't, but I wasn't quite sure if Kaiser had rubbed off on you."

Payne laughed at the suggestion. "Believe it or not, Kaiser wouldn't steal it either. At least, I don't think he would steal it. Then again, well, who the hell knows?" Payne hoped to ask Kaiser someday, assuming his friend was still alive. "But that's neither here nor there. The point is *we* won't try to steal it."

Jones picked up from there. "And to make sure we don't break any laws, we kidnapped an employee of the Bavarian Palace Department to watch our every move."

Heidi smiled. "Is that why I'm here? To watch over you?"

"That and your butt. You have a *great* butt."

She rolled her eyes. "Well, you should know—since you're an *ass*."

Jones laughed. "Heidi, you crack me up. We're definitely not killing you."

Sensing a face slap in Jones's future, Payne slowed his pace and eventually stopped. Not only to bail out his friend but also to clarify his previous statement. "Before we go any farther, I'd like to make sure we're in total agreement on our current objective. If we find a treasure at the end of this tunnel, the treasure belongs to Bavaria. Is that what we're saying?"

Everyone nodded in unison.

Payne continued. "On the other hand, if we find something of value—like a map or a journal—that leads us *off* of castle grounds, then whatever treasure we might find is fair game. I don't care if it's six inches past the castle wall. If it isn't on the castle grounds, we claim it as our own. Does that sound fair?"

Everyone nodded once again.

"Are you sure?" Payne demanded.

"Yes, I'm sure," Ulster replied.

Heidi nodded. "Sounds fair to me."

Jones stared at him. "Duh!"

Payne smiled and pointed over his shoulder. "Good, I'm glad to hear it. Because I spotted something up ahead."

63

✳

At the end of the tunnel, there was a thick wooden door that had been closed since Ludwig's death. Its handle was black and shaped like a swan. Payne brushed away a century's worth of cobwebs and pounded on the wood. It felt as solid as steel. It was the type of door that would laugh at a battering ram. It was meant to keep people out.

Payne knew the odds were long, but he tried the latch.

As expected, the door was locked.

Jones patted him on the shoulder. "I believe that's my job."

Payne suddenly remembered the golden key they had discovered inside the statue of cupid. The bow of the key resembled the swan on the door handle. With any luck, it would get them access to the room. "I believe you're right."

They switched positions without complaint while the others looked on. Enjoying the group's attention, Jones milked the moment for all it was worth. He stuck the key in the hole, then pulled back his hand and blew on his fingertips like he was preparing to crack a safe. The tension in the tunnel was so great that Heidi linked her elbow with Ulster's and buried her face in his shoulder. She simply couldn't bear to look. Finally, after a few more seconds of drama, Jones grabbed the key and gave it a twist.

Click.

Everyone breathed a sigh of relief.

Instead of rushing into the room, Jones showed remarkable restraint. He had been involved in too many missions to act without thought. He glanced back at Heidi. "You said Ludwig built secret passageways in all of his castles. Were any of them booby-trapped?"

She shook her head. "None that I know of."

Jones glanced at Ulster. "Petr?"

"I don't believe so," he replied.

"Just checking."

With gun in hand, Jones gave the door an easy shove. It squeaked open on its ancient hinges and hit the concrete wall behind it with a thump. In unison, all of them shined their lights into the darkness, hoping to see mountains of jewels and gold.

What they saw next was tough to comprehend.

Nearly every inch of space in the rectangular room was covered with stuff—a wide assortment of blueprints, sketches, letters, and more. Some of the items were attached with glue. Others were attached with nails. Every once in a while, objects were drawn directly on the walls, as if Ludwig had run out of paper but didn't have time to stop. The entire place looked like his brain had exploded and these were the ideas that stuck.

Jones gasped at the sight. "Holy shit! Ludwig was a serial killer."

Heidi took exception to the joke. "Disturbed, maybe. But certainly not violent."

Payne glanced around the room, trying to make sense of things. The only furniture was a fancy desk and chair in the center of the space. "Violent or not, this guy had a lot on his mind. The last time I saw something like this . . ." He paused in thought. "Actually, I've *never* seen something like this before. The PSYOP guys would have a field day."

"The who?" she asked.

He continued to look around. "It's a unit in the U.S. Army. It stands for Psychological Operations. Their job is to study the human brain and figure out how to break it."

Jones smiled. "In this case, they're a little too late. Ludwig's brain was already broken."

"I'm not sure about that," Ulster declared from the back of the room. He was staring at a series of letters that ranged in date from 1873 to 1886. There were so many pages they filled half of the wall. "I think I know what's going on."

Payne walked toward him, skeptical. "We've been here less than a minute, and you know what's going on? I find that hard to believe."

Jones agreed with Payne. "It looks like a scrapbook puked in here. How does any of this make sense?"

Ulster scanned the documents, doing his best to translate them. "Believe what you want to believe, but I'm not exaggerating. I think I know what we're looking at."

Heidi hurried to his side. "What did you find?"

"Letters to Franz von Löher."

"From who?"

"A team of global researchers."

She blinked a few times. "Are you serious? I thought that was a myth."

"So did I," Ulster exclaimed. "Several years ago, a scholar friend of mine gained access to the Geheimes Hausarchiv in Munich and searched through Löher's papers, but he never found what he was looking for. Now I know why. The letters were hidden down here."

She shined her light on one of the documents. Addressed to Löher, it had been sent from a small village in South America. "Did he find a site for Camelot?"

Ulster shrugged. "Unfortunately, my dear, it's far too early to tell. But if he did, wouldn't that be exciting?"

Payne cleared his throat. The sound was so loud it echoed in the room. "Pardon me for interrupting, but what in the hell are you talking about?"

Jones nodded in agreement. "I heard 'Heimlich maneuver' and 'Camelot.' Everything in between was gibberish."

Ulster laughed. "Actually, I said 'Geheimes Hausarchiv,' not 'Heimlich maneuver,' but I get your point. You'd like me to explain."

Jones sighed. "That would be nice."

Ulster gathered his thoughts. "During the past few days, you've undoubtedly heard enough stories about Ludwig to grasp the basic philosophy of his life. Whether it was the costumes he wore, the castles he built, or the fantasies he created, he did whatever he could to escape reality. As early as 1868—a mere four years into his reign—Ludwig started searching for a way out. At first, he masked his sorrows with music and architecture. He worked on preliminary designs for Neuschwanstein and added the opulent Winter Garden on the roof of the Residenz Palace. In addition, he became a major patron of the arts, sponsoring composer Richard Wagner and building elaborate theaters. Through it all, he remained unhappy because he was unable to break away from the one thing he despised the most."

"What was that?" Payne asked.

"Bavaria."

Heidi clarified Ulster's statement. "More accurately, Ludwig hated the *politics* of Bavaria and the pressure of being its king, not the country itself. According to his journals, he loved the woods and the mountains of his homeland but was never fully able to enjoy them because someone was always looking over his shoulder—whether that was his advisors, his cabinet, or his rivals. During his early twenties, he had to deal with the Seven Weeks' War between Austria and Prussia, the war with France in 1870, and the foundation of the German Empire, which took away Bavaria's status as an independent kingdom. That would be a lot for anyone to handle."

Ulster nodded. "That last event in particular had a profound effect on Ludwig's psyche. The kings he admired the most, both historical and mythological, were sovereign rulers who answered to no one. They had the autonomous authority to build their kingdoms as they saw fit, which was a power that Ludwig never enjoyed. He always had to answer to someone."

Payne shined his flashlight on the rear wall and stared at the letters addressed to Löher. They had been mailed from all over the world. "Where do those fit in?"

Ulster explained. "Remember that crazy story I told you about Ludwig's staff? How he sent his butler and cooks to rob a bank in Frankfurt when he was turned down for a loan?"

Payne laughed. "How could I possibly forget?"

"Well, robbing a bank is *nothing* compared to his task for Franz von Löher, who was the director of the state archives in Munich."

"What did Ludwig ask him to do? Forge some paperwork?"

Ulster shook his head. "Ludwig asked him to start a new country."

64

❧

Payne stared at Ulster in the semidarkness of the room, trying to figure out if he was serious. Based on their years of friendship, he knew Ulster didn't joke about historical data. Yet there was something so ludicrous about Ulster's statement that Payne found himself doubting what he had heard. "Löher was supposed to start a new country?"

Ulster grinned. "I thought that would get your attention."

Jones chirped in. "How does someone do that? Because I would *love* to start one. It would be like the Playboy Mansion, but with even less clothes."

Payne ignored the joke and focused on Ulster. "Back in Ludwig's day, was something like that possible? Or was this just another pipe dream?"

Ulster shrugged. "Historians have been debating that for years. Obviously, it would have been preposterous for a normal citizen to plant a flag in the ground and start a new country, because no one would have recognized his autonomy, but someone with Ludwig's clout might have made it work. After all, he was beloved in Europe and known around the globe. That gave him a reasonable chance to pull it off."

Payne pointed at the letters on the wall. "And Löher was his ambassador?"

Ulster nodded. "Ludwig had always been enamored with the concept of building the perfect kingdom on the perfect tract of land. He figured if he couldn't make Bavaria live up to his high ideals, then he would start over somewhere new. It would give him the chance to rule a country as he saw fit—even if there were no citizens except his servants."

"Did Löher take him seriously?" Payne asked.

"As a matter of fact, he did. Unlike the amateurs who went to Frankfurt with no intention of robbing a bank, Löher approached his mission with verve. Ludwig had given him a specific list of requirements for his new kingdom, and Löher traveled the globe searching for a tract of land that would meet his needs. Keep in mind, this was during the 1870s, long before air travel and cars. Löher was forced to travel by horse, train, boat, and everything in between."

Heidi picked up from there. "Amazingly, Löher did all of this in total secrecy. If word of his mission had leaked, think of the damage it would have done. The king of Bavaria, a ruler who was loved by his countrymen, was looking to abandon them? There would have been riots."

"How did they keep it quiet?" Jones asked.

Ulster explained. "Löher, who had traveled extensively in his younger years, posed as a travel writer or a wealthy foreigner looking for land. When he arrived in a new country, he would talk to the locals and figure out who owned the most scenic real estate. Then he would tour the properties and determine if they suited his needs. Not surprisingly, Ludwig was more concerned with pastoral beauty than anything else. He wanted breathtaking views and crystal-clear water, the utopian world he had dreamed about for years. But Löher was levelheaded. Although beauty was an important factor, he viewed the land through the eyes of a bureaucrat. He made sure the soil was fertile and ready for crops. He inquired about fish, and wildlife, and other sources of food, because Ludwig and his servants needed to eat. He asked about droughts, and storms, and the weather in all four seasons. He studied the local history and made sure the land was defensible from invading forces. In other words, he made sure the kingdom would be sustainable for the long haul."

Payne was impressed. It sounded like Löher was the perfect accomplice for the crazy king. One was a dreamer, the other a realist. "What did he determine?"

Heidi answered. "After his first journey in 1873—a trip that took him to Spain, Africa, Greece, and the Turkish Isles—he presented Ludwig with a detailed report on a number of locations. No one knows how the king reacted, because their conversation was private, but it's assumed he told Löher to keep looking."

Payne asked, "If their talk was private, how do you know about the report?"

"Löher's reports eventually turned up in the Geheimes Hausarchiv, the Secret Archives of the Royal House, two years after Ludwig's death. The reports are still there today."

Jones glanced at Ulster. "I thought you said your friend searched through the archives and didn't find what he needed."

Ulster smiled. "He wasn't looking for Löher's reports. Those have been scrutinized for decades. My friend was searching for documentation on what happened next."

Payne furrowed his brow. "What do you mean?"

"According to the Munich archives, Löher made a second journey abroad in 1875. He visited Cyprus and Crete and inquired about Crimea, an autonomous republic on the Black Sea. Unfortunately, nothing seemed suitable for their needs. By this time, Ludwig was getting antsy and Löher was getting too old to be traipsing around the globe. Understanding the importance of secrecy, Ludwig trusted no one except Löher to work on this sensitive project, which forced Löher to refine his approach. Instead of touring the world, he collected journals from travelers, read books on foreign lands, even interviewed tourists from different countries—all in the hopes of finding a kingdom for his king. Despite all of his effort, he reached a regrettable conclusion. The perfect spot for Camelot did not exist."

Löher explained his verdict in his final report to Ludwig:

I have myself visited a large part of the inhabited world and have read and researched in countless books. Yet I could find only very few places which might be remotely suitable, and in not a single case would I like to guarantee that the enterprise could really succeed . . . On the whole earth, there is not a single spot which totally fulfills the conditions for a satisfactory outcome. The goal can be only partly attained, and certainly not without great sacrifice and trouble.

Heidi added a few more details. "Unfortunately for Löher, he was vilified by the public when these reports were uncovered by the media. Most people were still angry about Ludwig's murder, so they lashed out at Löher, saying he had taken advantage of the delusional king by getting Ludwig to finance his extensive travel. Eventually, the Bavarian government pressured Löher to give up his position as director of the archives even though Löher was the person who added the reports to the archives in the first place. He felt they were an important part of Ludwig's legacy, but he was punished for his honesty."

Payne stared at the letters on the wall. Even though he couldn't translate the language, he was able to read the handwritten dates on the documents. Most of the letters were sent in 1886, the year of Ludwig's death. "When did Löher file his final report?"

Ulster grinned with delight. "That, my boy, is why I am so excited. This wall of letters, dated years after Löher's final report was presented to Ludwig, contradicts every scrap of evidence that has ever been collected. There have been rumors, but never this kind of proof."

"Proof of what?" Jones asked.

"That Löher hired a team of researchers to travel the globe for him and compile data for an unnamed client. That these researchers found a piece of land for a modern-day Camelot, and Löher's final report—in which he claims that no such place exists, so it would be a waste of time and money to keep searching—was simply a smoke screen to throw off Ludwig's rivals."

Payne took a deep breath and tried to make sense of the claim. During the past few days, he had received a crash course on the history of Bavaria, and his head was starting to spin. Prior to his current trip, he had seen pictures of Ludwig's castles but had been completely unfamiliar with Ludwig's life. Now he was standing in a secret room, hidden underneath one of those castles, talking about Ludwig's plan to abandon his country.

Payne stared at Ulster. "I think you better explain."

Ulster nodded. "As I mentioned earlier, my colleague visited the Munich archives on a very specific quest. He wanted to find out more about the ongoing relationship between Ludwig and Löher in the months leading up to Ludwig's death. As you know, Ludwig was a loner and the friends he made were artistic in nature. If that's the case, why did Ludwig and Löher continue to communicate for years after the end of their secret project? Löher was an elderly historian, not a painter or a musician. Trust me when I tell you this: Most historians are painfully dull!"

Payne smiled. "Aren't *you* a historian?"

"Obviously, I'm the exception to the rule."

"I beg to differ," Jones teased.

Ulster laughed. "Anyway, when Löher's travel reports were leaked to the media in 1888, some people speculated that they were the real reason that Ludwig had been deposed. Not because he was insane, but because his cabinet had learned about his crazy plot to start a new country and had punished him for his disloyalty."

Payne shrugged. "That seems reasonable to me."

Ulster shook his head. "The problem with this theory was the timing of things. Löher's final report was given to Ludwig several years before his murder. If the subject had been closed for that long, why did the cabinet act so viciously when they discovered Ludwig's foiled plan? What's more, why would they have waited so long to react? If the final report was indeed intended as misdirection, Löher would not have concealed its delivery. In fact, it would have been essential that Ludwig's cabinet learn of the report immediately to reassure them that Ludwig would not be leaving. Obviously, I'll know more once I read through these letters, but my guess is the subject *wasn't* closed. That Ludwig was *still* looking to leave Bavaria, and his cabinet killed him before he had a chance."

65

❂

While Ulster and Heidi focused on the letters, Payne and Jones examined the rest of the room, searching for information about Ludwig's secret mission. Unfortunately, their inspection was hindered by a lack of electric lights, a surprising oversight considering all of the special effects in the grotto but one that was probably done to avoid incriminating power cables. Jones noticed ventilation shafts in two of the corners, which would have allowed Ludwig to use candles or lanterns without fear of asphyxiation.

Shining his flashlight on the left-hand wall, Payne stopped in front of a series of sketches that caught his eye. None of the artwork had been signed, so he didn't know if Ludwig had drawn them or not, but they highlighted the rocky coastline of a scenic island. Most of the sketches featured a spectacular palace, whether real or imagined, that made the Linderhof look like a shack. Built on the edge of an imposing cliff, it was designed with an assortment of whimsical details—decorative chimneys, ornamental turrets, steep gables, and stone sculptures—yet the structure seemed to sprout out of the earth as if it had been there forever. With beautiful gardens and sweeping views of the endless sea, it appeared to meet Ludwig's definition of Camelot.

A few feet to his right, Payne noticed a collection of architectural blueprints hanging from two hooks that had been mounted on the wall. Having grown up in the offices of Payne Industries, he was familiar with a wide variety of technical drawings, but these blueprints' combination of age, language, and scope was unlike anything he had ever seen. Drawn in the 1880s and labeled in Bavarian, the pages showed the interior rooms of a massive palace that was larger than most cathedrals. Payne studied the floor plans and tried to imagine what the building would actually look like. When he did, he realized the designs matched the sketches to his left.

Apparently, Ludwig's scheme wasn't just a pipe dream. They had started the planning process.

In the center of the room, Jones sat on the carved chair and sifted through the drawers of the antique desk. A version of the Bureau du Roi (King's Desk)—a richly ornamented rolltop desk that was commissioned by Louis XV of France—it was inlaid with an intricate variety of colored woods. The original desk, which still stands in the Palace of Versailles, has a miniature bust of Minerva on top, but

Ludwig's featured an elaborate bust of the Swan Knight. On the public side of the desk (away from where the king would sit), there was an oval filled with the carved head of Silence, a symbolic figure that held a forefinger to its lips. It was a reminder that discretion was required in matters of the king. Down here, where the desk had been locked away for more than a hundred years, the symbol seemed to have extra meaning.

Unable to read Bavarian, Jones searched through the desk for anything that seemed *unusual*—although that was a tough term to define in the underground lair of a man with his own secret grotto. Still, he attacked his search with zeal, realizing it was a unique opportunity to investigate the death of an important historical figure.

At first glance, most of the objects in the desk seemed to be artistic in nature. He found dozens of pages of sheet music and the vocal scores of Ludwig's favorite operas. There was a sketch pad filled with doodles ranging from clouds to mountains to horses. In addition, one of the smaller drawers was stuffed with nineteenth-century office supplies, including pencils, fountain pens, and stationery. Like most people in the modern world, Jones was tempted to steal some items for personal use, but decided against it since they belonged to the king.

Jones was nearly ready to abandon the desk and focus his attention on the right-hand wall when he came across a handwritten receipt. The paper itself was an early sheet of letterhead that had been printed from a copper engraving. The emblem at the top of the page was a fierce-looking lion holding a shield. At the bottom, there was a name and an address. Jones tried to translate the words but struggled with the language.

"Hey, Petr," he said over his shoulder, "are you familiar with a city named Minga?"

Ulster, who was reading one of the letters on the wall, stopped and turned around. "As a matter of fact, I am. Minga is the Bavarian name for Munich."

"Really? I thought München was the name for Munich."

Ulster shook his head. "That's the *German* name for Munich, not the *Austro-Bavarian* name. Most people get them confused. Why do you ask?"

"Minga is written on this letterhead."

"What letterhead?"

Jones handed it to Ulster. "I found it stashed in Ludwig's desk. I think it's a receipt. Then again, it could be a grocery list. My Austro-Bavarian is kind of rusty."

"So is mine," Ulster admitted as he shined his light on the document. "But as luck should have it, I believe you are correct. This *is* a receipt."

Jones stood from his chair. "A receipt for what?"

"Honestly, I have no idea. It's one of the most cryptic receipts I have ever seen."

"Wow, I guess your Bavarian does need some work."

Ulster smirked. "No, it's not that. I can read the words just fine. It's just, well, the receipt doesn't say very much. According to this, the item will be available on July 1, 1886."

"What item?"

"That's the cryptic part. It simply doesn't say. There's

no price, or description, or item number. There's a date of availability and nothing more."

Jones considered the possibilities. "Well, if you think about it, I guess it isn't too surprising. I mean, how often does a king order something from your store? They're bound to remember what he bought."

Ulster nodded. "That's a very good point."

Heidi turned from the rear wall. "What kind of store?"

Jones laughed. "We mentioned shopping and you came running. That's a shocker."

She smiled. "I *am* a woman."

"Trust me, I've noticed."

Ulster stared at the letterhead. "Actually, I don't know if it's a store or a law firm. The enterprise was called Hauser & Sons. With a name like that, it could have been anything."

Payne entered the conversation. "What about the address?"

"What about it?" Ulster asked.

"Different parts of a city are sometimes known for different things—like Wall Street or Madison Avenue. Maybe the address will give us a clue."

Ulster struggled to read the tiny print at the bottom of the page. "Hauser & Sons was on a street called . . . Briennerstraße. Wait! Why do I know that name?"

Heidi giggled with excitement. "I used to work near there! Briennerstraße is one of the best shopping districts in Munich. It's where wealthy people go to shop."

He shook his head. "Sorry, my dear, that's incorrect. I know it for some other reason."

She laughed at Ulster. "I wasn't answering your question. I was telling you why *I* know the road. The reason you're probably familiar with Briennerstraße is because it's the oldest road in Munich. Plus, it's very close to Nymphenburg Palace, which is where I used to work."

Ulster nodded. "Yes, of course, Nymphenburg Palace! The summer residence of Bavarian kings. How could that have slipped my mind?"

"And," she added, "the birthplace of Ludwig II."

Jones stared at her. "Ludwig was born near the street on the receipt?"

She nodded. "A few blocks away."

"And when was he murdered? Something like two weeks *before* his order was ready?"

Ulster reread the date on the receipt. "I'll be darned. I failed to make that connection. I must need a snack to recharge my brain."

Jones patted him on the back. "Don't worry about it. In fact, don't worry about *anything*. Call me crazy, but I think Ludwig is trying to tell us something."

Ulster glanced at him, confused. "Really? And what is that?"

Jones grinned. "He wants us to go to Oktoberfest."

66

❋

Everyone assumed Jones was kidding about Oktoberfest. He assured them he wasn't. "Go ahead and laugh, but I'm completely serious. I think the receipt is a major clue."

Ulster graciously disagreed. "As much as I hate to squabble, I think our time would be far better served in this environment than the party atmosphere of Munich." To illustrate his point, he shined his flashlight on the walls. "Please take a moment to glance about this chamber. The room we're standing in is filled with more information about Ludwig than a hundred modern textbooks. And all the history you see here is completely unfiltered. It's as if we stumbled across the tree of knowledge and were given permission to pick the fruit."

Heidi nodded in agreement. "I love Munich as much as the next gal, but I'm with Petr on this one. We've barely had time to read any of the letters. Who knows what we could learn?"

Jones looked to Payne for support. "Jon?"

Payne took a deep breath. He knew his friend wouldn't be happy. "Listen, I respect your hunches, you know I do. But right now we're not even sure if Hauser & Sons still exists. I mean, that's a long way to travel for a store that might have closed its doors in 1890."

"Yeah, but—"

Payne cut him off. "Even if I voted for you, we still would have lost the tiebreaker."

"Tiebreaker? What tiebreaker?"

"Petr *owns* the chopper."

Jones growled and snatched the receipt from Ulster's hand. "In that case, I'm taking this and walking to Oktoberfest."

Payne laughed. "Have a nice hike. Don't talk to strangers."

Ulster waited until Jones had left the room and disappeared into the darkness of the hallway. Then he glanced at Payne, concerned. "Good heavens! Is David miffed at me?"

Payne shook his head. "Relax. When he comes back, everything will be fine."

Ulster gasped. "Comes back from *where*?"

"Don't worry! He didn't go to Oktoberfest. If I had to guess, he went outside to get some air. Trust me—when he returns, he won't even mention Munich."

. . .

Jones climbed the ladder on the far side of the tunnel and opened the secret hatch. Thirty seconds later, he was sitting on the fake tree stump and glancing at his waterproof cell phone. Reception had been nonexistent in the grotto and the tunnel. Now that he was outside, he could finally make a call. He quickly entered a number from memory.

"Research," said Raskin from his office at the Pentagon.

Jones instantly recognized his voice. "Randy, my man, it's David Jones. I wasn't sure you'd be working this late. I'm glad you're on duty."

Raskin typed away furiously. "Let me see if I got this straight. You're *happy* that I'm working the graveyard shift? That's awfully sweet of you."

"Come on, man. You know I didn't mean it like that."

"Then how did you mean it?"

"I meant I'm glad you're the one on duty because I need your expertise."

Raskin adjusted the microphone on his headset. "Damn, DJ, that's even worse! You're *glad* I'm working the graveyard shift because you want to *use* me. You didn't even say hello or ask how I'm doing. Yet you expect me to jump to attention."

Jones groaned. "Wow! You, Jon—everyone's giving me shit today."

Raskin leaned back in his chair. "Please tell me you aren't getting a divorce. I'm too old for joint custody."

"No, nothing serious. Just a disagreement about something we're doing."

Raskin played dumb. "Something you're doing *where*?"

"Germany."

"Really? What are you doing in Germany?"

"Long story. I'll tell you about it some other time."

"Maybe you should tell me right now. You know, since you need my help."

Raskin had a better security clearance than he did, so Jones wasn't worried about him blabbing to anyone. Still, Jones was reluctant to tell him anything too juicy. "I wish I could, but I'm temporarily sworn to secrecy. As soon as I get permission, I'll be happy to fill you in."

"I can respect that. It doesn't mean I like it, but I can respect it."

"So," Jones said, "about that favor of mine . . ."

Raskin cracked his knuckles. "Fire away."

"I'm staring at a receipt from 1886. I was hoping you could tell me a little bit more about the store itself. What business they were in, and so on."

"What country?"

"Germany."

Raskin opened a database on one of his screens. "What city?"

"Munich."

"Munich," he mumbled as he dragged a chunk of data from one screen to another with his mouse. "Please tell me you have a name or address. Otherwise, this is going to take a while."

"Actually, I have both. The store was called Hauser & Sons, and it was located on a road called Briennerstraße. It's the oldest road in Munich."

"Whoop-dee-fuckin'-doo. The age of the road doesn't

help at all. But do you know what *would* help? If you could spell that for me. That would help a bunch."

Jones laughed and spelled Briennerstraße. "Anything else?"

"Just give me silence so I can do my thing."

The sound of typing filled the line for the next several seconds. Every once in a while, Raskin would curse at one of his databases, but it was usually followed by some sort of taunt that let the computer know who owned its ass. To Jones, it was like a progress bar on a computer screen. When the taunts increased, it meant Raskin was getting closer to the end.

"So," Raskin eventually said, "do you want the good news or the bad news? Because I have a little bit of both."

"No games. Just tell me."

"Hauser & Sons was a family-owned jewelry store that opened in 1845. It stayed open until 1933, when the National Socialists—i.e., the fucking Nazis—took control of Germany. After that, the city of Munich changed dramatically. As you know, the Allies bombed the shit out of the city during World War II. I'm talking seventy-plus air raids, not to mention a ground assault. By the time we took control of Munich in 1945, the city was mostly rubble."

Jones cursed under his breath. He had been confident that the receipt would lead them to Camelot. Now he'd have to go down below and admit his mistake to everyone. "What about the Hausers? Are any of them still around? Maybe I can—"

"Hold up! I'm not done. The best part is yet to come."

"Sorry, my bad. Please continue."

Raskin collected his thoughts. "As usual, our government felt guilty about blowing up a city, so Uncle Sam rebuilt Munich with American tax dollars. Which, on a personal note, didn't sit well with my grandparents since they were Jewish. Seriously, do you know how many holiday meals were ruined by stories about the past?"

Jones smiled. "You're Jewish, I'm black, let's move on."

"Anyway, it didn't take long for Munich to start thriving again. In 1955, Hauser & Sons opened a new store at a new location, which is still open today."

"Please tell me you're serious."

"Of course I'm serious. I just sent the address to your phone."

"That's awesome! I can't wait to rub this in Jon's face."

"Wait. So you two really are fighting?"

"Not fighting. Just competing, like we always do."

Raskin smiled. "In that case, I gotta ask: Is he pissed at me?"

"At you? Why would he be pissed at you?"

"Because of his ringtone."

Jones burst out laughing. "*You* changed his ringtone?"

"Of course I changed his ringtone. Twelve times on three different phones. You're telling me he *still* hasn't figured it out?"

"Nope. He's clueless."

Raskin grunted in frustration. "I have to admit, I'm kind of insulted by his confusion. Who else does he know that could pull a hack like that?"

"Actually, he thinks it was me. Well, at least he did until yesterday."

"What happened yesterday?"

"I was flying a chopper when you switched his ringtone to 'Little Bunny Foo Foo,' so he knows I couldn't have done it. Great song, by the way. It totally pissed him off."

Raskin grinned in triumph. "Speaking of which, the next time you take Petr Ulster's chopper, you really should get permission."

"Permission? What are you talking about?"

Raskin groaned at his mistake. He didn't want Jones to know too much about his cyber-stalking, for fear it would upset him. "To change Jon's ringtone, I've been forced to track his phone. Because of that, I know you guys spent the night at the Ulster Archives."

"And?"

"I was bored, so I ran a search on Petr's latest projects. You know, just to see if he was working on anything exciting."

"And?"

"And I noticed his personal chopper had been reported stolen."

"When?" Jones demanded.

"About an hour ago."

"By whom?"

Raskin quickly pulled up the information. "No name on the report, but it was filed by the Bavarian State Police in Munich. They're tracking the beacon as we speak."

"Son of a bitch! Can you stop it?"

"Of course I can stop it."

"Then stop it! *Immediately*!"

Raskin typed furiously for the next several seconds. This time, there was very little cursing. "Okay . . . done! The beacon is toast."

"Thanks, man, I appreciate it. I really do. But I gotta go."

"Why? I told you, I stopped the beacon."

Jones opened the secret hatch. "I know you did, but we've been sitting still for the last hour. Whoever was tracking us knows where we are."

67

❦

Using the camera feature on his phone, Payne started taking pictures of the artwork and blueprints that hung from the walls. He knew from experience that missions, particularly those in uncharted territories, were prone to interruptions, so he compiled as much documentation as he could while he still had the chance.

His foresight proved to be invaluable when he heard the sound of footsteps in the tunnel. Worried, he pulled his weapon and headed for the door. "Be quiet. Someone's coming."

Ulster dismissed the warning. "It's probably David."

Payne listened closer. "Then why is he *running*?"

Heidi and Ulster immediately tensed and looked to Payne for further instructions. Unfortunately, he didn't have many options. They were in a windowless room with only one exit, which led to a concrete tunnel with no protection. The best they could do was stay put and hope for the best. With that in mind, Payne swung the door until it was nearly closed. The gap was just wide enough to keep an eye on the hallway.

Then he pointed at the desk. "Turn off your lights and stay low."

They quickly followed his orders.

As the footsteps got louder and louder, Payne calmly aimed his Sig Sauer into the hallway. For the next few seconds, shot discipline would be essential. The only way he would fire was if he saw men with automatic weapons or explosives. Otherwise, violence wasn't warranted. Still, it was wise to take the necessary precautions. In the darkness behind him, Heidi and Ulster crouched near the floor, the two of them huddling together for support. Hearts pounding, palms sweating, they prayed the noise in the hallway was Jones and there wasn't an actual threat.

Only half of their prayers were answered.

"Jon!" Jones called as he ran toward the room.

Payne recognized his voice. "What's wrong?"

"Someone tracked Petr's chopper. We gotta go!"

If anyone else had sounded the warning, Payne would have asked for additional information before he gave the order to abandon the site. But he trusted Jones far too much to question his judgment. "You heard the man. Let's go!"

Heidi stood up and started to complain. "We're leaving? Why are—"

"Now!" Payne growled. "Or you're on your own."

She looked to Ulster for support. "Petr? It's your helicop—"

Ulster, like a father quieting his child, put his fingertip on her lips. "Hush, my dear. It's time to go. Not another word."

Heidi wasn't happy, but she scurried out the door.

Payne fought the urge to smile. "Follow DJ. He's got the lead."

Ulster glanced around the room one last time, disappointment etched on his face. There was so much more he wanted to learn about Ludwig and his final years as king. Ulster hoped he would have a chance to return someday soon to finish his historical research. If not, he would always be filled with regret. "Will you be locking the door?"

Payne nodded. "I'll even let you hold the key."

Ulster thanked him, then lumbered toward the others.

Meanwhile, Jones was already approaching the vertical shaft that led to the fake stalagmite. Although the deep water of the Venus Grotto would temporarily slow them down, he realized it was the fastest route to the chopper. Plus, he wanted to grab their personal belongings and the map, which had been stashed by the control panel, before they left the castle grounds. No sense in giving anyone else a head start in finding them or Ludwig's secret room.

Jones waited for Heidi's arrival before he climbed the ladder. When he reached the top, he made sure they were safe, then signaled for her to join him. One by one, they popped out of the stalagmite and jumped into the Grotta Azzurra. As usual, Payne was the last one out. He made certain the hatch was secure while the others headed for the shore. According to his watch, it was already past nine. That meant the Linderhof gates were officially open. An influx of tourists would make things messy, especially if gunplay was involved. Payne hoped it wouldn't come to that, but he didn't know what they were facing since he hadn't been fully briefed.

Less than a minute later, they were gathering their things and rushing toward the door. As an ex-employee, Heidi knew where supplies were stored in the bowels of the grotto. To protect the map and the black swan envelope, she placed them in a clean plastic bag and handed it to Ulster—not to avoid the responsibility, but because she assumed she would be driving the golf cart back to the chopper. Nevertheless, Ulster thanked her for the sign of respect.

"Okay," Jones said as he hustled toward the secret entrance, "keep your eyes open. If you see anything suspicious, call it out. Understood?"

Soaking wet, they nodded in agreement.

Jones continued. "I'm out the door first. Stay here until I give the all clear."

With gun in hand, Jones cranked the handle that held the door in place. There was a soft click followed by a loud rumble as the giant boulder turned on its center axis. Unlike before, Jones knew exactly what to expect, yet he couldn't help but smile. It really was a cool special effect, the type of thing that was commonly used in movies but rarely seen in real life. The fact that it was over a hundred years old made it even cooler.

When the boulder stopped moving, Jones peeked through the resulting fissure. He hoped to see their golf cart and a deserted path. Instead, he was greeted by a four-man hit squad. They were armed with semiautomatic pistols and sound suppressors. Ordered by Mueller to follow the chopper's beacon, the squad would have entered the grotto a lot sooner had they been able to figure out the secret door. Now that was no longer an issue. They were standing in a semicircle in front of the opening, all of them poised to shoot.

Schultz, the lead goon, stepped forward. "Raise your hands!"

Jones cursed under his breath. He was severely outgunned, and he knew it. Even if he killed their leader, the other three would mow him down in less than a second. Things would have been different if he had been alone. He would have bolted back inside the grotto in hopes of losing the goons in the darkness, but he couldn't risk it with Heidi and Ulster standing behind him. Without instructions, they wouldn't know what to do or where to go. So Jones decided to stand his ground as long as possible, hoping to give Payne a chance to hide them inside.

To buy some time, Jones replied in Spanish. *"No hablo inglés."*

Unfortunately, Schultz spoke *español* a lot better than Jones did. *"¡Levanten sus manos! ¡Deja su arma!"*

Jones grimaced. His tactic had backfired. So he decided to switch to Russian. He had learned some on a recent trip to Saint Petersburg. "Я не говорю по Испански."

Schultz wasn't stupid. He was willing to give Jones the

benefit of the doubt with Spanish, but he knew damn well that Jones wasn't Russian. "Stop stalling. I know you and your friends can speak English. Your pilot told us that and more."

Jones glanced over Schultz's shoulder and spotted Baptiste in the back of the golf cart. His hands were tied and his face was bloodied. "What do you want?"

"I want you to raise your hands and drop your gun."

To buy more time, Jones decided to press his luck. "Are you sure about that? Because if I raise my hands *first*, I'm liable to drop my gun on my head. And between you and me, scalp wounds are rather messy."

Schultz smiled, then calmly pulled his trigger. A silenced round whizzed past Jones's ear and burrowed into the rocky mound behind him. "So are bullet holes."

Jones quickly dropped his gun. "Good point."

"Now take three steps forward, then kneel."

"Big steps or baby steps?"

Schultz didn't answer. He simply readjusted his aim. His new target was a spot between Jones's eyes. From close range, it would be tough to miss. With Schultz's patience wearing thin, Jones decided to follow his orders. As things stood, he had already bought Payne more than enough time to hide their friends in the grotto and to plan an attack.

If the goons went inside, Payne would kill them.

If they didn't, Payne would escape through the tunnel.

Either way, Jones had done his duty.

The rest would be up to Payne.

68

❖

Payne refused to take any chances with Heidi and Ulster. Instead of stashing them in the darkness of the grotto, he ordered them to hide in the secret tunnel. He knew the concrete would protect them from gunfire, and in a worst-case scenario, they could exit through the fake tree stump and escape the castle grounds. Surprisingly, neither of them complained. They jumped in the water and swam toward the Grotta Azzurra, where they would enter the stalagmite.

Meanwhile, Payne eyed his surroundings and planned his assault. Unless the goons had recently toured the Linderhof, he knew he had the tactical advantage inside the grotto. Thanks to the man-made cavern and the special effects, it would be like fighting a war in an amusement park. To tilt the terrain in his favor, he hustled to the control panel and turned on the waterfall. Within seconds, water gushed from its spout and splashed into the lake. Next he turned on the wave machine and turned off the underwater lights. Suddenly, the dark water resembled an angry sea, its waves crashing against Ludwig's boat and the nearby path.

Payne smiled at the sight. Back in the Special Forces, he had spent many nights in similar conditions, sneaking onto foreign shores and taking out targets. He had enjoyed it then and he would enjoy it now. About the only thing missing was Jones by his side. And yet somehow Payne knew that his best friend was fine and that they were still working in unison.

Jones would lure them in and Payne would take them out.

Just like old times.

Near the bottom of the control panel, Payne spotted a large dial that looked like the volume control on a stereo. Hoping to limit his opponent's communication, Payne turned the knob. Instantly, the soaring vocals of Richard Wagner's *Tannhäuser*, one of Ludwig's favorite operas, filled the grotto. Payne grinned and cranked the volume even louder. In a confined space, the music and the darkness would conceal his movement until he was ready to strike.

Now all he had to do was wait.

The goons entered the grotto completely unprepared. No flashlights. No maps. No advance surveillance. They just stormed into the darkness en masse, a cluster of three soldiers on a well-lit path. Apparently, they hadn't been briefed on the shoot-out in the gorge; otherwise, they would have thought long and hard about a frontal assault against a highly skilled soldier.

Of course, that was the problem with most goons.

They weren't trained to think.

Payne crouched in the dark lake, allowing his body to rise and fall with the surging tide. He was close enough to the path to be accurate, but far enough away to be unseen—until his muzzle flash lit up the cavern like a lightning bolt. If he'd had more time to work with, he would have picked them off silently, using his bare hands and his blade. Unfortunately, Jones was in immediate danger, so the clock was ticking.

He was forced to make his move now.

For Payne, the first shot would be the easiest. He raised his Sig Sauer above the waterline and aimed at the lead goon's throat. Because of the undulating waves, Payne knew his aim might be affected vertically. If he shot high, he would hit face. If he shot low, he would hit chest. If his aim was true, he would hit jugular. No matter what, the goon would go down. After that, Payne would have to swing his weapon to the right and get off two more shots before the last goon spotted Payne's position in the water. If that happened, things would get interesting.

The blaring music masked the blast as Payne pulled his trigger. The bullet caught the lead goon under his chin and killed him instantly. He collapsed on the narrow path, effectively blocking the two men behind him. Payne wasted no time and fired at the second goon. The rising water pushed his aim high, but not high enough for the guy to survive.

Just like that, there was one goon left.

His name was Faust, and he was smarter than the others.

He quickly fired a shot toward Payne's muzzle flash, then jumped into the dark lake even though he wasn't a good swimmer. For Faust, it had been a spur-of-the-moment decision, one that had helped him survive since the lit path had been a shooting gallery and his team had been the targets. Another moment up there and he would have been killed like his colleagues.

In the water, at least he had a chance.

Three days earlier, Payne had been swimming on the bottom of the Ohio River, blindly looking for a lost bottle opener. Now he was searching for prey in a man-made lake.

In his mind, this would be far easier.

With a knife in his hand and his lungs full of air, Payne glided underwater toward the panic-stricken Faust. The lake was deep enough and dark enough to conceal Payne's approach, so he wasted no time once he spotted the thrashing legs of his target. Attacking from behind, Payne grabbed the back of Faust's collar and yanked him under the surface of the water. Faust bucked and flailed, trying to break free, but Payne ended the battle with a quick slash of his blade. Blood gushed from Faust's neck as he dropped his gun and tried, in vain, to hold the fluid inside of his body. But it wasn't to be. Within seconds, the life had drained out of him.

Payne held on until the struggling stopped, then he pushed the corpse aside and swam hard toward the shore. He sprang from the water and landed on the narrow path, not far from the second dead goon. Normally, Payne would have been reluctant to use someone else's weapon unless his own gun was damaged or out of ammo, but in this case, it made sense strategically. The goon's Beretta was equipped with a sound suppressor, which would be useful outside of the grotto—especially if more men were positioned around the Linderhof grounds. The last thing Payne wanted was to make them aware of his presence. With that in mind, he picked up the Beretta, fired a test shot into the water, then headed toward the fake boulder.

While kneeling on the hard ground, Jones could hear the music seeping from the opening behind him. Although he wasn't familiar with this particular opera, he found himself humming along to the music—partially to calm his nerves and partially because he was bored.

Based on Schultz's tactics, it was fairly obvious that he had been ordered to follow the beacon and question the chopper's occupants before anyone was eliminated. Otherwise, Jones and Baptiste would already be dead, and Schultz would be inside the grotto looking for Payne, Heidi, and Ulster. Once Jones figured that out, his attitude changed. If given the opportunity, Jones would still make a move on Schultz, but he wasn't about to do anything desperate. At least not until Payne had a chance to wipe out the rest of his crew. In the meantime, he would do everything he could to keep his captor distracted.

Jones stared at Schultz, who was fifteen feet away. "What time is it?"

"Time to shut up."

He acted offended. "Damn! Why are you so mean? Have you always been like this? If so, you got in the right line of work. Lots of angry men in the goon business."

"I'm not a goon."

"Really? What are you, then?"

"I'm a soldier."

"Me, too. How long have you worked for Mueller?"

Schultz glanced around. He wasn't used to chatty prisoners. Normally, they were quivering in fear, not trying to make conversation. "Two years."

"Good employer?"

"Not bad."

"Benefits?"

Schultz caught himself before he answered. "That's it! No more talking. I know what you're trying to do."

"Really? What's that?"

"You're *trying* to distract me."

"Is it working?"

"Not a chance."

During the past few seconds, Jones had noticed the music getting softer behind him. Either someone had turned down the volume, or someone was standing near the fissure, blocking the sound as it tried to escape the grotto. If he had to guess, he would say it was probably the latter.

"One last question, then I *promise* I'll shut up."

Schultz glared at him. "What is it?"

"Do you know why we're here?"

He sneered. "I'll find out soon enough."

Jones smiled, confident Payne was behind him. "No, you won't."

A moment later, Payne squeezed the trigger and ended the conversation.

Jones didn't even turn around. "Took you long enough."

"Screw you," Payne snapped. "It was one against three."

Jones stood and brushed off his knees. "Actually, it was three against three. Or don't Heidi and Ulster count?"

"In this case, they don't. I sent them to safety."

"Then you better go get them. We need to lift off, A-SAP."

"Me? What about you? What are you going to do?"

Jones pointed at the golf cart. "I need to check on Baptiste. If he can't fly, I'm the pilot."

"Fine! We'll meet you here in five."

Jones suddenly turned serious. "By the way, thanks."

Payne nodded, then disappeared into the darkness of the grotto.

69

Munich, Germany

Oktoberfest is the world's largest fair. Held annually in Munich, the sixteen-day festival attracts more than six million visitors a year. The original Oktoberfest occurred in 1810 and commemorated the marriage of Princess Therese of Saxe-Hildburghausen and Crown Prince Ludwig, who later became King Ludwig I. (He was the namesake of Ludwig II and his paternal grandfather.) The event is held in the Theresienwiese—which translates to "Therese's meadow"—an open space of four and a half million square feet that is southwest of center city. The festival is so important to Munich's economy that the massive field has its own subway station. During the event, the U-Baun station handles roughly twenty thousand people per hour in each direction.

Because of security concerns, Payne was thrilled that

Hauser & Sons was located on the opposite side of the city, far away from the madness. Baptiste landed the chopper on a corporate helipad six blocks from the store, then took off as soon as his passengers hustled to safety. Although Jones was convinced that Raskin had handled the beacon problem, Baptiste was instructed to fly around the city to confuse would-be pursuers.

As a former resident of Munich, Heidi led the way to the store while Payne followed closely behind. Unlike the crowds of foreigners that filled the sidewalks, she knew exactly where she was headed. Energized by the palpable buzz in the city, she walked so quickly at times that Ulster struggled to keep up. Eventually, Payne grabbed her elbow and urged her to slow down—not only for Ulster's sake, but also for the group's safety. The farther they were spread apart, the tougher it was to keep an eye on everybody.

Ironically, Heidi wasn't the least bit excited about their trip to the store. She thought it might result in a small tidbit about Ludwig but didn't think it was worth their time and effort, not at this stage of their search. In fact, the only one who truly believed in the significance of the receipt was Jones. For some reason, he just sensed it was critical and wouldn't let it rest. In the end, Payne and Ulster were willing to play along in order to shut Jones up.

Located in a brown brick building on a commercial street, Hauser & Sons had the glossy look of a high-end store. Its name was written in gold calligraphy on an elegant sign above the tinted glass doorway. Display cases, filled with a wide assortment of jewelry, sat behind the shatterproof windows that lined the sidewalks. Lit by over-head lights that were discreetly hidden from public view, the jewels sparkled like stars in the desert night.

Heidi wanted to stop for a longer look, but Payne dragged her away from the window and toward the door. For the next few minutes, he needed her to focus on the receipt, not the diamond necklace she had been admiring. Heidi nodded and promised she would be on her best be-havior, but the moment they entered the store, she was distracted by a pair of earrings. Then a tennis bracelet. Then a gold ring. Before he knew it, she was in shopping mode.

Dressed in a designer suit, Friedrich Hauser watched the action unfold from his desk near the back of the store. Over the decades, he had witnessed a similar scene play out more times than he could possibly remember. The truth was he made his living on the type of excitement that she was displaying. He only hoped the woman (or one of her friends) had the bank account to match her expensive taste. If so, it would be a great afternoon.

"Guten Tag!" he said as he strolled forward.

Payne waved and said, "Hello."

Hauser, a man in his mid-sixties, smiled warmly. "Ah, you are visiting our city. I should have known. Everyone is a visitor during Oktoberfest. Where are you from?"

"America."

"That is a long way to come for jewelry. I guess our reputation is growing."

Payne laughed and shook his hand. "From the looks of

things, your reputation is well deserved. You have a beautiful store."

Hauser beamed. "I thank you—and so do my ancestors."

The comment caught everyone's attention, including Heidi's. She turned away from the main display case and joined the others.

"You're the owner?" Payne asked.

"One of them. My name is Friedrich Hauser."

Payne introduced his group. "I'm Jon. This is David, Petr, and Heidi."

Hauser nodded. "Nice to meet you. How may I be of service?"

Payne took a step back. "DJ, the floor is yours."

Hauser smiled and waited for an explanation.

Jones took over. "We found something from your store, and we were hoping you could give us some additional information about its owner."

Hauser arched his eyebrow. "Let me guess: You found a ring! People lose them all the time. Thankfully, we keep wonderful records. Can you describe the piece?"

Jones shook his head. "No, not a ring. We found a document."

"A document? I don't understand."

Ulster pointed at one of the display cases. "May we show you?"

Hauser nodded his approval and walked to the opposite side of the case while Jones placed the receipt on the freshly cleaned glass. Over the next several seconds, the group watched in silence as Hauser inspected the antique document. Strangely, he seemed to go through a wide range of emotions in a short period of time—confusion, followed by excitement, and finally trepidation. Meanwhile, his body went on a similar journey. Gone was the relaxed posture of a moment before, replaced by the rigid stance of a prison guard.

His eyes narrowed to slits. "Where did you get this?"

Jones answered. "We found it in a desk."

"Whose desk?"

"For the time being, I'd rather not say."

Hauser grimaced and returned his attention to the document. It was painfully obvious that he knew what he was looking at, yet something prevented him from admitting it. Payne was tempted to go on the offensive and question him, but before he had a chance, Hauser looked at him directly. "May I take this into the back? I'd like to show it to my father."

Payne shook his head. "Actually, we'd prefer if he came out here and talked to us in person. We'd love to meet him."

"That will be difficult. He doesn't move around very well."

"I'm sorry to hear that, but we go where the receipt goes. If you'd like, we're more than willing to visit him. Just lead the way."

Hauser stared at the document and sighed, the weight of the world on his shoulders. He looked like a man who truly didn't know what he was supposed to do. "Wait right here. I'll see which my father would prefer. In the meantime, can one of you lock the main door?"

"Why?" Heidi asked.

"Whichever he decides, this matter should be handled in private."

Payne nodded. "You talk to your father; we'll get the lock."

Hauser hustled into the back while Heidi took care of the door. Meanwhile, Payne, Jones, and Ulster tried to figure out what was going on.

Jones whispered. "Did you see Hauser's face? The guy was scared—almost like I'd handed him a ransom note. If this receipt says 'give me your money' in Bavarian, we're fucked."

Payne shook his head. "That wasn't fear. That was anxiety. He's nervous about something. For the time being, I think it would be best if we spread out in the store."

"Why's that?" Ulster wondered.

"If he comes back with a shotgun, I don't want to be an easy target."

"Are you serious?"

Payne shrugged halfheartedly. "Kind of, but not really. It's obvious we've stumbled into something important. Until we know what that is, I think it's best if we took precautions."

"Like what?" Heidi asked.

"Like spreading out in the store."

Jones moved first, grabbing a defensive position near the front door, while Heidi and Ulster scattered to opposite corners. Meanwhile, Payne stood off to the right, where he had a clear view of the entire room. From there, he could see everything and control the action.

Five minutes later, Hauser emerged from the back. Although his hands were weapon-free, he was armed with a question—one that would determine what happened next. He spotted Payne off to the side and walked in his direction, sensing he was the leader of this group. Hauser stopped a few feet in front of him and lowered his voice to a whisper.

"My father," he said, "is nearly a hundred years old. During his lifetime, he has suffered through two world wars and the death of his entire generation. In the last decade, he has buried the love of his life and two of my sisters, so the man has endured far more than most. Because of that, I'm willing to respect his wishes—even in situations that I don't fully understand."

Payne stared at Hauser, trying to figure out where this was going. "What does any of that have to do with us?"

"I spoke to my father about the receipt, and, well, to be perfectly honest, he got upset."

"Upset?"

Hauser nodded. "He said he didn't have the strength to talk to you. Unless . . ."

"Unless what?"

"Unless you can answer a question."

Intrigued by the whispering, Ulster crept closer. "What's the question?"

Hauser sighed. "That's the thing. It isn't even a question. It's more like a statement that you're supposed to finish. If you finish it correctly, my father will speak to you. If not, I'm supposed to escort you from the store."

Ulster welcomed the challenge. "How fun! What's the statement?"

"Yeah," Heidi said as she approached, "what's the statement?"

Hauser took a deep breath, then whispered the words his father had told him to say. "He who holds the key . . ."

The group answered in unison. "Gets to wear the crown."

Hauser blinked a few times, stunned. "That's correct. How did you . . . ?" His voice trailed off as he thought about the past few years with his father. They had been more than difficult. "Do you know what? It doesn't even matter. I'm just glad *someone* knew what he was talking about. He's been babbling about your receipt forever. Until today, I thought maybe it was a figment of his imagination. I'm thrilled to know it wasn't."

Payne cut to the chase. "Does this mean we can talk to him?"

Hauser answered cryptically. "Not only that, it means you get to open the case."

"What case?" Jones demanded.

Hauser smiled. "You'll find out soon enough."

70

Hauser led the group into the stockroom at the rear of the store. To their right was a walk-in vault that protected the most valuable merchandise at Hauser & Sons and any currency that had been collected during the course of the week. To their left was a small office filled with a desk, chair, computer, printer, and three filing cabinets. Everything was simple and clean.

"Where's your father?" Payne asked as his eyes darted from side to side, looking for danger. While he walked, he kept his hand near his gun. "I thought he was back here."

Hauser glanced over his shoulder. "He's in his workshop, which is in the rear corner of the building. We put it back there so the noise wouldn't disturb the customers."

Jones whispered. "If he's chained up and making sneakers, we're going to set him free."

Hauser didn't hear the joke. "I wanted him to retire years ago, but he says work is the only thing keeping him going. If that's the case, he can stay here as long as he wants."

Heidi asked, "What kind of work?"

"Jewelry design and repair. Despite his age, he still has the hands of a surgeon. Unfortunately, his eyes are a different story."

They walked down a hallway and came upon a well-lit repair shop where an old man was sitting on a metal stool, hunched over a counter. Dressed in a long-sleeved shirt and a pair of dark pants that were held up with suspenders, he stared through a high-powered magnification lamp that allowed him to see the necklace clasp he was working on. He was also wearing a thick pair of glasses that were attached to a black cord that hung around his neck.

Without turning his head, he sensed the group's approach and calmly laid down his tools. After all this time, someone had *finally* come to claim the item. It was a moment his family had been waiting for since 1886. Although his role had been small over the years, he was honored to be a part of the conclusion and thrilled to share the moment with his son. With great effort, he swiveled on his seat until he faced the doorway. He wanted to get a good look at the group that had found the receipt and had answered his question correctly.

"Please come in," he said with a thick Bavarian accent. "I apologize for not coming to greet you, but as my son surely mentioned, my mobility is poor."

Payne smiled warmly. "If anything, we're the ones who should apologize for showing up unannounced. I'm sorry if we've inconvenienced you in any way."

Appreciative of the sentiment, the old man stuck out his hand and formally introduced himself. "My name is Alexander. It is a pleasure to meet you."

"The pleasure is ours," Payne said as they shook hands. "My name is Jon."

Jones followed his lead. "I'm David."

"I'm Heidi."

Ulster went last. "And I'm Petr."

Strangely, Ulster's handshake lasted longer than all of the others combined. After a few uncomfortable seconds, Ulster tried to release his hand from the old man's grip, but Hauser held tight, his yellow fingernails digging into Ulster's skin. Everyone, including Hauser's son, was confused by the development. The old man finally blinked and released his grasp.

"I am sorry," he said, obviously embarrassed. "It's just, well, I saw . . ."

With empathy in his eyes, Ulster looked at Hauser and tried to figure out what had just happened. For a split second or two, it seemed like the old man had gone somewhere else in his mind. "You saw what?"

He swallowed hard and tried to explain. "As a jeweler, I could not help but notice the ring on your finger. With your permission, may I take a closer look?"

Ulster stared at his right hand. The gold ring was a permanent fixture. Not only because of its personal significance, but also because of his weight gain over the years. "Unfortunately, I'm unable to remove the ring. My fingers are a tad too plump."

"That is fine," Hauser assured him. "I can work around that."

With some effort, Hauser reached up and grabbed the magnification lamp. It was attached to a maneuverable spring arm and clamped to the counter. As everyone watched closely, he slowly pulled the powerful lens toward Ulster's hand and adjusted the settings on the light so he could get a better look at the family crest on the ring. When the image—an eagle with a sword in one talon and a scroll in the other—came into view, the old man gasped in recognition. He hadn't seen the coat of arms in more than sixty years.

"Are you an Ulster?" the old man asked.

Petr was taken aback. "Yes, sir. My name is Petr Ulster."

"And your grandfather, what was his name?"

"Conrad. Conrad Ulster."

The old man trembled slightly. A few seconds passed before he lifted his eyes to meet Ulster's gaze. For the first time, everyone noticed that the old man had started to cry. "Then it has come full circle."

Hauser's son rushed forward. "Papa, what is wrong?"

The old man shook his head for several seconds. When he finally spoke, his voice quivered with emotion. "Nothing is wrong, my son. Everything is *right*. The right people have come for the case. Please retrieve it from the vault."

The son nodded, then hustled off to fulfill the request.

Meanwhile, the old man slowly regained his composure. First he wiped away his tears with his sleeve, then he pointed to a stack of folding chairs in the corner of the room. After years of being hunched over a counter, his spine was so curved he had trouble lifting his head.

"Please grab a seat. I'd like to look at you while we talk."

As they carried their chairs across the room, the son returned from the vault with a plain wooden crate. It was nondescript in every way. He set it gently on the floor next to his father's stool, then he grabbed a chair for himself. From this point forward, he was like everyone else. He wanted to know what was going on, because he, too, had no idea what was about to be unveiled.

Hauser cleared his throat. "By now, all of you must think that I am a crazy old man. I assure you I am not. My body might be failing, but my mind is still sharp. As for my tears, they came from an unexpected source. I have always known that *someone* would come for the case. I have been prepared for that for half of my life. What I didn't know was who. At my age, nothing in the world surprises me. I have lived too long and seen too much to ever be astonished. Nevertheless, I was caught off guard by your ring."

Ulster pointed at his finger. "My ring?"

Hauser nodded. "I have not seen it for decades. But, even with failing eyes, I recognized it at once. An artist always remembers his art."

Ulster quickly connected the dots. "You *made* my ring?"

"I did indeed. I carved the crest myself."

"I don't understand. This was my grandfather's ring."

"Yes," Hauser confirmed, "it belonged to your grand-father, but I was the one who made it. My father gave it to him after the war as a token of our thanks."

"Thanks? Thanks for what?"

"For everything," Hauser explained. "For hiding our jewels during the war. For keeping his word when others had lied. For protecting the case from Nazi hands. Your grandfather was an amazing man. Without him, the item would have been lost forever."

Payne heard the words and breathed a sigh of relief. Only two days had passed since he had called Ulster and warned him about the bunker in Garmisch-Partenkirchen. At the time, the discovery of Ulster's coat of arms on a crate of missing artwork had been potentially devastating. It threatened to stain Ulster's name and tear apart every-thing that the Archives represented. But after hearing Hauser's heartfelt speech, he knew the Ulster legacy was safe.

He patted Ulster on his shoulder. "Your grandfather was a hero."

Ulster beamed with pride. "I guess he was."

The old man waved his finger. "There is no guessing about it. Conrad Ulster was a hero. He saved countless treasures across Europe, then returned them to the rightful owners. If not for him, this store and many others never would have reopened. That is why my family gave him the ring. And that is why I'm glad you've come for the case."

71

✤

Payne stared at the wooden crate, which was sitting on the floor next to Hauser's stool. Nothing about it seemed special. It was made of wood and looked eerily similar to the crates found inside the hidden bunker. As far as he could tell, the main difference was its size. He guessed it was two feet in width, length, and height. Certainly not large enough to hold an enormous treasure.

"Sir," Payne said, "you keep mentioning the item. Can you tell us about its history?"

Hauser paused in thought, trying to figure out where he should start a narrative that had been going strong for more than a hundred years. After a while, he decided to pose a question to the group. "Tell me, are you familiar with Nostradamus?"

Payne and Jones exchanged knowing glances. Both of them were quite familiar with the sixteenth-century French prophet who was renowned for his ability to see the future. Less than a year ago, they had discovered one of his lost manuscripts, and it had nearly gotten them killed.

Ulster answered for the group. "Yes, sir."

"And what about his connection to Ludwig?"

Heidi shook her head. "That's news to me."

"Me, too," Ulster added.

Hauser smiled. "Then that is where we shall begin— way back in 1864 when Ludwig was still a prince and his father was slowly dying."

The group leaned forward, not wanting to miss a single word.

"King Maximilian II summoned his son to his bedside and warned him of a prophecy that he believed foretold the death of Ludwig. Though it did not appear in his book *Les Prophecies*, the quatrain has long been attributed to Nostradamus, a man who has influenced many a king across Europe and many a man across time."

Ulster interrupted him. "What was the prophecy?"

The old man answered in fluent French.

*Quand le Vendredi Saint tombera sur le jour de Saint
    George,
Pâques sur le jour de Saint Marc,
Et la Fête Dieu sur le jour de Saint Jean,
Tout le monde pleurera.*

From personal experience, Ulster knew that Payne and Jones weren't language experts, so he translated the verse into English.

When Good Friday falls on Saint George's day,
Easter on Saint Mark's day,
And Corpus Christi on Saint John's day,
All the world will weep.

The group pondered the quatrain for several seconds, trying to decipher its meaning. Even though Ludwig's name wasn't mentioned, they knew the verse could have been written about his death. Or not. That was the problem with most of Nostradamus's prophecies; they could be interpreted in a number of different ways. Of course, that was also part of their allure.

Heidi spoke first. "Have those events ever occurred in the same year?"

"It's happened once. The year was 1886."

She grinned. "The year Ludwig was murdered."

Hauser nodded. "For two decades, Ludwig feared the approach of 1886 like a sailor watching an approaching storm. In his heart, he knew he wouldn't survive that ill-fated year no matter what he did. Somehow that gave him the courage to finish his dream of creating a kingdom across the sea. Ironically, it was his pursuit of that dream that ultimately got him killed."

Ulster frowned at the irony. "His cabinet found out?"

Hauser nodded again. "First Ludwig was arrested, then they silenced him forever. The Bavarian government proclaimed its innocence in the whole affair, but I know the truth. Everyone who was living in Munich back then knows what happened. They murdered our king."

Jones did the math in his head. "Wait. You're not *that* old . . . are you?"

The old man laughed. "Sometimes I feel like I am, but all of this occurred three decades before I was born. It was my grandfather, not me, who lived during Ludwig's reign. When I was a young man, he told me about Ludwig's life and death, so I could pass the story on to future generations. It had great impact coming from my grandfather, since he actually knew the king."

Heidi stared in amazement. She was talking to someone who had secondhand knowledge about Ludwig. "Your grandfather *knew* him?"

Hauser nodded. "They worked together. Over a period of six months, they met more than a dozen times to discuss the item's design. I'm sure you have heard rumors about Ludwig's controlling manner. According to my grandfather, the rumors were quite accurate. Everything had to be perfect. Then again, for something this important, I can understand why."

Payne didn't want to be rude, but his curiosity was starting to get the best of him. The crate was sitting on the floor, a mere five feet away, yet he didn't know what was inside. "Sir, you keep mentioning the item and talking about its importance, but none of us know what it is. If it's okay with you, we'd love to know what's inside the crate. It might help us understand."

The old man smiled sheepishly. The item had been in his family for so long, he was having trouble letting go. Still, he knew it had to be done. Tears filled his eyes as he thought about the three men—his father, his grandfather, and Conrad Ulster—who had protected the item before him. Selfishly, he wanted his son to be a part of the process, even if his duty was symbolic in nature. "Friedrich, it is time. Please remove the case and hand it to Petr. After all these years, that only seems fitting. The item is being passed from our family to yours."

His son picked up the crate and placed it on a counter behind him. The lid had been nailed shut, so it would take a moment to pry it off. While he worked, his father filled the silence.

"If you look past his quirks and all the rumors, Ludwig was nothing more than an idealist. It was the main reason he tried to leave Bavaria. He wanted the opportunity to create a perfect kingdom, one that he would be proud of. Some rulers would have started with a code of laws or a new system of government, but Ludwig was bored by bureaucracy. Instead, he focused his attention on the arts, for that was the one thing he was passionate about."

The crate creaked behind him as his son worked on the lid.

"Ludwig started with the basics, several years before his death. First he designed his country's flag, which featured an image he had drawn himself: an elaborate black swan. Then he contacted Richard Wagner, his favorite composer, and asked him to create a national anthem. Before long, Ludwig had hired Christian Jank and Eduard Riedel, the men responsible for Neuschwanstein, to design the most spectacular castle the world had ever seen. If that wasn't difficult enough, they were asked to design it with no knowledge of the building site. Ultimately, by the time Ludwig acquired the land, both builders were approaching death."

Heidi gasped at the news. "Ludwig *found* a location?"

Hauser nodded. "According to my grandfather, Ludwig selected a large parcel of land on the island of Capri. His goal was to start a city-state, similar to Monaco's relationship with France. Ludwig would have independence, but Italy would be responsible for his defense."

Jones instantly thought about the map of Capri that he had found inside the grotto. Currently, the document was locked in the helicopter for safekeeping, but he was willing to bet that when they examined it closer they would find more than just the entrance to the secret tunnel. He was confident the map would reveal the exact location of Ludwig's land—the place his kingdom would have been established if he had lived long enough to build it.

Ulster pondered the selection. "Actually, Capri makes a lot of sense for a creative soul like Ludwig. During the 1800s, it was a haven for artists, writers, and musicians. Plus, it was one of the few spots on earth where men and women were able to enjoy open lifestyles."

Heidi asked, "Out of curiosity, did he have a chance to visit his land?"

Hauser shook his head. "It was never *his* land."

The statement confused Heidi. "I don't understand."

Hauser explained. "Travel was far too difficult in those days to make a quick trip overseas, and Ludwig was being watched too closely to risk a long journey. Instead, he was forced to send a representative to Capri to make the arrangements for him. Unfortunately, the land was never officially purchased because of Ludwig's paranoia."

"What do you mean?" Ulster wondered.

"Ludwig had never been the trusting sort, so it should come as no surprise that he didn't give his delegate the funds to purchase the land. He gave his delegate the authority to negotiate a final price and to reach an agreement in terms, but Ludwig refused to give him the money to complete the transaction. According to my grandfather, Ludwig planned to deliver the gold himself when he left Bavaria for the final time."

Payne's ears perked up. "Did you say *gold*?"

Hauser nodded. "Legend has it that he was going to finance his new kingdom with a collection of gold bars that had been stamped with the black swan emblem. Of course, it's only a legend. As far as I know, the gold has never been found."

Somehow Payne, Jones, and Ulster managed to keep a straight face, despite their recent discovery in the secret bunker. Meanwhile, Heidi, who knew nothing about the crate of gold, asked a follow-up question: "Where did the gold come from?"

Hauser started to address the topic but stopped when a loud crack emerged from his son's workstation. Everyone glanced in that direction, worried that something important had broken.

Friedrich quickly assured the group that everything was okay. It was merely the sound of the lid being removed from the crate. "It's ready, Papa."

Hauser reached out his arms. "Come, my son. Help me to the case. We shall do this together."

Even with his son's assistance, it took a minute for the old man to get off his stool and walk to the counter behind him. By the time he got there, Payne, Jones, Ulster, and Heidi had already gathered around the wooden crate. They were more than anxious to see its contents.

While Hauser caught his breath, Friedrich removed the lid from the wooden crate. After a nod of approval from his father, he reached inside. A moment later, he pulled out an elaborate gold case and handed it to Ulster, whose eyes widened with surprise. In all of his days, he had never seen anything like it. Inlaid with rubies, emeralds, sapphires, and pearls, the case measured slightly less than two feet in width, length, and height. In the middle of all six sides, the black swan emblem had been discreetly carved into the gold.

Ulster spoke in a reverent tone. "It's magnificent. It truly is."

The elder Hauser, who hadn't seen the case in years, reached out his hand and traced the symbol with one of his crooked fingers. "My great-uncle built this himself. He worked nonstop for many months, using jewels and gold that had been donated to Ludwig's cause. Ludwig had requested the materials via a series of letters."

"The black swan letters?" Heidi asked.

His mind drifting elsewhere, Hauser nodded as he ran his hands down the left and right sides of the case. With his index fingers, he pointed to matching sapphires near the bottom of the cube. "To open the case, you must push these jewels at the exact same time. Ludwig loved his secret contraptions, and he chose sapphires to match the color of the water in the Blue Grotto."

The old man pushed the jewels.

Click.

All of a sudden, a horizontal seam appeared an inch above the bottom of the box. To open it, the top would have to be lifted straight off the base.

Hauser continued his explanation. "Ludwig did not want a hinge in the back. He wanted his case to be in two separate pieces: the base and the lid. That way he could display the item in the base without interference from the lid."

Ulster looked at him. "You mean the cube *isn't* the item?"

Hauser shook his head. "This merely holds the treasure within."

Payne and Jones exchanged glances. They found it hard to believe that something more valuable was waiting inside. A few seconds later, their doubts were proven wrong.

Hauser wiped his eyes on his sleeve. "As you probably know, Ludwig was a vain man who always wore the finest clothes and robes. Even as a child, he valued beauty above all else. With that in mind, he wanted to look his absolute best when he sat on his throne for the very first time. He wanted to look like the king he had always pictured in his dreams."

Hauser took a deep breath and lifted the lid off the gold case. For the first time in decades, he stared at his grandfather's handiwork. It was more beautiful than he had remembered—more beautiful than anything he had ever seen. The group gasped at the sight.

"To be that king, he needed the finest crown ever made."

EPILOGUE

The Hofbräuhaus, the most famous beer hall in Munich's old town, has its own tent at Oktoberfest. Known as the Hofbräu-Festzelt, it is the largest of the thirty-four tents on the festival grounds, with a total capacity of nearly ten thousand people. During the sixteen-day festival, more than a half-million liters of Hofbräu beer would be served inside, not to mention a million pounds of meat. With many guests dressed in traditional costumes and a Bavarian oompah band playing on the large stage, it was easy to get caught up in the fun.

As he made his way into the tent, the man spotted Jones at a large wooden table and decided to sneak up behind him. Well aware of Jones's training, he took no chances with the ex-MANIAC. He patiently waited until Jones set down his mug before he wrapped his arm around his friend's throat. Then he gave it a friendly squeeze.

Jones glanced back and saw the unmistakable chin of Nick Dial. It was the physical trait that defined him. "It's about time. We were wondering when you'd show up. Or *if* you'd show up."

Dial patted his shoulder. "Sorry about my tardiness. But some idiot shot a bunch of people in the grotto at the Linderhof. I had to go check it out."

Jones grunted. "The *nerve* of some people!"

Payne, who was sitting across from Jones, stood and shook Dial's hand. "Long time no see. We're glad you could sneak away—if only for today."

"And I'm glad you're still alive. Seriously, you guys are retired. You need to relax."

Jones handed him a beer. "That's exactly what we're doing."

Dial pulled out his chair. "Not to be a downer, but it's getting harder and harder for me to clean up your messes. My badge can only do so much."

Payne nodded in understanding. "Just say the word and we'll quit calling."

"And miss invitations like this? Not a chance."

"Come on, Nick. You know what I mean."

Dial nodded. "We're not there yet, but we're getting closer."

"Understood."

Jones glanced at Dial. "Any news on Mueller?"

Dial took a sip of beer. "Well, those were definitely his men at the Linderhof. Fingerprints and arrest records prove it. According to my calculations, you've killed ten of his men in the past week. That's bound to get you noticed."

"Define *noticed*."

Dial chose his words carefully. "Mueller is a cold, calculating son of a bitch. He isn't the type of guy who will challenge you to a gunfight at dawn, unless he knows he can win. My guess is he'll take his time to find out everything he can about you. After that, he'll come after you with a small army—or a very good assassin. Whatever he thinks will work best."

Payne scanned the room. "Great."

Dial forced a smile. "Don't worry, it won't be today. Oktoberfest is far too important to the local economy. If he struck here, the German government would destroy him. No way he would risk his entire organization for two Americans he's never met. Even assholes like you."

Jones poured another beer. "Good to know."

"So," Dial said as he noticed two empty chairs at their table, "where's Petr? And didn't you say something about an attractive blonde who might like handcuffs?"

"They'll be here soon. They're flying in from Switzerland."

Dial lowered his voice. "And what about Kaiser? How's he doing?"

Payne answered. "He'll live, but he's pretty pissed off. During the assault, he caught some shrapnel in one of his eyes. The doctors tried to save it, but they weren't successful."

Dial winced. "I'd be pissed, too, if I lost an eye."

Payne shook his head. "Actually, he can handle losing an eye. It's the joking that's got him pissed. We stopped by the hospital to see how he was doing, and DJ playfully called him 'Long John Kaiser.' He even brought him a pirate eye patch as a gag."

Jones grimaced. "In retrospect, it was a little too soon."

Dial laughed at his friend's antics. "If I were you, I'd buy him a gift. A *really* nice gift. This is someone you don't want pissed at you."

"Trust me," Jones said as he thought about the crate of gold that was waiting in Ulster's vault, "we have just the thing to cheer him up."

Over the next twenty minutes, the trio caught up on old times. They had known each other for years but rarely had a chance to get together because of the distance between Pittsburgh and France. Halfway through his story about the salami, Jones stopped and rubbed his eyes. Even though he'd had very little to drink, he was pretty sure his mind was playing tricks on him.

Jones asked, "What's the alcohol content of this beer?"

Payne shrugged as he ate some roast pork. "I don't know—why?"

"I think Petr just arrived."

"And?"

"Unless I'm imagining things, he's wearing leder-hosen."

A few seconds later, Payne was laughing so hard he started coughing up food. The sight of Ulster, one of the most respected historians in the world, squeezed into the traditional knee-length leather shorts—his outfit completed with matching suspenders and a pointed hat with a red feather—was too much for him to handle. Not wanting to embarrass his portly friend, Payne quickly excused himself before Ulster reached their table.

Thanks to the massive crowd, Payne slipped away unseen. At least he thought he did until he felt a faint tap on his shoulder a minute later. He turned around, fully expecting to see a drunken tourist with a handful of beer. Instead, he saw Heidi. She was standing there in a gathered skirt with a low-cut bodice, a white apron, and thigh-high white stockings. Her blond hair, which was normally in a ponytail, had been separated into two braids, each tied with white ribbons that dangled in front of her cleavage.

"Hey, stranger," she said before she kissed him on his cheek.

Payne struggled to catch his breath. "Wow."

She smiled and curtsied. As she did, she swooshed her blue skirt back and forth with her hands. "Do you like it? It's called a dirndl. It's very popular in Bavaria."

"I can see why. You look incredible."

She blushed slightly. "If that's the case, why did you run away from me?"

"When was that?"

"Just now. I showed up with Petr, and you ran away."

He apologized. "Sorry, I didn't even see you. I started choking on my food and needed to clear my throat."

She patted him on the back. "Are you okay?"

He nodded. "I am now."

She linked her arm in his and pulled him off to the side of the tent. "Before we go back to the table, I just wanted to take a moment to thank you."

"For what?"

"For letting me tag along on your adventure."

He laughed at her description. "Yeah, like I had a choice."

She gave him a playful shove. "Come on! I wasn't *that* bad, was I?"

"You mean, before you blackmailed your way onto the chopper, or after?"

Heidi laughed at the memory. "After."

"In that case, you were great. We couldn't have done it without you."

"Well, I don't know about that, but I appreciate the sentiment."

He turned and faced her. "Maybe you're right. Maybe we could have done it eventually, but the truth is your presence really sped up the process. I hope you know that."

She smiled at the compliment. "I do now."

"So," he said, "how are things going with Petr?"

For the past few days, Heidi and Ulster had been working together at the Archives, trying to organize all of the information that they had learned about Ludwig. Eventually, their group would have to contact the local government about their discoveries at the Linderhof, and Payne wanted Heidi to be a part of the process since she worked for the Bavarian Palace Department.

"It's been unbelievable," she gushed. "I've learned more history in the last week than I did during my four years of college. Suddenly, my eyes are open to a whole new world, and I'm looking forward to exploring it."

"Wow. You're pretty young to be having a midlife crisis."

She laughed. "Trust me, it's not a midlife crisis, although I am thinking about changing jobs."

"Really? Do you have something in mind?"

"As a matter of fact, I do. Earlier today, Petr offered me a position at the Archives, working as a paid intern. The money isn't great, but the contacts I'd make would be invaluable."

"Congratulations! That's awesome news. When do you start?"

"I don't know. I haven't accepted the position yet. Petr just offered it to me on the flight here, and I told him I needed some time to think."

"Personally, I think it would be foolish not to take it. With the Archives on your résumé and a letter of recommendation from Petr, you can get a job at any museum or research facility in the world. His name carries that much weight."

"I agree, which is why I'm going to accept the offer."

He threw his arm around her. "In that case, we need to celebrate your news. And since you'll be taking a major cut in salary, everything is on me tonight."

She snuggled against him. "If I drink enough, that *might* include me."

Payne laughed at her comment, then ordered another round.

AUTHOR'S NOTE

The first time I saw a picture of Neuschwanstein, I didn't think it was real. I figured it was a make-believe castle, drawn by a talented artist for an upcoming movie or the cover of a new game. I mean, who in their right mind would build something so whimsical? If you've never seen the castle, take a moment to look at the photos on my website. Then you'll know what I'm talking about. (The Internet address is listed on the next page.)

Of course, I would later discover that the castle *was* real, and the man who commissioned it was downright crazy. Whether he was dressing up as the Swan Knight or riding his horse in circles for hours at a time, Ludwig II seems like a fictional character. But his eccentric behavior—including his dream of starting a brand-new kingdom—has been well documented in several nonfiction sources.

For more information, take a trip to your local library. While you're at it, buy ten more copies of this book, make your friends and family read them, and then have a lengthy discussion on the topic. In fact, I recommend that for all my novels. Especially the *buying ten more copies* part. (Actually, just to be safe, better make it twenty.)

By the way, here's one last thing I didn't mention in the story, but I found it interesting nonetheless. Toward the end of Ludwig's reign, one of the biggest concerns of the Bavarian government was the enormous amount of personal wealth that he had spent on his castles, yet since his death in 1886, more than sixty million people have toured Neuschwanstein alone. Once you factor in visits to Linderhof Castle, Herrenchiemsee Palace, and the King's House on Schachen, Ludwig's architecture has brought in billions of dollars of tourist revenue to Bavaria—far more than he ever spent on his building projects, even after adjusting for inflation.

In retrospect, maybe Ludwig wasn't so crazy after all.

Please visit **www.chriskuzneski.com** for additional information about my writing, answers to frequently asked questions, and a brand-new section detailing the locations visited in my books. I'm really excited about this new addition to my website, and I encourage anyone interested in a visual tour of my books to check it out.

ACKNOWLEDGMENTS

This book wouldn't exist without the collective effort of many people. I've tried my best to personally thank everyone for his or her contribution, but there are a few I'd like to recognize here.

As always, I'd like to start with my family (especially my mom). Without their love and support, I wouldn't be the person or the writer that I am today. Thanks for putting up with me.

Professionally, I want to thank my friend and agent, Scott Miller. Before we teamed up, I couldn't find a publisher. Now my books are available all around the globe. Not too shabby for two guys from Pennsylvania. Speaking of geography, I'd like to thank Scott's assistant, MacKenzie Fraser-Bub, and her sweet Southern accent. I smile every time she calls or answers his phone. (Of course, then she puts Scott on the line and he instantly ruins my mood!)

To say that I've been thrilled with Putnam and Berkley would be an understatement. How they managed to turn an unknown writer like me into a *New York Times* bestseller is a miracle—especially since my surname has way too many consonants to look pretty on a book cover. Believe it or not, even I don't know how to pronounce it. In particular, I'd like to single out my editor, Natalee Rosenstein, and her amazing assistant, Michelle Vega. Working with them has been a wonderful experience. I'd also like to thank Ivan Held, Neil Nyren, and Michael Barson.

Next is my awesome friend Ian Harper. I want to thank him for reading, rereading, and then re-rereading everything I write and for all the suggestions that he makes. His advice and expertise are, well, awesome! If anyone's looking for a freelance editor, please let me know. I'd be happy to put you in touch with him.

Finally, I'd like to thank all the readers, librarians, booksellers, and critics who have read my thrillers and have recommended them to others. At this stage of my career, I need all the help I can get, so I would appreciate your continued support.

FROM *NEW YORK TIMES* BESTSELLING AUTHOR

Chris Kuzneski

THE
LOST THRONE

Carved into the towering cliffs of central Greece, the Monastery of the Holy Trinity is all but inaccessible. Its sacred brotherhood has protected its secret for centuries.

In the dead of night, the monastery's sanctity is shattered by an elite group of warriors carrying ancient weapons. One by one, they behead the monks and hurl the bodies from the cliff top to the rocks below. The holy men take their secret to their graves.

Halfway across Europe, Richard Byrd has uncovered the location of a magnificent treasure, but there are those who will stop at nothing to prevent its discovery.

Hoping to save himself, Byrd contacts Jonathon Payne and David Jones and begs for their help. The duo rush to Saint Petersburg, Russia, and quickly find themselves caught in an adventure that will change their lives forever.

"A fresh new voice that you won't forget."

—W.E.B. Griffin, *New York Times* bestselling author

penguin.com

FROM *NEW YORK TIMES* BESTSELLING AUTHOR

Chris Kuzneski

SIGN OF THE CROSS

Three crucifixions on three different continents.
A secret that could destroy the faith of billions.

On a Danish shore, a Vatican priest is found—
hanging on a cross. Within days, the same crime
is repeated…this time in Asia and Africa. Meanwhile, deep in the legendary Catacombs near
Orvieto, Italy, an archaeologist unearths a scroll
dating back two thousand years, revealing secrets
that could rock the foundations of Christianity. Its
discovery makes him the most wanted criminal in
all of Europe. But his most dangerous enemies operate outside the law of man…

penguin.com

M14G0610